THE LEGEND MacKINNON

DONNA KAUFFMAN

BANTAM BOOKS

New York Toronto London
Sydney Auckland

THE LEGEND MACKINNON
A Bantam Book / April 1999

ISBN 0-553-57923-1

Bantam Books are published by Bantam Books, a division of Random
House, Inc. Its trademark, consisting of the words "Bantam Books" and
the portrayal of a rooster, is Registered in U.S. Patent and Trademark
Office and in other countries. Marca Registrada. Bantam Books, 1540
Broadway, New York, New York 10036.

PRINTED IN THE UNITED STATES OF AMERICA

OPM   10 9 8 7 6 5 4 3 2 1

*The destinies of two ancient clans are
entwined for all of eternity. . . .*

MAGGIE CLAREN—A week ago, she thought she had the perfect life. Then she uncovers a shocking secret that sends her running for her life . . . straight into the arms of a gorgeous, kilt-clad ghost.

DUNCAN MacKINNON—For three hundred years, he'd sworn vengeance against the family who'd destroyed his own. Now the ruthless warrior may have betrayed his clan, all because of a woman who could be his redemption . . . or his destroyer.

CAILEAN CLAREN—Haunted by visions she cannot explain, she flies halfway around the world to save the life of a cousin she has never met. And finds herself drawn to a man from another time and place—a man who will stop at *nothing* to get what he wants.

RORY MacKINNON—He was fierce, proud, and merciless, but his skills with the sword weren't enough to save him from a Claren witch. Now John Roderick MacKinnon has another chance to break the ancient curse when a modern sorceress unlocks his heart.

DELANEY CLAREN—All her life she'd yearned for adventure. Now in the ruins of a magnificent castle, she will cross paths with the eldest of the brothers MacKinnon, a man who is every bit her match.

ALEXANDER MacKINNON—For years he has hidden in his castle lair, searching for a way to change history and turn the tables on his enemy. But the battlegrounds have shifted, and one spirited woman just may save his heart and everlasting soul. . . .

Romance novels have always celebrated the power, fortitude, and resilience of women. I am very fortunate because I'm surrounded by a number of real-life heroines. Without them, this book could not have been completed.

This book is dedicated to Susann Brailey, Jean Hobday, Cassie Goddard, Linda Hayes, Jill Shalvis, Wendy Chen, Jean Brashear, Carmen Ardura, and Leanne Banks.

And because no heroine worth her salt goes through life without a wonderful hero by her side, this book is also dedicated to my personal hero, my husband Mark. The quest continues . . .

PART ONE

DUNCAN

"True love is like ghosts, which everybody talks about and few have seen."

—FRANÇOIS, DUC DE LA ROCHEFOUCAULD

ONE

H E'D NEVER FIND her here.

It was twilight when Maggie Claren finally wound her way to the end of the gravel and dirt road and parked in front of the old cabin. Madden County, North Carolina. It was impossible to believe that anyone lived in such a remote area. On purpose.

From the looks of the place, no one had been living here for quite some time. The cabin was part stone, part log over log, put together the way she imagined Abe Lincoln's folks had probably built theirs. If she'd been standing in Kentucky instead of the Smokey Mountains, she could easily be convinced they'd built this one personally.

Maggie forced her fingers to release their death grip on the steering wheel. She rolled her shoulders, wincing at the pinches of pain. She didn't care what the place looked like. It was hers. She could be safe here. She had to be.

The deed had been rerecorded over the years, but at least part of the cabin and all of the land was the original Claren property as it was first claimed almost three centuries ago. She could not fathom it.

A shivery sensation raced over her skin. How many of

her ancestors had stood on this spot, walked this land, stepped up on that porch?

Until recently Maggie had never given much thought to her family tree. Aunt Mathilda hadn't spoken of it, most likely because she didn't care. They'd both been too busy living the present to dwell on the past. As Mathilda had been right up until her death at age eighty, Maggie was happy, well-adjusted and excited about the vast opportunities life presented to her. That had always been more than enough.

Had been. One of those opportunities had, unfortunately, been Judd. Suddenly the opportunity to delve into the past was a tantalizing proposition.

She looked upward. "Thank you Great-Uncle Lachlan, whoever you are. Were. You saved my life."

She eyed her timely inheritance again. Old Judge Nash had not been a fount of information, but now she understood why he'd spared the extra minute to explain where she could find a room for the night. She hadn't thought to ask about basic matters like electricity and running water.

She looked down at the key in her hand. Who was she fooling? There was a good reason Judd would never think to look for her here. Ellie Mae Clampett she was not.

She seriously debated tracking down that motel room and tackling this tomorrow. Then she thought of Judd, who was probably taking her condo apart right this minute, looking for any clue to her whereabouts. Well, he wouldn't find any. Judge Nash's letter telling her of her recent windfall could not have arrived at a more perfect moment. Judd knew nothing about it and since the letter was in her purse, he never would.

He'd certainly never picture her living in a run-down shack and driving a rusted out hull of a car. She smiled a bit smugly at her vehicle. Little had she known just how well the junker would suit her new life.

She slid out of the car, groaned as she stretched, then

marched up the steps of the creaking front porch. She slid the key Judge Nash had given her into the lock, then shoved at the warped door until it opened enough for her to squeeze inside. She had no idea what she expected.

It definitely was not a six-foot-plus Scotsman wearing a kilt. And nothing else.

Her mouth dropped open. Too stunned to do more than blink, she simply stared. The man was a giant. His long legs resembled roughly hewn oak trees, looking oddly all the more masculine for the skirt he was wearing. Her gaze moved upward when he crossed formidable arms over an even more formidable chest and glared at her. His face was full of magnificent angles, accentuated by dark slashes of eyebrows and sculpted lips that, for all their beauty, looked as cold and hard as the rest of him. His hair was long, black, and as wild as the light in his fierce gray eyes.

He took a menacing step forward. "I dinna ken who ye be lassie, but I'll thank you to get the hell off my land."

He was entirely overwhelming and more than a little terrifying. None of which explained why a bubble of semi-hysterical laughter emerged through her lips. She held up her hand. "I have a key," she said, as if that would explain everything. "Lachlan Claren left the cabin to me."

The man's face twisted in rage and he stormed across the room toward her, dust rising from the floorboards with each thundering footstep. "This is MacKinnon land," he roared. "And MacKinnon land it will stay! Auld Lachlan dinna own this place, nor lass, do you. Now be gone!"

By all rights she should be running screaming down the mountain. Perhaps it was because less than a week ago she'd had a loaded gun held to her head and had spent several terrifying minutes believing she was going to die. Maybe you only really believed you were going to die once.

She stepped back and said, "I don't know who you are or how you got in here, but this is my cabin now. I have the deed to prove it. If you have a problem with that then I suggest you take it up with Judge Nash. In the meantime, it's late and I'm tired. When I come back, I expect you to be gone."

She turned and walked out to her car where she grabbed her duffel bag and the can of pepper spray she'd tucked into the glove compartment. She glanced at the rest of her inheritance, which occupied almost the entire back of the car. Later, she decided. She'd unload Lachlan's trunk tomorrow, though she had no idea how she was going to get the thing inside. She cast a look toward the cabin, then shook her head. She doubted Braveheart in there would be willing to play bellboy.

She could hear him swearing and stomping about as she walked back to the porch. Her moment of bravado wore off and she paused at the foot of the stairs. She read newspapers, she watched CNN. She'd heard of wild loonies living in the woods doing horrible things to unsuspecting campers. She looked back at her car, then down at the can of pepper spray in her hands. This was stupid. Going back into that house armed with only a can of chemical spray was asking for trouble. God knows, she'd had enough of that.

She turned back to her car. The motel it would be after all. She'd confront her houseguest again in the morning, with the police in tow.

She grabbed the door handle, then stilled. It was quiet. Suddenly, completely silent. No swearing, no stomping. And she could have sworn she heard the faint echo of bagpipes echoing through the trees. She shook her head, then warily turned around.

She half expected to hear a bloodcurdling war cry as Braveheart launched himself from the door or the roof. Maybe he was getting a rifle or flaming arrow launcher. She could easily picture him wielding a battle-ax.

But she didn't hear anything. After all the racket, the total lack of it was odd. More than odd, it was curious.

From where she stood, she peered at the two windows fronting the cabin but they were too dingy to see beyond. Still, there were no curtains and it wasn't dark enough yet for a man to stand on the other side without being seen. *Find the motel and come back tomorrow with that nice deputy sheriff,* she told herself.

She opened the door of her car, then froze. No curtains in the windows? There had been curtains. Lacy ones. She closed her eyes and pictured the inside of the cabin as she'd seen it the instant before he'd filled the room. The furniture had been basic. But she definitely remembered lace curtains. Her neck prickled and she spun around. No curtains. Had she imagined them?

She crossed the clearing. "Hello," she called out. "It's the owner here." She half-ducked on the off chance she'd provoked him to blow her head off. Still nothing. She climbed the steps, almost certain that she was alone.

She stepped inside and was immediately proven right. The cabin was one open room comprising both living and dining area. A large stone fireplace and hearth framed one end, old oak cabinets were mounted above a scarred countertop that ran along the back wall of the cabin. There was a window over the sink and an old fashioned refrigerator in the corner.

There were no interior walls, only a curtain that could be drawn across a corner at the opposite end where a claw foot tub and an antique toilet crowded each other in the limited space. A small loft ran across the narrow end above the bathroom area, but that was completely visible from below . . . and completely empty.

A quick glance showed there was no back door and the one rear window obviously had not been touched in decades.

But it wasn't the mystery of where her kilt-clad madman had disappeared to that had the room tilting and her peripheral vision growing narrow. It was the fact that not only had he disappeared, he'd somehow managed to make an entire cabin full of furniture and belongings disappear right along with him. What did remain was covered in a thick layer of dust. Including the rustic floorboards.

Floorboards that showed only one set of footprints.

Hers.

Maggie capped off her day of surprises by adding another personal first. She fainted.

MAGGIE SNUGGLED IN his embrace, feeling safe for the first time since escaping from her Manhattan condo, and unwilling to wake from her peaceful nap.

She shifted her head, then sneezed violently as dust tickled her nose. Her chin connected solidly with the hard wood floor. Groaning, Maggie opened her eyes to pitch blackness. She was alone. And yet, the sensation of being held had felt so real.

She rolled slowly to her knees, carefully taking inventory of all movable body parts. Hitting the floor in a dead faint had to have left her bumped and bruised. But other than feeling the stiffness of lying on a cold, hard floor, she felt relatively fine. She stood carefully, then brushed at the dust on her jeans and shirt.

Her eyes adjusted to the darkness, and she turned and groped for the door handle, yanking hard to pull the warped door open enough to step outside. She tried to ignore the fact that she *knew* she hadn't closed the door behind her, because if she thought about it too much, she was liable to do what most sane women would have done hours ago—run screaming down the mountain.

She picked her way carefully toward her car, rubbing at her arms as the cold night air crept through her sweater. She walked a little faster, making a determined effort not to look over her shoulder. She climbed behind the wheel, locked all the doors, then let out a sigh of relief—*as if loonies and goblins and things that go bump in the night couldn't breach the inside of her car.*

It wasn't until she forced herself to slowly replay the incidents of the afternoon that she finally felt some semblance of control. Unfortunately, she also felt terror. Hadn't she had more than her share of that already? Apparently not.

"Only I could go from running from a lunatic ex-fiancé, straight to running from a . . . a" She couldn't say it. Not because she wouldn't believe in it—given enough proof—she just wasn't exactly sure what "it" was. Or wasn't.

She knew what she'd seen . . . then not seen. She simply needed a rational explanation.

Being a rational woman, waiting until daylight to determine what this explanation was seemed like an entirely, well, rational, thing to do. She turned the key in the ignition. But instead of the rumbling sound of an old clunker badly in need of a tune-up, all she heard was a series of clicking noises. An old clunker badly needing a tune-up and a new battery, she amended. Wonderful. Simply wonderful.

She swore and rested her head on the steering wheel. *Now what?* Hiking down the rutted mountain road even in broad daylight would be an arduous undertaking. Doing so in the middle of the night would be downright foolhardy. But was staying in her car all night any less so?

At that moment, the cabin came to life. Warm yellow light glowed from the windows. Smoke was coming from the stone chimney. Someone had started a fire in the fireplace.

A fireplace that had been swept clean, save for the dust of disuse. And there hadn't been so much as a stick of kindling stacked nearby.

The cabin looked cozy and inviting now, nestled in the small clearing, backed by centuries old hemlock and birch.

The fire inside was seductively welcoming on a cold night. Lace curtains fluttered against the windowpanes.

Lace curtains.

Oddly it was the lace curtains that sent her out of her car. She might get hurt on the twisting road, but at least she was trying to save herself.

She hadn't gone a hundred feet when a large shadow eclipsed what little light she had.

"I'm already doing eternity for the death of one foolish lass," a booming voice intoned. "I'll not be payin' for another."

Oh God. She looked up. Way up. She hadn't heard a sound until he'd stepped in front of her in all his kilt-clad glory. In *front* of her? She looked over her shoulder. The cabin was still glowing.

He took her arm in a none too gentle grasp. "Come on wi' ye." He dragged her several steps toward the cabin.

She tugged hard at his hold and dug her heels in. Perhaps he wasn't used to being thwarted. Whatever the case, she managed to free herself and immediately took off.

She heard him swear loudly. Though she understood little of the words, the intent was clear enough to make her run even faster.

Only me, she canted silently, her breath forming white puffs in the night air, *only me*. She'd escaped from one monster and run directly into another one.

Even as the thought crossed her mind, she slammed into something solid enough to send her flying backward, landing painfully on her backside. Anger and fear made her glower up at him. "How do you do that? Or do you have lookalike brothers?"

He braced his hands on his hips. "Brothers I had, aye. I am but one man now. One you should heed unless ye've a mind to freeze to death." He extended an oversized, callused hand to her. "Take it, lassie. Or you can ride over me shoulder. I care not which."

Maggie got to her feet unaided. "First you order me out of here, now you're commanding me to stay?"

Then she recalled what he'd said. *I'm already doing eternity for the death of one foolish lass . . .*

So that meant he was what, an escaped convict? A murderer? A murderer whose face she had clearly seen? Oh, lovely, just lovely.

"Who are you?" she demanded.

If it was possible, he stood even taller. "Duncan MacKinnon." Even in the weak moonlight, his eyes took on a fierce light. He said his name as if it alone should strike fear and awe in her.

She stuck her hand out. "Maggie Claren. Listen Duncan, I think if you—"

"Yer a Claren?" His roar was so loud she was surprised the trees didn't shake.

He turned and stomped away from her. "I shouldna even tried," she heard him rant. "Shoulda known they would do something like this." He shook his fist at the sky. "I'll no' be a part of this, ye hear me? She can freeze her bloody arse off, ye ken? It's no more than a bloody Claren deserves."

Maggie took a step backward, then another.

She turned to run, but froze before moving an inch, her gaze riveted to the spot where he strode from her sight. Literally. One second he'd been storming toward the cabin, the next instant, he vanished, as if walking into a fog. Only it was a crystal clear night. He'd been yards from the cabin or the cover of any trees. He'd simply . . . vanished.

"Who are you really Duncan MacKinnon?" she whispered, awestruck and half-disappointed that she felt no sign of another faint coming on. "Rather, *what* are you?"

She felt the key weighing like a lodestone in her pocket. It was her cabin, dammit. Her one place to be safe.

She started across the clearing toward the cabin, stopping at her car to grab her duffel bag and tuck the pepper spray in her back pocket.

Feeling like a cross between Alice in Wonderland and every stupid horror movie heroine, she hitched the bag up higher on her shoulder and headed for the front porch. "Ready or not, here I come."

TWO

MAGGIE HALF EXPECTED the cabin to go dark when she opened the door. She was only partly relieved when it didn't. "Hello," she called out as she shoved at the wooden door. "I've decided not to freeze me bloody arse after all."

He was poking at the fire with a long iron pole. She tried not to view it as a weapon. The flames danced shadows across his skin, enhancing his menacing appearance.

"Yer smarter than most of yer kind then." His gaze stayed on the fire. "Take the loft. I'll no' be usin' it. Clarens," he snorted under his breath. He grumbled something about not taking to being tested like this and why in hell couldn't they leave him to what little peace he had.

Maggie knew leaving here was not an option. Duncan, whatever he was, seemed the lesser danger. For the moment, anyway.

"Well, goodnight then." She turned to the ladder.

"G'night lass."

She glanced over her shoulder, surprised he'd answered. He was no longer by the hearth. He wasn't anywhere inside the cabin.

Don't think about it, she schooled herself firmly. Be thankful he left the fire. Heaving her bag over her shoulder she climbed quickly, as much to find a place to sleep as to escape the shadowy questions crowding her brain. She gasped in delight: A large bed piled with the thickest comforter she'd ever seen filled most of the loft area. An antique washstand topped by a small mirror was tucked under the slanted eaves. An oak nightstand stood next to the iron headboard.

She ached with fatigue. It was all too much. She pulled off her shoes and her sweater, sliding her bra off from underneath her T-shirt. Too tired to do more, she undid the top button of her jeans and crawled into bed. Her body felt like it sank forever into a cloud of softness.

"Goose down," she sighed. She pushed the jumble of thoughts to the far reaches of her mind. They'd all be there tomorrow. For now, she'd found sanctuary. She snuggled deeply into the pillows. No more living in her rusted junk heap. "Thank you for the bed, MacKinnon," she murmured as sleep claimed her. "Yer a saint."

"HARDLY THAT," DUNCAN spoke into the quiet night. Murderer. Betrayer. Coward. Those were words used to describe the second son of Calum, Laird MacKinnon.

He stared down at her sleeping form. A Claren. In as fair a package as her ancestors before her. He frowned. And, like her ancestors, she brought with her naught but trouble. Trouble she would make his, as had that wretched Claren lass centuries ago.

Three hundred years had passed but the rage inside him had not diminished. Nay, three millennia could pass and he would still feel the same.

"A test you are," he said, certain *They* had contrived to bring her to this place, this place of his annual, month-long incarceration. "And it is a test I will fail," he said, his hushed tone doing nothing to soften his words. "You can parade a hundred, a thousand Claren lasses before me and I will fail you a hundred, a thousand times."

Aye, he'd caught her when she'd fainted. It meant nothing. Fool woman would have likely split her skull and made matters worse. There was no denying that fatigue lined her face, even in sleep. There were shadows too, some visible to any mortal, some visible only to him.

"I am not responsible for her folly nor will I be responsible for freeing her from it. I'll stay in this void for eternity before I help one of the clan that destroyed mine. You have naught to offer me beyond it. No solace great enough for me to endure the getting of it. Only hell." He looked to the dark shadows of the mountains beyond the window. Mountains that weren't his own, land that would never be Scotland. "Aye, and isn't this hell enough?"

He climbed down the ladder, using his mortal muscle and sinew, needing to expel the strange energy plaguing him and knowing naught how to do it except through the physical use of the body that housed his soul. His damned soul.

He poked at the fire, restless in ways he cared not to analyze. This was not the first time he had been tested. Yet in this, his three hundredth month of exile, They had, for the first time, crossed his path with a woman. And not just any woman, but an ancestor of the clan against which he'd sworn vengeance. She was Claren. She could not be his absolution.

For there would be no Higher Place for him. There was no way to correct the wrongs he had committed in the name of his clan. Wrongs he'd wrought because of the treachery of a Claren.

If he failed again this month, would he finally descend into hell? And what hell could possibly be worse than knowing his clansman had died without his help? What hell could be worse than having an eternal view of all history except that which took place on Scottish soil? They allowed him to see what he wanted of the world, except that which mattered to him most. Hell could not be worse than what he had suffered these last three centuries.

Thirty days to endure, then perhaps he would find out.

Perhaps he'd take a Claren to hell with him. "Enjoy yer soft bed whilst ye can, lassie."

MAGGIE OPENED HER eyes to a misty gray morning. She'd slept dreamlessly for the first time in weeks. She was tempted to stay nestled in the depths of the covers.

Coward. She wrestled a foot out. Cool, but not chilly. The sweet smoke-scent of wood in the fireplace below proved that a fire still burned in the hearth. She closed her eyes and listened, but heard nothing else stirring. No one else, to be more exact.

Was she ready to face whatever waited for her below?

She didn't chance a shower, but was heartened that the antique toilet flushed properly. She splashed her face and brushed her teeth at the kitchen sink after figuring out how the pump handle faucet worked. Feeling refreshed, she stoked the fire, then climbed the ladder and made the bed, gaining confidence with each normal chore she performed.

She would spend the morning checking cupboards and making a grocery list. After a quick trip to town, she would get Lachlan's chest inside and spend the afternoon going through whatever was in it. She might even buy a paper and see how Wall Street was doing in her absence.

She could almost let herself believe everything was under control. Until she hauled her bag onto the bed and began sorting through her recently purchased, very scaled down wardrobe.

Just because there had been no sign of MacKinnon this morning, didn't mean he wouldn't return. And even if he was a figment of her imagination, he was still a bit too real.

Enough so that getting naked made her uncomfortable. The idea of climbing under the covers to change was too adolescent to consider. She gripped the edges of her T-shirt and started to pull it off, then stopped midway and hooked her bra around her and slid it up under the shirt first, fumbling on the straps. After a quick peek over the loft railing, she yanked off the T-shirt, put on a sweatshirt, then sat on the bed and changed into new panties and sweatpants, all in under sixty seconds with her rump barely leaving the mattress.

Judd is trying to kill me and I'm worried that some hallucination is getting his bagpipes off watching me dress? Disgusted, she climbed down the ladder. Tonight she would strip fearlessly. She might even sleep in the nude. So there.

"Do ye always sleep the day away?"

Maggie almost fell from the last rung. "It's you."

"You were expectin' someone else perhaps?"

Maggie made herself straighten and took a steadying breath. He was more . . . massive than she'd remembered, which was hard to believe. Today he wore a loose-fitting white linen shirt, with strings dangling untied at the neck. His kilt was the same, with more plaid and a bag of some kind tied around his waist. His calves were covered with heavy socks and leather boots. His long black hair was pulled back and gathered at the neck. He was nothing short of magnificent. *Mel Gibson, eat your heart out.*

"I was, uh, expecting to be alone," she managed.

He stared hard at her. "This won't be the first time I'll be disappointin' ye."

She took a bold step forward, heartened when he didn't move away from the fire. "As I told you last night, this is my cabin. I own it, all legal and proper."

"And what if I said I don't give a bluidy damn for your laws?" He leaned casually against the mantle. "What will you do then, lass?"

His brogue wasn't near as thick now as it had been

yesterday when he'd been angry and shouting. Yet his relaxed pose and quieter speech rattled her more—he didn't seem remotely loony today.

"Then I'll be forced to go into town and deal with the local law enforcement on this matter."

He tipped back his head and laughed. It was a robust sound that filled the cabin. "You do that, lassie," he said, still chuckling. "You do that."

Maybe this wasn't going to work after all.

It wasn't difficult for Maggie to foresee the end of that scenario. She'd drag Deputy Branson up the mountain and the cabin would be empty and dusty with only her footprints as signs of recent occupancy. It also wasn't hard to foresee her future if she left the mountain. It would be very brief.

She needed this cabin, dammit. And as much as she hated to admit it, having Duncan around might not be such a bad idea if Judd were to suddenly show up. Having furniture and a fire wasn't a bad bargain either.

"Well, much as we'd each like the other to go, I have a right to be here. We'll have to work out a compromise."

He frowned. She smiled. "This probably won't be the only time I'll disappoint you either."

He grumbled something about lassies too bold for their own good and turned toward the fire once again.

Maggie studied him while she reviewed her options.

"You going tae gawk at me for what's left of the morning, or do you have something else that might be needin' your attention?"

She scowled at his back then stalked to the kitchen where she began flinging open cupboard doors. No food. No dishes. Nothing.

"It's going to be more of a list than I thought." She turned to go up to the loft for her purse . . . and found a pen and pad of paper lying on the kitchen table. She darted a suspicious look at him, but MacKinnon's back was to her as he poked in the fire. *At least he was still visible.*

Okay. She took a deep breath. I'm fine. *So then how did the paper and pen get there?*

She started writing. Lunchmeat. Bread. Cereal. Milk. Water.

"The well water here is a bit of an acquired taste. A lot of minerals in these hills. Buy several gallons."

She slapped her hand over her list and looked up. He was still across the room. There was no way he could read what she was writing.

She tore the top sheet off and folded it in her hand. Why make a list? What *didn't* she need? She studiously ignored him as she climbed the ladder, retrieved her purse and climbed back down again. She was going down the porch stairs when she heard him in the doorway behind her.

"Take yer time," he said, sounding almost friendly.

She was immediately suspicious. "I'm sure you'd like it if I went down the mountain and never came back." She stopped at her car door and looked back. Her throat closed over. Arms crossed, feet braced, he filled the doorway, looking like a wild warrior hero. Simply speaking, he took her breath away.

Yeah, well, he wasn't taking her cabin, too. It would take more than his bizarre presence to scare her off.

It wasn't until she was turning the key in the ignition that she remembered her dead battery. *Just what I need, a dose of Highlander humiliation.* Even as she prepared to meet his smug smile, the engine roared to life with nary a sputter. She darted a quick glance to the doorway of the cabin. It was empty.

"I'll be back, MacKinnon," she grumbled. "Bet on it."

THREE

S HE DID COME back, but it took Maggie longer than expected. She'd been so aggravated when she'd left she hadn't remembered her disguise. It was only a baseball hat and a pair of dark sunglasses, but along with the baggy sweats, it would have been enough to keep anyone with a photo from recognizing her. Thinking of her newly-acquired "look" she cringed. She missed her tailored Donna Karan suits and her Magli pumps. Judd would pay for that, too.

Maggie remembered with chilling clarity the exact moment she thought she was going to die. She'd come home from work to find Judd waiting for her in her apartment. Apparently the restraining order she'd sworn against him wasn't going to work. He'd had a gun to her head when he'd been paged to an urgent meeting with the division president. There was only one thing Judd valued more than keeping his possessions, of which she'd unwittingly become one, and that was keeping his prestigious rung on the corporate ladder. He'd tied her up and locked her in her own closet, making it clear he'd finish when he returned.

Maggie was proud of her Houdini-worthy escape, which

hadn't been easy considering the silk hose he'd had tied around her wrists at the time. Judd would know she'd run and she'd need money to do it, which was why she'd emptied her savings account. All he'd be able to find out was which branch and the time of withdrawal, nothing of use to him.

What Judd didn't know was that she'd become an heiress. The investigator Nash had hired to find the next living kin had tracked down her birth certificate while researching her deceased father, Lachlan's original heir. From there he'd been able to track down her social security number and eventually her address. Thanks to modern technology, Nash's investigator hadn't talked to anyone.

No one would look for her in Madden County, North Carolina. She hoped.

She shoved the car door open, and got out. The entire hatchback was crammed full of bags, all stuffed around Lachlan's trunk. She doubted MacKinnon was going to offer her any assistance. Maggie wrestled out several bags and headed for the door. She used her hip to bang her way inside. "I could use a hand here." She heaved the bags onto the trestle table, then turned to the crackling fire. He wasn't there.

She checked the loft. Nobody was home but her. Good. Now she had all the comforts of home and no irritable ghost hovering about.

She slapped a hand over her mouth, as if she'd spoken the word. But she'd thought it, and that was just as bad. And, worse than that, she realized she wasn't all that relieved to be alone either.

She sunk down on the wooden bench and dropped her forehead to the trestle table. "I have lost it for sure."

"Not surprising, lass," a deep voice said. "You could lose a highland cow in that heap you dragged in here."

Her head jerked up. "Will you stop doing that!"

"Asking questions?"

"Popping up and scaring me half to death. Make some noise. Stomp on the floor when you walk. Knock on the door, clear your throat or . . . or something."

"I'll no' be knocking on the door to me own cabin."

"It's my cabin!"

He stalked to the table, planted two very large fists on the oak planks, and leaned over. "If ye don' like the company yer keepin', lassie, then leave. I'll do as I please. Just as I have every November for the last three hundred years."

"Oh God," she whispered. "You couldn't just disappear and leave me alone, could you?" She buried her head on her arms. "If you'd just go away, back to wherever it is you come from, I'd eventually come up with some rational explanation that I could live with."

Silence.

She raised her head. He hadn't moved an inch. Her shoulders slumped forward. "You're not going to do that, are you?"

He shook his head.

MAGGIE BEGAN TO laugh. It increased until it took on a decidedly hysterical edge. "This isn't happening."

Duncan frowned, but more out of concern than anger. What was wrong with the chit? Aye, he'd wanted to drive her off, but she'd seemed to be made of sterner stuff than this. The last thing he needed was her going daft on him. "If yer goin' tae fall apart, don't do it here, lassie," he ordered.

She just wiped the tears from her eyes, and laughed harder. "Sure, no problem," she said between choked gulps of air. "I meet ghosts everyday. No reason to get hysterical."

"Just what is it yer doing here? Why dinna ye leave this place?"

She finally looked at him, her expression a bit hollow. "I can't leave. I have nowhere left to run."

He didn't want to know, but he heard himself ask anyway. "What is it yer runnin' from, lass?"

Maggie smiled mildly. "I had the nerve to end a relationship. My fiancé didn't take that too well."

Duncan lowered himself to the bench opposite her. "He was good tae ye, provided for you and made you happy?"

She eyed him warily. "Initially."

"Yet ye run from him?" He smacked the table, making her jump. "Just like a Claren! Have you no' learned anythin' of honor in three hundred years? You can so easily shame your family and forsake a man and his family to suit your whim?"

Fire lit her eyes again. "I didn't shame anyone but myself for staying as long as I did. I have no family left, thank God. Aunt Mathilda would have kicked my butt for not leaving sooner. Trust me, Judd Templar is no prince." She rubbed at her temples. "Why am I even trying to explain?"

Aye, Duncan thought. And why did he want her to? It was an emotion he cared not to feel. In an abrupt change of subject, he demanded, "What is all this?" He gestured to the pile of bags strewn on the table.

"Food. Supplies. Stuff." She swung her legs over the bench and stood, her back to him. "There's more in the car. I guess I'd better get this put away."

He didn't want to feel concern. Not for a bluidy Claren. She'd gotten herself into this mess by running. A Claren trait that hundreds of years had not bred out of them. He'd have no part in helping her. "Yer stayin' then?"

She met his gaze. "I don't have a choice."

"Because of this Judd?"

"Because of this Judd."

Certainly not because of you. The words were clear in her expression. Good, he told himself. If they must be exiled together, keeping her as distant as possible was most preferable. He cared not one whit how she would resolve her circumstance, nor did he care if she drove herself into the far reaches of exhaustion whilst doing it. In fact, he had every intention of speeding up that drive. Perhaps she would decide to leave all the more quickly.

She didn't wait around for a response but shuffled toward the door. She was halfway out, then turned back. "Do you eat?"

He did not at all like the tinge of guilt that colored his conscience. He had no conscience. Else he would not be plotting to expedite her defeat. If she chose to be considerate to him, 'twould be her own folly. Though most likely it was a Claren trap. She was probably planning on poisoning him. A slow, hard smile curved his lips. She couldn't kill a dead man. Her ancestor had beat her to that triumph. "I need nothing from you."

She stiffened. "Fine. I'll stay out of your way." Her eyes narrowed and her voice dropped. "And you best stay out of mine." He heard her stomp down the porch stairs.

Didn't need him did she? Duncan was tempted to leave and take the fire and furnishings with him. But he'd already expended more energy than was wise popping in and out as he had been doing. Instead he sat heavily on the bench and brooded.

Maggie Claren might prove to be a more formidable foe than he'd imagined. She had mettle. She was not going to be any easier to deal with than her ancestor, Mairi, who'd run them both into death's arms rather than marry him.

He scowled and slid off the bench to prowl the confines of the cabin. Apparently his fate was to be hounded by Claren women for all eternity. He couldn't keep Mairi Claren, and couldn't get rid of Maggie. At the very least, discovering he was a ghost should have led to terrified screams, perhaps some staunch protestations. Instead she'd laughed. Laughed! Not at all what he'd expected.

Duncan paced to the fireplace, then abruptly turned and

slammed a fist against the aging beam of oak that was the mantlepiece. "Saints be damned!" he roared, though he knew railing against fate would only gain him a sore throat and naught else. "Trapped, I am."

Grabbing the iron poker, he shoved it into the dying embers of a stout pine log, creating a shower of ash and final spears of flame. He stared at the sap, crackling and popping as it oozed from the last remnants of wood. Clear and sweet, it dripped slowly into the ash, turning black as it hardened. "Like a Claren heart," he muttered, poking savagely at the small bits, burying them deeper in the soot.

MAGGIE MADE IT all the way to the rear of her car under her own power, then collapsed on the rear fender. The metal groaned under her weight. She didn't care if the whole thing tore off and dumped her to the ground.

Her legs were shaking. A man just calmly, or not so calmly actually, announced he was three hundred years old. She squeezed her eyes shut. Had she demanded proof? No. Had she even tried to deny it was anything but the truth? No. She opened her eyes. Why? *Because I already knew it, I already knew exactly what he was.* She rubbed at the goosebumps that rippled over her skin.

In fact, she should be commended for having such savoir faire in the face of such an incomprehensible reality. Yeah, that's right, she hadn't run screaming, she hadn't tried to deny the obvious. No, not her, she'd stood there and dealt with him. So why did she feel stupid?

"You asked him what he wanted to eat for Christ's sake."

She stood and brushed her palms on her sweats. "And by now the mint chocolate chip is probably all melted. Great. Just great."

Duncan brooded by the fire, not sparing her so much as a glance as she shouldered in the rest of the bags. Maggie

tried not be unnerved as she stuffed everything into the
cabinets. She sighed in relief when the ancient refrigerator
proved functional. She'd noticed the huge propane tank
outside and made a mental note to find out who to call to
fill it when it got low.

Soggy ice cream all stored away, she closed the freezer
door, then wasted several more minutes folding the paper
bags and storing them in the cabinet under the sink. Well,
that was ten whole minutes she hadn't had to deal with the
fact that she was living with a ghost. Now what?

She could haul Lachlan's trunk inside . . . or spend the
afternoon staring at Duncan's backside. It disconcerted her
to find her gaze straying toward that particular kilt-clad
part of his anatomy. Instead of his tartan-covered backside
however, she encountered a pair of ruddy masculine knees.

Caught, she figured she might as well be hung for a
thief and took her time raising her gaze. He wore the same
unlaced white linen shirt, no tartan sash. She supposed she
should be grateful that he didn't have a sword. Though he
probably had a dagger on him somewhere. Didn't they
tuck daggers in their socks? She wished she'd spent more
time watching Liam Neeson's clothes in *Rob Roy* and less
time watching his face and his legs and his, well . . .
kilts really were amazingly masculine garments, weren't
they?

She raised her gaze boldly to his, not about to let him
know how badly he unnerved her. "I . . . I appreciate the
use of the furniture, and the bed. And the fire." The small
living quarters demanded that they come to at least the
bare minimum of accord. She was doing her part.

"I do you no kindness, lassie."

"So you furnish this place for yourself? Why? I mean, do
ghosts need creature comforts too?"

"If ye mean do I like looking at bare walls and dusty
floors, the answer is no."

"Is that how Lachlan left it, then? Empty? Judge Nash said he rented the place to hunters."

"Auld Lachlan hasn't set foot here or rented the place in ages. Och, what peaceful months those were." He sent a pointed look her way.

She ignored it. "I understand he never lived here himself." She wanted to keep him talking—she almost liked him when he wasn't shouting at her and blinking in and out.

"No, he never did. He lived out his last years in Scotland." His gaze drifted to the dying fire. "The bastard."

His expression had gone from wary to bleak. He looked almost . . . lost. He was a ghost, wasn't he? Obviously he had unresolved stuff he was dealing with or he wouldn't be haunting this place. Maggie felt a tug at her heart and quickly squashed it. She had other things to worry about. Like how to get her life back and keep Judd from killing her.

"Only one Claren has ever made this a home."

Maggie's attention went back to Duncan. No way could she ignore that tantalizing bit of information. He was still staring at the fire. She doubted he was even aware he'd spoken out loud. Still bleak, his expression held anger now, too. It tightened the skin around his eyes, drew his mouth into a flat, uncompromising line.

"I take it you weren't too fond of that particular Claren," she said.

He turned and looked at her then. It wasn't something as benign as anger coloring his expression. There was rage in those gray eyes of his. And it ran deep. Three hundred years deep?

"Mairi." He paused and she watched him visibly grapple for control. His jaw was locked tight when he said, "She was my betrothed."

The idea of him marrying anyone took her aback. She swallowed. "Then you loved her."

"Love had nothing to do with it." He hadn't yelled or even raised his voice. Somehow, the statement seemed even more lethal—and sad—for the complete lack of emotion vested in it. "Something you know of, I ken."

Maggie didn't even stop to wonder at the wisdom of pursuing this path. If Lachlan was indeed her blood relative, then so was this Mairi Claren. She swallowed hard. Which meant she had ties beyond mere unfortunate circumstance to this ghost of a Scot. "Why marry her then?"

"This was no feeble matter of the heart," he stated with clear disgust. He leaned forward. "It was a matter of honor."

Maggie shrank back slightly at the fury in his eyes. A slight tick twitched the skin beneath his right eye. His jaw jutted out a bit further and from the corner of her eye, she saw he clutched the iron fire poker like a sword. When he spoke again, the deadly calm of his voice turned her skin to gooseflesh and made her scalp prickle in warning. Duncan MacKinnon had been a warrior, had likely died a warrior, and was a warrior still.

"Our union would have ended too many years of feuding between Clan Claren and Clan MacKinnon. Mairi did not stand in honor to her clan. She chose to run, leaving my clansmen to die on Claren swords."

Maggie swallowed hard, understanding his earlier rage. She'd run too. She prayed Mairi had had different reasons than she had. "Didn't she want your clans united?"

"It was not up to her to make that decision. She was betrothed by her father, the clan chief."

"So her opinion meant nothing. It didn't matter if she didn't want to ally her clan to yours."

"She didna want to ally herself to *me!*"

Maggie smiled. "Ah, so now we get to the truth. It wasn't politics. It was love. Or rather the lack of it."

"Love has nothing to do with these unions. Can you no' hear me woman? 'Tis about honor."

"It's about pride, you mean. And stupid male ego. Could she have refused you and not run away? Could someone else have taken her place? I know that arranged marriages were common back in your time, but certainly it's understandable even to you that a woman might choose to marry for love. What difference did it make which Claren woman you married? Certainly there had to be at least one who—" She paused. His expression turned murderous. "Oh, is that it? *No one* would have you?"

"*She* was the chosen one!" He clenched the poker next to his thigh, when she knew he'd wanted to swing it. "She should have done what she was born to do. Her da was Laird. Her duty was to him, and to her clan." He stepped closer. "And as my betrothed, to me."

Maggie crossed the room. "She didn't love you. She didn't want you. Committing herself to a lifetime with you would have been a lie and she knew it. What good is that? You would build your truce on a lie? On a false union between two people who hated each other? How could you build a harmonious future for your people on a platform of anger and hatred and lies? Just because you two marry doesn't mean your people will stop hating her people. You're a hypocrite if you think otherwise and so was her *da.*"

Maggie tossed up her hands and turned away from him, not sure why she was so angry on behalf of an ancient ancestor, but it felt good to vent over someone's injustice. Especially good since she couldn't rail over her own. She whirled and poked a finger in the air. "You know what I think? I think she was courageous to do what she did. It took guts to walk away from a bunch of strutting men who could find no better way to solve an argument than to bind some innocent woman into unholy matrimony with the enemy. That's what I think."

Only when Maggie was done with her tirade did she question the intelligence of giving into it in the first place.

Duncan looked as if he was going to pop several main arteries, some of them hers. His face was a very unhealthy dark red, and his chest was heaving as if there suddenly wasn't enough oxygen in the room to fill the massive thing.

She wondered where she'd put her pepper spray and if it worked on ghosts. She took a step backward, trying to appear humble and harmless. "But then, what's my opinion worth anyway?" she said, smiling weakly. "I'm one of those headstrong nineties women and you know what a pain in the ass we can be." Her attempt at a chuckle sounded more like a death wheeze.

Duncan stared at her a moment longer, then suddenly swung the poker high over his head. He might be dead, but that poker was terrifyingly real. Maggie skirted the table and ran for the door. A war cry filled the air and rattled the walls. Her heart pounded its way up into her throat and her stomach wrenched violently. The floor began to shake with his thundering footsteps and the damn door wouldn't unstick!

Well, if she was really meant to die, she was not going with a poker in her back. If the bastard was going to kill her, he was going to have to look her in the eyes and do it. She whirled and plastered herself to the door, eyes wide in terror as he bore down on her, iron rod raised above his head like a lance.

Duncan clearly hadn't expected the turnabout and could not pull up his charge in time. At the last second Maggie squeezed her eyes shut. So, maybe she was a teensy bit of a coward. But at least she hadn't run. There had to be some honor in that.

There was a bone-shaking crash as the poker buried itself into the old oak door a foot above her head. She only had a second to savor the sweet relief that it wasn't buried in her as she braced herself for the slamming weight of his body. There was a rush of cold air; then nothing.

Maggie squinted one eye open. He was gone.

Adrenaline, fear, and a second near death experience combined to make her temper rise. She yanked the door open so hard it flung back, banging the iron rod into the wall and rattling the rusty hinges. She stormed onto the porch and down into the yard. She turned a circle, found nothing out of the ordinary, then looked to the sky. "Goddamn you, Duncan MacKinnon!" she yelled. "Stop playing your disappearing games with me!"

"Would you rather I had run you through, lass?"

She whirled around. He was leaning against the open door frame, as calm as you please.

"I'd rather you kept your temper."

"Like you, perhaps?"

Her chest was heaving, her hair was hanging in her face and she was probably wild-eyed. Well, who wouldn't be under these circumstances? "I was doing just fine until you tried to skewer me with the poker. You'll have to pardon me if that gets me a wee bit riled up."

"You'll have to pardon me if having my name and honor desecrated gets me *a wee bit riled up.*" He stepped off the porch and walked right up to her.

Maggie worked hard to quell her heart rate and get her pulse somewhere near normal, but the closer he got, the more ground she gave on that particular battle. But she didn't step back. She wouldn't give him that satisfaction.

He stopped less than a foot away and stared at her for several seconds. "Why di' ye turn around?" he asked, his burr making the question sound almost gentle.

"I couldn't get the door open."

"That's no' what I asked you."

She suddenly found she couldn't hold his gaze. The intensity she found there was too demanding, too knowing, too . . . much. He reached out a hand, but she jerked her chin away before he touched her. Somehow she knew she'd be lost if he touched her. And it had nothing to do with being spooked.

"Why did ye turn to face me, Maggie?"

Hearing her name, the way he said it, made her turn her gaze back to his.

"Because if you were going to kill me," she said quietly, "I wanted to make you look me in the eyes when you did it."

He reached out and, despite her attempt to duck away, caressed her cheek with a callused thumb. "Then perhaps you understand more about pride and honor than you thought, Maggie Claren. A shame ye were no' around three hundred years ago."

FOUR

Maggie held his gaze for several long seconds then stepped back. "I . . . I need to get something from the car."

Duncan remained silent as he watched her walk to her car. His touch had bothered her. Far worse, however, was how much it had disturbed him.

Uncomfortable with those thoughts, he switched his attention to her car. He couldn't say much for her choice in conveyance. He'd seen better, and not much worse.

He had found himself drawn to one or two technological advances over the years. Cars, airplanes, military armament. He'd learned that no matter the level of sophistication of weaponry achieved by man, the warring continued, with the outcomes differing little. Clan MacKinnon and Clan Claren could have feuded with ground-to-air missiles and exploding land mines and the outcome would have been the same. Weapons didn't win wars. Men did.

Cunning, skill, strategic command, aye, they had their place. As did folly, cowardice, and betrayal. In the end, it was man who defeated himself as well. Three hundred years of observing the rise and decline of warring nations hadn't taught him that. His gaze narrowed as Maggie swore under the awkward weight of the trunk she was levering from the car. A woman had. One woman. Had he not learned his lesson?

There was a loud thud followed by a cloud of dirt and more swearing. Duncan folded his arms across his chest and continued to watch. Aye, he'd watch. And stand clear. Maggie Claren was not to be dealt with lightly. Or directly. He rubbed his fingertips along his sleeve, the fine linen not comparing well in softness to that of her skin. He curled his fingers and muttered a curse of his own.

She blew her hair from her face and planted her hands on her hips. "Why are you grumbling? I'm the one breaking my back." She looked at the trunk sitting at her feet. "I don't suppose you could help me out here. Like blink this thing inside. All your poofing stuff in and out ought to be good for something."

Well clear, he repeated silently, disgruntled to find himself actually having to take a step back to his original spot. "I'll no' be draggin' a Claren trunk into my home."

"It's no' your *hoome*," she said in a poor imitation of him. "It's our hoome, at least for now. And since you have a whole Claren human draggin' hersel' into yer hoome, what difference can a measly Claren trunk make?"

"I didna say you couldna have the trunk inside, lassie. I merely said I wouldna be helpin' ye wi' it."

She let out a heavy breath. "I guess it's long past time for me to stop relying on men anyway." She bent to the task of grabbing a worn leather handle, dismissing him entirely. "You'd think I'd have learned that lesson well enough by now."

He gritted his teeth as she pulled on the strap, the strain showing in her shoulders and in her face. A grunt escaped her clenched jaw as, with a mighty effort, she moved it two entire centimeters. She turned and grabbed the strap with both hands and pulled in another breath. Another mighty tug . . . and she went flying back onto her rump when the strap gave way with a rending thwack. A smile twitched his lips, but he quickly tamed it.

Without so much as a look in his direction, she stood and brushed herself off and walked to the back of her car. She bent inside and began digging about.

He should be inside tending the fire. It was getting damnable cold outside. During his time in purgatory there was no physical sensation since he had no physical self. But for his one month annual term on earth he was essentially mortal, inasmuch as he regained usage of all the human sensations. Yet he could never seem to get warm enough and he spent the entire month chilled to the bone. Perhaps They thought to remind him of the dank cold of Stonelachen, the MacKinnon stronghold on the Isle of Skye. He rubbed his palms along his arms. In his mortal life, he didn't recall ever feeling the cold quite like this. Perhaps a specter's blood did not heat a man like lifeblood did.

The slamming of the hatchback snapped his attention back to her. She stomped back over to the trunk, then walked around it once, then again, all the while ignoring him as if he didn't exist.

As the second son to Calum MacKinnon, he was used to being accorded the full, respectful attention of every man, woman, and child whose presence he encountered. Yet Maggie ignored him as easily as if he were a . . . a . . . . A ghost. Bah! To hell with the Clarens.

Duncan scowled and began to turn away, then stilled, caught by the sudden change in her expression. Her eyes lit up and a smile spread her lips wide, making her features somehow glow, even on such a gloomy day. She looked little like her ancestor, but then, he couldn't say what Mairi would have looked like had she ever smiled.

Maggie wasn't as delicately made as Mairi. She was broader of shoulder, a bit squarer of jaw. Her hair was a darker brown and her eyes a shade lighter blue. But it was her mouth that defined the true difference, and her beauty, if truth be told. Where Mairi's mouth had been small and bow-shaped, Maggie's was wide and even. Where Mairi's usually had been cool, her lips pulled into a tight, disapproving line, Maggie's was alive and inviting, always animated and usually moving, no matter her disposition. And in their brief acquaintance, he'd seen her in many forms.

This look of joy, however, was a new one to him. He didn't at all like it. It did odd things to the beat of his heart.

She scrambled back to the car, yanking open the passenger door and diving into the glove box. She emerged triumphant, a small manila envelope clutched in her hand and, once again, turned her back to him as she knelt in front of the lock dangling from the front of the trunk.

She fished in the envelope and came out with a key, her lips quirking. "Another skeleton key." She tossed him a quick glance. "If I'd only suspected when I got the first one just how appropriate it would be."

He held her gaze without comment, merely recrossing his arms and settling his weight on his other foot. She didn't seem to notice as she went to work on the lock. It took several tries, but eventually it sprung open. She was a determined lass, he'd give her that.

Her sudden intake of breath caught his full attention.

"Would you look at this?" Her face fairly glowed with wonder.

He took a step closer despite himself, all thoughts of returning to warm himself by the fire vanished. He didn't feel any chill at the moment.

Maggie covered her mouth with her hand as she stared at the contents of Lachlan's trunk. It was filled with plain leather bound books that looked like journals of some kind. The idea that there might be something of her heritage recorded inside those pages filled her with excitement. For the first time it felt odd that through her entire life she'd never questioned her family history. Staring at the journals it seemed impossible to fathom. Her interest in what lay between the burgundy and deep blue leather covers close to consumed her.

She felt Duncan come up behind her. There wasn't enough sun for a shadow, but then, she wasn't sure he'd cast one anyway. Not that he needed to—ghost or mortal, Duncan MacKinnon had presence in spades. She recalled his touch. For a dead man, there had been an incredible amount of energy generated by that simple brush of his fingers on her skin. She'd been well aware that the disturbance hadn't been totally one sided. What had he been like in real life? His life.

"A stack of musty old books." Duncan all but sniffed in indifference.

Maggie ducked her chin and smiled. She was beginning to understand Duncan MacKinnon. Perhaps better than he could imagine. That he'd troubled himself to wander over to look inside the trunk at all belied his lack of interest. That he'd bothered to make a comment all but proved he was as consumed with curiosity about their contents as she was.

"Yep. There go my dreams of buried treasure. No gold coins or lavish silks." She sighed in feigned disappointment. "Just musty old books."

Duncan's eyebrows drew together as he considered her in silence. He was no fool either, she decided. Something she would be wise to remember.

She considered him for a moment too, then couldn't help herself. "Probably should have left the old thing in the car and taken it to an antique store to have it appraised."

"You would sell yer heritage?"

She had no intention of selling anything, still she was surprised at the vehemence of his reaction. "You say that like it's blasphemy or something."

" 'Tis worse than that, lass."

"It's just an old, moldy trunk. Not the crown jewels."

"What of the volumes?" he demanded. "You would sell them off as well?"

"Oh no, they wouldn't be worth anything to anyone else. We can use them for fuel I suppose, when the logs run out."

She'd only said it to get a rise out of him, but he looked so sincerely aghast at the suggestion she felt a moment of shame.

"Just like a Claren! Ye have no need of a thing, toss it awa' like so much excess baggage." He raised his arms in the air and she almost shrank back at the imposing figure he made. "Burn it, sell it, give it awa'. Wha' do ye care? 'Tis only yer history yer sellin' and destroyin'." He stared at her with a mixture of disgust and resignation, then made a swiping gesture and spun on his heel. "Och, to hell with ye and yer blasted trunk. Do what ye please as Clarens 'ave been doing since the dawn of time. More the fool I am fer carin'."

Maggie scrambled to a stand. "Wait."

He continued to stalk toward the cabin.

"You're not a fool. I know how important history is to you and I shouldn't have teased you. I'm sorry."

He stilled, then slowly turned to face her. "Wha' did ye say?"

"I said that I know family heirlooms aren't something to be taken—"

"No' that. The other, the last part." He took several steps closer to her. "Repeat that last part to me again."

Maggie tried not to scowl. The blackguard. Couldn't he just take a sincere apology for what it was worth without rubbing her face in it? She almost wished she hadn't said anything and let him storm off believing the worst of her. Perhaps then she could have had some peace and quiet, some time alone without him looking over her shoulder to look in Lachlan's books. But his horrified expression when she'd suggested selling her inheritance was etched in her mind.

She squared her shoulders and leveled her chin. "I said I was sorry for teasing you."

He walked closer, stopping a foot or two away from her. Feet braced apart, he crossed his arms as he regarded her. "Ye were lyin' then, about sellin' the trunk and burning the journals."

"Not lying," she said, maintaining her own proud stance in the face of his questioning glare.

"Then why did you tell me what you did?"

"Because you stand around looking so distant and sounding so pompous slandering my family all over the place and I was tired of it. I just wanted to get a reaction out of you, that's all."

He seemed to ponder this for a moment. "You say I slander the Clarens' yet you make no attempt to defend them."

"I defended Mairi and it almost got me skewered with a poker. You'll have to forgive me if I don't like debating with you."

He waved away her concern. "I wouldn't have run you through, lass."

Now it was Maggie's turn to snort and cross her arms. "You'll have to forgive me if I don't believe that. From where I was standing, I thought my time was up. I already saw my life flash before me once. I don't like repeats."

Duncan stepped closer. Maggie struggled to maintain her stance as he invaded her personal space for the second time that afternoon.

"What are you doing?" she demanded.

"You said I was distant. I'm trying to improve on my shortcomings."

Maggie swallowed hard. "You took me too literally."

She looked up into his eyes. "You can be physically close to me, but you still come across as distant."

"Dinna forget pompous." There wasn't a trace of a smile on his face, but she thought she detected the hint of it in his eyes.

"I call them like I see them."

"Am I really so bad as all that, Maggie?"

"You come from a different time, Duncan. You're used to commanding people—I'm simply not used to being commanded."

The sudden flare in his eyes caught her unawares. It made her temperature spike along with her heart rate. He moved closer, inclining his head toward hers.

In a voice more gentle than she'd ever heard from him, he said, "Yer no' so different from yer ancestors as you think, Maggie Claren."

She dipped her chin under the intensity of his gaze. "You asked me why I don't defend my clan. I don't know anything of my family's past. I know nothing of who they were, what deeds they did, dastardly or otherwise. I suppose that damns me in your eyes as much as my supposed similarity to them." She straightened a bit, holding his steady regard, watching him just as closely.

"Do ye care so much what I think of ye, Maggie Claren?"

The answer stunned her. "Yes, apparently, I do."

"A pompous, distant man like me?" The twinkle returned. Along with it came a slight twitch at the corner of his mouth that was the closest he'd come to a true smile since she'd met him. It did amazing things to her heart rate.

He's not real, she reminded herself. But Lord he sure looked real. "You—" She broke off to clear her throat. "You, um, don't seem so distant. At the moment."

"Aye. And I'm no' feeling so pompous." His lips twitched again, then smoothed, the look in his eyes deep-

ening to something serious and sincere. "While yer a lot
like yer ancestors, Maggie, I'm beginning to see that in
many ways, yer nothing like them at all."

"Because I swallowed my pride and apologized?"

He tapped a finger on her chest above her breast, then
let it rest there with a small caress. "Because ye have a
heart. Somethin' I've been accused of no' being able tae
claim."

"You have to have one, to recognize one." Maggie tenta-
tively raised her hand to cover his. He was warm. She felt a
pulse thrum beneath her fingertips. Alive. She looked down
to where they touched, then back up to him. "What are
you Duncan MacKinnon, man or ghost?"

FIVE

"RIGHT NOW, I'M a man, wi' blood running through my veins." He lifted his fingers so that they wove between hers. "And my blood is runnin' hot and heavy wi' the touch of you under my fingertips." He pressed her own fingertips against her chest. "Aye and yer heart is beating strong and fine as well." He dipped his chin and angled his head, holding her gaze as he moved his face closer to hers.

Maggie couldn't have so much as blinked in that moment. Her breath was stalled in her throat, her mind was drunk on the sensations rocketing through her, an intoxicating thrall created by his touch, his words, his heat, his overwhelming nearness. She waited for him to close the distance, to take her mouth in a devastating kiss like any good rogue Scots hero would. Her eyes drifted shut, her lips parted . . .

"Open yer eyes."

She did and found him staring intently at her. "Ye want to be ravished, is that it?"

Maggie felt embarrassment heat her skin clear down to her neck. She tried to pull away, but he locked his arm around her back and pulled her against him. The feel of him hard and strong against her threatened to buckle her knees. She had to get away before he let her fall into a heap at his feet while he had a good laugh over her silly female sensibilities. She should have heeded her own advice and steered well clear of her supernatural roommate and put her mind to more important things, *real* things, like determining how to escape the last man she'd gotten weak-kneed over.

Although Judd had never once made her feel a sliver of the awareness pulsing through her at this moment.

He hugged her tighter still, jerking her full attention to his face, which was now a mere breath away from hers. Duncan was disturbingly real.

"Aye, I could ravage ye lass and we'd both be the happier for it I'm certain."

She tried to struggle from his grasp, then went totally still and held him in as cool a regard as she could muster. "I no longer wish to ravish or be ravished," she lied, "and I'll thank you to unhand me immediately."

With a deep, honest laugh that moved her when it shouldn't have, he hugged her to his chest, then set her back a space, still holding her captive with both hands. "Och, but you have the Claren spirit in abundance." His laughter subsided, but his smile did not.

It transformed him so completely, she stood there, mouth open, basking in the amazing glow of it.

He bent his head close and spoke in a whisper against her ear. "I'll have that kiss, Maggie, but I'll no' be takin' it from you. I've had my fill of taking without receiving. We'll share it when it's done. And it will be done. Many times if I'm to be the judge of it."

Shared, he'd said. Demanded. Macho, yes, egotistical, yes, but she wanted his kiss. Perhaps many of his kisses. And he was right about one other thing, damn him. She didn't want to be taken.

"Where is yer smart mouth when it would do ye the most good, bonnie Maggie?" Duncan asked softly.

"I think my smart mouth was doing too well for its own good," she said faintly.

Aye, that it was, Duncan thought, coming abruptly to his senses. He should be backing away. She drew him in, made him feel a warmth the likes of which he had not felt in three hundred years. Nay, perhaps ever. And yet it was precisely that she so easily drew him in that alarmed him the most. With more control than he'd expected to be able to drum up, he let her go, stepping away from her as further insurance.

"If yer as smart as that mouth of yours, Maggie, you will be well warned to stay away from me."

He took the loss of her smile as if it were a physical injury to him. That the look of hurt and confusion was quickly masked only made him feel worse. She had pride, that one did. And he was hard-pressed, despite their twined history, to do anything but admire her for it. "Yer pride will stand you in good stead, where I canno'." He braced his feet and crossed his arms as if needing a shield. "Take yourself off with Lachlan's journals and learn something of your ancestors. Perhaps there you will learn why I warn ye awa'."

He waited for her rebuttal. When she did not deliver one he realized just how badly he'd wanted to be challenged to change his mind. After a long quiet look, she turned and walked back to the trunk, retrieving a batch of Lachlan's leather volumes.

"Maggie."

She paused, then finally looked at him, her brow raised in a silent question.

"Where do ye want the trunk?"

"I can handle—"

"Where do ye want it?" he demanded, somewhat more

forcefully than he'd intended. Och, but she tried him in ways he didna ken and perhaps would be wise not to.

"The loft," she answered evenly. "But don't think you can blink it away and make amends for your rude behavior."

"I've been pompous and distant, now rude, have I? Those are the least of the names ye'd have called me if I'd continued."

"You're taking an awful lot for granted where I'm concerned, Duncan MacKinnon. I can make up my own mind on what I want and don't want."

"As can I, Maggie, as can I. Like as no' it will be another sin I'll be paying for, but less of one against you."

"What are you talking about? We're both adults. Why can't we do whatever the hell we want to if we both agree to it?"

"I'll no' listen to yer swearing and carryings on. If I say we are done wi' it, we are done wi' it. Now move out of my way."

She merely glared at him and folded her arms. "You're scared aren't you? You were actually feeling something there and it scared you, didn't it?"

Duncan decided to ignore her. She'd live longer if he did. He bent to lift the trunk. With a groan he hoisted the unwieldy thing and began a labored walk to the stairs. He prayed he did not disgrace himself by tripping on them.

She walked behind him. "Why are you doing this?"

He had no breath to answer.

After several more strong opinions regarding his stubbornness, she ran past him and called out instructions, guiding him up the warped stairs and around the rotted boards. She then held the door for him as he maneuvered himself and the trunk inside. He lowered the thing beside the base of the ladder in a dust-raising thud.

"Couldn't you have just, you know, blinked it in here?"

He straightened and looked at her. "Aye," he said, gathering his breath.

"Then why—"

"Because I have only thirty-one mortal days a year and I wanted to use my God-given strength where I could." He gave her a pointed look, but as usual, she did not heed his warning.

"Then you are mortal?"

"As much as a soul in purgatory can be."

"Purgatory? Why? Penance for Mairi's death? Surely you don't bear the guilt of her choice."

"It is not I who makes the choice of purgatory, but Them who do. I merely exist in it, to feel guilt or no'."

"Them? Who are *They*?"

"*They* control the passage of souls." He sighed, not sure if this was a wise discussion. But her curiosity was fired up. He could see it in her eyes and he knew not if he was strong enough to deny her the knowledge she sought. Nor was he certain he could deny himself the comfort her presence and her conversation were affording him.

"Is that it then? You're stuck in purgatory for all eternity because They say so?"

"Until I learn the lessons They deem necessary, aye, that is the way of it."

"What lessons?"

Duncan rubbed a hand over his face. "I do not wish to discuss this wi' you."

"I didn't wish to have you invade my cabin or my life either, but you're here and I don't seem to have any choice in the matter. You say your past is mixed up with one of my ancestors. Doesn't that give me some right to understand why you're here?"

"Read the journals. Perhaps Lachlan explains it."

"Maybe he does. But if so, that will likely be the perspective of my side of the family. Mairi's not wandering the hillsides of North Carolina as a ghost. *You* are. I'd like to hear it from you."

"And I'd like to be left alone."

She stepped closer to him. "Then you should have left me alone. But you didn't. So it's too late—you involved me. So deal with it."

"Don' step too close to me, Maggie," he warned softly. "Or we'll be involved, as you say, in every way a man and woman can be. I gave ye a warnin' as much for yer own good as fer mine. I ask you to leave me be before we both take steps better not taken."

"Speak for yourself," she said.

"Now who's bein' stubborn and unwise?" he asked, tamping down the sudden urge to smile. Bluidy hell, but she riled him up in ways he did not understand.

She looked up at him then, her eyes no longer filled with anger and righteousness. There was doubt and fear behind all that soft blue. He wanted to think her a pretender as her ancestors had been, using their arsenal of feminine wiles to urge a man to do as they bid.

He was having a hard time ascribing that character to Maggie. He released a short sigh. Perhaps he'd learnt more over the centuries than he'd been aware of if this chit could simply walk in here and move him in these strange ways. Whatever the cause, he could not have looked away from her at this moment even had someone swung a claymore at his head. Daft he was. Daft and soft.

"My life as I know it is gone," she said quietly. "I had to leave my job, my home, and all my possessions. Everything I worked for is gone. I can't call or write to anyone. I'm a virtual prisoner here. Very much like you. You have lessons to learn here. So do I. I have to learn how to survive. I have to learn how to get myself out of this mess I'm in. I have to find a way to keep the man I once thought I loved from killing me."

A thread of steel entered her expression and she straightened a bit. "You're right. I guess I was too eager to find a diversion from my very real problems. The last thing I need to do is get caught up with you." She tried a smile and a laugh, but both wobbled on a sudden gulp of air. "I mean, I don't even believe in ghosts."

He realized that bit of steel he'd spied in her was more thin shield than the thick walls protecting a fortress. He also realized that his own shield was thinning where she was concerned. He wanted to rail at the deities for finally conjuring so perfect a teacher. He could not tear his eyes away from hers. More proof of his quick descent after three hundred years of solid resistance.

What demon was this They had sent him? Bluidy hell. The deities be damned, but reach out he did. He held her chin with the tips of two fingers, his attention drawn by the sight of his scarred hands so near to something as perfect and soft as her skin.

"I'll make you a compromise," he said. "The first a MacKinnon has ever willingly made with a Claren."

Her expression turned wary. He smiled. "Tell me yer story and I'll see what I can do to help ye leave this place." *And me,* he thought, not liking the instant pang of regret that followed. "Then we can both have what we want, you your life back and me my peace, such as it is. And if yer still interested when we're done, I'll tell you the story of Duncan MacKinnon before you go."

She didn't say anything for the longest time, but the fear receded a bit from her eyes and she finally lifted her chin away from his touch. He curled his fingers back by his side, rubbing the tips against his palms as if he could rub away the feel of her. It only seemed to burnish the softness deeper into his skin.

"I don't know what you could do to help. But no matter what happens, I will hold you to your end of the bargain," she warned. "I might agree that we shouldn't get any more involved than we have, but I doubt I'll ever meet up with another ghost again in my life, so you get elected to satisfy my sudden curiosity about the afterlife."

"So is that all I am? A curiosity?" Why he goaded he had no notion. "Yer a smart and bonnie lass, Maggie. You make me wonder how it is you were foolish enough tae have a man huntin' you down, wantin' tae kill you."

Her eyes flashed and that shadow of vulnerability mercifully disappeared. "*I* thought we were sharing our lives together. *He* thought I belonged to him. He didn't understand that loyalty and devotion aren't earned by threats and commands."

Duncan's heart stilled. Did she know how close she had come to pricking his own shamed heart?

"All I wanted was out. He wouldn't accept that."

"To the point of death?" he asked, even as his own heart taunted him with the same question. *Didn't you chase your betrothed to her own death and yours because you couldn't accept her refusal of you?* That was different! he wanted to roar. Mairi's refusal of him hadn't just spurned him as a man, it had condemned an entire clan to their deaths!

"He's a vice president in charge of international investments for one of the largest banks in Manhattan. I'm a stockbroker, or was anyway. We were very compatible and though he wasn't my dream man, he was certainly closer than anyone else I'd dated. He was a bit on the domineering side, but I figured I could handle that. I'm thirty, it was time, we both wanted it, so I agreed to marry him.

"As soon as the ring was on my finger, his behavior changed. He became annoyingly possessive. We argued constantly and eventually I realized, as much as it hurt me, that the man I'd chosen to marry wasn't going to change, and that, as his wife, he would only get worse. So I broke it off with him."

"How di' ye leave him? Di' ye sneak off in the middle o' the night or di' ye confront him wi' how ye felt?"

She shot him a sharp look. "I didn't sneak off, not the

first time anyway, though in retrospect that might have been the wiser move. He knew I wasn't happy, so I told him my feelings had changed and that I couldn't marry him."

"And his reaction?"

"He was furious and refused to accept it."

Duncan swallowed his retort and shifted his weight from one foot to the other, suddenly wanting to pull at the already loose laces around his throat.

"Here I thought I'd finally met a true gentleman and he was really a barbarian in a designer suit. Maybe there was some aura of danger that initially attracted me. But after the episode in the stairwell of my condo, I know there is absolutely nothing remotely romantic about danger, restrained or otherwise."

Duncan came to full attention. "What incident? Wha' di' the bluidy bastard do to ye?"

She appeared startled by his vehemence. No more startled than he was himself, to be sure.

"He'd been hounding me day and night, threatening me. I didn't really think he'd do anything, but one night he was waiting for me behind the door to the stairs of my building. He pulled me in the stairwell and shoved me around a bit. When I got angry and told him to lay off before I started screaming, he grabbed me by the throat and shoved me up against the railing. I'm fifteen stories up, so it was a long drop. He bent me backward and laughed in my face. He was choking me and I honestly had no idea if he was going to push me over." She rubbed one hand along her arm and wrapped the other protectively around her throat. "I had never been so terrified. I think that scared me the most. That this man I'd once made love to could— and would—terrify me."

Duncan stared at the fear in her eyes and a rage filled him. He wanted nothing more than to storm from the cabin and track down the cowardly whoreson himself so he could personally choke the life from his heart and lungs. He was already turning toward the door when two thoughts stilled him. First, he could not leave the mountain. Such was his lot in purgatory.

But it was the second reason that had him turning toward the dying fire. Here he was wanting to kill a man for behaving the barbarian to this bonnie lass, this bonnie *Claren* lass! A more brutal irony he'd yet to face in his three hundred years of this hellish existence.

He might not have ever laid his hands on Mairi's throat or struck at her in anger, but he had been more barbarian than gentleman to her throughout their ill-fated betrothal. He had never once given serious thought to any of her protests, thinking only of his clan. Her wants and needs mattered naught.

"He let me go just before I blacked out," Maggie said. "He warned me that he'd have me back or kill me trying."

Duncan felt his skin grow hot and his chest grow tight. The ancient scene flashed fully before him. He watched the snowflakes coming down as he grabbed Mairi, wrapping her frail form in blankets, so intent on leaving the cabin that day the ghost of Argyll himself could not have stopped him. He listened yet again as Mairi flayed him with her sharp tongue, chiding this ultimate stupidity, and him telling her he'd made it through far worse. A little snow was not going to stop them from making the shore and the ship that awaited them. The snow fell harder. Mairi's health, already worn from a sickness she'd caught during the long trek over the sea, failed more rapidly than he could believe. The snow turned into a blizzard. He huddled them under a bush as any progress became impossible. Bundled her closer, wrapping them both in tartan and blanket, even though they both knew warding off the freezing temperatures would quickly become a losing battle.

Her accusing eyes stared into his before she finally closed them in what became her eternal sleep.

"I immediately went for a restraining order," Maggie was saying. "I hoped he'd decide I wasn't worth the effort at that point and leave me alone."

"He wouldna have," Duncan said hoarsely. He continued to stare into the fire, watching the wood turn to ash.

"It's not like we were the love match of the century."

Duncan faced her. He reached out before he could stop himself and stroked his hand down the length of her tangled hair, his touch as gentle as he could make it. His fingers trembled. "There is no effort too great when honor is at stake, lass. However misguided that honor might be."

"So I'm to die because his ego is wounded?"

The weight of his shame threatened to crush him. "You wouldna be the first, lass."

"That doesn't make it right."

Duncan sighed and released her. He turned back to the fire. "No, it doesna make it right. I, of all people, am beginning to understand the truth of that."

SIX

WHEN THE BOOK hit her face for the fifth time, Maggie finally agreed to call it a night. She'd barely made a dent in Lachlan's volumes, but she was already enraptured by the rich, detailed way he related his family history.

Her family history.

Maggie was sorely tempted to sit up and peer over the loft railing to see what Duncan was doing. Still brooding? After their earlier discussion, he'd descended into one of his blacker moods, helping her lift a small stack of the journals up to the loft before retreating in silence to stand and poke about in the fire.

He'd said nothing more about her problems with Judd and she'd decided not to press him on the matter. If she'd thought him cold and unapproachable before, the stony countenance he currently sported made his earlier moods seem festive by comparison.

She'd planned to talk to him when she came down to rummage for dinner, but she'd been so caught up in the journals, she hadn't even noticed the sun going down. Now her eyes were tired and her stomach rumbling. She raised her eyebrows when she noted that the nightstand lamp had lit itself at some point during her immersion in the past.

She carefully marked her place in the book and slid her legs over the bed, indulging in a long stretch. So far her reading had barely taken her as far back as the turn of the current century. She'd been disappointed to discover that the first journal began with her grandfather, whom she now assumed was one of Lachlan's many brothers, so there was no mention of her father. From what she gathered, Lachlan had been doing more than tracing his family history and recording familial anecdotes. It seemed as if he were on a hunt of some kind, a quest almost. To prove what, however, she had no idea. But the lives of the Claren clan were so vividly and colorfully drawn, she had all but forgotten her curiosity about Duncan's life . . . and that of his be-trothed.

She recalled with sudden clarity how remote and haunted his expression had become as she'd gone on about her past with Judd. She crept to the edge of the loft and spied down on the cabin.

Empty.

"Damn," she muttered. She hadn't realized how badly she'd wanted him to be there. Then her gaze lit on the plate sitting on the trestle table. A napkin covered it and an apple sat beside it. Dinner? À la Duncan?

She smiled dryly as she scrambled down the ladder. The apple was probably poisoned. She hadn't even heard him moving about down here, her attention so caught up in her reading. There were still beads of water on the freshly washed apple and the ham and cheese sandwich beneath the napkin was soft and fresh, the lettuce still crisp. She devoured the meal quickly, wondering where Duncan had gone off to this time.

The front door suddenly burst open. Duncan entered the cabin with a fresh armload of split wood.

Maggie leaped off the bench. "You scared me half to death."

"Your nose has been buried so deep, I didna think a bellowing elk would rouse you."

"There are no elk in North Carolina." Silence. Still grumpy, she mused. "Thank you for the meal. That was thoughtful of you." Her appreciation only seemed to darken his mood further. He dumped the lumber in a small stack on the stone hearth and proceeded to add fuel to the low fire.

"Is that the whole of your existence when you're on earth?" she asked, deliberately prodding him. Even a blast of anger was better than this dark silence. "If you're not poking at it and feeding it, you're out chopping wood for it. You're the only man I know who can turn fire-tending into a full time job."

His back was still when he spoke. "Wha' I do is no' any business o' yours."

She changed tactics. "Where do you go when you pop out of here? I mean, when you're not chopping wood."

He surprised her by answering. "I canna 'blink' out of here, as you say. For this one month each year, I am relegated to this mountain and this mountain only."

"But you do blink," she persisted. "I mean, you popped out of here when I first came into the house, taking the furniture with you. Which made me think I'd gone crazy, by the way. And you did it again when you tried to run me through with the poker. How do you do that?"

He let loose with a long suffering sigh. Maggie hid a smile, just in case he could see things without actually looking at them. And that was another question she wanted the answer to. Preferably before she got ready for bed.

"I can move my spirit out of my body if I choose, but only to land with it somewhere else on this godforsaken hill. I canna go back to the spirit world. No' that this is any better or worse." He poked a bit viciously at the log, creating a shower of sparks and ash. "Although you don't always feel so damned cold in purgatory. Ye don't feel anything."

"You're cold? This place is like an oven." Maggie regarded him for a moment, not liking the softening she felt in her heart. "Is that why you maintain the fire so fiercely, Duncan? You're always cold when you're on earth?"

"I've lived in colder climes than this, lass, wi' no fire to warm my hide, nor clothes to cover my back."

It was a dismissal, if she'd ever heard one, and an evasive one at that, but Maggie was learning to read beneath his blustering statements and stony countenance.

"So," she began, smiling freely when he stiffened in continued frustration, "when you pop out of here and take all this stuff with you, does it pop down wherever you do? I bet that gets real interesting."

No response.

"Is this the furniture that was here originally? Or do you get to pick what you want? 'Cause I don't see you as a lace curtain kinda guy. And can you conjure up anything? That would explain the empty cupboards. But you know, a satellite dish would be most appreciated." She paused, gauging the tension mounting in his stance. "If it wouldn't be too much trouble."

Still nothing. She stifled a short sigh. She didn't really want him exploding in anger. She recalled what had happened the last time tempers had risen. Her temperature had risen right along with it. Along with several other things.

She'd managed to repress the memory of the kiss they'd come so close to sharing all afternoon and evening. Until now. Just the thought of it brought back the rush of sensations she'd felt, every touch, every—"

"What is wrong with ye, lass?"

Maggie abruptly stopped fanning her face. He'd turned

toward her, but rather than a smug expression, she found concern. And frustration. He didn't want to care about her. But could it be that he did? She recalled the meal he'd prepared for her. Even if he'd just conjured it up, it was still proof he'd worried about her. The idea of him caring made her feel . . . well, good. That was bad. Wasn't it?

God, shouldn't there be some lesson learned in what Judd put her through? Shouldn't she be a better judge of men now? The simple answer was no. Different man, different set of criteria. And no two men were alike.

She almost laughed. Most certainly there was no man on earth like Duncan MacKinnon. God only knew what lessons she was about to learn this time.

"I, uh, I think I'll go on up to bed," she said finally. Whatever she'd thought she'd seen in his eyes moments before was gone. The implacable mask was back in place. If only he'd keep it that way for another couple of weeks or so. Maybe they'd both escape this incarceration with their emotions unscathed.

She went to the small bathing area and drew the curtain, then poked her head back out. He was staring at the fire once again, but she knew he'd watched her leave. The ripple of pleasure that knowledge sent through her should have been warning enough. *Shut the curtain and wash up for bed, Maggie.* But she had to know. "Just how far do your powers of observation extend? When you're on earth?"

He kept his back to her. "If yer worried about your privacy, I've no intention of invadin' it."

"But could you, if you wanted to? Without, you know, physically invading it?"

He turned to face her. "Is there something ye have so unique that I should be sneakin' about tae see it?"

Maggie flushed. "Point made. I'll just take my excruciatingly average self to bed then. Sorry, to have bothered you, my lord." She yanked the curtains shut and started to turn on the water, but paused when she heard him speak.

"I am no lord, lass. No chieftain either. I am but the shamed second son." This quiet statement was punctuated by the loud thump of another log joining the fire.

She opened the curtain, but when she came out, he wasn't there. She found herself thinking about going outside to see if she could find him. Just to see where he goes, she told herself, not to do anything rash.

She could hear the wind whipping through the trees. It was dark, and the mountain was still unfamiliar territory. But that wasn't what made her decide to stay. No matter what he said about his limited powers, she was certain Duncan MacKinnon was only seen when he chose to be seen.

Snuggled in bed—after changing under the covers—her thoughts shifted to the journal she'd been reading. She'd already rummaged to the bottom of the trunk, but Lachlan's rambling didn't seem to follow any sort of chronology. Information on Mairi and Duncan could be in any one of the lengthy volumes, if it was there at all. She wondered yet again what it was Lachlan had been searching for, but drifted off to sleep before she could match action to thought.

BY THE AFTERNOON of her fifth day in hiding, Maggie was ready to tear out her hair, one strand at a time. Duncan had made himself all but invisible, the irony of which had ceased to be amusing days ago. They had little if any conversation and even her best attempts at goading him had fallen on seemingly deaf ears.

His offer to help her with her problems hadn't come up again and her pride and his silence kept her from mentioning it.

Other than a daily foray or two into the woods which just happened to coincide with Duncan's daily disappearances, she'd spent most of her time tucked away with

Lachlan's journals. So far she hadn't gone further back than the 1800s but she was still as fascinated by the people Lachlan wrote about as she was by Lachlan himself.

She wished she'd had the opportunity to meet Lachlan Claren. From his frank, no nonsense observations and dry wit in describing his own ancestors, he sounded like quite the character. She imagined he and her Aunt Mathilda would have made quite the duo.

Maggie stared out the front porch window and wondered where Duncan had gone off to this time. In all her attempts, she'd yet to find a trace of him in the woods. She scowled, remembering early this morning, when she was certain she heard the chopping sounds of wood being cut, yet each clearing she'd sneaked up on had turned out to be absent of man or chopped wood. All she got was the faint moaning of the wind and the occasional echo of bagpipes mocking her.

She slanted a look at the freshly stacked pile of wood by the fireplace that had been there when she'd returned. Damn the man's ghostly hide!

She'd been here almost a week. A week with no newspapers, no CSPAN, no cell phone, no stock reports. She couldn't recall ever being that cut off from the day-to-day workings of her world. Even one week out of the race and she wondered how she'd ever catch up. Or if she could.

For that alone she'd never forgive Judd. She'd been good at her job and she'd enjoyed the sweat and grit it had taken to climb the ladder. So, maybe she'd daydreamed once or twice while twirling her engagement ring around that Judd's demands that she give up her career to become the perfect corporate wife didn't rankle as badly as they should have. That he'd made them rankled, but . . .

But now she'd have to start over from scratch. After escaping from the condo, she'd gone straight to the police station. They'd told her they could arrest him for violating the restraining order, but that if she had anywhere else to go, preferably a place Judd didn't know about, it would be best if she went there. Immediately.

She read stories like this in the papers all the time. They didn't have to spell it out for her, that with Judd's money and connections, it was likely he'd be back on the street in no time . . . and there was nothing they could do about it. What they didn't have to tell her was how much angrier he'd be after getting bail posted.

She had no family to run to, no friends she would put in the middle of a dangerous situation. She clearly recalled the sickeningly irrational look in Judd's eyes. There was no vacation long enough to make him forget his determination to have her or destroy her.

So she'd emptied her accounts, bought the junk heap and called her boss about an extended vacation while she sorted out some personal problems. She was a climber, a go-getter, he'd said, but he'd noticed her work had been suffering of late. He had to be able to depend on her and if he couldn't, there were others in her department that he could.

And so ended her illustrious career on Wall Street.

Which was why she needed to get her butt in gear and figure out what in the hell she was going to do. She couldn't stay here forever. She shivered despite the roaring fire. Judd had connections all over the country, hell, all over the world. And Judd always got what he wanted. He'd find her. She didn't know how, but she couldn't believe he'd just let things go.

And she'd been sitting here for a week with her head in the sand, pretending things would just fix themselves. Maybe she'd head back over to the neighboring town of Griffith again and look into hiring a private detective. If she had someone following Judd, at least she'd know if he was tracking her down. And maybe, just maybe, she'd get some indication that he'd given up and was moving on to possess and control someone else.

Shuddering, she knew she didn't believe that. Judd would never give up, even if he had ten women on his arm. Duncan was right. It was about pride and honor, as twisted as Judd's was.

It hit her hard that she truly might never go home again. And just where in the hell *was* home for her anymore? Madden County, North Carolina?

Well, hiring the detective would at least give her some peace of mind while she figured out where she'd go to start over. It was a plan. She felt immediately better.

She hurried up the ladder and pulled on a thick sweater. She dragged her purse out from under a pile of laundry, then swore when she realized she'd better take that to town with her. She laughed humorlessly. Another life adjustment for the woman who had been a slave to her dry cleaner.

Her gaze fell on the journal lying open on the bed. She might as well take it with her, something to read during the spin cycles. Though she was still disappointed that she hadn't seen any mention of Duncan or Mairi, the MacKinnons made frequent appearances in Lachlan's roaming stories. Lachlan had time and again referred to something he termed the "Legend MacKinnon," but he tended to ramble and go off on tangents.

She scooped up the book and reread the last paragraph.

My digging has brought me yet another tragic story from The Legend MacKinnon. I see my theory might have some weight to it. I am none too happy to be proven right. Too much tragedy between our clans. So much so the tales surrounding them have spawned a legend. And I must wonder how long these tales have endured? How many generations does this legend touch? And what was the spark that began it? These are the questions I must answer if I am to find my peace.

The mystery of this "legend" had definitely sparked her curiosity. She would corner Duncan this evening, one way or another, and question him on what he might know about it.

Not that she was looking for excuses to talk to the man or anything.

She was halfway down the ladder when she heard the unmistakable sound of a car engine. She dropped her things and moved quickly to the front window, careful to stand to one side as a dusty black four-wheel-drive Jeep pulled up behind her car. There was no Sheriff's Office decal on the side, or any other official looking markings.

It couldn't be deputy Branson, and she doubted it was Judge Nash.

Dear God. Had Judd found her? Maggie's heart rose to her throat even as it pounded so loudly she couldn't hear herself breathe. She turned and looked around for a weapon, any weapon. The poker! She dashed for it, bending as low as she could, to avoid being seen through the windows.

Oh God, why hadn't she left earlier? What in heaven's name had she been thinking? With shaking hands she grabbed the poker, slippery in her sweaty palms. Stay cool, think cool. She crawled over to the door, and stood behind it, poker raised over her head. Where in the hell was Duncan now, when she really needed him?

"Maggie? Maggie Claren?"

It took Maggie a moment to realize it was a woman's voice calling out her name. Could Judd have hired someone to find her? And if so, what was this person supposed to do? Kidnap her and drag her back to Manhattan so Judd could kill her? Or maybe Judd had decided he wanted her dead but didn't want blood on his vice presidential hands. A female hitwoman? She hitched the poker higher and braced her legs. It was the nineties. It could happen.

She inched over to the side of the window and peeked out. A tall woman with long blonde hair pulled back in a loose braid, wearing worn khakis, a mountaineer-style jacket and hiking boots, was looking inside her car. The woman straightened and turned toward the house. "Hello. Is anyone home?"

Maggie snorted. *Did Judd assume I would think she was a neighbor stopping by to borrow sugar and just invite her in?* "You're going to have to work a little bit harder than that if you want to kill me, sweetheart."

SEVEN

MAGGIE HEARD STEPS on the creaking porch. She tensed, then froze when a knock sounded on the door. Every muscle locked in terror, perspiration trickled down her temples and beaded on her upper lip. Could she really strike a total stranger with deadly intent? She'd have to. If the woman out there moved first, it would likely be the one and only move made.

"Maggie Claren?" A short rapping followed. "Judge Nash told me where I could find you."

Judge Nash? Maggie didn't budge. If Judd had tracked her down, he'd have already found out about Judge Nash and Maggie's inheritance.

"My name is Cailean. Cailean Claren." There was a pause, then a short laugh that sounded both amused and a tad disbelieving.

Cailean Claren, my ass, Maggie silently sneered.

"I'm your long-lost cousin. You have something that was supposed to be sent to me. The solicitor in Scotland couldn't find me." There was a pause, then, "So he sent it here and Nash gave it to you. A large trunk. With some journals in it. From our Great-Uncle Lachlan."

Our Uncle Lachlan? Maggie almost snorted, then stopped. If Judd had somehow found out about her inheritance, he'd know about Lachlan. But no one, not even Judge Nash himself, knew what was inside the trunk. The original solicitor might know, but Judd couldn't have gotten to him that fast. Could he?

Her head started to hurt. It couldn't really be a long-lost cousin. This was simply too surreal.

"Look, Judge Nash warned me you weren't too keen on receiving company, but I've traveled a long way and I'd really like to talk with you. Could you just, please, open the door? I promise I won't stay long."

Maggie slowly moved to the other side of the door and peered again from the very edge of the window. The woman was pulling her backpack off, and loosening the string to reach inside. Maggie swung the poker back over her head and braced her feet, ready to swing or dive, depending on the size of the gun.

But she didn't pull out a gun. She pulled out two leather bound journals. Two very familiar looking journals.

"Are you at least interested in looking at the rest of his journals?"

Maggie lowered the poker slowly. She was for real?

"Fine, okay," Cailean said in defeat. "God knows I didn't want to be here anyway. I didn't even want the damn trunk or the damn journals," she continued as she walked to her Jeep. "I'll just throw these out and the hell with all this."

Maggie moved without thinking. She yanked open the door. "Don't you dare toss them out."

Cailean swung around, but there was no smug smile of a battle craftily won. She looked as sincerely disgusted as she sounded. "It's about time."

Maggie folded her arms. "Judge Nash did warn you."

"I believe you have something that belongs to me."

"Something you've already stated you don't want."

"Maybe so, but it's mine nonetheless." She reached into her backpack.

Maggie realized she was still carrying the poker when her hands flexed around it. She lifted it waist high.

Cailean's stony expression cracked a little as her lips curved. "It's the papers from the solicitor. I'm unarmed." She flashed the folded documents.

Maggie didn't lower the poker. "If you don't want the journals, I'd like to keep them. You can take the trunk."

Cailean merely raised an eyebrow. "Such generosity with my property."

"Property you don't want."

"What I want has little to do with anything." She paused, then impatiently brushed at the loose hairs framing her face. Maggie had the impression what she really wanted to do was massage her temples. "I need to see the journals and the trunk too. Listen," she said abruptly, "do you think I could get something cold to drink? I've been on the road for a long time and—" She broke off. Her features looked pinched and drawn.

Concerned now, Maggie lowered the poker and stepped off the porch. "Are you okay?"

"Just tired." She tried to smile but didn't pull it off very well. "A cold drink would help. Water is fine if you have it."

So much for her trip to Griffith. "Follow me."

Once inside Maggie took the papers from Cailean and motioned toward the old rocker that faced the hearth. "Have a seat. I'll get a glass." She scanned the documents. They looked legal enough.

Cailean nodded. "It's like a furnace in here."

Maggie found herself smiling at that. "Yeah, it is." She wondered when Duncan would put in an appearance. That was going to be interesting. She should probably warn Cailean, but Maggie discovered she wasn't as anxious for her to leave as she had been several minutes ago. A cousin.

She had family. Maggie shook her head, unable to grasp it. She just hoped she could get a few questions answered before he made his grand entrance.

She eyed Cailean as she drank the water. Her features were still strained, but not as pinched as they had been. Her khakis looked well worn and more than a bit rumpled and her hiking boots looked like she might actually have hiked here in them. "Where did you travel from?"

"Peru." She handed the glass back. "Thank you."

Maggie raised her eyebrows.

"I was working. I'm an anthropologist. The executors of Lachlan's estate had all but given up on finding me."

"When they passed on the documents to Nash, they told him I was the last remaining heir. I guess they shipped his trunk here when they couldn't find you. I didn't know."

"Saved me a trip to Scotland, anyway."

"I would gladly have traded places." Maggie waved a hand. "All this luxury could have been yours."

Cailean's smile was mild, but appeared more heartfelt. "You could have it all if it were up to me."

"Are there more family relations out there to meet?"

She shook her head and gently dropped her backpack and the journals to the floor beside her. "Just me."

They lapsed into silence, openly studying one another. Maggie smiled first and stuck out her hand. "Margaret Mary Claren. Pleased to meet you, cousin Cailean."

Cailean's hand was strong and callused. "Likewise."

"So, exactly how are we related? I don't know much about my family."

"We have something in common then. Neither do I."

Cailean didn't seem all that upset about it. A week ago, Maggie would have understood the feeling completely. "I've been reading Lachlan's journals. He apparently made genealogy a sort of life quest."

"As far as I can tell, the confusion with the property was because Lachlan hadn't updated his will recently."

Maggie nodded. "He left my inheritance to his nephew, my father. How did they find you?"

"These other journals were found in some things he'd left to a friend in Scotland. They had some information on my parents in them, so the man who had them contacted the solicitor. I guess that was the missing link to me. I was on a dig, but they finally tracked me down. He forwarded the journals to me, along with the information about the trunk." She laid the journals on top of her pack.

"I wonder why they told me I was the last heir?"

"I guess when they couldn't locate me, they figured you were."

"So, you haven't read the journals you have?"

Cailean's smile faded, the pinched look returned to the corners of her mouth and eyes. "No. I haven't."

"Well, if Lachlan was one of my grandfather's brothers, then you must be descended from another brother."

"You're probably right."

"That would make us what? Second cousins?"

"If our grandfathers were two of Lachlan's brothers, it makes our fathers cousins. Or would, if mine were alive."

"Mine died, too, when I was little. Both my parents did. Sort of spooky, the similarities."

"Spooky. Yeah." Cailean's laugh rang a bit hollow. Maggie wanted to chalk it up to her obvious fatigue, but she sensed there was something more disturbing running through her cousin's mind.

"So, you didn't know about Lachlan at all?"

Cailean shook her head. "I was raised by my mom's best friend. There was no family stuff left for me to go through. House fire," she added at Maggie's questioning look. "That's how my father died."

"That's awful!"

"I was an infant, so I have no recollection of him. My mom died of cancer when I was six." She waved away Maggie's condolences with an appreciative smile. "Lachlan must have been living in Scotland. I never heard about him."

"Well, he knew about your father anyway. And mine. They needed a detective to track me."

"Seems odd that he hadn't updated his will in all this time. I mean, our fathers both died decades ago."

Maggie shrugged. "I think he was more interested in digging deeper into the distant past. As for me, I was raised by my maternal grandmother's sister, Mathilda. She wasn't much for dwelling on the past."

"I think I would have liked her." There was a wistful note in Cailean's voice as she stood and walked to the window.

Maggie's curiosity nudged her to probe a bit. "Isn't it a bit unusual for someone who studies ancient human cultures and peoples to seem so—"

She spun around. "Disinterested in her own?"

Maggie sat back in her chair. Cailean might have been road weary, but that hadn't diminished the sudden heat in her green eyes. Funny, she hadn't noticed their color until now. Maggie decided not to back down. After all, the woman had tracked her down, not the other way around. "Exactly. Why did you come here today?"

"I had to. My inheritance is here."

"Oh, right. More family history stuff. Yeah, I can see how you'd be dying to get a hold of that." Maggie stood. "I'm sorry, I don't mean to sound so harsh. But it's obvious you don't care about any of this. Why would you want the rest of the journals?"

"I don't want them. But it's . . . they are . . . well, they're my destiny. You couldn't possibly understand. I have to have them whether I want to or not." She stared defiantly at Maggie, then seemed to deflate. Her chin dipped, her eyes went flat and her shoulders slumped.

At first, Maggie thought she'd simply lost the will to argue, that fatigue had finally won out. But several seconds passed and Cailean neither moved nor so much as blinked. Her gaze was fixed past Maggie's shoulder, in the direction of the fire. Maggie thought she might pitch forward in a faint.

"Cailean?" Uh oh. Had Duncan returned in a poof somewhere behind her? Maggie shot a quick look over her shoulder at the fire, but there was nothing out of the ordinary. Frowning, she stepped closer to Cailean, but her cousin didn't move in any way. Feeling ridiculous and scared at the same time, Maggie waved her hand in front of Cailean's gaze. "Cailean? Are you all right?"

She had no idea if Cailean was having some sort of seizure or what to do for her if she was. Should she try to snap her out of it? Shake her? Move her to a chair in case she passed out? She waved her hand in front of Cailean's face again. "If your head starts spinning, I'm out of here," she said quite earnestly.

In that instant, Cailean blinked, then turned her head and looked at Maggie. "Could I have another glass of water?" she asked, as if nothing had happened. She paused while Maggie stared at her, then added, "If it's not too much trouble."

Maggie looked closely, but other than the pinched lines around her eyes and mouth being a bit more pronounced, and her skin being a shade paler, she seemed fine. "Ah, sure. Be right back."

Maggie shook her head as she filled the glass. *I've inherited the* ADDAMS FAMILY.

"So," she said calmly as she handed Cailean the glass, "does that happen often? You blanking out like that?"

Cailean accepted the glass just as calmly and sipped. If she was bothered by the question she didn't show it.

"Are you ill? I mean, is there something I should do for you if you gap out again?"

Cailean let out a short laugh, startling Maggie. "Ill? I've often thought so. Plagued, actually."

"You want to tell me about it?"

"Not really." Cailean eyed her steadily, then sighed in resignation. "But you're not going to leave it alone, are you?"

"Let me ask you this," Maggie said, relenting a bit. "Does whatever just happened to you have something to do with why you're here for family heirlooms you don't want?"

"You could say that." Cailean sat down in the rocker once again. She gestured to the couch. "You might want to sit. It's been my experience that it's the best way to hear what I have to say."

Maggie folded her arms and held Cailean's gaze. "It can't be all that bad." Though the sudden lifting of the hairs on her neck warned her that she might be wrong about that. Cailean was looking at her almost too intently. Perhaps she should have left things alone.

"Have it your way," Cailean said at length. "You don't seem like the fainting type to me anyway."

Maggie laughed despite the sudden tightness in her chest. "Oh, you might be surprised." She gave in enough to sit down across from Cailean and offered a smile. "I'm an open-minded person. In fact, my mind has made some amazing expansions lately."

Cailean's smile was part indulgent, part apologetic. "Since you've witnessed one of my 'spells,' I might as well tell you. Just remember, you wanted to know. Whether you choose to believe me is up to you." She stopped, took a small breath, then said, "Since I was little, I've had the ability to . . . know things." She looked Maggie dead in the eye. "Before they actually happen."

Maggie was proud of herself. She hardly blinked at the news. "So you're saying you're . . . what's the word . . . clairvoyant?"

"Something like that."

"So that's what's happening when you blank out? You're seeing something? You have like, visions or something?"

Cailean kept her chin as level as her gaze. She was neither embarrassed nor boastful. In fact, she seemed emotionless, simply delivering the facts. "Yes."

"And you have no control over when they hit you?"

"Very little."

"Wow, I'll bet that can be a major pain in the butt."

A smile curved Cailean's lips. "An understatement, you can be sure."

"Do you have them often?"

"Fortunately, no. Until recently, I'd almost begun to think that they were going to stop altogether." Cailean looked away for a moment. The light streaming in the window revealed the strain beneath her calm outward expression. "I started getting them again about two months ago. They were mercifully brief, vague. More of a pain than anything. I was more annoyed that they'd come back than by what I was seeing. I tried to ignore them, but that was wishful thinking. I learned that a long time ago, but it had been so long . . ." She trailed off and looked away again. "I just hoped."

Maggie felt a tug in her heart and reached out to cover Cailean's hand. It was then she realized just how tense her cousin was. She wasn't simply weary and stressed, she was on edge. She had her fingernails dug so deeply into her knees, Maggie imagined they were making marks through her pants.

"Listen, you don't have to tell me any—"

Her eyes locked on Maggie's. "But I do. You're part of it now. You're part of the reason I'm here."

"Is that what you just saw? In your vision? Something about me?"

Cailean nodded. "You're in danger." She swore suddenly under her breath and pulled her hands from Maggie.

"That's the hell of this." There was anguish and a wealth of frustration in her voice. "I get to know this much," she put her forefinger and thumb close together, "but never the whole picture. I know who you're in danger from, but not why, when, or how."

"Cailean—"

She abruptly grabbed Maggie's hands and held them so hard her fingertips went numb. "No, listen. You don't understand. I might be part of the course fate set you on. I never know if I'm deliverer or deliverance. But I have to try anyway. I *have* to try."

"Well, of course. Anyone would feel they had to do that, but listen—"

"No, you don't get it." Cailean was growing more agitated by the second, pulling on Maggie's hands, her expression ferociously intent. "I'm not here because I'm some kind of Good Samaritan. Far from it. If it was up to me, I'd ignore the visions, force fate to happen without my help or hindrance. God knows I'm sick of feeling responsible for things I have no control over. But that's not the way it works. It just gets worse and worse until you think you're going insane and—"

"Cailean," Maggie interrupted, first gently, then with some force. "Cailean, stop! Listen to me." She would have been more worried about the state her cousin was getting herself in if she hadn't felt such a profound, almost ridiculous sense of relief. "It's okay. I already know about the threat. That's why I'm here." She gently pried her hands loose, then took Cailean's in her own. "That's why I wouldn't greet you at the door." It was a mark of just how strange a turn her life had taken that she grinned, when there was actually nothing funny about the situation at all. "I actually thought you were a hitwoman."

Cailean finally stilled.

"I know it sounds weird. You have no idea how relieved

I was when I saw those journals in your hand. I really didn't want to kill you with the fireplace poker."

Cailean pulled her hand away. "I have no idea what you're talking about."

"The danger you saw in your vision. My ex-fiancé is stalking me. That's why I'm here."

"You're joking." She looked at Maggie like she wasn't too certain of *her* mental stability all of a sudden.

"Of course I'm not joking." Maggie frowned. She would think Cailean, of all people, would have an open mind. "Listen, I believe you about the visions." She smiled wryly. "God knows, there's not much I won't believe these days." Cailean continued to appear concerned. With a sigh, Maggie said, "You should be happy. Your job is done. I'm warned. I know I'm in danger. You can stop worrying about me."

But Cailean wasn't listening. "I have no idea what other trouble you may be in, but your life is in jeopardy from another source. A source that has plagued Clan Claren for centuries. You are going to cross paths with—"

At that moment the front door crashed open and Duncan strode in carrying an enormous armload of firewood. He was kilt-clad but bare-chested and sweaty from his labor despite the cold mountain air. His hair clung damply to his neck and shoulders.

Maggie sprang to her feet. "You're back!" she said, a bit too brightly. *Oh great, what timing.* Cailean still had a death grip on her arm and now she had to explain Duncan. At least he'd entered the cabin like a mortal.

She started to pull her arm loose so she could move aside and introduce Cailean, but froze when Duncan dropped the entire load of firewood to the floor in a resounding crash. He pointed at Cailean, simultaneously reaching for a broadsword that—thankfully—wasn't there. "You!" he thundered.

Maggie turned toward Cailean, but she skirted in front of her, arms spread wide as if to protect her. "MacKinnon! Don't come near her!" Keeping her gaze locked on the advancing Duncan, she said to Maggie, "This man is going to be the death of you."

EIGHT

"THE ONLY ONE who'll be dyin' today is you, Edwyna Claren!" Duncan roared as he charged across the room.

Cailean retreated a step, bumping Maggie backward. "Stand back, MacKinnon," Cailean warned.

"Di' ye think waitin' three hundred years was long enough to make me forget wha' ye did?"

"I haven't done anything to you. I'm not Edwyna Claren. My name is Cailean."

Duncan's advance ended with him less than a foot away. "Cailean? What devil is this now?"

Maggie whispered, "Maybe your vision was a bit off."

"I know what I saw," Cailean said clearly, resisting Maggie's attempts to push by her. "You are in danger here."

"Aha!" Duncan shouted. "A *taibhsear*. You have the *dha shealladh,* two sights. You're a key. Ye've admitted it."

Cailean stiffened.

Maggie ducked under Cailean's arm and stood between them. She turned to Cailean. "I thought you didn't know anything about your family—our family. How do you know his name?"

Cailean never took her eyes off Duncan. "I didn't until a few minutes ago. What I saw was distant past. There is danger between our clans." She swore under her breath. "I didn't see it all, I just . . . know. There is a threat here."

Maggie looked uncertainly at Duncan, then at Cailean. She blocked Cailean's attempt to pull her back. "I appreciate what you are trying to do, Cailean. Don't worry, I'll take full responsibility for whatever might happen to me." She glanced at Duncan. "But I don't think it's me he's after." She moved back so she could eye them both at the same time. "Now, would one of you like to clue me in on exactly what's going on here?" She turned to Duncan. "*Do* you know each other?"

Duncan eyed Cailean with clear distaste. "Perhaps no'," he said, though it was clear he didn't completely believe it. "I've met her kind, sure enough. Cailean, you say? Yer no' wraith then?"

"You think I'm a ghost?" Now it was Cailean's turn to look at Maggie in confusion.

So she didn't know. Yet. "Humor him," Maggie said.

Cailean looked back to Duncan. "I'm quite alive, thank you." She straightened her spine. "And I will remain that way. As will Maggie."

"We all die sometime," he said darkly. "Doona expect me tae beg yer pardon, Cailean Claren. First one Claren descendant, now another." He slashed at the air with his hand. "Aye, as if They thought one wouldna be enough of a test, they put a Claren Key in my path." His eyes narrowed and he took a menacing step forward. "Even if yer no' Edwyna Claren, yer a descendant of her. You have her look exactly. Yer a seer, as she was. I'll warn you now. I've no more use for you here today, than my brother did three hundred years ago. If you think tae come charmin' me onward to hell with your fey ways, then you'll be sadly disappointed. I willna be followin' my brother's path. You'll go alone." He raked his gaze insultingly over her, then, with a snort of disgust, turned away from her in clear dismissal.

Maggie stared after him, more curious about the things he'd said than worried for her or Cailean's safety. She pasted a smile on her face and turned to Cailean. "He's not entirely housebroken yet. You'll have to excuse him." She eyed Duncan over her shoulder.

Cailean still had a semi-glazed look on her face. "Did he say brother? Does he really believe his brother is three hundred years old?" She was staring at Duncan's back with a combination of disbelief and fear.

"It's a long story." Maggie took her by the arm and led her quickly to the front door before she recovered enough to start asking. She had some questions of her own anyway. Judging from her reaction, Cailean seemed to understand a whole lot more of what he was talking about than Maggie did. She skirted the pile of wood and tugged Cailean behind her until they were safely on the front porch. Did all this somehow tie in to Lachlan's quest?

The firewood kept her from closing the door, so she moved on down the stairs and across the small clearing. "Why don't you come with me to Griffith? It's a little town about forty-five minutes from here. We can talk on the way."

"Maggie, I want you to explain. . ."

Maggie wasn't sure how long Duncan would brood—given his usual pattern, it could likely be days, but she couldn't take the chance. "I promise I will. I really have to get to Griffith and make a call. Come on. We'll take the Jeep, my wreck isn't all that dependable. I'll pay for gas." She was trying to usher Cailean along without actually grabbing her by the arm and dragging her. Then she realized she'd have to go back in the cabin and get her purse. Despite her instincts telling her Duncan wouldn't really hurt her, there was too much going on for her to be certain Cailean wasn't in danger here. "You'll feel better if I'm away from Duncan, right?"

That seemed to push the right button. "I'll drive."

"I need to get my purse from the house." Maggie was already jogging toward the porch. "Don't worry. I'll be right out." She ran up the stairs, checking the front windows to make sure the curtains were still there. She smiled at herself. It seemed like a perfectly normal thing for her to do now, like checking to see if the porch light was on. "You're deeper in that rabbit hole than you think, Alice," she whispered.

She half expected Duncan to be gone, but when she found him in front of the fire, her relief surprised her. She was filled with questions for him, but she wanted to talk to Cailean first. She'd probably have better luck getting information out of her anyway. Maybe she'd learn enough to figure out how to prod more information out of Duncan when she returned.

She went to sidestep around the wood, but it was already stacked neatly by the fireplace with the other piles of wood. "Nice trick. You could make a killing in the housecleaning business."

Duncan grumbled, "The only thing I'd like to kill are nosy Clarens with their *dha shealladh,*" but he didn't turn to look at her.

Maggie scooped up her purse and the stuffed pillowcase, knowing she should make a quick retreat. It was killing her not to toss a barrage of questions his way. She was at the door when he stopped her.

"Maggie."

Something in the quiet way he said it made her skin chill. She looked over her shoulder. He was facing her.

"Doona bring her back here. I willna have her in this cabin again."

"Don't be ridiculous," Maggie said, though it was clear

Duncan was serious about his demand. "I didn't invite her up here, but I won't just toss her out."

The look on Duncan's face told her he'd have no problem doing just that—literally.

"She's my cousin, Duncan." She took a step toward him. "I didn't even know I had family left."

"You dinna need family of her type."

"Her type?" Maggie frowned and walked back into the room. "And who are you to go 'typing' people, Mr. Ghost?"

"She's a Claren Key. 'Tis said their talents were given to them by the *sidhe.* Faery folk," he clarified. "She's dangerous."

Maggie laughed. "You're afraid of fairies?"

"I'm dead," he said flatly. "I'm no' afraid of anything." Then he spun abruptly around and plunged the poker into a flaming log.

Maggie jumped.

"But I'll no' be havin' the ancestor of the Claren Key who killed my brother Alexander in my cabin. No' as long as I'm inhabitin' it."

His declaration stunned Maggie into silence. "Cailean didn't kill anyone," she said at length. "In fact, she doesn't want to be here any more than you want her here."

"Good. Then it's settled."

Maggie strode across the room, dumping her things on the small couch. "It is not settled. She came here to warn me. She thinks you're going to kill me."

Duncan turned slowly and faced her. They were less than a foot apart. "What makes you so sure she's not right?"

Maggie shrank back despite herself.

"They who have the sight are rarely wrong in what they see. Unless it's trickery on her part tae make you do something she wants done."

"What could she possibly want from me? She didn't even know I existed until just recently."

"What is she here for, Maggie? Besides the warning. There is something else, isn't there?"

"Lachlan's trunk and journals." At his victorious smile, she added, "They're her inheritance from Lachlan. She doesn't even want them, but she feels she has to have them for some reason. It's all part of her vision and the warning."

"Don't trust her, Maggie. It's trickery, I tell you. The only one who will bring ye tae harm here is her."

"You are the one talking in circles. First you say seers are always right, then you say she is lying and trying to trick me. If all she wants is the journals, she can have them." Maggie spun around, but Duncan was suddenly right behind her. His firm hand on her shoulder stopped her from taking a single step. He turned her back around.

"Doona go off wi' her alone, Maggie."

It wasn't the warning that gave Maggie pause, nor the earnest sincerity with which he'd delivered it. What stopped her was the real concern she found lurking behind the frustration and anger in his eyes. "I think you're the one who'd better be careful," she said. "For a moment there I actually thought you were really worried about me."

She'd expected an oath and a quick dismissal, but he shocked her further by caressing her cheek with a blunt fingertip. "Aye, and that's the truly mad thing, Maggie. For a moment there, I was."

Before she could respond he turned and walked back to his fire.

She opened her mouth twice to say something, but closed it both times without uttering a word. Perhaps getting out of here for a while was a good idea. She picked her things back up and walked to the door.

"Will you be here when I get back?" She hadn't meant to ask, but now that she had, she wanted an answer.

He was silent for a moment, then said, "Where else am I to go?"

She did smile then. "Well, I think there are still a few trees left on the mountain that have somehow escaped your axe."

He seemed to relax slightly then. When he spoke, the edge was gone from his tone. "I'll be here."

It was more than she'd expected. And it filled her with a warmth she knew was foolish. She nodded, even though he wasn't looking at her, and smiled at his broad back.

"It's been a long time since someone worried about me. It shouldn't feel so nice. But . . . well, thanks."

"If you mean that, then listen tae wha' I say tae ye. Leave that one in town. Come back tae the cabin alone."

"Duncan." But he stood there, such a magnificent picture, with the roaring fire at his back, white shirt framing his shoulders so proudly, kilt wound around his waist and hips so perfectly, and legs so sturdy and fine, all topped off with concern for her clear in his fierce eyes. She couldn't find it in her to deny him anything at that moment. "I'll work something out with Cailean."

He seemed to relax a little then. And the fierce light that shone from his eyes had somehow managed to capture a bit of the heat of the fire he so carefully tended. She felt warm all the way to her bones. And tended to in a way she'd never been made to feel. Judd had wanted to possess her and to that extent he'd paid her a great deal of attention, but he'd never tended to her. Not to the parts of her that mattered. No one ever had. Because she hadn't let them. To her, needing was a weakness and she wielded her independence like a sword and her self-sufficiency like a battle shield.

Perhaps that had been her mistake. Perhaps needing wasn't the weakness. Maybe pretending you didn't have needs, or needed someone other than yourself to fulfill them was the real weakness. It was a tantalizing thought.

The idea that Duncan was the one to teach her that was the epitome of irony. What was the point in finally discovering the meaning of life if the man she wanted to explore this great insight with was dead?

Boy, can you pick em or what?

"I'll have questions for you," she warned.

"I'll do what I can tae gi' ye the answers."

"Fair enough. I'll come back alone."

Cailean was out of the Jeep and halfway to the porch when Maggie finally came out of the cabin. "All set," she said a bit too brightly and hoped that Cailean's gift didn't extend to mind reading. She knew her cousin had as many questions as she did and the task of explaining Duncan wasn't going to be easy. Explaining her feelings about Duncan would be downright impossible. She wasn't sure herself what the complicated mass of emotions he stirred up inside her would all boil down to, but she was certain that she wanted the chance to figure it out in private before sharing them with anyone.

Cailean looked her over, spending a few lengthy moments on her face, but in the end she nodded. "Let's go."

They climbed in the Jeep. On the long drive down the mountainside, Cailean fell deep into thought and Maggie didn't push it. They would eventually talk. For now, her thoughts strayed back to Duncan. She touched her cheek where he'd stroked her and remembered their almost kiss. A light shiver raced over her skin and her pulse notched up a level or two. Yes, maybe finding Cailean a room in town was a very good idea after all.

NINE

DUNCAN WALKED TOWARD the small clearing with something close to dread filling his stomach. He had never come back here, not once, in all the months he'd spent on this mountain. It surprised him how little of an impact centuries of time had had on the small meadow. It looked much the same as it had that November afternoon he and Mairi had started across it. They had never made it to the other side.

Early on in purgatory, when he'd made it clear he had no interest in returning to this place, They had made it known to him that small markers had been erected by the family Mairi had traveled across the ocean with. The same family had helped her find the small hunting cabin after their arrival and had taken turns tending to her when she was so very ill. For the first time he wondered what it must have been like for her. To him, her decision to leave her clan had been the mindless act of a coward.

During his trip over and the subsequent hunt for her in America, he'd thought only of her betrayal and the cost it would levy on both their clans. Never once had he considered that she could not have been either mindless or a coward to have made such a journey with no fellow clansmen to see to her safety.

He'd seen her illness as a manifestation of her foolish act and her just due for her betrayal. He had not listened to one word of her attempts to explain her actions to him. She was his betrothed and, as such, his property. To his mind, her rights began and ended at that point. He had refused her even the basest courtesy, not even demanding she return, but simply arriving and exercising his rights by taking possession of her. His only goal had been to return them both to Scottish soil where they would be married and thus end the long feuding between their clans.

Duncan hadn't expected to find the small stones still standing. And, in fact, he found only one. It was small and rounded, blackened with time until the name etched in the stone was almost unreadable. Almost. But to him the letters and numbers shone as if lit from an inner fire. Mairi Claren. Born 1680. Died 1698.

Eighteen. Had she really been so young? She'd been considered well past the age suitable for marrying and he'd never given thought to the difference in their ages. Almost eleven years had separated his birth from hers.

He sank down in the cool dampness of the grass, heedless of the gray skies and chilling air. There was no sign of his stone or that he had ever walked this meadow. Why that made him feel hollow he could not have said. He frowned, irritated further by yet another sign of his sudden sensitivity.

He certainly was a man who was clear about his contributions to his family and his time on earth, deeds both good and bad that had shaped the man he was. That there was no mark of his time spent on this continent should not concern him in the least. Scotland was his country, his home, his heart. He would have given his life for it without pause. This land meant less than nothing to him. It had

taken and not given. He felt no true loyalty to it . . . or
to the woman whose bones lay beneath it.

He wondered where Mairi's spirit had ended up. He'd
been certain upon learning of his destiny in purgatory that
she was burning in hell for her sins to her countrymen and
to him.

Now, for the first time, he was not so certain. Who had
been sinner . . . and who had been sinned against? That
uncertainty was what had driven him from the cabin. It
had eaten at him, badgering his mind and soul with questions he did not wish to ponder.

He had first blamed Maggie. All her talk of her mis-
treatment at the hands of Judd had made him think and
react in ways completely foreign to everything he'd previously believed of himself. Then to compound things, The
Key had shown up. This was faery trickery he was certain.
They had wearied of his stubbornness and contrived to
force him into madness and complete his descent to hell by
putting these Claren women in his path.

And yet it was a path from which he did not seem able
to stray. When Maggie walked out of the cabin earlier that
afternoon, he'd actually worried that he'd not see her face
again, hear her laughter, taste her lips. He'd worried of this
obsession for days now, taking care to steer clear of her
presence all together until he had his thoughts once again
under his control. And yet one glance, one word, and his
heart and thoughts and desires were no longer his to master.

His first impulse had been to restrict her from leaving
by using his greater strength. If she was too foolish to see
to her own safety, then he would see to it for her! But he
had listened to her words, taken her promises . . . and
trusted her to act on them. Trust a Claren? What spell had
she cast?

Was this how Alexander had been drawn to his death?
Had his younger brother, John Roderick, fallen to a Claren

Key as well, or a Claren sword? After Duncan's failure, it would have fallen to Rory, the last of Calum's sons, to bind the clans in some way. What did it matter? They'd all ended up dead.

It was because it did indeed matter that he had finally ended up here in this spot, certain he would come back to what he knew and had always known as truth. He had done the right thing in trying to take her back. Never before had he questioned his actions and he would stop this insurgence now before it went any further.

"Aye, so ye've finally come."

Duncan froze, then forcibly relaxed. Her voice was soft, the lilt musical where he'd only remembered shrillness. Mairi. Had his thoughts conjured her?

Mairi gathered her roughly woven skirts and sat down beside him in the grass. "From yer frown I'd say yer not here to grieve me." She paused and he felt her silent censure. "Some things no amount of time will change."

He should have been surprised by her sudden appearance, yet he was not. "A thousand years could pass. I'll no' grieve the death of a woman who killed my family, my clan."

" 'Twas no' my act, but your stubbornness and that of every man in both our clans that killed them."

Because he was terrified to look at her, he made himself do so immediately. She was taller, broader of shoulder, less fragile, than he remembered. Where he remembered it pinched and tight, her mouth was wide and generous, as if made to smile often, though he couldn't remember a single one. It was not that he found her lovely where he'd only remembered ugliness, that shocked him. It was that, with few exceptions made for the decade or so difference in their ages, she looked like Maggie.

"Ye look like yer seein' a ghost." She smiled faintly. "Perhaps yer seein' now what you didna let yoursel' see before." She reached out a hand and it took all his considerable will not to shrink away. Her touch on his arm was not weak and grasping, but surprisingly warm and firm.

"Yer beauty or lack of it doesna change your actions," he said coldly.

"Nor does yer sudden appearance here change yer brutality and arrogance," she said evenly.

"You condemned us to death, Mairi. No' just you and me, but our clans as well." He looked her in the eye. "Is that the sin yer paying for in purgatory? Why are ye no' rotting in hell where ye belong?"

She seemed shaken by his accusation. "Our union would no' hae stopped the killin' or the feudin'." She spoke fervently. "Ye still havena seen that in all this time? Our clans were destined to decimate each other."

"And yet rather than stay and fight alongside yer kinsmen, you fled, compounding the sin of death with tha' o' shame as well."

There was a fierceness in her blue eyes he had never seen before. It reminded him of another set of blue eyes, ones that had moved him as Mairi's never had. Had the fault of that been Mairi's alone?

"Aye, I grieve for what happened to them," she said heatedly. "But 'twas their own foolishness and misplaced pride that warred them to their deaths. I couldna make them listen. Nothing ever would. I knew that, as my sister had before me."

"Doona speak tae me o' Edwyna!"

"They killed her ye know. After we left. Raped and murdered her, yer clansmen did. Because of their fear of her 'kind' and what she tried to tell them. Should I have stayed and endured the same fate?"

Duncan hadn't known. It shouldn't have bothered him, she'd been the cause of Alexander's death after all. But no woman deserved such a fate. Not even Edwyna.

"I tried tae make ye understand that marryin' alone would not end the wars, that we had to do more. Ye wouldna listen to me. Tae you I was chattel. I didn't expect yer love, yer admiration, or even yer respect. But because I truly wanted to save my clan, I had planned to earn them over time. Together, we might hae saved them, Duncan. But if ye wouldna grant me so much as a second of yer time, how was I tae earn anything in yer eyes? How would we ever forge the bond necessary tae truly end the anger and begin to heal the pain o' so many years o' death and destruction between us?

"Marrying me was only an act of faith tae our clansmen. It was wha' we did wi' that union that could have changed history. But you made it clear that was no' tae be. I refused to let you condemn me to die by your side."

Duncan flung her hand from his arm and stood. He walked a good distance across the field before stopping.

"As it was, ye killed us both anyway," she said.

She was standing behind him. He could vanish, but he was certain she would follow him through all levels of hell.

"If ye want to lay blame, it belongs as much on yer soul as it does mine," she said. "But it also lies wi' each of our clansmen. They knew they were warring themselves out of existence, yet their foolish pride wouldna let them seek any other solution than a marriage bond."

Duncan spun around and gripped her by the arms. His rage was so complete he envisioned himself simply snapping her in two. And yet her calm acceptance of his violence proved the stronger weapon. Her knowing visage was like a mirror thrown up to him. He was barbarian first, acting with strength of hand instead of strength of mind, just as she had accused.

He released her, his hands curling into fists at his sides. Swallowing centuries of hate and anger was like acid on his throat, making his voice rough. "Why di' ye no' come to me before this?"

"Would ye have heard my words?"

He didn't bother to answer.

"Ye had to come to me," she said.

"I did no' come to ye."

"Did ye no'?"

He didn't answer that either.

"It has taken me a long time, though not as long as you, to understand and accept my faults and the sins committed because of them. I have done so. My sentence on earth is finished."

He looked at her then. She smiled and he almost cringed at what he saw in her eyes. He saw understanding. He saw supreme knowledge.

He saw forgiveness.

"I am no' here for me, Duncan. I am here now because ye needed me tae be here." Concern colored her eyes. "Be warned. I willna be here for ye again. If ye hae any last questions of me, ask them now."

So many thoughts and revelations vied for attention, and with such fury, none could surface. One thing he could not deny. Now that he had seen her again, spoken with her, he would forever think of her differently.

She smiled and reached up to place a soft kiss on his cheek. "Good-bye Duncan MacKinnon," she said softly. "May your soul find its final resting place."

As she stepped back, he understood more than he wanted to. "God rest yer soul, Mairi Claren."

"Fear not. I willna be burnin' in hell, Duncan. There is forgiveness for you as well if ye but seek it."

Her image shimmered and he stepped forward and gripped her arm with unnecessary strength. He tempered his hold on her even as desperation crawled through his heart. His eyes burned into hers, the sting behind them unexpected but accepted. "I do have one final request," he said gruffly.

"Aye?"

"Alexander and Rory. What happened to them?"

"Tha' I canno' tell you."

"Find them, then. Tell them . . . I'm sorry."

Her smile surfaced once again, serene and knowing. "Ye'll be tellin' them yersel' soon enough, I think."

"Promise me!" He struggled yet again to temper his desperation. "In case I dinna make it there." Pride was an awesome burden to fit down one's throat. "Ye dinna owe it tae me," he said roughly. "But ye asked . . . and I'm . . ." His voice broke deep. He squared his shoulders, chin jutting forward. "I'm beggin' ye."

She seemed more stunned than pleased by his humbling. It made it no easier.

She moved out of his grasp easily like the wraith she was. "Trust me, Duncan. All will be as you wish it. But you must wish." She stepped back and her image shimmered once again, then was gone before he could speak again.

He stood there for several long moments, feeling oddly empty.

"Good-bye, Mairi Claren," he said finally.

He bent down and plucked a late bloom, then knelt beside her grave. He placed the slender-stemmed flower on the soft ground in front of the stone.

"May ye rest in eternal peace," he said quietly. After a moment, he added, "May we all one day."

It was a long time before he rose and began the walk back to the cabin.

TEN

MAGGIE WATCHED FROM the front porch as Cailean headed back into town, where she had reluctantly booked a room at the only motel, which was owned by Deputy Branson's sister. They had argued about it almost the entire drive back from Griffith, but Maggie had held firm, saying she would take full responsibility for whatever happened to her while alone with Duncan. "The MacKinnon" as her cousin called him.

On the way to Griffith, Maggie had told Cailean about what she'd read in Lachlan's journals so far about the Legend MacKinnon. Cailean agreed that she needed to read the journals. Her sense of dread and foreboding had increased, not diminished, since their confrontation with Duncan. Maggie's mention of the legend only seemed to cement this.

She'd tried to get Cailean to talk more about what she'd seen in her vision but she was as adamant about not discussing it until she'd read the journal entries, as she was about Maggie not staying in the cabin. That was when the arguing began. It ended abruptly when Maggie blurted out that Duncan did indeed believe his brother died three hundred years ago. It was true. He had died with them. He was a ghost. Cailean had gone dead silent and just as pale. When Maggie refused to return with her to town, Cailean had taken the trunk and the journals and left, angry and upset.

While in Griffith, Maggie had other, more important worries at the moment. She had called directory assistance in Manhattan and asked for the number of any detective agencies close to Judd's office address. The first one was less than a block away, but very posh and way out of her ballpark. The man she'd spoken to had been nice enough to refer her to another smaller agency. Relieved, she'd been about to hang up when he'd asked her to repeat her name, there had been a pause, then he'd politely put her on hold. A sick ball of dread had formed in her stomach. She'd been about to hang up when another man came on the phone, all smooth voice and placating talk. He'd apologized for his partner and said he'd be more than willing to help her for a reduced fee, gave her some song and dance about his sister getting knocked around once and how he'd made it a personal pledge to help women like her.

Problem was, she'd never gotten far enough with his partner to explain she'd been abused. She'd made some garbled response and slammed the phone down. Had Judd hired someone to track her down? Very possible. Just as possible he'd pick the priciest agency closest to where he spent most of his time. His office. Abused sister my ass. She could only hope he'd be unable to trace that call.

Maggie stared sightlessly at the road leading down the mountain, the dust long since settled after Cailean's departure. For half a second, she wanted to run to her car and follow Cailean to town. A useless move as her new-found cousin was all caught up in the past and visions of murdering Scots. Maggie had a real violent man to deal with. Her clan ancestors would have to wait in line.

It was getting dark and the air was decidedly cold. Maggie let herself into the cabin. It was as dark as it had been when she and Cailean had come in to get the trunk. The Jeep ride had been drafty and she'd looked forward to one of Duncan's roaring fires. But there wasn't a roaring fire. Nor was there any Duncan. Would he come back now that Cailean was gone? He'd given his word.

The furniture was still there. The wood he'd chopped earlier was still stacked on the hearth. The poker he'd angrily driven into the burning log what seemed like a lifetime ago, was now laying flat on the hearth, the pointed end laying useless amidst the ashes.

She shivered and rubbed at her arms. She needed to talk this out with someone. She wanted that someone to be Duncan.

First things first, however. She'd used up the stash of matches she'd found earlier in the week repeatedly lighting the finicky pilot light on the old propane stove. She'd meant to get more in town, but she'd completely forgotten. A quick search didn't turn up any more of them. "There's never a good ghost around when you need one."

Swearing loudly, disparaging Duncan's entire lineage in the course of it, half-hoping it would make an effective ghost-call, she climbed the ladder to the loft and pulled on another sweater and grabbed the duvet off the bed. She heaved it over the railing, then descended to the kitchen, still grumbling. She grabbed a package of cinnamon crackers, looked longingly at the tea kettle, and made a nest on the small couch.

Munching her way through one cracker after another, heedless of the crumbs or the encroaching shadows, her thoughts turned back to her phone call. Even if the detective managed to trace her call, all he'd find out was that she'd been in the Sip N' Suds in Griffith, North Carolina. He wouldn't be able to track her from there. Would he? Just having Judd narrow her down to the state she was in, much less the county, was much too close for comfort.

"Think, Maggie, think," she said, wiping cinnamon crumbs from her hands.

She couldn't go to the police. Hiring a detective agency wasn't against the law and she wasn't sure what good it would do if it did violate some restriction. Judd had grown to omnipotent proportions in her mind, but the reality wasn't so farfetched from that vision.

Whom could she trust? She thought of deputy Branson in town, but shook her head. Branson was a nice guy, in a Gomer Pyle sort of way. Well meaning and loyal, but not exactly hardened to the ways of the big bad world. Judd would make a light snack of him. Where did that leave her?

Dead. That's where it left her.

Just then Duncan pushed the front door open and let himself quietly into the cabin. It was the quiet that caught her immediate attention. She was used to screeching door hinges, warped wood dragging across the floor and the thundering footsteps that usually announced his arrival.

He walked right past her toward the hearth. It was darker than she'd realized and she'd turned on no lamps, but she didn't think he'd miss noticing her sitting there.

He didn't bend down to lay fresh wood on the ashes. Instead he stood and stared into the cold hearth in silent contemplation, as if the flames still danced and beckoned his attention.

"Duncan?"

Maggie watched him for a moment. He didn't move so much as a muscle. She was tempted to ignore him as well, Lord knew she had enough to deal with at the moment, but something about the way he stood there, so still, so contained, held her attention until she finally gave into it. She shifted the comforter off her lap and stood, shivering almost immediately as the chill night air hit her skin.

"I'm sorry I didn't get the fire going," she said. "It was out when I got back and there were no matches."

Still nothing.

She stepped to the end of the couch. Something was wrong. Very wrong. She took a step closer. "Are you okay?"

When another eternal minute passed she couldn't stand it any longer. "Well, I can't keep up with your scintillating conversation, so I'll turn in." She walked toward the ladder. "If you could get a fire going, I'd appreciate it."

She clutched the ladder with one hand, the duvet gathered in an awkward bundle in her other hand. She was halfway up when he finally spoke.

"I didna mean tae upset you."

She started at his voice and gripped the ladder hard, then balanced herself and the duvet before looking back at him. "Well, you're doing a good job of it."

There was a pause, then, "Good night, Maggie."

His tone was more vacant than dismissive, like something else was so dominating his attention he could barely focus enough to form words.

Go on up to bed, she told herself. He's got problems, so what. You've got problems of your own. And he's already dead. You're not. Yet.

Still, she couldn't help staring at him. "Do you want to talk about it?" The words just came out. Maybe if she could get him to talk, she could get him to listen to her as well. It still surprised her how badly she wanted to talk to him about her situation.

He didn't answer. He was lost once again in his inner world. She only hoped he surfaced enough to make a fire before she froze to death.

"Well, good night then."

She climbed the rest of the way to the loft then took off her boots, pulled on another pair of wool socks and crawled into bed fully dressed. She tried to get her mind back to her problems, but found her thoughts drifting relentlessly back to the man standing downstairs in the dark. What had happened while she was gone? Why had he let his fire go out?

Sleep claimed her as she wrestled with worry. As she drifted off, she saw a glow spring to life down below and smiled as the heat slowly invaded her limbs.

She woke up in the middle of the night, sweating profusely. More asleep than not, she kicked grumpily at the heavy covers and sat up, already tugging at her sweater and shirts. The jeans took a bit longer, but she dumped them on the floor in a heap along with the rest, and sighed in relief, her eyes already shut as she curled blissfully naked back beneath the covers.

WHEN SHE WOKE for the second time, she was sweating again, but this time it was cold and clammy. Her heart was racing and her head ached from the nightmare. She blinked hard and rubbed her eyes as she sat up, working hard to focus on reality and escape the last vestiges of the dream. She frowned as she woke the rest of the way up . . . and was forced to accept that the nightmare was real.

"Judd will kill me," she whispered. Saying it out loud only made it more real. "No matter where I go Judd will find me." She wondered if the torture she'd suffered would hurt as badly in real life as it had in the dream. Could the subconscious really know?

"Yer right, lass. He will kill you."

Maggie let out a small scream as she clutched at the covers. Duncan was standing on the other side of the bed, looking out the small window above the headboard. His face was devoid of expression.

Then he turned to look at her and whatever words had been on her lips slid down her throat in a solid mass. His gaze was so pointed it all but pinned her to the bed. "And ye will suffer."

She struggled to breathe, to get her bearings.

"Shouldn't—" The word came out on a gargle of air. She had to pause to clear her throat. "Shouldn't you be wearing a black robe and be carrying a scythe or something?" Her attempt at humor didn't help either one of them.

"I am no' the angel o' death."

She tucked the covers more firmly under her arms and scooted back. "You're not exactly the life of the party either."

Duncan moved closer, towering over her. "Maggie, you will die."

She could hear the finality in his voice. He knew. But she knew it on a deeper level than that, had known before he'd spoken, before she'd dreamed her own imminent death, before she'd made that phone call. She could stay here in Madden County, North Carolina or run to the ends of the earth.

"I can't live my life running." She looked up at him. "Maybe I can avoid him for a while. But he'll catch me, won't he?"

Duncan merely nodded, watching her.

Maggie began to shake. Terror and tears fought violently for the upper hand. "I don't want to die like that, Duncan," she whispered roughly. Tears burned past her eyes, terror took over her body, rattling it hard. "I don't want to die." She held the edge of the duvet in two fists beneath her chin and fell apart. "There should be a way for me to do this, but there isn't, is there? Oh God, there isn't, is there?"

Duncan moved around the bed and sat next to her. He took her chin in a firm grip and forced her to look at him. "There is a way."

"How? Find him first? I can't kill someone. Not even Judd. I don't think I could. Duncan—"

He stopped her with a kiss.

He'd humbled himself far more than he'd ever thought possible by going to Them in the first place. They'd called his appearance before them proof of his strength of soul. He knew it had only proved his ultimate weakness. A Claren woman would send him to hell. It was his fate.

Yet he had gone forward, had asked for help and guidance. They had given it.

But he had not planned on touching her.

He took her mouth, swallowed her plea, tasted her tears, hoping to drown his own anger, to find an end to this need he had of her. It wasn't a soft claiming, but a fierce declaration that he could take and not give in to her. He was already prepared to sacrifice for her. But it was a sacrifice of the mind, a saving of his choosing. He would not surrender his will. And he would certainly not surrender his heart.

And yet simply by bending to his need to taste her, to have her, he knew the destruction of his will had begun. Telling himself it was a selfish act he committed for his own pleasure was a lie even he could not dwell on for as long as it took to think it. This was not about pleasure.

This was about need. Basic, fundamental need.

Even knowing that, feeling his will begin to erode, to crumble as Stonelachen had against the battering rams of the Claren warriors, he continued to feed his needs, plundering her mouth for the spoils of war. But where it had taken centuries of time and thousands of Clarens to defeat the MacKinnons, it would take only one week and this one Claren woman to destroy him.

He made to pull away then, but she lifted her hand to his cheek and opened her mouth under his. He stiffened further, experiencing something close to terror at the feelings a simple touch of her fingers could wring from him. She slid her hand to the back of his neck and with needy, urgent fingertips, held him close.

He told himself there was resistance in him still, that the battle might be compromised, but the victory of wills was still his to claim. But she chose that moment to release him, and will it or not, there was no denying the instant and absolute abandonment he felt at that sudden disconnection. He could not devise a lie clever enough to make himself believe that his will would ever again be solely his to control.

She stared at him, her skin flushed, her lips wet, her soft eyes filled with emotion. The confusion was understandable. It was the rekindling of hope that tore at him. "You said there was a way," she said finally.

"Aye, there is." He stood. His long discussion with Them had yielded many disturbing things, but only two solutions. "I can give you two choices. Only one is certain tae keep ye safe from the death Judd has planned."

"And that is?"

"I have less than three weeks left on this mountain. When that time is up I return to purgatory." He shifted his weight, still disturbed by this next bit. "They will allow you to ascend with me."

Her mouth fell open. "Excuse me?"

Duncan straightened further. Trust a Claren to make a difficult situation even more so. "I said, ye can join me in the afterlife. Ye'll be safe there."

Maggie tucked the sheet under her arms and scooted into a cross-legged position, a look of disbelief on her face. "Let me get this straight," she said. "In order to keep Judd from killing me, I'm to kill myself now."

He scowled. He should have known better. Why had he felt compelled to intervene on her behalf? Her lips were indescribably sweet, but her tongue certainly wasn't. "Ye would be wise tae heed this offer."

He watched her struggle to regain her composure, but there was very real fear behind those blue eyes. Still, she would not give into it. His irritation lessened somewhat. A MacKinnon recognized and admired bravery when he saw it. Even, he supposed, in a Claren.

"There is another way."

She brightened immediately.

He silently cursed the responsive chord that struck in him. He tried to tell himself that he was only doing this as a means to hopefully be reunited with his clan. With his brothers. They had presented him with an opportunity and he had been wise enough to avail himself of it. He had not offered to save her life to make her happy, nor to settle any debt he had to Mairi or the Clarens.

Liar.

He swallowed the truth and it went down hard. "I could try and see to yer safety here on earth before I go. Because I've offered tae do that for ye, They are willin' tae allow me to have my leave o' this place to see it done."

She took a moment to assimilate his words. "You mean, they'll let you leave the mountain?"

"Aye. I can go where I wish, do wha' I wish."

Her eyes all but sparkled with the possibilities. "And you get to keep your . . . ghostly powers?"

Duncan frowned at her description. "Nothing else changes."

Maggie clapped her hands together, then made a wild grab for the slipping covers. "That's wonderful, that's—" She broke off as suddenly as she'd started, a frown creasing her forehead. "Wait a minute. Why?"

"I told you why, so I could help ye—"

"I know that part. Why would you do this? I can understand dragging me along to the afterlife when your three weeks are up. All you'd have to do is sit here until we're called. But this . . . This way you'll have to physically do something. You'll actively have to help me."

"And I warned you there were no guarantees this way. I'll do wha' I can, but it may no' be enough."

"That still doesn't answer my question. Why would you do this for me? Just to get off the mountain?" Her eyes widened. "If I don't agree to just go with you and ask you to help me instead, what happens if you—if we—fail?"

"I am free to spend my time here where I wish no matter. When my time is done, I return to purgatory."

"So why do it? Why put yourself out for me if offering alone was enough?"

Duncan stared at her sitting there in her downy nest, hair tangled, skin glowing in the firelight from below. There were a hundred answers to her question and not one had anything to do with being reunited with his brothers. "Does it matter as long as I'm willing?" he asked quietly.

She assessed him in silence, her gaze so intent it was as if she thought she could intuit his thoughts, ferret out his secrets, if she but looked long enough and deep enough.

"Yes. Yes, it does," she said, just as quietly. "If you succeed, do you get out of purgatory?"

"I have no way of knowing that." He stilled her question with a raised hand. "If I've passed some test with Them by doing this, so be it. It was not why I offered."

She straightened, her gaze turning more challenger than inquisitor. "I swore when I left Judd I'd never let myself get into a situation where I had to rely on someone else ever again. I'd have to be sure I was in control, at least of my own share. Well, I'm still not in control, of anything. I'm still having to rely on someone else to help me. That's hard enough to deal with. Maybe I should just be grateful for your offer and not care about the motivation behind it. But I'm already trapped by one person's agenda. I can't risk getting trapped by yours, too." She commanded his full attention and a great deal of his respect with nothing more than a look. "Tell me the truth, Duncan MacKinnon. Why do you really want to help me?"

ELEVEN

MAGGIE WATCHED HIM intently, yet his eyes betrayed nothing of what he felt. A part of her was still reeling from his kiss.

"There is nothing sinister in my motives, Maggie."

She reluctantly drew her gaze away from his mouth. "But you're not going to tell me," she stated.

His expression was as closed as it had ever been since she'd first met him. "I have the days to fill no matter what." He didn't shrug, but his words were the equivalent.

"So I'm supposed to put my trust—not to mention my life—in your hands because you have nothing better to do then help me hunt down a killer?"

"Have you got a better offer, Maggie?"

He hadn't said it unkindly, but it didn't matter. Her cheeks stung, but she didn't look away. "If I refuse both of your generous offers, then what?"

His stony façade began to crumble, frustration and strain began to tighten the skin around his eyes and mouth. "I didna question Them at length about it, lass." His voice was rising and his hands were clenched at his sides. "If I'd have known how stubborn ye'd be about acceptin' my help, I'd have reconsidered. Now, will ye take my help or no'?"

Maggie's first instinct was to tell him exactly what he could do with his offer, but it was one thing to be self-reliant and quite another to throw away what very well might be her only chance to save her life.

"Well, I suppose you are the perfect man for the job." She'd said it less than graciously, but his anger seemed to curb a bit at her admission.

His hands relaxed and his expression smoothed. "And why would that be, lass?"

She tried on a smile, surprised when it fit more easily than she'd expected. "You're already dead. Judd isn't exactly a threat to you, now is he?"

When Duncan returned the smile, she was more relieved than she'd thought possible. A warning if there ever was one. She hadn't realized how badly she'd wanted to take the solution he was offering her. She determined right then and there not to let him have any more control over the situation than was absolutely necessary.

"True." His expression grew serious once again. "But remember, I canna promise you I'll be able to stop yer fate from claiming you this way."

A cold chill snaked down her spine. She knew that, had understood it before she'd accepted his offer, but hearing him say it now stilled something inside her. "I know." She looked up at him. "I haven't been very gracious. I've been suspicious and difficult and, while that probably won't change, I'm sorry for seeming so unappreciative. Thank you for doing this, Duncan. Whatever your reasons might be."

He didn't respond, but merely studied her in silence, a silence that grew steadily more uncomfortable. His gaze roamed over her in the lazy manner of someone in no rush to move on to other things. Maggie grew almost excruciatingly aware of her nakedness, could feel every inch of the fabric that touched her skin, his gaze making the linen feel as intimate as the touch of his hand. And yet she had no idea what was going on behind those gray eyes of his. There was heat there to be sure, but he seemed to keep it easily under his command . . . while merely being the object of his considered attention was slowly unraveling every last thread of her control.

Her pulse thrummed, hot and heavy beneath skin growing flushed with awareness, damp with excitement. "Maybe you'd better leave," she managed. "So I can get dressed." Had the heat in his eyes flared? Her body certainly reacted as if it had. "I'll . . . uh . . . meet you downstairs." As long as he kept staring at her like that, she would be incapable of regaining a toehold on her composure. "Please."

Duncan held her gaze for another moment, then walked slowly, purposefully, toward her side of the bed. Her breathing grew shallow, her pulse raced wildly. Thoughts of what he'd done the last time he'd gotten close invaded her mind, diminishing any further resistance she might have. Resistance? Yeah, right.

He stood less than two inches away from her, the sheer force of his presence drew her gaze along the lean lines of his body until it collided with those implacable gray eyes.

She trembled. He missed nothing, not even the tiniest movement. *Do it, dammit!* she wanted to scream as he continued to look at her. *Take me, ravish me.* Even as the truth of that struck her she didn't—couldn't—back away.

"Don't worry, Maggie. I'll not take your mouth again."

What? She couldn't hear him for the pounding of her heart echoing in her ears. She must have misunderstood.

"Ye need no' look so fearful. I'll no' be touchin' you again. My offer of help was not a trick, nor an attempt to get ye to trade anything. I willna compromise yer pride more than I have. I know it is important to ye to do this as much on yer own as ye can."

Fearful! If she could have uncurled her fingers from the

death grip they had on her blankets she would have flung them away and lunged at him. She'd show him self-reliance!

"I never thought I'd be saying this to a Claren, but yer a proud woman, Maggie, with strong principals and a fierce determination to see your own way. I suspect you need that to survive in the world you live in." He stepped back then. "I'll leave you to yer dressin'."

In the next instant, he was gone. It was only after she'd blinked several times, that Maggie saw in her mind's eye the way he'd held his hands tightly clenched just before he'd disappeared.

Maggie went from the dazed confusion of hyper-libido drive to the smile of a woman who knew crumbling restraint when she saw it. "Your control is not what you think it is, Duncan MacKinnon," she whispered beneath her breath.

The question was, did she want to test that control? Well, naturally she *wanted* to. But how foolish would it be to give into that dangerous, yet sublime temptation?

Maggie defiantly tossed the covers aside and stood. The cold air made her skin prickle, but she welcomed the shock of it. She salved her ego by contemplating boldly descending the ladder with nothing more than a sheet wrapped around her or perhaps wrapped in nothing more than her own skin. *Let's see how long you last then, granite man.*

But she quickly gave up on that idea. She didn't need the humiliation of him refusing her twice. He couldn't have missed the bald desire she'd made no attempt to mask. She yanked on her clothes. So what had just happened between them? And it had been *between* them, almost palpably so. Hadn't it? Maggie sat heavily on the side of the bed and pulled on thick socks. There was no way she could be the only one affected by their kiss.

He had to have been fighting it too or why bring it up? Why had he purposely misread her trembling with need for trembling in fear? He had to know she wanted him to touch her again, kiss her again. Dear God. She shuddered with remembered pleasure. The man knew how to kiss.

She tied her boots, yanking the knots tightly. *And what if he does want you, Maggie?* He's a ghost. A spirit who will disappear in less than three weeks. Forever.

She shook her head then rubbed her temples, the beginnings of a vicious headache beginning to settle in behind her eyes. The whole thing was insane. For a ghost he sure felt, touched, and tasted like a real live, warm-blooded male. As for the short-lived time frame . . . well, he had a point there.

What would she gain from pushing him or herself into an intimate relationship, knowing full well she would only suffer for it when it was done?

She sighed deeply. Maybe Duncan had thought of exactly that and that was why he'd made his little speech, even as he'd been staring at her like he wanted to consume her whole. She made herself stand. He'd done the right thing, setting the boundaries right from the start. She hated to admit it, even if it did somewhat assuage her ego.

Maggie walked over to the ladder. It didn't matter if they talked right now, or two days from now, it would still be there between them, waiting to be confronted. Perhaps it would always be there.

Another thought struck her as she climbed down. What if they weren't successful and Judd managed to kill her after all? If she were going to die anyway, wouldn't it be foolish to pass up what little time she and Duncan could have together?

An even more provocative thought crossed her mind. If Judd killed her, would she still get eternity with Duncan as a consolation prize?

Maggie took a seat on the couch, her brain cramping under the pressure of too many thoughts, too many decisions to make. Duncan had the fire going once again and stood before it. He hadn't turned from it once.

The heat began to seep through her socks and sweater. "Are you hungry?" she said. She suddenly realized she was famished.

The look Duncan flashed over his shoulder made her toes curl. He was hungry all right, starved even. But if she weren't mistaken, it wasn't for anything in the kitchen cupboards. So far, not so good on the resistance and control thing. If he looked at her like that again, she'd be lucky to last three minutes, much less three weeks.

Maggie scrambled off the couch, his promises not to touch her again echoing in her ears. She wondered who was kidding who. "Never mind," she said quickly. "I'll just make some coffee." She glanced out the window before moving to the kitchen, only then realizing how overcast it was. She'd thought it close to dawn when she'd awoken upstairs, but now she wasn't too sure how late in the morning it actually was.

She smiled at the matches she found next to the stove. Duncan said nothing while she put the coffee on to perk, but she swore she could feel his gaze along her back. How did a ghost make her feel so incredibly alive? Only a dead woman wouldn't wonder what it would feel like to make love with a man who kissed like that.

Only a dead woman. Prophetic thoughts? She swallowed hard as the rest of their unbelievable conversation ran through her mind. She grabbed a bagel from the bag on the counter and chewed thoughtfully as she crossed back to the living room area. Duncan's attention was firmly on the fire and Maggie decided it might be wiser to keep some space between them. She detoured to the couch with her breakfast. "So, where do we start?"

"You can contact this Judd?" he asked, his back to her.

"Why would I want to?" She paused, the bagel halfway to her mouth. "You mean lure him here? Then what?"

Duncan turned, the poker gripped in his hand. She had a sudden vision of what he must have looked like in full battle armor.

"I kill him."

She dropped the bagel. "Excuse me? Ghost or not, you can't just go around killing people."

"Why not? He is trying to kill you, aye? You canno' bring yerself tae end his life. I dinna have that problem."

"Well, I don't care. It's not right."

Duncan took a step toward her, looking alarmingly fierce. "Just how di' ye think this was going tae end, lass? Wi' a slap on his wrist? Ye said yerself he would hunt you down until you were dead."

Maggie knew he spoke the truth. "I . . . maybe in self-defense I could—" She shuddered. "No. This is insane."

"What is this if no' self-defense?"

"It's setting a trap, that's what it is. It's calling him up here and then murdering him."

"I already told you I'd take care of it. Ye'll have no blood on yer hands."

"If I'm part of it in any way, then my hands are as bloody as if I drove that poker through him myself!"

Duncan swore and spun back to the fire.

"What if we call the police and have them waiting here for him?" she suggested. "They could hide and we could get him to admit he wants me dead. They could witness him threatening me. With everything else he's done to me, surely that would have to help get him a prison sentence."

He turned on her once again. "Maybe. Even then, he'll likely get out."

Maggie propped her forehead on her hands. "I know you don't understand why I'm opposed to this. But things are different now. You don't take the law into your own hands."

"He seems to have no such morals."

"As much as I want this to end, and as much as I want Judd punished, unless he was actually coming at me with a knife or a gun, I could not cut him down in cold blood. No matter who pulls the trigger." She put the bagel aside and stood. "If I were to do it your way, I would have to set aside my own principals. Then I would be no better than he is. Can you understand that?"

Duncan stared into her eyes, his expression unreadable. "And these are principals yer willin' tae die for?"

Maggie shrugged helplessly. "Yes, I guess that's what I'm saying." She turned away and paced the length of the couch. "There has to be another way."

It was silent for several long moments. "Ye say you would agree to this if he were actually tryin' to kill ye?"

Maggie spun around, eyes narrowing. "I think I know where you're going with this and you can just stop right there. If I thought I could protect myself against him by using deadly force if he came after me then I wouldn't be hiding in a cabin in the middle of nowhere, would I?"

"Perhaps I could simply persuade him to leave you alone."

Maggie paused at the icy steel tone that had entered Duncan's tone. "Persuade?"

Duncan crossed his arms over his formidable chest. "I might be able to make him think twice about wasting his time with you."

For the first time in what felt like forever, Maggie smiled a genuine smile.

"For a woman so opposed to killin', you seem quite taken with the idea of torturing."

"Well, I might be angry enough to justify a little pain. As long as he survives it."

Duncan shook his head. "Three hundred years and I still dinna understand the mind of a woman."

Maggie walked dangerously close to him, her smile still firmly curving her lips.

There was a long silent moment as Duncan looked down into her eyes. "Yer willin' tae trust me so much, Maggie?"

Maggie's throat went dry as his words stroked her senses like a silky caress. "Yes," she said, her voice shaky, "I guess I am."

"I thought ye didna want anyone to help ye."

"If I thought *I* could put the fear of God into him, I'd do it myself."

Duncan grinned and Maggie felt the heat of it singe a path straight through her. They really shouldn't stand so close.

"I dinna think ye credit yerself enough, Maggie lass," he said far too gently. "Ye put the fear into me often enough."

Kiss me. The words just formed in her mind. The way he was looking at her, close enough that all she had to do was reach up and— She curled her fingers inward, an ache in her heart at the empty feeling it left her with.

"I'm only afraid of one thing at the moment," she whispered.

"What would that be?"

"That I won't be able to stay around you like this much longer and not have you touch me again. Not when you look at me like that."

A wicked glint sparked in his eyes. "You'd have made a terrible warrior, Maggie. Never give away yer weaknesses to the enemy."

"Is that how you see yourself? As my enemy? Still?"

"Perhaps no'." His eyes darkened.

A nervous laugh found its way past the knot in her throat. "We aren't managing the truce too well. It's been what, an hour?"

"I'm beginnin' tae think I've been waiting a lot longer than that to touch ye, Margaret Mary Claren."

Maggie's knees felt decidedly weak. "Tell me again why we have to fight this—whatever it is between us?"

"Yer a Claren and where there is Claren blood, there

should be hate and suspicion, yet I feel none of those things when I look at you. Maybe I am a fool, maybe this is Claren trickery."

"What have you to fear from me?"

"I know no'. But the fear is there. Why else do my fingers tremble?"

She made this man tremble? "There is no trickery here, Duncan. I have no special powers."

"Aye, but you do."

Her fingers ached to touch him. "Duncan, I—"

"Why do ye want me, Maggie? You are runnin' from one bad choice. I am no' a better bargain. I have but twenty-one days left here."

"I know that. And I didn't say it was wise, but if we both understand where the boundaries are, then why pass on the only chance we'll ever have to explore whatever it is we're feeling."

"Yer making too much sense." He stepped closer, his hand coming up to her cheek, but hovering just shy of touching her.

"For once we agree on something. Kiss me, Duncan."

His eyes flashed dark. "Aye, I want to, lass, but I dinna know if we can stop at just one. I swore I wouldna touch you, partly for that reason. You wear at my control, Maggie, that ye do."

Maggie found a wry grin of her own and stood an inch closer to him on legs that shook with need. "It has been three hundred years. That's enough to make any man . . . edgy."

"Yer playing with fire, Maggie."

"You're the expert at fanning the flames."

He chuckled at that and she found herself swooped up into his arms.

"Duncan! Put me down." She was laughing as she said it, which might be why he didn't heed her demand.

He was halfway to the ladder. "If ye want to be ravished,

then I mean to ravish ye properly." The grin he aimed at her made her toes curl and her fingers grip his shoulders a bit more tightly. "Why do ye think I let ye keep that fine feather bed?"

"What . . . what about Judd?"

"I doona wish tae ravish him."

Maggie laughed. "That's not what I meant."

Duncan nestled her closer to his chest. "We'll find a way to take care of Judd."

He had one hand on the ladder when a loud rapping came on the front door.

Maggie went stiff in his arms. "I didn't hear anyone pull in," she whispered, "did you?"

"I heard nothing but my blood poundin' in me ears," he grumbled.

Maggie's heart now pounded in fear as much as desire. "Put me down. We should peek out front before we—"

"Maggie?" came a voice through the door. The pounding came again. "Open up, it's urgent!"

"Damned Claren!" Duncan roared, as he put her down.

Maggie scowled at Duncan, but her heart wasn't in it. "I'll be right there, Cailean," she called out. "You owe me one, cousin," she said under her breath as she stalked to the front door. "A major one."

TWELVE

MAGGIE YANKED THE door open as Cailean was shoving it from her side. She stumbled back as her cousin charged in. There were deep shadows under Cailean's eyes and she wore the same clothes she'd had on the day before.

"Did you stay up all night reading those journals?" Maggie asked

Cailean grabbed Maggie's arms, desperation in her eyes. "Shut up and listen to me. I found out why I'm here. There's a curse."

"A curse? You mean the legend Lachlan wrote about?"

"It's real. Read this." She shoved a journal in her hands and flipped it open to where she had a paper stuck inside. Cailean stabbed her finger halfway down one page. "Here."

I've exhausted all my energy and too many years of my life, but it has been worth it. The Legend MacKinnon is no myth but truth. And I have found the source from which these tales were spun. And what is more fitting between two warring clans than a curse? The tragic endings to each and every Claren-MacKinnon union from that time forward is no coincidence. The tales these doomed unions spawned created a Legend of truth. A truth that began three hundred years ago.

Maggie looked up to find Cailean's gaze boring into hers. "He's really Duncan MacKinnon, isn't he?" she asked. "The Duncan MacKinnon that was born in the late seventeenth century." Desperation still tinged her expression, along with acceptance and a healthy dose of fear.

Maggie looked over her shoulder, expecting Duncan to answer. In fact, she was surprised that he'd remained silent this long.

There was no one behind her. Blast the man!

Maggie gently pried Cailean's fingers from around her biceps. "It's okay, Cailean. He won't hurt me. Or you."

"You don't understand."

"That he's a ghost? Believe me, I understand more than I want to."

"I read them all, Maggie," she persisted. "Lachlan is right. It's legendary, but it's no myth. He has it all clearly documented. Every MacKinnon-Claren union he researched ended in tragedy. The MacKinnon's have been a curse to the Claren family for a long time." Her steely-eyed gaze bore into Maggie's. "Three hundred years to be exact."

"I know about Duncan's ill-fated betrothal to Mairi if that's what you mean. As to the rest, well, it is weird that MacKinnons and Clarens have continued to have such bad luck in their marriages, but you can hardly blame Duncan for—"

"Did you know we're both descended from MacKinnon-Claren unions? Your mother was a MacKinnon descendant."

Maggie's mouth dropped open. "That's not—"

"He has it all documented. It seems your great-grandmother was married twice. She had Mathilda with her second husband, and your grandmother with her first. He was a MacKinnon." Cailean waved away Maggie's confusion. "Trust me, it's all in there."

The information jolted Maggie and she struggled to assimilate it all. Her mother was the daughter of a MacKinnon and her father was a Claren. "Lachlan had all this recorded?"

"Yes. There's more."

"But wait. If he knew all that, why weren't we listed in the will by name? He knew about us, right? He knew our parents were dead?"

She nodded. "There is a notation of the children born to our parents' generation. He had us listed by birth date and gender, but not by name. I don't know why we weren't listed as heirs in the will, maybe he just never got around to updating it. He never did any research on us, at least in the journals anyway. He was mostly interested in documenting the unions, so maybe it's because we never married."

Maggie rubbed her temples. "And every union failed?"

"Not just failed. Ended in tragedy. The stories that were told about them have been passed down for hundreds of years, hence The Legend MacKinnon." She paused. "He traced my background too. My mother was also descended from a MacKinnon."

"And you think your mother and father died as the result of a centuries-old curse?"

Cailean nodded. "Just like yours did. It's all in there, Maggie. Lachlan started the whole thing when his own wife, a MacKinnon herself, died in a climbing accident."

"He mentioned it in the journals I read, but I didn't read the one where he explained it."

"He was disconsolate after she died. He was going through her things and found a family bible. He noticed the odd number of fatalities and was curious. He did some digging and saw a pattern."

"Pattern," Maggie repeated, but she didn't need it spelled out for her. "Surely there were some happy unions? Some happy endings?"

Cailean held her gaze solemnly as she shook her head. "The only unions that didn't end in disaster or tragedy were those that married outside the clans. Naturally, some of those ended poorly as well, but that's normal."

"So maybe that's the cause of the others. Just a freaky string of coincidences."

"For three hundred years? Without a single exception?"

"Did Clarens and MacKinnons marry so often? I mean, just how many relationships are we talking about?"

"That's part of it too. There are dozens of them. So many it's weird. They come from all over the place, branched down from many different members of the Claren and MacKinnon clans. But every one that Lachlan tracked, and he was amazingly thorough, could all be traced back to the two original clans. Back to the mid-seventeenth century, right before the clans destroyed each other."

Maggie's headache was full-blown by now. "I know that part of the story. Duncan explained it to me. But I don't understand where the curse began." She lifted her head. "And I'm not saying I believe there is a curse."

"You will when you read the journals." Cailean relented a bit, her expression softening, allowing the fatigue to be even more clearly etched on her face. "I didn't want to believe it either, but Lachlan's documentation is very detailed. It's amazing, Maggie. Genealogists work for a lifetime and don't gather the immense amount of data he managed to collect."

Maggie took a deep breath. "Okay. So there's a curse between the Clarens and the MacKinnons, or at the very least, an incredible run of bad luck. What does this have to do with Duncan?"

"Lachlan has traced the descendants from each ill-fated couple back to members of the clans during Duncan's time. They were centered on the Isle of Skye, in Scotland. Prior to Duncan's father being clan chieftain, the two clans had been bitter enemies for dozens of years. Duncan's father and the Claren chief sought to end the trouble by uniting the clans through marriage. They made three attempts, but none of them ended in a union. And in the end, the Clarens decimated the MacKinnons to the point that the clan collapsed. From that point on, the curse began."

"But why do you think it was Duncan, specifically?"

"He was one of three sons of the chief. The oldest, Alexander, disappeared shortly after being betrothed to Edwyna, the eldest daughter of the Claren Laird."

Maggie's eyes widened. "He called you Edwyna."

"If he thought I was her, I can understand now why he was so angry. It was rumored that she had something to do with Alexander's disappearance. After that, it was up to Duncan to bind the families together. He failed."

"I know that story," Maggie said quietly, feeling somewhat battered by the onslaught of information. She didn't want to hear any more statistics, she didn't want to know anything more about Duncan's ill-fated past. "What about the third son?" Maggie heard the defensive, almost desperate note in her voice. "And what of the first son? Why did he disappear? And why are you so sure it was the MacKinnons who started the curse?" Another memory niggled at her brain. "What about this 'Claren Key' Duncan mentioned? Could our descendants be responsible for this curse?"

Cailean shook her head wearily. "I don't know. Maybe. There are rumors, tales, whatever, surrounding the Claren sisters, too. It's what I have to find out. It's why I came up here." She slowly lifted her gaze to Maggie's, looking tired and haunted. "I'm going to Skye. I have to find out the root of all this and end it once and for all."

"Why are you doing this to yourself?" She tried a smile. "As long as we don't marry a MacKinnon, we'll be okay, right?"

"The visions — I won't be able to rest, I won't be able

to sleep. . ." She let the words trail off and shook her head. "I don't have a choice."

"Then why the warning? Why did you come racing up here?"

Her gaze darkened once again. "I had to. You're falling in love with a MacKinnon."

"He's a ghost," Maggie said simply. "He's already dead."

"But you're not." The warning was all the more ominous for the soft tone in which she delivered it. "There's another reason I'm going to Skye." She took a breath. "There is another cousin listed in the journals. Female. Born a few years before you, which makes her about five years older than me."

Maggie froze. "What? Who is she?"

"There's no name, just a birth date. I have no idea who she is or if she's even still living."

"Don't you think the solicitor would have looked for her? If she's alive, she's a surviving heir, too."

"I'd think so, but I don't know. I want to look into that too."

"Couldn't you just call him?"

"I tried. I couldn't get through. But I need to be there, to talk to him in person." She walked to the door.

"Wait a minute. You're leaving now? Right now?"

There was a plea for understanding in her tired eyes. "As soon as I can make the arrangements. I have the journals in the Jeep. You need to read them."

Maggie wasn't sure she wanted anything to do with them, she was totally spooked out at the moment. "You don't need them? To help with research?"

"I made notes. Legal pads full. If I have any other questions, I'll contact you through Judge Nash." She stepped back, then suddenly moved forward and caught Maggie in a hug. "Please be careful," she whispered fiercely in her ear. "You're the only family I have." She moved back and her eyes glistened. "I'm discovering just how important that is to me. Promise me you'll leave here as soon as you can." She grabbed Maggie's hand. "Better yet, come with me."

Maggie turned her hands over and linked them with her cousin's, feeling for the first time just how fragile the link was that held them together. "I can't do that." Cailean's expression collapsed and Maggie's heart tightened painfully. She didn't want Cailean to leave upset with her. "Not because of Duncan. Or not only because of him," she added honestly. "I can't run from the situation I'm in. I have to finish it, one way or the other. I'm afraid for my life, Cailean, I won't lie to you. But not at the hands of Duncan. He's agreed to help me."

At that news Cailean's expression turned downright distraught.

"You wouldn't let me talk you out of what you have to do, would you?" Maggie forced a smile. "Does Lachlan's research say if all Clarens are as stubborn as the two of us?"

Cailean's eyes watered and she pulled her hands away to wipe them on her sleeve. "No, but we must be a stubborn lot if we keep insisting on banging our heads with Mac-Kinnons. Stubborn or stupid."

"Let me know where you're staying when you get to Skye, okay? Send a note via the judge or deputy Branson."

"You contact me if you need anything," Cailean demanded. "Anything. And let me know what happens. Promise."

"I promise. And if you find this mysterious third cousin, you have to send word immediately — whatever you find out."

She nodded. "Be careful, Maggie."

"You be careful, too." She tried to put into words the fear she suddenly felt on her cousin's behalf, but she couldn't. "Just be careful."

"I will."

Maggie helped Cailean move the trunk to the porch,

then waved good-bye once again, watching as the Jeep flew around the bend. She avoided looking at the trunk as she went back into the cabin. "If she drives like that she'll be lucky to live to see town, much less Skye."

"Skye?"

Maggie startled and turned. Duncan was standing in his usual spot in front of the fire. "Thanks for all your help."

"You seemed to be doing fine wi' no help from me."

"So you listened in?"

Duncan didn't respond, his gaze remained steady on hers. "Yer cousin is chasing a faery tale, Maggie. She willna find naught but dust and perhaps an old pile o' rocks on Skye."

"What do you know of MacKinnon or Claren history?"

"I know the clans were formally wiped out soon after my death, the remaining men scattered about to be taken in by other clans. What more does she need?"

"Then you're saying there is no curse? That you and your brothers just happened to be the first in a long string of strange tragedies between Claren and MacKinnon unions?"

Duncan leaned the poker against the wall and crossed the room toward her. "I thought you didn't believe in Cailean's talk of curses either."

"Lachlan's curse," she corrected.

"Aye, auld Lachlan and his stories. Auld man let his love for a MacKinnon twist him up inside until he was seeing ghosts in every corner and faery spells 'neath every bunch of heather."

"You sound as if you knew him."

Duncan shrugged. "As ye said, lass, he claimed to own this place. He was here from time to time."

"Did you see him? Speak to him?"

"I saw him, aye."

"Did he see you?"

Duncan scowled. "No. Now tell me about this fool journey Cailean's taken it in her head to make."

"Why are you so worried? What is it to you if she's off on a wild goose chase?"

"I didna say I was worried. I just don't see why she has to go poke around in what should be left alone. What's past is past. There is no changin' it."

Maggie stepped closer, her head tilted slightly to one side as she studied him. "You really are worried," she mused. "What is it you think she's going to find?"

"She'll find nothing! There is no curse! Clarens have been bad luck for MacKinnons forever. I am proof of that, if nothing else."

"I thought you were just proof of your own ignorance in how to treat women." Maggie's blood pressure rose along with her voice.

His eyes blazed. "Claren women cost the lives of two MacKinnon brothers and I'm betting they claimed Rory as well. It would no' surprise me if their descendants held claim to their fey faery ways and claimed men for centuries to come. If there is a curse at work here, it be a Claren one." He spun on his heel and stalked to the fireplace.

Maggie was right behind him. She grabbed his sleeve just as he reached for the poker. "What are you so upset about? What are you afraid she's going to find, Duncan?"

He stared at her for a long time, then quietly said, "Let it go, Maggie. She'll find wha' she will. You canna do anything about it."

"But you could." Why was she reminding him? He was likely the only chance she had of straightening out the mess her life had become. "You could return home, Duncan."

"I havna forgotten, Maggie."

"Then why don't you go after her," she said quietly. "Or blink yourself over there, or whatever it is you ghosts do."

"I made ye a promise." He blew out a harsh sigh, then reached up and tucked a strand of hair behind her ear.

Maggie trembled as his fingers brushed her cheek. Cailean's unwanted warnings echoed in her mind. "I told you before, I'll take care of my own problems." She stepped back slightly. "If you're worried about Cailean, then follow her. Your time is limited and I can't ask you to—"

"I dinna recall you asking me. MacKinnons have always tried to do the honorable thing, even if their efforts didn't reap the rewards they sought. I canna make amends for my past actions, nor those of my clan. What's past, is past." He stepped forward, closing the space between them until she had to tilt her head back. "But whether they be righteous or false-hearted, one answers for one's actions. I didna fully understand this until now. Until you. For that I pledged my help to ye, Maggie, and ye shall have it."

A small sigh slipped from her lips as he cupped her cheek, his warm, rough skin claiming hers as his fingers slipped into her hair and tugged her forward.

He bent his head to hers. "Time has become a precious commodity for me, Maggie. I would not waste a moment arguing with ye about that which we canno' change."

"No," she whispered. "No more arguing."

He claimed her mouth only, but in that moment Maggie felt as if a far more important part of her had become his and his alone. Yet instead of feeling vulnerable, she felt quite the opposite. He moved his lips on hers, and slid his tongue inside to claim her deeply, intimately, and she felt full and strong, rich beyond her wildest dreams.

She couldn't explain it, couldn't think clearly enough to put words to it. She'd been kissed passionately before, but this claiming had nothing to do with his mouth or lips or tongue. This bond between them had been forged with words and actions and his kiss merely sealed it.

She slipped her fingers into his hair, loosening it from the slip of white fabric he'd used to tie it back. She rose onto her toes and took the kiss deeper. It no longer mattered if they had weeks or decades or a lifetime. The time they did have together would be cherished, savored, indulged in to the fullest. Precious time indeed.

There was a sudden, loud rapping on the door.

Duncan's hold on her tightened, but Maggie was already pulling away, anger blazing.

"For heaven's sake, I swear Cailean—" She stormed toward the front door. Duncan swiped for her arm and missed.

"Maggie, don't!"

Duncan lunged for her just as she yanked open the door.

"What is it this—" She broke off abruptly, shock and terror rooting her to the spot.

"Hello, darling."

It took a heartbeat too long to realize Judd was pointing a handgun at her chest.

She heard the loud explosion even as something slammed into her side. She went down hard, knocking her head on the wooden floor. Darkness crept in from all sides. There was a loud scream.

It must have been hers. It echoed again and again inside her head as she was pulled under.

THIRTEEN

DUNCAN BARELY AVOIDED rolling on top of Maggie. She had been knocked unconscious, but at least she hadn't been shot. The slice of pain shooting across the back of his arm was proof of that.

He was quite aware that Judd was still armed, which made Maggie a vulnerable target. The crack of the gunshot still echoed as he shifted to his feet, squatting low to shield Maggie and to give himself leverage. He launched himself at Judd's knees.

Duncan's size and force knocked Judd down and across the porch. Judd's head glanced off the side of Lachlan's trunk and snapped forward. Duncan was more than happy to meet it with his fist. Blood spurted from Judd's nose and he howled in pain as Duncan rammed a shoulder into his middle, driving him backward down the stairs.

Duncan grunted in pain himself. He should have used the other shoulder. He could feel the warmth of his blood seeping through the back of his sleeve. It had been a long time since he'd felt the pain of a battle wound. He'd never thought to live through that again and, in truth, he hadn't missed it. Yet, a black rage had filled him when he'd spied the gun aimed at his Maggie's heart, and he would not be satisfied until Judd's heart no longer beat inside his chest.

Duncan pushed himself upright, then scraped the tangle of hair from his face. Judd lay in a dazed heap halfway down the stairs. His suit was dirt-smeared and torn, blood had dripped from his chin, marking his white shirt, staining his tie. He looked beaten, another foe vanquished.

But the gun was still in his hand.

For the first time, Duncan felt real fear. Even when he had charged into battle against the Clarens, willing to give his life to the honor of defending his people, he had not felt emotion of this magnitude. Yes, he'd fought for all members of his clan; man, woman, and child. But never for one particular woman. It had never been Maggie's life at stake.

A roar began low in his chest. This sniveling blackguard had come here intent on doing battle with an unarmed woman. *His* woman. The roar erupted with the force of a volcano, the hills echoed his raging battle cry as he launched himself off the porch.

Judd turned his head at the sound, barely managing to roll away in time to avoid being crushed by the massive force of Duncan's body. Duncan twisted to his side, grunting as his shoulder bore the brunt of his fall. He rolled to his belly and reached out, latching a firm hand around Judd's ankle as the bastard tried to scurry out of reach.

"Ye willna hurt her." Duncan growled through bared teeth as he dragged the man toward him. "No' ever again."

There was terror in the smaller man's eyes, but he quickly regrouped. He had been using his hands for leverage, trying to resist Duncan's greater strength by grappling at the ground. Now he gave up and rolled to his back, bringing the site of the gun down, resting his hand on his stomach for balance. The muzzle was pointed directly at Duncan's head. "I don't know who the hell you are or where Maggie dug you up, but it looks like you lose." He spat out the blood that streamed into his mouth. "And here I thought she understood the balance of power." He cocked the gun. "You know, brains win over brawn every time."

"Think again, mister."

Judd turned to look at Maggie, who stood over them, holding the fireplace poker like a spear. Duncan could only see her in his peripheral vision. He didn't dare turn, instead keeping his gaze fastened firmly on Judd . . . and the gun.

"Go awa' from here, Maggie," he said. "I said I'd handle him and I will." Even as he said it, he was busy trying to calculate just how fast he'd have to move if Maggie followed his command. Judd could swing the gun wide and shoot her through the back in the blink of an eye. Would he be fast enough? Beads of sweat trickled down his neck and under his collar. His palms grew damp. He tightened his grip on Judd's ankle.

"He's holding the gun, or hadn't you noticed that?"

Eyes widening at her thankless tone, Duncan growled. "I see that bump on the head didna knock any sense into ye."

"It gave me a helluva headache is what it did." She shifted her weight. "Another thing I owe you for, Judd."

"The one paying here will be you, Maggie," Judd spat out. "I explained everything to you, but you wouldn't listen. I could have given you everything you ever wanted if you'd only understood. Don't you see? We would have been perfect together. You belong to me, Maggie. Mine. All mine. But you ruined it all. Why did you do that? Why? I loved you and you ruined my life."

Maggie let out a shocked laugh. "*Your* life? I ruined *your* life? Why I ought to—" She swung the poker up and Judd flickered the gun in her direction.

"Maggie, don't!" Duncan yelled.

Judd moved the gun firmly back toward Duncan, his

aim maddeningly sure-handed. "Listen to the man. Unless you want to see him shot through the head first."

Maggie froze, the poker high over head, then slowly lowered it.

"Dinna let him use me tae bargain wi', Maggie," Duncan warned. "He canno' hurt me."

Now it was Judd's turn to laugh. It ran on the side of irrational and made Duncan's skin crawl. The man was truly mad. "Where did you dig this guy up, Maggie?" Judd demanded. He narrowed his gaze on Duncan now. "Let go of my ankle." He flickered the gun toward Maggie. "Do it."

Duncan gritted his teeth and swallowed just enough rage to keep him from clawing his way up Judd's narrow frame and ripping his heart out through his throat. He was certain he could kill this man. But he wasn't certain that a bullet wouldn't pierce Maggie's heart before he got his hands on Judd's. He let go.

"Very good." Judd scrambled to his feet, wiping his mouth along his sleeve. He waved the gun, motioning Duncan. "Join her. You'll be joining with her eternally anyway."

"If you only knew," Maggie said under her breath.

Duncan got his first good look at her. She was pale and there was a noticeable bump on the side of her head. Despite her bravado, she was clearly hanging on by a thread.

"Steady, Maggie. Dinna do anythin' rash," he said softly. Her eyes flickered to his briefly. There was stark apology and regret. He motioned to her with a short shake of his head. "It's no' over yet," he whispered.

"When did you switch to the brute savage type?" Judd goaded, clearly smug now, but his eyes glittered with a mad rage. "Slumming it, Maggie? Is that what turns you on? I never pegged you for a slut, but then it seems I was mistaken about many things. Too many things. Blinded by my love for you and you think to mock me like this?"

Duncan vowed that he would be wiping that smile from Judd's face. And he planned to take a good deal of pleasure in the doing of it.

"I'm not slumming anywhere. It's not money or slick Wall Street charm that gives a guy class."

Hatred flickered in Judd's eyes, sending a renewed jolt of fear and anger through Duncan's body. "Maggie—"

"No, let her talk." His grin could only be described as feral. "And since when did you choose men based on class?" he taunted. "I thought you got off on power. Who has the power here, Maggie?" He waggled the gun.

"If you were truly powerful, you'd have been able to take a simple no from me, Judd."

Only Duncan saw the tightness at the corners of her mouth, or the way she held her head and shoulders so rigidly. She was terrified but damned if she'd let anyone see it. She was standing up to Judd as fiercely as any warrior he'd fought with or against. She'd fight until the battle was done. Duncan felt something shift inside him.

He'd lay down this life and any other for her, proud to have known her, whatever the duration.

It hadn't escaped his attention that if Judd killed her, Duncan could spend eternity with her. But the thought of her dying ripped at the heart he had not thought he owned.

She would not die here today. No' if he could help it.

"Well, this little reunion has been fun, but I've got more pressing matters to attend." Judd smiled again. There was a desperation to it that made Duncan's gut tighten in dread. "Who wants to go first?"

"You said I ruined your life," Maggie said. "Seems like the only one ruined here is me. Certainly you have enough things going for you, big man in the world of high finance, to not feel ruined because one woman walked out on you."

Hatred twisted Judd's face into an ugly mask. "You have no idea what your run-in with the police cost me! I should have wrung your neck the first time I had my hands around it."

"Why didn't you?"

Veins popped out on Judd's forehead. Duncan balanced his weight, and flexed his hands against his legs, ready to shove Maggie down and launch himself at Judd if he moved so much as a muscle toward her.

"My boss got wind of our little domestic dispute. He wanted to know if I was handling the matter." Growing more visibly agitated, Judd was clenching and unclenching his fist, the gun bobbing dangerously. "I was up for promotion, but he wasn't going to promote someone who couldn't control his own personal life. I had to make you understand that." Sweat was beading on Judd's forehead now, too. "Why wouldn't you understand that? You had to come back to me."

Maggie shifted her weight, moving slightly closer to Duncan. "Just how did you find me anyway?"

Judd puffed up a bit, his irritation smoothing out somewhat. "Power, Maggie. So what if Henderson is a tightass who can't see beyond his idiotic family values. He should never have fired me, Maggie. I might be having some difficulties, but I'm still a powerful man." He snapped his fingers. "People jump when I do that, Maggie. Your timely little inheritance situation came to light when your cousin tried to contact you.

"It's all over now, Maggie. I've lost everything. It's only fair that you lose everything too." He swung the gun out, straight-armed.

Duncan could remain silent no longer. "Maggie, move back."

"Come on, Judd," she said, her voice wavering a bit. "You're a money man, not a killer. Can you stand here and gun me down in cold blood?"

There was a roar of an engine just as Judd slipped his

finger across the trigger. His attention was diverted for one split second. It was all Duncan needed.

He lunged at Maggie, shoving her down and covering her with his body. A stand of trees jutting out prevented Duncan from seeing the vehicle he heard spewing gravel as it swung around the last bend. Judd was just far enough out in the clearing to be in sight of the oncoming car. Duncan could only pray it was not Cailean.

Duncan lifted his head just in time to watch Judd turn back, and fire . . . directly at him.

"Freeze! Police! Put down your weapon!" It was Deputy Branson.

Duncan had been hit in the side, but even with the red haze of pain blinding almost all his senses, he was able to focus enough to watch as Judd swung around and fired at Branson.

Branson took him down with one clean shot to the head.

Maggie was safe. Maggie was safe. The words echoed in his pain-fogged head. She began to struggle beneath him and another realization dawned. As soon as Branson stepped toward Judd's body, he would be able to see Duncan and Maggie, sprawled on the ground.

"Are ye okay, Maggie mine?" he said in a low whisper next to her ear. "Yer no' hurt?"

"Other than having two hundred pounds of Scot on me, no," came the muffled reply.

Duncan laughed, sucking in his breath at the resulting pain. "Och, Maggie Claren, ye'd have made a fine warrior."

She tried to wiggle from beneath him. "Are you okay? Duncan, what hap—"

He kissed her and held her down one moment longer. "Shh. It's all right now. Yer safe." Then he squeezed his eyes shut and concentrated hard . . . and disappeared.

•   •   •

MAGGIE ROLLED TO her back as the weight on top of her suddenly vanished. "Duncan?"

"Maggie?"

Deputy Branson's shout jerked her head around. She choked on a gasp at what she saw just beyond him: Judd's lifeless form, sprawled awkwardly on his back in the dirt. There was another uniformed man kneeling over him. Branson's partner, she guessed. She hadn't known he had one.

God, was it really all over?

"Are you hurt? I called for an ERT team, but it will take them a few more minutes to get here. Just lie still."

"It's okay, I'm—" She moved to sit up, but her head reeled. "What happened?"

"I'm sorry, Ms. Claren. He stashed his car halfway down the mountain on an unused service road and hiked in. We didn't know he was up here until your cousin told us."

"Cailean? Is she okay?" She struggled again to sit up, but stopped short of standing when Branson put his hand on her shoulder.

"She's fine. She'll be up here in a few minutes. I almost had to hog-tie her to stay in town.

"Your cousin was in the middle of checking out and she got all funny, sort of spacey. My sister was worried and called me over. She was okay when I got there, but she was adamant that you were in danger. She told us about your former fiancé and we decided to follow up. We found the rental car with his name on the papers." He touched her arm anxiously when Maggie laid back down. "Everything is okay now, Ms. Claren, he can't hurt you again."

"Who . . . ?" She closed her eyes.

"I did. It's okay. There's no question of responsibility. You're in the clear. It's all over."

Maggie saw Deputy Branson through completely different eyes. He looked and sounded amazingly competent for a good ol' boy cop. Apparently she'd misjudged him as well. Boy, she was on a roll. "Are you okay? I'm sorry you had to . . . what I mean is . . . thank you, you saved my life."

"It's my job." His eyes were steady on hers. "Thank your cousin. You know, I've got an aunt who knows things like that. Mighty handy to have around at times." He grinned. "A dang nuisance otherwise."

Maggie managed to smile. "Yeah," she said weakly.

The ERT truck rolled in just then, along with two other cars. Branson's partner called to him. "Will you be all right?" the deputy asked her. "Just lie still until the medic gets over here." She nodded easily, but he grinned and dipped his chin. "Promise?"

Maggie's smile was easier this time. "Promise. Thank you again, Deputy Branson."

Maggie was reassuring the medic she was fine and submitting to some tests while she held an ice pack to her forehead when Cailean rushed over.

"My god! Are you okay?" She knelt in front of Maggie. "I didn't know until it was almost too late. I swear. I'm so sorry. Oh Maggie, I—"

Maggie looked to the medic who was taking the blood pressure cuff off her arm. "Can I have a few minutes here?" The young woman nodded and moved to the front of the truck. Maggie turned to Cailean. "It's okay. I'm okay. You saved my life, Cailean. Maybe it's not such a curse after all." She tried to smile.

Cailean looked around and whispered, "Where's Duncan?"

Maggie hadn't been able to think straight for two seconds since he'd blinked out, but she felt like something was wrong. Very wrong. "I don't know."

"You mean he wasn't here for you? I can't believe—"

"He was here." She held Cailean's hand. "He saved my life, too."

"I thought Branson shot Judd?"

"He did. But Judd fired at me first. Duncan tackled me and—" She gasped. "Oh God." The sequence of events flashed back through her mind in crystal clarity. He'd been shot! She'd seen the blood on his sleeve from the first time he'd been grazed, shoving her to safety. She tightened her grip. "I have to find him. I think he took a bullet meant for me. Twice. Oh God, I have—"

She started to get up, but Cailean stopped her. "Maggie, calm down. You're not making any sense. He's a ghost, he can't die."

"I'm making perfect sense. He can bleed, Cailean. If he can bleed, can't he die again? I can't just let him go like that. His time might already be up and then we'll never, I'll never . . ." Her breath hitched and she swallowed hard. "I have to find him. And I can't with all these people around." She looked to Cailean imploringly. "Please, help me get rid of everyone. He won't pop back in until they all leave." At least she prayed he would.

"But you have to be checked out—"

"I'm fine! Why won't anyone believe that?"

Just at that moment, Branson stepped around the back of the truck. "I hate to do this, but we need to ask you some questions. You too, Ms. Claren," he said to Cailean.

Maggie forced a smile on her face and tried to look more relaxed. Gauging from Cailean's expression, she wasn't fooling anyone, but she had to try. "I understand. But is there any way I can come down tomorrow? I have this bump on my head and I'd really like to just lie down for a while."

Branson's face creased with renewed worry. She cut him off before he could speak. "It's nothing. The medic already checked me out, not even a mild concussion. It's just been a lot to deal with."

Branson smiled reassuringly. "We'll have plenty to keep us busy today. Why don't you two come down as soon as you're able in the morning."

"Thank you." She hoped she didn't look overly relieved.

It took another fifteen minutes, but with her cousin's help, she was able to assure everyone she'd be fine, then she and Cailean retreated into the cabin while the various personnel dealt with everything else. She tried to shut that out. As soon as the door was closed, she turned to Cailean. "Thank you for helping me out there."

"Of course." She frowned, worried. "But you really should rest. Duncan will be back when he's ready."

"You don't understand, Cailean."

"I know he was hurt, but, really, I'm sure he has ways of dealing with that, wouldn't you think?"

Maggie dipped her chin. "I don't know what to think. I'm worried." She looked to Cailean. "What if he doesn't come back?"

She hadn't wanted to voice her deepest fear, especially to Cailean, given how she felt about Duncan in the first place, but her cousin surprised her by pulling her into a hug. "I'm sorry, Maggie. Truly sorry. But maybe it's better this way. You're done here. You can come to Scotland with me. Or go back to New York. Whatever. Maybe it's best to put all this behind you."

Maggie was already shaking her head. "I can't. I know you don't approve, but I'm not going anywhere." She moved over to the sink and pumped out some water. "I know you have to do what you have to do." She raised her hand to stall Cailean's response. "I won't have you stay here because you're worried about me. Nothing has changed except now you don't have to worry about Judd. And now you know you don't have to worry about Duncan either."

Cailean nodded reluctantly. "Would you like me to stay until morning?"

Maggie shook her head. "Not because I don't want you here or appreciate what you've done. Cailean, I can't tell you—"

"Don't. I'm just glad that for once it worked out right. But I can't just leave you here."

Maggie saw the fatigue and strain around her cousin's eyes. "I can't imagine how hard this is on you. You need to go to Scotland and find out what is behind all this. I need to stay here. At least for a while."

Cailean sighed in defeat. "Okay, okay, I'll go. I know Duncan will be more likely to pop back in if I'm gone. But you have to promise to speak to Branson in the morning. I'll go down and talk to him before I leave." Maggie nodded. "Is there anything else I can do for you before I go?"

Maggie smiled. "I really need to get out of here and look for Duncan. Create a diversion and cover for me until everyone is gone?"

Cailean rolled her eyes and sighed. "You're incorrigible."

Maggie winked. "It runs in the family."

FOURTEEN

It was dusk by the time Maggie gave up and returned to the cabin. She kept her eyes averted from the spot where Judd had died. She'd had plenty of time to think about what happened while she'd searched the wooded trails for Duncan. It was horrific how things had ended and she could honestly say she hadn't wished Judd dead. She'd just wanted him to leave her alone. But he'd chosen otherwise and she refused to feel guilty for the relief that she felt now that it was over.

She sat down on the middle porch step, allowing the doubt and fear to creep past the relief for the first time since she'd begun her hunt. The cabin was dark. She hadn't realized how much she'd been counting on finding smoke curling from the chimney. After everything else, this was simply too much. If she'd had the energy, she'd have yelled and screamed at the sky, threatening anything, promising everything if They'd just send him back for one more minute.

What came out instead was a soft, tear-clogged whisper. "You can't leave me like this, Duncan MacKinnon."

In the next instant he materialized in front of her, and

she found herself swooped up in his arms. He was bare-chested, his hair a wild mane, all loose and tangled.

"Duncan, what——? Where——?" All the emotions that had roiled inside her churned past the wall she'd forced them behind. "I've spent hours looking for you." The pain and fear were all there in her voice, her eyes burned with the release of it all. "I thought you weren't coming back," she choked out.

"Och, Maggie mine, it wasna my choice to leave ye as I did. I'll explain, but there is somethin' I must do first." He bent his head to hers.

All her anger and fear vanished at the emotions she saw mirrored in his eyes. He'd been afraid for her, too. She pulled his head to hers and met his lips eagerly.

He didn't stop at one kiss. Once his mouth was on hers it was as if he would never be satiated. She knew the feeling. When he finally released her, she was holding onto him as much from need as to keep from melting through his arms to the ground. "Wow," was all she managed.

His grin was a bit wild and a lot cocky. "Aye. Wow."

She smoothed a hand over his face and his grin turned to a tender smile that softened her heart and tugged at her soul. "Are you okay?" She remembered the blood on his sleeve. "You saved my life, Duncan. Twice you put yourself in front of a bullet for me."

"I canno' be hurt, Maggie. And even if I could, I couldna let anyone harm ye."

"But the blood, I saw——"

He pressed a finger to her lips. "Aye, I bleed, and I feel pain, but I'm no' a mortal, real and true, Maggie. I canno' die." His smile faded completely. "For you can only do that once."

She craned her neck and ran her hand along his arm. "You're healed? But how? Is that where you've been? In some sort of purgatory health clinic?"

Duncan laughed. "Ye are quite a woman, Maggie mine,

and I love the sharp side of yer wit. I was with Them. The wounds I sustained no longer plague me."

There was something more, something he wasn't telling her, something she wasn't sure she wanted to know. But there would be no secrets between them. Not now.

"What did They want with you? I thought you couldn't return to purgatory until your month was up?"

"I willna lie to ye, Maggie. My time here is done, my lesson, for this visit perhaps, has been learned."

Her heart felt like someone had snatched it into a fist. "Because you saved my life?"

He nodded.

"Then it's not true," she said quietly, her heart breaking. "You can die twice."

"Ah, Maggie, please dinna cry."

Cry? She realized then that tears were coursing down her cheeks.

"I never want to hurt you, lass. I never meant—"

She silenced him with a finger pressed against his lips. Lips she'd never taste again. God, could one person really bear so much in one day? "No, don't apologize," she managed. "You saved my life, Duncan." Her voice caught, but no matter how hard she tried, she could not stem the tide of tears. "I'm sorry I'm crying, it's just . . ." She buried her head against his shoulder and held on tight. "I'll miss you."

She felt his finger beneath her chin but did not want to look into those eyes again. Fierce gray eyes that were capable of saying so much. But he persisted and she reluctantly lifted her head.

"Ye have a choice to make, Maggie. I'll no' bring ye more pain then ye can bear, but if ye'll have me, I've asked to complete the remainder of my time on earth. With you."

"Don't tease me," she warned.

"Never."

"Really?" Hope blossomed inside her.

"Aye. We have twenty-one days."

Maggie refused to let her mind progress beyond that deadline. If it hurt this much to think about losing him now, in three weeks it would kill her. But could she really let him go right now?

"I want them all," she said, knowing there had never been any other choice. "This thing with Judd and now with the journals and Cailean coming into my life . . . I have a lot to think about. I don't know what the future holds for me. But for the next three weeks, I want you. Will you have me, Duncan? This Claren woman?"

He grinned. "Aye, that I will. And often if ye'll allow it."

Maggie laughed, suddenly delighted and overwhelmed with this latest twist of fate. "Well, I believe, before we were so rudely interrupted earlier, you were about to ravish me."

"Was I?" He leaned down and planted a searing kiss on her lips that left her breathless. "I seem tae recall it as bein' the other way around."

"I can think of a really great place to settle this argument."

Duncan didn't need a map. She liked that in a man.

THE FEATHER BED seemed to absorb their bodies like a cloud, just as her clothes somehow disappeared.

"Ye were wrong, Maggie," he said hoarsely.

"About?"

"Ye said yer body was excruciatingly average. And here I find you are perfection."

"If I recall, you were the one who said I had nothing you hadn't seen before." She arched a playful brow.

"I was a cad, Maggie. And a bastard fer certain. You are an exquisite creation of God's own hand and it is blessed I am to have the honor of touching you."

Spoken so sincerely; his words stunned her. He reached for the sash that surrounded his waist, but she put her hand on his, stopping him. "If you don't mind. I'd rather do this part the old-fashioned way."

Duncan's wicked grin surfaced. "Yer just wantin' to see wha I wear beneath me kilt."

She laughed. "I'll finally discover what women have been wondering about for ages." She slid her hands up his hard thighs.

Duncan leaned back and crossed his arms behind his head. "I'm yours to explore." He winked at her. "Go gentle with me, Maggie. It's been a long time."

Maggie didn't know whether to laugh or choke. "I'm not sure I'll be worth the three hundred year build up," she said. "Of course, *any* woman would probably be—"

The rest of the sentence left her on a whoosh of air and she found herself on her back, Duncan's heavy weight pushing her deeply into the duvet.

"I didna manage to exist without a woman for so long because any would do, Maggie. There is only one woman for me in all eternity and she is here in my arms."

Maggie's throat closed. There had never been anyone in her life who had made her feel so singularly special, so cherished. How had she found this immense gift in the one man fate had proclaimed she couldn't have?

Duncan smoothed a fingertip along her temple and down over her cheek. "My declaration brings you sorrow, Maggie?"

Her eyes burned. "I promised myself I'd enjoy what we would have and not mourn what we could not." He pressed his forehead gently to hers and she squeezed her eyes shut as an enormous pain threatened to crush her very soul.

"Och, Maggie," he said roughly. "Dinna fash yerself over that which is to come. The future can hold many wondrous things that we canno' foresee in even our wildest imaginings. You are testament of that." He kissed her cheeks. "Open yer eyes, Maggie." When she didn't respond, he kissed them gently. "Look at me." He kissed her nose and the corners of her mouth. "Please."

She opened them. "I thought I could handle this." She began to tremble. "I'm not sure I can. I look at you and I want you so badly and . . . and . . ."

"Share that kiss with me now, Maggie."

Confused, she stopped and sniffed. "What?"

"I said once that when we kissed, it would be sharing, not taking or giving. This is a gift. Doona waste it away. Share it with me." He moved his head, closing half the distance between them. "Meet me here, Maggie."

Her breath came in shallow gasps as her lips met his. He opened his mouth on hers, then with a deep groan pulled her into a fierce embrace. And she was lost. Thrillingly, willfully lost.

It was a kiss, a sharing, like none she'd ever known, all the more intimate for its patience and indulgence. In that moment she felt she could kiss him for all eternity and still want for more.

When his lips finally left hers, he dipped back quickly for a small kiss on the corner of her mouth, as if he had to have one last taste. She kissed the curve of his chin, knowing exactly how he felt.

He raised his head enough so she could look into his eyes. If she'd thought she'd seen intensity in them before, she hadn't known the true meaning of the word. She wondered if the same emotion was reflected in her own eyes. She certainly felt it. How could one kiss rock her so deeply, affect her so unquestionably?

"Will that be enough to last you, lass?" His voice was rough with emotion, but there was a twinkle in the depths of his eyes and the slightest of curves to the corners of his mouth.

"If I had to go through my life and be allowed only one kiss, I would choose one of yours, Duncan MacKinnon."

She smiled and reached down to tug at his waistband. "Now about that other demonstration . . ."

There was a faint sound of bagpipes floating through the air and then she felt his bare chest pressed against hers. He nudged a knee between her thighs and she welcomed him instantly.

"So," she said a bit breathlessly, "am I not to know the answer?"

He settled between her legs and nudged upward, making her gasp as he himself groaned. "Ye have yer answer."

Maggie laughed and gasped again as he pressed just inside of her. "I'll remember that."

Through clenched teeth, he said, "I'll see to it that ye do."

She shifted her hips and pulled him deeply inside her. He groaned long and loud, his hands diving into her hair as he angled her mouth for a searing kiss. He claimed her with his mouth as surely as he did with his magnificent body.

Their bodies moved together easily, the rhythm increasing, both of them panting, almost drowning one another in feverish kisses. Then Duncan broke free from her mouth and reared up on his hands, thrusting deeply inside her, making her back arch fully to meet him.

His eyes held an unholy light and she wondered, in that moment, if he too felt the sensation of timelessness that she felt. He held her hips and pulled her to him even as he thrust more deeply into her. Her body clenched, wound tighter, spiraled higher, then shattered, into a million sparkling pieces of perfect pleasure.

He bent down and with a deep, guttural groan, thrust into her one last time. "You are mine, for all eternity." He shuddered and held her tightly as he came inside her, rocking her over and over as his body continued to convulse.

• • •

SOME TIME LATER Maggie opened her eyes and found
herself nestled against his chest. The duvet had somehow
found its way over them. She felt as if she were floating
inside the perfect cloud. She never wanted it to end.

"I want to go to Scotland," she said into the comfortable
silence.

He hugged her. "I would love tae show ye my home."

"I want to see it from your eyes. Share it with you." She
swallowed and added, "I'd also like to help Cailean."

She felt the sweet pressure of his kiss on her hair. "It is a
kind and gentle heart ye have, Maggie. And I'd be less than
truthful if I said I wasn't a wee bit concerned for her myself."

Maggie lifted her head, truly surprised by the admission, but his eyes narrowed before she could speak.

"Doona expect too much. I simply want to make sure
she doesna trample too heavily on MacKinnon history."

Maggie sighed and smiled, settling back against his
chest. She let her eyes drift shut. "Tell me about Scotland."

He settled deeper into the bedcovers and sighed. "It is a
wondrous, magical place."

Maggie listened as he went on to describe the land of his
birth, creating vivid mental pictures and starting a craving
deep in her heart. There was pain and anguish there too,
despite his best attempts to quash it. She knew that these
next three weeks would put an indelible mark on the rest
of her days, define who she was to become and how she
would live the remainder of her life.

"Why the bagpipes?" she asked, forcing the pain away.
"Every once in a while, when you wink in and out, or do
something ghostly, I hear bagpipes."

"My clan were pipers to the great Clan MacDonald," he
said. "The pipes and their music played a significant role in
our lives. I know little of Scots history beyond the time of
my death, but They have let it be known to me that shortly
after the end of my clan, the highland clans were stripped

of many rights under a new royal regime intent on dismantling their power."

She could feel the tension grow inside him as he spoke, his voice began to vibrate with emotion.

She flattened her palm on his chest. "Duncan, don't. I didn't mean to bring up a subject that would hurt you."

"Ye wanted tae know, now let me finish. They banned the wearing of the plaid and the playing of pipes and that was only part of the tyranny they perpetrated on the highlanders in their efforts to control them and their land." He sighed heavily and Maggie felt her heart break. "I wasn't there to help save my clan when I should have been. Even if I had, I don't know if I would have lived through that devastation of all I ever knew and loved. So, in honor of my people, I kept the sound of the pipes. It is the one piece of home that I can carry with me into the afterlife, the one reminder of all that has been done . . . and all that I left undone."

"Oh, Duncan." Maggie didn't know what else to say. She simply held on to him as tightly as she could.

He pulled her on top of him and wrapped her tightly in his arms. He pressed his face to her neck and she thought she felt the hot sting of tears on her skin. "I've failed so badly, Maggie."

She clasped his face between her palms. "You haven't failed at anything, Duncan. You're a man, not a god. The only thing you did in life was to prove you are human." She pressed a quick kiss on his chin. "We do our best, Duncan. That's all we can do. You did what you thought was right. So did I. I think I've learned from my mistakes. I think you have too." She smiled. "Some of us just take longer than others."

When he went to argue, she kissed his mouth shut. He was still frowning, but he said, "I think I might like arguin' with ye." He looked into her eyes. "But I confess it scares me a wee bit to think I might make a mistake with you. Our time—"

Maggie pressed a finger to his lips, unsure she could survive seeing that bleak despair that threatened to fill his eyes. "You were the one who said we shouldn't worry about what is to come."

"I don't ever want to forget you, Maggie."

"You won't," she promised. "I'll always be here." She touched his forehead. "And you'll always be here." She placed his hand on her heart.

They met halfway, their kiss as fierce and claiming as any that had come before it.

Scotland waited for them both. But first, they would make time for this.

PART TWO

RORY

". . . yet spirit immortal the tomb
cannot bind thee."

—LEONARD HEATH

". . . To save, to ruin, to curse, to
bless,—"

—THOMAS HOOD

FIFTEEN

CAILEAN LOOKED DOWN from her second-story hotel window, at the quaint strip of buildings on the lower port street of Portree. Boats bobbed in the harbor under overcast skies. Below, people were leaving for work, dashing in and out of the corner market, driving their cars down to the town square and disappearing beyond. Children were off to school, laughing as they bustled along the street. A classic west highland small town. The scene should have been calming, reassuring.

She shivered even though the radiator had kept her room toasty warm all night. From the moment she'd paid the toll and driven the tiny red Citroen she'd rented from Kyle of Lochalsh onto the Isle of Skye, she'd questioned her decision to come here.

Her work as an anthropologist had taken her to a wider variety of locations than even the best travel agency could detail. She'd been awed by the natural wonders of some and chilled by the sheer desolation of others. But never once had she felt such an intense sense of dread.

It was here, in the town where Lachlan had lived . . .

and died, that she would stay until she put the demons that badgered her to rest once and for all.

Looking at the map the solicitor's secretary had drawn for her, it seemed a fairly easy trek to the cemetery where Lachlan was buried. It was a bit off the track, but Miss Marchant had no doubt Cailean could find it.

But did she want to find it?

Cailean's hands grew clammy and the porridge she'd forced down this morning rolled in her stomach. She shoved the map in her pocket and snagged her keys, trying to smile at the clerk as he waved cheerily to her on her way out.

She had no idea what she expected to find at Staffin Bay. She'd hoped to speak to Lachlan's lawyer directly, but he was out of town until tomorrow. She knew enough about the confidentiality of wills to know that there was little chance he'd explain the contents to her, but she did want to at least question him about the third cousin.

As much as she hated her visions, Cailean hoped seeing the places where Lachlan had lived, and talking to people who knew him, might trigger a clue for her to follow. His research had claimed his attention from the time his wife had passed away, almost to the exclusion of everything else, but he'd died before finding the one thing he was after. The key that would unlock the curse.

Cailean hadn't told Maggie about that particular aspect of Lachlan's research and the personal conclusions he'd come to. Maggie was already dealing with enough.

Lachlan had discovered that each generation of the Clarens had produced at least one daughter with *dha shealladh*, the second sight. She was known as the Claren Key.

Stories about the curse had been handed down in tales known as The Legend MacKinnon. And Lachlan had originally believed that the Claren seer held the secret to ending the curse, but as his research continued, he'd come to believe the real key might be an actual, tangible thing, a thing that only a Claren seer could control. He'd died without ever finding it or proving its existence.

Now it was up to Cailean to take up his quest — whether she wanted to or not.

She realized now that the visions had returned right about the time that Lachlan had died. Cailean clutched the steering wheel more tightly as she went over the rest of the history yet again. She had shivered as she'd read about Kaithren Claren, the youngest Claren daughter, known at the time for being a *taibhsear*, having the second sight. A Claren Key, as was her oldest sister, Edwyna.

She knew the story of Mairi and Duncan now. Edwyna had been Mairi's older sister, betrothed to Duncan's older brother, Alexander, in the first attempt to bind the two clans through marriage. That attempt had ended in tragedy when Alexander disappeared the night before his wedding, never to be seen again. He'd been labeled a coward by the Clarens but there wasn't a member of the Clan MacKinnon who believed it. They had all thought him to be their next chief and knew him worthy of the task. The MacKinnons placed the blame on Edwyna. Most, if not all of the clansmen were a superstitious lot and there had been much recorded about the Claren Keys and their ties to the faery realm, and all the havoc that could wreak upon their clans if a union was allowed.

The disappearance of Alexander brought all that to the fore and the unrest grew to the point where Edwyna was sent into seclusion. Duncan, now the heir apparent, was then betrothed to the middle daughter, Mairi. According to Lachlan's research, after Mairi fled and Duncan left to retrieve her, the feuding between the two clans climbed to disastrous proportions, leaving them vulnerable to other, larger clans, who were also warring for more land and more power.

And still, Calum, the MacKinnon laird, resisted betrothing his sole remaining son, Rory, as John Roderick was called. Then Edwyna's body was found behind a brae, less than a mile away from Stonelachen, the MacKinnon stronghold.

The Clarens naturally blamed the MacKinnons and the warring escalated, continuing unabated for several years, with the Clarens always emerging victorious. Calum was ailing and could no longer lead his clan into battle, leaving Rory to that undertaking. He was a formidable warrior, yet it wasn't enough. Calum hadn't reached his ripe old age without understanding the power of union and the wisdom of compromise. Despite the resistance from his clan, he sought a meeting with Angus, the Claren chieftain.

Calum used his allegiance with Clan MacDonald as his bargaining chip, and after much discussion and more than one bloody brawl between members of the chiefs' counsels, the deal was made. There would be an end to the fighting in return for his remaining son's hand in marriage to the Claren's youngest daughter, Kaithren.

Kaithren was rumored to possess even stronger powers than her sister, though the Clarens spoke little of it after the disastrous attempt to wed Edwyna to Alexander. The MacKinnon clansmen, wary and angry though they were, heeded their chief's decision, as did Rory. It was just after the turn of the century and both clans began to hope for a brighter future.

Then, on the morning of the wedding, Kaithren refused to marry Rory. With both clans collected together for this union, all hell had broken loose. Calum was slain and there were many accounts stating that Rory fought with what some called demonic power. But in the end, the Clarens vanquished the MacKinnons, whose formal rights to Stonelachen and all clan properties were forfeited to the Clarens.

The Clarens had also suffered severe losses in manpower and weaponry and supplies, and shortly afterward, their lands, including Stonelachen, were taken over by the MacDonalds.

There was no record of what became of Rory or Kaithren, but all felt certain he'd died on the same field as his father, that fateful day. As the Legend MacKinnon was passed down and embellished, it was rumored that Kaithren had escaped to the realms of the faery world when the destruction began and from that time forward, the faeries would rise and destroy any union between descendants of the original two clans.

The Claren Curse had begun and only the real Key could reverse the spell.

Cailean stared out at the vista of brown hills to her left that rolled onward to the steeper mountains above in the distance. It was in those mountains, above Staffin Bay, that her destination lay. The area known as the Quiraing. Even the name evoked mysterious images.

Miss Marchant hadn't been able to answer her question as to why Lachlan had chosen this place instead of being buried closer to his home in Portree or with his wife, who'd been buried on the other side of Skye in Dunvegan.

Her shoulders slumped. In the last ten days she'd taken a month-long sabbatical from a dream dig in Peru, she'd withdrawn a substantial chunk of her life savings, hopped a jet and flown halfway around the world, all because she was convinced a strange inheritance was the reason she was having a renewed onslaught of visions.

She wanted control of her life back.

She wanted control period. Control of her thoughts, of her mind, control over her ability to make decisions based on *her* needs and wants, and not those dictated to her by some quirk of genetics that had cursed her with the ability to occasionally see things that hadn't yet happened.

She wanted peace. Was that so crazy?

She wound her way up the narrow road into the Quiraing. It was even more majestic up close than it had been from a distance. Steep craggy spears and cliffs jutted out of the side of the mountain, forming a bowl behind them that

cattle rustlers had used hundreds of years ago to hide their
stolen goods. Spring water raced over the edge of the cliffs,
only to be blown straight up and back over the edge by the
strong prevailing winds. If she looked behind her, she
could see the whole of Staffin Bay spread out below.

It was stunningly beautiful, but it was also incredibly
desolate. Mostly rock, it was home only to sheep. Not even
the sturdiest croft would survive back here.

Then she spied the tiny dirt and gravel road. It was
exactly where Miss Marchant had said it would be, and in
about as good a condition as she'd described. Deeply rutted
and weathered, it was the only way to the cemetery, and
she had no choice but to go slowly.

It was early afternoon now and days were short in November. She glanced at her watch. She had roughly two
hours before she needed to head back. It would be dark
when she returned, but she knew the small town of Portree
well enough to find her way back.

She wound around another bend and there it was. She
was surprised by the orderly cluster of headstones enclosed
by wrought iron fencing. With a shaky sigh, she climbed
out of the car.

The wind was strong and she had to lean forward to
make any headway. She had to work at the latch to the gate
for a few minutes, before finally figuring out how to open
it. She shoved it forward, wincing at the squeal it made,
then left it open so she wouldn't have to fight it again later.
The cemetery was well maintained. Still it was obvious
which grave was Lachlan's—all the other headstones looked
weather-beaten with time. She stood at the foot of Lachlan's grave:

Lachlan Claren, Born 1919 Died 1999.

She knew he'd died of a heart attack, but she'd always
thought of him as robust and hale, younger than an eighty

year old man must be. Maybe it was his bold handwriting, which never wavered from his first journal to his last, in which he'd made entries right up until his death.

Someone had placed a bouquet of silk flowers in front of the headstone, wedging them well into the rocky earth. She wondered who'd left them. And who'd arranged for the funeral and the headstone.

He'd never mentioned anyone's name unless it was directly related to family history. He struck her as a loner who'd wrapped himself up in his grief and spent all his time searching for a way to end it.

She edged closer to the headstone and noticed there was something inscribed below the dates.

" 'Born and Died a Claren, but his heart belonged—' " The flowers blocked the rest from view. A chill raced over her that had nothing to do with the wind. She leaned over farther and carefully brushed the flowers aside. " 'His heart belonged to a MacKinnon.' "

She looked around at the other headstones. There were a few other surnames scattered about, mostly belonging to women, she noticed, but one name showed up again and again. MacKinnon. This was a MacKinnon family cemetery. This was MacKinnon land.

How had he finagled space in what looked to be an ancient MacKinnon family cemetery?

Cailean struggled to stand from her awkward position and grabbed hold of the headstone behind her for support.

The vision struck without warning.

SIXTEEN

EVERYTHING WENT BLACK. Then, just as suddenly, there was a spear of blinding light. In the center of that white dagger stood a man.

His face and clothing were cast in shadow, but she could tell he wore a cloak of some kind. She could determine only that he was slightly above average height. His shoulders appeared broad, but it was hard to tell if it was him or the coat.

The man didn't move or do anything to reveal himself or his motives to her in any way. Yet she felt . . . threatened.

Not physically, but . . .

Damn this! She hated feeling so powerless, so victimized, so . . . inadequate. This man meant her harm, but not physically. So that meant, what? Emotionally?

She was yanked from her musings when another piece of information popped into her mind, knowledge that wasn't there one second and an instant later it was as if she'd always known it.

He was the guide.

The guide to what?

Then it struck her. Would he be the one to take her to the key Lachlan believed existed? She knew better than to expect an answer to that. Heaven forbid she be given any practical information. *Just step out of the shadow,* she urged silently. *Let me see who you are.*

He remained where he was, frustratingly silent.

Without warning, the vision ended as abruptly as it had begun. She was standing in the cemetery, holding on to the headstone. She turned, scraping back the wisps of hair that had come loose from her braid, and froze.

The stone she'd gripped for support had blackened with time, the rounded shape worn down so much so that the top part of the first name was gone. The letters were shallow and some had eroded altogether, but still she could read what it said.

Calum MacKinnon.

She rubbed her hand over the corroded stone, as if that would clean the blackened surface. The dates had worn down to the point where they were impossible to read. She traced her fingers over the lettering several times, but nothing. No feelings, no more visions. Just more unanswered questions.

She stood and brushed her hands against her pants. There was nothing left to do but head back to town and wait for her morning appointment with the solicitor.

And think about the man in her vision.

She did take the time to wander around the remaining stones. Of the ones she could read, there were none older than the early 1800s. Some of the names looked similar to the ones she'd read about in the journals, but no exact matches that rang a bell. There were too many Williams, Johns, Marys and Sarahs to place a particular name to a particular story. And yet Lachlan had chosen this place for a reason. And there was the matter of Calum's headstone triggering her vision.

She rubbed her temples, knowing from experience that

the splitting headache coming on would turn into a migraine if she badgered herself with this. Experience had taught her it was best to leave it alone, let it simmer until something came forward to guide her once again. There was that word again. Guide.

She climbed into her car, only now noticing how deep the shadows had grown. Had she really been here for hours?

She'd just started the car when the sky opened up and rain thundered down like a waterfall. She wasn't certain about the flash flooding statistics of the area, but it didn't take a meteorologist to see the rutted dirt track was rapidly becoming a river.

The tiny Citroen would likely wash right down the mountainside, along with God knew what else. How did the sheep stand it up here? she thought crossly.

Thankfully it wasn't all that cold, so she turned off the engine and decided to wait it out. She was on a relatively flat piece of ground next to the narrow cemetery, so she'd be safe enough. This couldn't last that long. She'd be fine once she'd negotiated the dirt track back to the paved single track that lead to the main road. All she had to do was wait. And think.

HE EMERGED FROM the mist of rain as if formed by the forces of nature. He was tall, with angular cheekbones and a strong jaw, both made all the more formidable by the hard slashes of his eyebrows and the even harder slash of his mouth. Rivulets of rain ran off the cape of his ankle-length brown duster, his heavy boots sunk into the mud as he walked toward her.

Cailean sat in her car, gaze locked on his, unable to move. He was the man from her vision.

He was the guide.

Her guide.

Heaven help her.

There was no use running. She was here to rid herself of her demons. Better to confront him right here, right now.

She climbed out of the car and yanked up the hood of her mountain jacket. She braced her feet against the wind and stood her ground. She waited until he cleared the corner of the iron fencing before she spoke. "Who are you?"

He stopped. It was only when the relief washed over her that she realized just how afraid she'd actually been.

"What are you doing out here?" he asked.

His voice was rough, though it might have been a trick of the wind. He didn't have to shout to be heard, though. In fact, his tone was calm rather than angry.

"Waiting for the storm to end," she responded at length. She looked uneasily at the graveyard, a cold chill snaking down her spine. "Where did you come from?"

"Here."

Not the answer she wanted to hear. "I didn't notice any crofts back this way."

"Are you stuck?" he asked.

Cailean shook her head, very aware that he hadn't answered her query. "I didn't want to chance the dirt track until the rain let up."

"I'm not too sure it will matter now."

Cailean didn't appreciate the way her skin prickled in warning. He wasn't supposed to be a physical threat to her, she reminded herself yet again. "I've waited out worse than this," she said, trying to sound confident. "I'll be fine."

He nodded toward the Citroen. "Not in that you won't. The ruts will be boggy now. Suck those tires in like rain on the desert sand."

"So what are you saying? That I'm stuck up here?" And what did this mountain man know of desert rains?

"The rain will end shortly," he said. "But you need to wait for the track to firm up. It'll take several more hours.

If you're smart, you'll wait until closer to morning to leave."

He was a good ten yards from where she stood, yet his voice carried almost eerily over the howl of the wind.

"What about you?"

"What about me?" he replied easily, like a casual stranger making conversation.

On the side of a desolate mountain next to an old, all but forgotten family cemetery, in the rain, in the dark.

This was anything but casual.

"Now that we've established that I'm neither stuck nor foolish," she said, careful to keep her tone as moderate as his. "There's no reason for you to be out in the rain."

"But it's not raining." And it wasn't. The wind still whipped furiously around them, whistling through the dagger-like peaks and rocky spears that towered above them, but the rain had stopped.

"Then you don't have to worry about me. You can go back home, wherever home is."

"You're wet."

She raised her eyebrows at the obvious comment. "So are you."

"What is it that you do that gives you such experience in poor conditions?"

"What is it that you do that brings you out to the wilderness on rainy nights to rescue damsels in distress?"

Could he be a caretaker of some kind? He didn't fit any definition of graveyard caretaker she'd ever imagined. He wasn't even a Scot. At least, he had no discernable accent.

A sick feeling assailed her. She strove to keep her eyes on his and not glance over to the graveyard again. He was not a ghost. Was he? And just how crazy had she become that this was actually the most plausible explanation she'd managed to come up with yet?

"I tend sheep," he said.

His answer startled her. "You're a shepherd?"

"Does that seem so surprising? You can hardly be in Scotland for more than an hour and not notice we have more than a few of the wee beasties. Did you think they tended themselves? We keep track of them."

"Even in the rain? In the dark?"

"It was neither when I left."

Left where? she wanted to demand. "So what am I then, a lost sheep?"

"There are many lost souls that need tending to."

She shivered under her coat. "Well, rest assured I am not one of them."

She thought about simply climbing back in her car and locking the doors. She thought about asking him if he was man or ghost. Neither seemed an entirely smart course of action.

And then it didn't matter. He was gone.

She hadn't even seen him leave, or disappear. Had she been so lost in her thoughts? Cailean shook her head slowly, resisting the urge to rub her eyes. Had he really been there? Or had he been some manifestation of her vision?

No. He'd been real. Well, maybe not flesh and blood real, but she hadn't been standing there talking to herself.

She walked to where he'd stood but it was too dark to make out any footprints. She'd check again before she left. She'd find those footprints, she'd find her proof. She needed proof.

VERY EARLY THE next morning, Cailean pulled gratefully into a space in front of her hotel. The road had been a challenge, but more because of the fog than the mud. Her night visitor had been right about the track firming up.

She pushed the bizarre night from her weary mind and hurried upstairs. She needed a long hot bath, a big breakfast, and a nice nap. A quick shower and a change of clothes

was all she was going to get, however. Her meeting with
the solicitor was in less than an hour.

THREE HOURS LATER Cailean pushed open the door to
her room and collapsed on the bed, so tired she could
barely keep her eyes open.

Donald Chisholm had been more than happy to talk
with her. And talk, and talk, and talk. Unfortunately, for
all that the man had stories to tell, none of them answered
the questions she'd most wanted answered. She sighed and
rolled onto her back, staring at the headboard curtains that
jutted out from the wall above her bed.

Mr. Chisholm had been Lachlan's attorney for ten years,
taking over when his previous solicitor had passed on. He
felt he knew Lachlan as well as anyone, which was, as she
was quick to discover, not all that well. She'd pretty much
pegged Lachlan correctly.

"We Scots tend to embrace our eccentricities, and auld
Lachlan was one of our better ones," Donald had said,
laughing and offering her more tea.

She had found out little information of significance.
When it came to Lachlan's property, his will, or anything
related to it, Donald tended to wave off her questions and
change the topic to some local story she'd be certain to find
amusing. When she'd pressed, asking specifically if there
had been anyone else besides Maggie and herself involved
in the disbursement of the will, Donald had finally said he
couldn't answer those questions other than to say that the
will had been fully executed now and the matter was
closed.

Frustrated, she pushed a bit more on her questions regarding Lachlan's choice of cemetery and Donald had relented enough to tell her that the cemetery plot was
Lachlan's right and proper, but beyond that he felt it
wasn't his place to speak of his former client's estate.

He did share the details of the funeral itself with her.
Donald had been present at the service, along with several
of the locals who knew Lachlan, including several personal
friends, the librarian, a few ladies from the church he rarely
visited, along with the clergyman who gave the brief eu-
logy. Cailean had pressed him for the names of Lachlan's
personal friends and those to whom he'd left his personal
property, but Donald had demurred once again, couching
his refusal with a kind smile and a pat on the hand.

It seemed the locals liked her great uncle well enough,
but no one really knew him. "Mostly just to tip their hat to
as he went on his way in and out of the local library."

Cailean had more or less pieced together that the people
Lachlan was most likely to have left anything to were his
housekeeper and the older gentleman who'd rented the
other half of his small home. There had been no mention or
even hint of a third cousin.

Cailean left Donald's office and followed his directions
to what had been Lachlan's home. It was a white, two-story
building, typical of the croft-like architecture on the is-
land, with a neat yard ringed with a white stone fence and
a tidy but very small garden.

Mr. Mackay was a kind enough old man and had poured
more tea into her, along with a few biscuits and some
cheese that the housekeeper put together. Mrs. Robbie was
almost as old as her employer, both of them easily contem-
poraries of Lachlan's.

They'd talked of Lachlan openly enough with what
might pass for reserved affection. Mr. Mackay had inherited
the deed to the cottage and planned to turn it into another
of the many bed and breakfast establishments that dotted
the countryside. His niece would be coming in the summer
to help him manage the place, he said with a warm smile.
Mrs. Robbie had received a six month stipend to find herself another job. But since she'd been kept on by Mr. Mackay, she'd been able to save her inheritance. She planned to

use it to pay a visit to her grandchildren in Glasgow. She couldn't have been more tickled.

But for all that they were fond of Lachlan, it was obvious that he had been an intensely private man who had shared little conversation beyond the basic social niceties, and even lesser of his thoughts.

Cailean had felt an odd twist of emotions. Lachlan had been consumed with curiosity about the lives and histories of his ancestors and Cailean easily understood how seductive it was to get lost in the history of a people and their culture. She liked thinking that she might have been someone who mattered to the old man, had they ever met. They'd have had something in common—a shared passion for the past.

From there Cailean had headed to the library, the only other place that Lachlan had spent a good amount of time. The librarian was friendly with a soft, delightful accent and a ready smile. She'd talked fondly of Lachlan and given Cailean a more vivid visual description of the man. He'd been short but stoutly built, with flowing white hair and bright blue eyes and a brown cap perched at the same jaunty angle when he arrived and again when he left.

But the librarian knew little of the man himself, other than his reading habits. He'd scoured every historical document in the building, with particular attention to information pertaining to the Clarens and MacKinnons.

"Faith, but the auld man must have had them all memorized as many times as he'd read the dusty volumes," the librarian had whispered as she'd pointed out the shelves he'd frequented.

Cailean had stopped into several of the stores and eaten lunch in one of the town pubs, asking questions and making casual conversation as she went. She'd spoken to more human beings that day than she had in the past year.

The Scots as a whole were a friendly lot. If she hadn't been there chasing demons, she might actually have enjoyed herself. They knew their history well, both personal and national, though they disagreed readily and heartily on many of the exact facts. Even the vaguest question usually elicited a spirited, jovial debate.

She'd found herself drawn to the colorful history of the isle and its inhabitants and wanted to know more, and not all of her curiosity was based exclusively on her reasons for coming to Skye in the first place.

For a self-proclaimed happy loner, it had been a bit unsettling to realize she felt a direct link. First to Maggie, now to her ancestors, her family history . . . herself.

But Lachlan hadn't been her only subject of discussion. As casually as she could, she'd brought up her awe of the Trotternish area, especially the Quiraing and surrounding mountains. As it was a popular tourist spot, it was easy to engage almost anyone in a conversation of the place, complete with stories and personal anecdotes.

She frowned, the slight pressure in her temples warning her that another headache was looming.

She'd asked about the sheep, making appropriate tourist noises about their cute black faces and the amazing number of them. She'd even managed to cleverly wind the discussion around to shepherding and how difficult it must be, especially in a place as remote as say, the Quiraing.

And that's when she'd hit pay dirt.

That was when she'd heard her first tale of the man known as The Remote.

SEVENTEEN

H E SAT ON a small tumble of stones and brooded. He wasn't used to brooding since there was little in life left for him to ponder at any length or with any real emotion.

That ceased to be true the moment he'd spied the woman standing in the middle of the cemetery, blonde wisps of hair blowing on the wind, transfixed as if by some unknown force.

She had disturbed him. Enough to make an appearance, to actually engage her in conversation, something he rarely did anymore. Who the devil was she?

She meant trouble for him, even if he couldn't say why, or how. Maybe it had been the shocked expression when she'd read the name on the stone she'd gripped.

Calum MacKinnon, clan chief, Laird of Stonelachen. He shook his head, surprised to find himself fighting a smile. Still turning ladies' heads after three hundred years. The old man would have liked knowing that, he would.

His mouth tightened as he stood and surveyed the small cemetery below. He'd returned to this spot on occasion, yet this was the first time he'd stayed. He'd followed the siren call of the earth until there was naught but a few wee notes left in her horn. Something had called him home. Maybe he would find peace here.

An odd supposition given how many men had found only death on the rocky ground beneath his feet. But then, that was the one thing he was assured of. He'd never find death . . . no matter how long and hard he searched for it.

CAILEAN TOOK HER time, driving slowly as she headed into the jagged pinnacles and cliffs of the Quiraing. She told herself the leisurely pace was so she could appreciate the view. But that was bull and she knew it. She was taking her time because she wasn't in any hurry to find what she'd set out this morning to look for.

The Remote.

Cailean swallowed hard as the looming pinnacles of the Quiraing came into view. The sky was cloudless today, a stunning vivid blue. The sun highlighted the grass, which clung like velvet to the harsh landscape that looked too rocky and unforgiving to grow anything so bright. The brilliance of the green was muted by the patches of heather, brown and twisted now that fall was turning to winter.

She turned up the single track road that twisted through the Quiraing to the graveyard . . . and perhaps to proof of The Remote's existence as something more than a hallucination or night specter.

She had always liked secluded places, feeling more at ease in areas where the only people around were the fossilized remains of the ones being dug up for analysis under her microscope. They were safer than people. She didn't have visions about fossils.

Cailean pulled into the lot and looked up the steep incline behind the cemetery. He'd have had to come from that direction, she thought, but she couldn't see how. Even the sheep weren't up this high. There were no obvious tracks or trails and with no knowledge of the area, mounting even a cursory climb alone would be foolish, even dangerous.

Blowing out a sigh of disappointment, she grabbed her notebook. She'd come all this way, she wasn't going back without some tangible progress.

She began near the gate and started listing the family names and birth and death dates. After several pages, she decided to change her tactics and began listing the information by dates first, rather than cross reference later. She wasn't surprised to discover that Lachlan was the only burial in the twentieth century.

Cailean found herself drawn deeper into MacKinnon history. She wasn't sure how she felt about it—wary? Especially when she considered that this was a MacKinnon cemetery and she was a Claren. To that end, she'd avoided physical contact with any headstones for the first two hours.

Then she came across the tiny stone for one Sarah MacKinnon, born 1868, died 1870. She found herself brushing her fingers gently over the stone face before she realized what she'd done. No visions assaulted her, but a strange melancholy had. Poor wee babe, she found herself thinking as she made note of the dates and those of her parents. Both of them had died young. She couldn't help but wonder what the wife's maiden name had been. She didn't want to know, yet in some corner of her heart she feared she already did.

She began crisscrossing her way back and forth through the stones, working from the latest dates back to the earliest. The stones were positioned in concentric oval loops, with a worn stone path circling the entire pattern. The open center appeared to have been a small garden at one time, judging by the pitted stone bench and bare scrabble of ground surrounding it. What an unforgiving place to be buried in, she thought, but then, this area was an entirely unforgiving place to have lived as well.

Cailean sat down on the stone bench, wondering if those who had sat here before her had appreciated the isolation and solitude of this remote place, or felt abandoned by it.

She had spent her adult life looking upon burial grounds as work, a place to be examined as a source of potential information to the lives and culture of those buried beneath. She'd never related to burial grounds personally. She'd been too young to remember anything of her parents' deaths, and when Adele Trent, the woman who'd raised her, had died, Cailean had been on a remote dig in northern Africa and had missed the funeral by the time word reached her. She'd been to the grave, but had never been able to connect the cold marble stone to the woman buried beneath it, or to herself.

So why did she feel such a strong sense of connection thousands of miles away from the land of her own birth?

She walked over to Lachlan's headstone and stared at the words etched there. "You stirred up something that should have been left alone, Lachlan Claren." She stepped closer. "I was doing just fine until you dragged me into it. And I'm damn sure I don't want to care."

"Now there is a sentiment I can relate to."

Cailean gasped and whirled around. Her night visitor sat on the stone bench she'd just vacated.

"This is a private conversation," she said.

He was wearing the same duster he'd had on earlier, but his head was uncovered. Dry now, his hair was still dark and unruly. In the sunlight his face was still unholy. That was the word that came to mind when she tried to describe the unusual beauty of him. It made no sense. His features were every bit as harsh as the landscape he seemed to arise from, all sharp angles and slashes. He should have looked angry, hard, defiant, anything but beautiful.

But he was beautiful. Enough to make her stare. If there

was anger in him, or defiance, or any emotion at all, he kept it cloaked. He simply . . . was. The word came to her again. Unholy.

Cailean resisted a shiver. "Why are you here?"

"You called me here," he said simply, when there was nothing remotely simple about any of this.

She did shiver now. She had come here looking for him, so there was no reason to feel so defensive, so intruded upon. So scared. But she was.

"And how do you figure that? I am not lost, nor am I stuck, and, as you can see, there is not a cloud in the sky."

"I didna say you required my assistance, lass, merely that your presence called tae me. Commanded me actually."

He said that last part as if it bemused him. He shook his head slightly and stood.

Taller than average. And the shoulder cloak was not enough to make him seem so broad if he wasn't naturally so. He took a step toward her and she reacted viscerally. He moved with an innate grace to even the smallest of movements. How did a man appear so smooth and unthreatening and strike such a soul-deep terror into her at the same time?

"Stop right there," she said, damning the quiver in her voice, one she had no doubt he'd picked up. She let out a slow breath. "You're a Scot?"

"Aye."

"I didn't notice your accent before."

"It comes and goes."

"As do you," she responded.

His lips twitched ever so slightly. "Aye, that is also true. One of the benefits of land ownership, a man can come and go on it as he wishes without drawing questions."

"You own this land?"

"In all ways that matter. No man can own the earth. At best he can lay claim to it for a time."

"That's not an answer."

"It is the only one I have to offer you."

"You own this cemetery as well, then?"

"It exists within the land I claim. I am its caretaker I suppose." His lips did more than twitch then, though there was no humor in it. "Laird of the dead, that would be me." He shook his head, an hollow laugh carrying softly over the ground. "Just when you think there are no more ironies left in life."

His smile had transformed the harsh lines of his face, making him look all the more like a fallen angel. His laugh had pulled at something inside her. She didn't think she'd ever heard anything so achingly empty.

An empty angel.

She tried to ignore the growing sense of panic. He was important to her in some way and she wasn't prepared for him to be anything to her, important or not.

Are you merely walking among the dead, she wanted to know, *or are you one of them yourself?* "Are these your ancestors?"

The question seemed to still something in him for the space of a second, but again, he answered smoothly. "Most. In one way or another, I suppose."

"You suppose?"

"I don't keep track of the comings and goings of each and every clan member who has the misfortune to be needing a burial."

"Well, from the looks of it, except for Lachlan, there haven't been many 'goings' of late. In fact, it doesn't appear anyone has been needing a burial in your family in some time."

"Your point being?"

"Nothing. I just guess I assumed you'd know something of who was buried in a cemetery you're responsible for, especially if it's a family plot. I mean, you've had at least a hundred or so years to check them out."

He visibly stiffened at her last words.

"Dead is dead," was all he said. "What matter is it if I know their names or their relation to me? Their stones remain upright and the gate opens and shuts. Beyond that my responsibility to them is done."

Though his tone held only the barest edge and his posture was still relaxed, there was no denying his defensiveness. She felt it roll off of him in waves.

"Have you lived out here long?"

"Long enough."

Cailean swallowed her frustration. "If you don't want to have a conversation, then why do you persist in showing up and beginning one with me?"

"As I said, you—"

"Summoned you, yes, yes, I heard you. Well, now I *summon* you to leave, okay?" She turned around. "It was more productive talking to a dead man."

"Is that what you were doing out here the other day?" he asked quietly. "Talking to the dead?"

She stilled. Had he been spying on her then? Had he seen—?

She turned slowly back around. "It is customary to show respect when someone dies," she said carefully.

"You have an unusual way of paying your respects."

Her eyes narrowed. "In what way am I unusual?"

"No flowers," he said smoothly.

She didn't even blink. "I wouldn't know where to purchase any. I felt it was most important just to be here."

"Why is that?" He took another step forward.

Her heart was pounding and her skin dampened in a cold sweat. *He will harm you.* The words echoed in her mind. *He is your guide.*

"Who are you that this dead man might need your words and your presence?" He took another step.

Crazy, she thought, that's who I am. Cailean locked her knees against the urge to step back. "I'm not here for him."

A smile ghosted across his lips. "In that you are quite right. The dead don't care who stands over them."

"You don't believe that the spirits of the dead somehow know who mourns them?"

"I believe it makes no difference. They are gone and you are here. You can do nothing to alter their existence, whatever it may or may not be. The only reason for talking to the dead is because the living soul believes he or she will benefit from it somehow."

"What a cynical view you have of human kind, Mr. . . . ?"

There was the barest hint of a smile at the corner of his mouth. "MacKinnon."

"I suppose I should have known that." This was The Remote, the man she hoped would provide some answers to the questions she had about her great uncle. This was the guide, sent to help her find those answers.

This was the empty angel who would haunt her. Harm her.

"Perhaps the only thing the living hope to attain is comfort," she said. "Is that such a bad thing to seek?"

"Not bad perhaps," he conceded. "Pathetic maybe. Foolhardy certainly."

Anger bubbled up through the fear. She didn't even want to be here, much less be lectured on the selfishness of her actions! "The fact that you actually believe that explains why you live out in the middle of nowhere with several dozen sheep as your only comfort. Anything with a higher intellect would search for comfort elsewhere, perhaps from someone who isn't too cold and harsh and full of himself to give it."

He seemed wholly unaffected by her outburst, which only served to further infuriate her. She blew out a harsh sigh. "Look. I'm sorry," she said, though she was truthfully anything but. "I'm not usually given to emotional outbursts. It generally takes more than one opinionated cynic to provoke me into a display of temper."

He moved again, only this time he didn't stop until he was standing a few feet from her. "I suppose I will have to work on that."

"It certainly wouldn't hurt," she responded evenly. "You might be surprised. You might actually make a friend or two."

"Oh, I'm no' interested in makin' friends, lass," he said. The smile this time was a slow transformation, the impact even greater as he gradually, calculatingly unleashed its power. He closed the distance between them.

Cailean was riveted to the spot. She couldn't run. She could barely breathe. Swallowing was impossible.

"I meant I'd have tae work on provoking ye," he said, ever so softly. "I find yer 'display of temper' and yer 'emotional outbursts' quite entertaining." He reached up and ran a single fingertip down along the side of her face. "And I have no' been entertained in a verra, verra, long time."

EIGHTEEN

"I'D PREFER THAT you didn't touch me."

"I'd prefer that I didn't want to," he replied easily, dropping his hand back to his side. "But then, many preferences of mine go unfulfilled. I'll survive this one. I survive everything."

Her brows furrowed as she detected the slight sarcasm he'd injected in that last part. Sharp, he thought. And too beguiling for her own good. She was no classic beauty. Her long hair was by far her best asset, he decided. Her green eyes were too widely set and her mouth too wide and lips too thin. He supposed the high cheekbones were what lent her face its character, along with a jaw that was entirely too rigid. What exactly had called to him to touch her he could not say.

And yet, one touch, he discovered, was not going to be enough. And he wasn't at all certain that she hadn't been as affected as he by their fleeting first connection.

"Who are you?" he asked, reminding himself that down the path of curiosity lay pain and eventual heartache, especially where a woman was involved. *Always* where a woman was involved. But by Christ those eyes of hers called to a man. Hell, a century had passed since he'd done something this foolish.

"My name is Cailean," she said at last, and grudgingly enough that he knew it to be the truth.

"I am John," he said. "But I am known as Rory."

He had no idea what had possessed him to tack on that last part. It had been so long since he'd spoken it, the name had felt odd on his lips.

But that was nothing compared to the reaction it struck in her. She went pale as white linen flapping in a cold breeze. "I've been known to irritate some, but hardly to the point where the mere mention of my name strikes terror into the soul."

His rare attempt at humor failed miserably. He should never have come back here. "Yer starin' at me as if ye seen a ghostie," he grumbled.

"Have I?" she whispered.

It took a second for her question to sink in. When it did, he laughed. It felt surprisingly good, so he laughed again.

"I'll take that as a no?"

Oh, she was a good one for arching that fine brow, she was. He decided he rather liked her when she was riled up. Far better than he'd liked seeing her pale and frightened. That made his insides react in ways he'd long ago learned would only bring him misery.

"I am mortal," he assured her. He found himself wanting to trace her lower lip, wanting to compare its softness to that of her cheek. "Irritatingly, eternally mortal."

"The alternative isn't all that great, you know."

"No, I wouldn't know."

Concern flooded those damnable eyes and he cursed his loose tongue. What was it about her that made him reckless?

"Has your life been so horrible that you'd rather it end?"

"I am not sure what it is I want." That wasn't entirely

true. He knew what he wanted, at least in part. He understood all too well the stirring in his blood, the hunger beginning to rise in him. He had thought that particular need had been permanently vanquished long ago. Apparently he was wrong.

There was still one woman on earth who could rouse him.

He should have stayed in the hills with his sheep.

"I can't believe you want death," she said.

"You have no idea."

He would have walked away then, back to his mountain, back to his sheep, back to his sanctuary. He would have, if she hadn't touched him.

She took hold of his arm. Perhaps she'd sensed that he was about to leave, about to run.

"Wait," she said.

Her grasp was firm and strong. Surprisingly so in one so slender. He looked into her eyes and found another surprise. Resolve.

"Now you suddenly prefer my company?"

A small smile quirked her lips, enchanting him in ways he didn't at all appreciate. "Someone once told me that many preferences go unfulfilled. I'll survive this one."

Damned if his own lips didn't twitch. She chose that moment to let him go. He immediately mourned the broken link.

"Did you know that you're practically a legend to the local townspeople?"

He had to work at concealing his reaction. Legend, was he? He took a moment to scan the empty horizon, then looked back to her. "I'm hardly local to anywhere. I doubt anyone knows of my existence."

"Tell that to the regulars at Tally's pub in Portree."

"Portree? That's hours from here."

She shrugged, obviously enjoying this. "Ever since you took on crazy Tommy's sheep and drove them into these

mountains your reputation has taken on mythic proportions."

He frowned, not at all happy with this bit of information. "What reputation? I don't even know them, nor they
me." He heard his voice begin to rise and worked to even it
out. Damn it all but this is what he got for interfering!
"And what do they care about Thomas Walpole's sheep for
God's sake? No one cared about the man when he was
alive."

He took a steadying breath. Maybe it was best she had
interfered. Better to know exactly what the folks were saying about him. He wasn't ready to leave here, but leave he
would if he must. An unexpected pang squeezed at his
heart. Dear God, what was becoming of him?

"Why did Tommy leave them to you?"

"Thomas was an interesting man, if a bit misunderstood. I met him while out wandering." And had found an
unexpected kindred soul. Not a friend exactly, Thomas was
too eccentric to allow that. But the man loved to spout his
ideas, and Rory had all the time in the world to listen. "He
said I needed a trade and taught me about sheep. When
he passed on, they became mine." Whether he'd wanted
the wee beasties or not. But he'd had nothing better to do.
Perhaps Thomas had been wiser than he'd known. He
snapped out of the reverie. "What else do they know of
me?"

"Nothing much actually. The tales are more folk legend
than truth. You're like a cross between Bigfoot and the
Loch Ness Monster. They call you The Remote."

"What nonsense is that? And why in hell do they care? I
dinna bother them and I ask for nothing but solitude."

"You took Crazy Tommy's sheep and left his land behind. Then you herded them up here into the Quiraing,
where no man survives. It spawned a tale or two in the
pubs. You know how that goes."

He did know and he didn't like it.

"Of course, no one agrees exactly. To some you're just another loony, as crazy as old Tommy, to others you're this mystery man. Everyone has a story to tell, but no one can claim seeing you themselves."

"And what is your interest in all this?"

His question startled the smile from her face. It was as if the clouds had suddenly covered the sun.

"Who said I was interested?"

"Ye dinna lie well, Cailean." He wasn't sure if it was his accusation or the use of her name that made her pupils suddenly dilate, nor was he sure why the reaction made his pulse rate speed up.

"Who said I—"

He stopped her with the barest touch of his fingertip to her lips. Och, but they were soft, like flower petals. He'd gone daft for sure, spouting thoughts like a poet. And yet he traced her lips before pulling his hand away.

"You listened to their stories. You came back here. You're interested."

"I came to talk to the dead, as you noted earlier."

"Ah yes, seeking comfort from a soul already departed. You strike me as a smarter lass than that. What has this man to offer you from the grave?"

"Answers."

"Did you get them?"

"No." She looked away. "I only got more questions."

He thought about how he'd first seen her, standing transfixed, her eyes unseeing. A dark cloud of suspicion moved into his mind. Anger, centuries old, flickered to life within him.

"Who is this Lachlan you come to ask questions of?"

"You don't know?"

He shook his head, beginning to think maybe he should have paid closer attention to his surroundings after all.

"I'm surprised. I mean, he's the only one who has been

buried here in a century. As the owner of this land, I assumed he'd bought the plot from you."

"I've only been here several years. Perhaps he arranged the purchase earlier. I don't keep track of such things."

"It didn't perk your interest when someone showed up and began digging a hole in your cemetery?"

"I saw it being dug, but what care is it of mine if another MacKinnon needs burying? God knows it happens to them all at one point or another."

"You don't know, do you?"

"Know what?"

She didn't answer right away. She studied his face, his eyes most of all. His patience came to an abrupt end. He grabbed her arms. "Know what?" He felt the dread crawling around in his belly. Christ, why hadn't he stayed in the damn hills with Thomas' sheep?

She pulled her arms from his grasp and stepped away from him. "The man they buried here is a Claren."

His face contorted in what could only be termed rage. He spun around to face the headstone, eyes blazing, hands clenched into white knuckled fists.

Cailean backed away carefully. "What difference does it make to you if—"

He whirled on her, making her stumble another couple of steps backward.

"The only good Claren is a dead Claren, but even dead he cannot lay his bones to rest in MacKinnon ground!"

His words, spoken with more emotion than she thought he contained, shook her hard. She struggled to keep her thoughts focused and her tone even. "The plot is his. I asked the solicitor. It's all legal. Who did he buy it from, if not you?"

It was clear he was struggling to maintain a toehold on his temper. Finally, she was getting somewhere. She just hoped her interpretation of her vision had been correct on the physical harm point.

"I have no idea how he got his hands on this plot."

"Well, the most logical person would be from whoever owned this land before you came here."

He said nothing, merely stalked away from her. He stopped at the bench, his back still facing her.

Understanding dawned. "You don't actually own the land, do you? Not legally anyway."

He didn't turn around. She could see his shoulders move as he took several forceful breaths, before blowing out one long sigh of disgust.

"Lachlan's solicitor wasn't too keen on discussing his will with me. Do you have any idea who owns this land?"

Still nothing.

"Well, they must not care overly much about it since no one has bothered you since your arrival."

She silently cursed Lachlan again for not including all the information in his journals. Maybe he thought it irrelevant. Maybe he'd assumed his quest would die with him. He hadn't updated his will in decades or searched out heirs and tried to impose his will on them directly. He hadn't purposely dragged her into this, but here she was. And since this was the only lead she'd been able to dig up, she wasn't letting it go. Nor was she letting go of one John "Rory" MacKinnon.

The name played across her mind. It couldn't be a coincidence. He might not be a ghost, but the whole thing was too amazing to be ignored. First Duncan, then Calum's headstone and now her vision about the man named Rory.

She walked toward him. "I know something of the history between the Clarens and the MacKinnons. So I understand why you aren't too thrilled with having Lachlan's remains here."

He turned slowly back to face her. His eyes were still lit with anger, the harsh slashes of his features were drawn so sharp they looked as if they could cut a person. She didn't intend to get that close.

"What do you know of it?" he said. "And what are you to Lachlan?"

"He left behind a trunk full of journals containing notes about the lives and loves of the Clarens and the MacKinnons. His wife was a MacKinnon."

Rory looked past her at the fresh grave. He seemed to relax a fraction. "Sorry bastard should have known better. They never learn." He looked back to her. "You have your answer. He was buried with his wife."

He didn't look happy about it, but neither was he as furious as he'd been moments ago. She almost hated to continue.

"His wife isn't buried here. She's buried in a family crypt in Dunvegan."

His eyes darkened. "Why do ye care about this auld man's remains? Or his scribblings." He stepped closer to her. "What is auld Lachlan to you?"

It was unnerving to be the source of his interest. Even more unnerving was the way she responded to it. She shifted her suddenly warm cheeks into the wind.

"I'm an anthropologist. I came into possession of his journals through professional channels."

"And of what scientific significance would they be?"

Cailean gave him a measured look. "Just how long have you been a sheep farmer, anyway?"

"I explained about Thomas."

"Yes, your sheep mentor. And before that?"

"I lived elsewhere." She gave him a look and he added, "A lot of elsewhere's."

"Doing?"

"How did we end up talking about me?"

"I find people's pasts fascinating."

Something close to amusement flickered in his eyes. "I thought you'd be more interested in the ancient past, rather than the recent one."

"All history fascinates me." Rory's in particular was beginning to fascinate her a great deal.

"What is your specialty?"

"I'm a molecular forensic anthropologist. My specialty is DNA analysis of the remains of ancient civilizations."

"So yer here to dig auld Lachlan up and examine 'is gray matter are ye?" The accent was intentional, as was the steely look he sent her way. He meant to intimidate. She tried her best not to allow it.

"Of course not."

He stepped toward her. "Then why are ye here Ms. Forensic Anthropologist?" He glanced at the stone. "He was old, but eighty hardly qualifies him as ancient."

"You never spoke to him?" she asked.

"Never met the man."

"I find that strange. Lachlan devoted his whole life to finding out as much as he could about the Clarens and the MacKinnons. After his wife's death, he charted as much of their history as he could. I would have thought he'd have interviewed you as well."

"Who says I've had anything to do with any Clarens?"

"Your reaction just a bit ago, when I mentioned he was one." When he merely held her gaze in his frustratingly silent way, she tamped down on her own growing irritation. "You said he was a sorry bastard and that they never learned. You know of the curse, Rory."

Her use of his name caused a palpable reaction in him. His eyes came alive again, boring into hers. He stepped closer and she swore she could feel heat emanating from him.

"Why are you so interested in him?" he asked quietly.

Cailean wasn't sure how long she could put off answering. If his reaction to finding out about Lachlan was any indication, finding out she was his great niece would not be pleasant. He was to be her guide. But only if she didn't screw things up.

"Lachlan found the origin of the curse. It's known as the Legend MacKinnon. He was searching for the key to it all when he died. His time ran out before he could finish his quest."

Rory went rigid. When he spoke, his words were measured and delivered through a tight jaw. "And you think to finish it?"

"I don't think so, I know so. I am part of the key."

NINETEEN

RORY KNEW IN that moment that life would truly never end for him, or he would have been struck dead that instant.

"The Key?" The words came out as a menacing whisper, when what he felt was a volcanic roar. He forced his fingers into tight fists so he wouldn't snatch her and shake the life from her, so great was his anger, so deep was his pain. "Why have you come here?"

Did she think to trick him as her ancestors had done before her? And what trickery was left to be played? Had he not suffered worse than any damnation he could have ever divined?

"You know why," she managed. He took little satisfaction in the tremble of her lips.

"I know nothing of how a Claren Key thinks, nor do I ever want to."

"How did you—"

He grabbed her then, shaking her once. "You said you were the Key. Did ye think I'd not know of it?"

"But—"

"But true to yer lying ways you didna come out and tell

me. No, you spin tales of being a scientist and of diggin' in the past as some academic endeavor."

With surprising strength, she tore herself from his grasp. "I didn't lie. I am a scientist."

"Yer a Claren." The word made his tongue twist.

"Yes, I am a Claren. Lachlan was my great-uncle." She leveled her shoulders and stared at him directly. There was no trembling in her now.

He refused to admire her for it. "And yer just now helping him? I'd say you've come too late."

"I didn't know about him until after he died. He left his journals to me. I didn't come straight out and tell you for obvious reasons."

"I dinna care about yer reasons or about yer search. I want you off this land and away from me."

"You can't order me off this land. You don't own it."

He actually shook, so consuming were the emotions that assailed him. "In every way that land can belong to a man, this land belongs to me! I dinna care about papers and deeds or the whims of kings. The Clarens may have laid claim to it through trickery and deceit, but a MacKinnon made this land his own and MacKinnon land it will stay."

The fear in her expression disappeared. She was a scientist again. "Wait a minute. You're saying this is the land the original clan owned? This land we're standing on?" She spun around, scanning the rocky pinnacles that soared above them. "This is the land they fought over? Then this became Claren land. Maybe . . . " She turned back toward the Bay of Staffin below.

Rory couldn't say which enraged him more, the audacity of her dismissing him or her easy supposition that this was Claren land. As if it ever could be!

She whirled back to him, her eyes shining. "Do you think Lachlan actually owned all this? It would explain a great deal."

She had an analytical scientist's brain, and he'd seen her

as something unusual, out of the ordinary. That was what had called to him. Or so he had thought. It had obviously been Claren trickery, more of their faery magic.

He'd seen through that now, so she'd metamorphosed into something else designed to draw him in. Her shining eyes, the hopeful cant of her mouth, the avid need to know everything painted so clearly in her expression. All designed to make him aware of her as a woman. It was trickery for certain . . . because it was working.

And for the first time in three hundred years, he was afraid.

"According to the laws of kings, this land has changed hands many times since the battles between the MacKinnons and the Clarens," he said. "There were many clans who laid claim to it over the years, though none has lived on it. If auld Lachlan owned it, it was a purchase he made, not an inheritance handed from Claren to Claren."

As he'd hoped, her smile faded, but the light remained in her eyes. "I don't care how he acquired it," she said, "but that must be why he picked this place to be laid to rest. He tried to find the exact location of that last battle, but he couldn't pinpoint it. There is no castle left standing, so—"

Rory stilled. "What of the castle?" There was no masking the intensity in his voice.

She looked at him curiously. "Stonelachen. Lachlan searched for the ruins but assumed they had disappeared since there was no record of them. He must have found this cemetery and decided that any evidence of MacKinnon ownership was enough, or as close as he was likely to get."

Stonelachen. The auld bastard had gone hunting for the MacKinnon stronghold, had he? "Why the interest in the castle?"

"He'd traced the curse back to the last battles between the two clans. He was convinced it began with the three sons of Calum MacKinnon."

Rory wanted to move away from her, far away from her. He had taken on many challenges, defying death again and again until he wearied of the monotony of survival. He'd lived in a state of near numbness for some time now, no longer wanting or desiring stimulus of any type. Why bother? It led to naught but frustration. He became a recluse, oblivious to old Lachlan's machinations, and he'd found a small measure of peace.

Until now. Until her.

His last run in with a Claren Key had lasted him an eternity. He could have lived throughout eternity without ever encountering another.

Then it struck him. Perhaps only a Claren Key could shatter the solitude he'd created.

"That's it."

"What's it?"

"The curse." If one Key had cast him into this hellhole of a curse, could another cast him out of it? Perhaps he should have spent this never-ending lifetime searching out a Key, instead of avoiding one.

Could he risk it? Could he not? What fate could be worse than the endless one he was already living?

"Then you do believe in it."

He ignored her. His mind was racing ahead to the future, to his salvation. "When you first came here, you had a vision, didn't you?"

"What does that—"

"What did you see, Cailean?"

"You." Her eyes were wide and wary now, her voice was a whisper. "I saw you."

He hadn't known what to expect, but it hadn't been that. Her steady regard unsettled him further. "And what of me?" He stepped closer. He hadn't missed the flashes of awareness he'd seen in her eyes. He didn't miss it now. She might be skilled in the ways of scientific research but he'd bet she wasn't nearly as skilled in the ways of seduction. Too many years spent with the dead, he supposed.

He raised his hand, touched her hair, then her cheek. "What of us, Cailean?"

"You're . . ." She had to pause to clear her throat.

He resisted the urge to smile. She was far from stupid, even if she did appear to be somewhat naive.

"You're to be my guide," she said.

He continued to stroke her face, holding her gaze with his own, challenging her to look away, step away. She did not. That he felt his own body begin to stir bothered him some, but he didn't intend to allow it to interfere with his plan. She had the power, but he planned to harness it and use it. Control would be his, one way or another.

"And what am I to guide you to?" He traced a fingertip around her ear, then along her jaw.

"I . . . I don't know."

"Does my touch disconcert you, Cailean?"

"No." She'd answered quickly. Much too quickly.

He raised a brow and traced a finger over her lip. It quivered under his touch. "No?" He lifted his other hand and framed her jaw with his thumbs, enjoying the leap of pulse he spied at her temple. "It's been a long time since I touched a woman. It's been even longer since I tasted one."

He bent closer, until he could feel her breath against his lips. "Do you want to taste me, Cailean? Are you wondering, right this moment, what my kiss will be like? Will he take me gently? Will he be a brute?" He shifted so that his eyes were level with hers. "Which do you want, Cailean? Shall I demand a kiss? Or coax one from you?" At her small gasp, he leaned in. "Do you want to be seduced?" His hands slid to the back of her neck and tilted her face upward. "Or do you wish to be taken?"

His own mind began to cloud. It had been a long time since he'd found even a shred of fascination in a woman. He'd exhausted the endless varieties centuries ago. Perhaps he hadn't come across the right partner. But there could be nothing "right" about a Claren Key.

But dear God, if this was to be his new hell, then he would be damned if he would not savor the darkest of the pleasures it had to offer.

"Answer me," he demanded hoarsely.

Cailean had never fully understood the term enthralled. She did now.

Her body was taut with the need he'd so easily and recklessly roused in her. The ache, and the soothing of it, was suddenly so central to her existence she thought she might shatter if he didn't kiss her. "What are you?" she managed.

His smile was a slow, wicked thing that only made her pulse thrum more loudly inside her ears. "I am your guide, remember? There are many paths I can take you down, Cailean. All of them will make you scream. With pleasure." He drew his tongue very lightly along her lower lip.

Run, her mind pleaded. Pull away. Stop this.

"Choose a path, Cailean," he went on. She felt his teeth nip ever so lightly on the edge of her chin. "Would it be easier for you if I chose? Do you like to be driven? Do you like to play victim?" He moved quickly and planted a hard kiss to her neck. "I play predator particularly well."

Dear God this was insanity . . . and all she could think about was what would he do to her next. And how much more of this intoxication could she stand. She shuddered as his tongue ran along her ear.

"You shouldn't—" It was all she could get out.

"Aye, but I will," came the rough whisper in her ear. "And you will enjoy it." He tilted her chin down. "Open your eyes, Claren Key, and look upon the man who will conquer you."

He was the darkest of magic spells. He would do more than make her want, he would make her care. Therein would be her pain. He would hurt her. And she still didn't want to stop him.

Her breath came out on a slow groaning sigh as he pulled her earlobe into his mouth and suckled it.

"I'm going to put more than my mouth on you, Cailean."

"Yes." It was a simple statement; it was a monumental acquiescence.

"I want to possess you. Body, mind, and spirit."

Dear God, yes.

"I will know your every thought, your every desire. Your every secret."

She began to shake.

His lips moved along her jaw, up across her temple. He buried his face in her hair and whispered in her ear. "In every way a man can own a woman, I will own you."

Heaven help her, she was sinking. Her thighs trembled so hard she was certain she would fall to the ground if he didn't take her in his arms.

He did not.

He was wreaking unholy havoc with every cell in her body, bending them, twisting them, wringing unimaginable pleasure from them . . . and he'd yet to do more than touch her face. He hadn't even kissed her. How on earth would she survive it? And goddamn it why hadn't he started?

"Please." The word was issued past lips still wet from his tongue. Had that plea really come from her?

"You haven't answered me. Seduction or demand?"

Christ, but if this wasn't already seduction she didn't know what was.

"Say it, Cailean. I will make you scream no matter which path you choose. But you must choose your own destiny. I will no' be accused of raping your will." He moved his mouth to her other ear, teased her with his tongue, eliciting another moan from her. "Say it."

"I . . . I . . . want . . ."

"You want me to take you?"

"Y . . . yes."

"All you have to do is ask." His mouth whispered over hers. "And I will. Until you tell me to stop, I will."

"Take me," she pleaded hoarsely.

He took her mouth, intimately and fully. His fingers dug through her hair, turning her head so that he could plunder her further, deeper. His lips were hot, his tongue wet, incessant.

"Do you dream of being taken like this when you are alone at night?" he said against her mouth.

She couldn't think, could barely make sense of anything but the feel of him on her. She felt strung out, stretched beyond the boundaries of endurance.

He's said he'd make her scream.

And she knew he would.

She reached for him. And the moment she touched him, he released her.

Only when she went reeling backward did she realize that at some point she had leaned into him, relied on him to keep her upright.

She ended up in a stumbling half-sit on the bench. The chilled wind slapped at her steaming cheeks, the cold stone bit at her bare palms. When had the sun begun to set?

She scraped the wayward strands of hair from her face, and, chest heaving, glared up at him.

"Why the hell did you stop?"

She took mild satisfaction that his breath wasn't quite steady either. Storm-tossed was the word that came to mind when she looked into his eyes.

"We will finish this," he said, his voice raw. "But not here."

A hard laugh burst out of her, shocking her like a slap to the face. She felt like she'd just emerged from a unwanted vision, a very visceral one. Dazed, confused, and frustrated.

"I don't think so," she said flatly, facing him.

"There is no turning back." He said it without menace, but there was no doubt he fully believed what he was saying.

"Watch me." She started to stand, but he moved forward, blocking her. In order to look directly at him, she was forced to look up. Had she actually begged this man to take her?

He looked into her eyes and she felt that tremble of need vibrate within her again. Terrified by the power he held over her, she looked sharply away, down at her hands. They were knotted tightly together.

"You will not crook your finger and expect me to follow," she said, marshalling her breath so that her words didn't waver. "I know I . . ." She trailed off.

"What? Begged me?"

"Arrogance is an ugly trait," she retorted.

"I am not arrogant. In fact, I have rarely been so humbled."

"You have a supremely odd way of showing it."

"I speak only the truth of what happened. Of what will happen."

"How have you been humbled? At what point did you feel you had less than total control?"

"Control has nothing to do with it. That I felt compelled to talk to you at all is a humbling fact."

"Yes, mingling with the Claren peasantry must be tiring for one such as you."

The harsh planes of his face seemed ever sharper in the dimming light.

"That I still talked to you when I knew you were a Claren is the most humbling of all."

"I am most sorry I shamed you," she said, her tone making it clear she felt no such thing.

"There was no shame in me when I touched you, Cailean Claren." His voice softened, alarming her in ways she couldn't name. "There was calculation, yes. There was manipulation, most assuredly. There was desire. For you to be conquered. For me to be the conqueror." He ran his gaze over her face and she felt as if she had been caressed. "It wasn't that way before. I will do whatever I have to, to make certain it is not that way again."

He stood over her, like some medieval warrior who intended to stake his claim. And his claim was her. "I have won nothing from you."

"Not you, but one of your kind."

"My *kind*? You mean a Claren?" Understanding dawned. "Have you been a victim of the curse? Is that why you hate the Clarens?"

His jaw clenched, making the muscles in his cheeks twitch. He all but growled the words. "It was one of you that laid this curse upon me."

"What curse?"

He went on as if she hadn't spoken. "And it will be one of you that will remove it. You will free me, Cailean Claren."

"I cannot free you, whatever it is. I have visions, yes. If you want to call me a Key, then fine, I'm one of them. But I have no power over what I see. I have no magic." She swung her legs around and stood shakily on the other side of the bench. "You can make me beg for you, Rory MacKinnon, but you can't make me free you from whatever curse you believe is upon you. I couldn't, even if I wanted to."

"You can. And you will. You are the only one, Cailean. You are the only Key."

"You don't know that."

He tilted his head just slightly. "You have the look of her, you know."

Bewildered, she said, "The look of who?"

"Kaithren."

Cailean's blood froze.

"You know of whom I speak," he said, almost gently. "Don't you, Cailean."

"I . . . I . . ." Dear God, who—what—was he?

"You know who I am, too. John Roderick, third son of Calum."

"But you . . . you said you weren't a spirit."

"I am most certainly not that. In fact, it is my mortality, or rather the lack of it, that I wish you to fix."

He walked slowly around the bench. He took her chin in his hand.

"Kaithren cast the spell of immortality over me. You, Cailean Claren, will be the death of me."

TWENTY

SHE COULD NOT take it in, and yet it fit. It was as if her whole life had merely been a path she was to follow that would lead her to this specific point, to this specific place, to this specific man.

"I will not kill you. I could not."

"Not directly, perhaps."

She moved out of his grasp. Something uncontrollable happened whenever he touched her.

"You can't leave," he said.

"I most certainly can." She ran toward the gate, not caring if she was half stumbling in her haste.

"Are you willing to go against your vision? Your destiny? How am I to guide you if you leave?"

He would guide her straight to hell. It would be a carnal journey, a sinful path of decadent exploration and erotic discovery. A wave of pleasure coursed through her. She cursed under her breath.

"You had a reason for coming here, too, Cailean. You won't be able to fulfill it if you leave."

She blew out a breath. "What do you want from me?"

"I want you to come with me."

"Where?"

"Stonelachen."

Her heart skipped a beat. "Stonelachen? But it's—"

"Very hard to find."

"Lachlan searched for it."

"He didn't know where to look."

"If there is a castle, or even a ruin of one back in those rocks, one that has been there for three hun—" Her voice broke as the enormity of what was happening to her, of just who she was talking to, assailed her.

He was right. She could not walk away from him, his past, her past . . . or their future. Not as a scientist, not as a woman, and most of all, not as a Claren. She gripped the gate for support. "Three hundred years is a long time for something to remain hidden."

Rory shrugged. "The MacKinnons were a crafty lot. Stonelachen was impregnable for good reason. The Mac-Kinnons lost down here, on this land, not up there." He gestured to the stone edifices that rose above them, beyond the boundaries of the cemetery. "The blood of battle was never spilled within the sanctity of Stonelachen."

"But the Clarens took ownership of it when they defeated your clan."

His expression darkened. "Aye, they did. And they lost it as well, to the MacDonalds. It was abandoned shortly after that. Stonelachen only gave her secrets to those born to her. It is useless to anyone else. She has been empty ever since."

"Except for you. How long . . . ?" She couldn't even phrase the entire question. It was too fantastical, despite the living proof standing before her.

"I've been here for several years, as I told you. I've been here before. Many times. This is the first time I have stayed. And now I know why."

"I don't—"

He raised his hand. "Enough. I'll talk no more of it here." He walked toward the back of the cemetery.

"Where are you going?"

"Follow me and find out."

"But—" She sighed in frustration. A mixture of fear and dread balled up inside her. Along with excitement. This was a once in a lifetime chance, she told herself. An incredible find. He was living history.

With a quick glance at her car, she snatched up her backpack and shoved her notebook inside, then hurried to catch up. And she knew that no matter what she told herself, it wasn't the scientist that followed the man. It was the woman. The Claren woman.

CAILEAN HAD ALWAYS considered herself to be in good physical shape. But there was no denying that every muscle in her body ached . . . and it had nothing to do with sexual urges. In fact, as she glowered at Rory's back as they traversed yet another impossibly rugged slope, she couldn't believe he'd made her feel anything other than pain.

She wanted to ask how much further, but she'd cut her own tongue out first. There had been no talk since they'd begun the ascent and she wasn't going to be the one to break the silence. It was almost full dark. And very cold. Certainly they had to reach Stonelachen soon. She diverted attention from her screaming muscles by imagining what the castle would look like. Abandoned as it had been for centuries now, certainly it had to be more ruin than functional building. Secrets, he'd said. What secrets could a castle contain? Secrets that had held civilization at bay for three centuries?

They topped the narrow ridge, and she held what breath she had in anticipation, only to be met with sheer rock. "No." The word, a wail, came out without permission.

Rory stopped and turned. "Yes."

"How?" It was all she could manage.

"You'll see." He turned and began to climb toward the towering wall of stone.

She could do nothing but follow, muttering several choice imprecations under her breath as she did. Even when they were less than twenty yards away, she could see no way up or around it.

Then Rory disappeared into the rock wall.

She stopped dead. "Okay." She ran a hand across her forehead. In the last week or so, she'd met a three-hundred-year-old ghost and now his three-hundred-plus-year-old brother. A brother who made her feel things . . .

"And I'm dealing with that pretty damn well, considering," she said aloud. "But I draw the line at a man who can walk through walls."

Rory reappeared as suddenly as he'd vanished. "Are you coming? It's getting cold out here."

"Sure. Fine. Just teach me that walking through walls trick and I'll be right there." She sounded more like Maggie with her sarcastic tone than her usual serious self.

A pang tugged at her heart as she thought of her cousin. For the first time in her life, she'd have appreciated the companionship and comfort of family. And a friend. Maggie was literally the only one who would understand. Cailean hoped she was okay.

And then it hit her. Duncan. Brothers.

She looked up at Rory, who stared down at her, hands on his hips. She'd have to tell him about Duncan.

"Come on. I willna harm ye."

Her heart tripped at the soft sounding burr. It occurred to her now that back in the cemetery, he'd spoken with the clarity of the King's English, almost chillingly so.

She'd reacted to his perfectly modulated commands with a depth of feeling she'd never experienced before, as if there had been no choice but to follow him down the darkly sensual path he was creating. And yet, the gentle rolling of his brogue affected her much more. She felt comforted, protected. It made no sense, but if he'd slipped into the patterns of speech of his early life, who knows what she might have done with him on that stone bench.

"Cailean."

"Okay." She carefully picked her way up the last stretch of scrabbling slope. She looked over the wall behind him, but still saw nothing. "I may have visions, but I can't move through stone. Sorry."

A small hint of a smile played at the corners of his mouth. He lifted his hand out to her.

Cailean studied the broad palm and long fingers as if the devil himself had offered her a treat. She looked back to his eyes, eyes that were glittering despite the lack of light.

She slowly lifted her hand, pausing slightly, then placed it in his. He didn't react in any visible way, but when his fingers closed over hers, she felt an energy flow between them that was so primal she couldn't deny the connection. She had truly committed herself now.

"Follow me."

As if she'd ever had a choice.

He turned and stepped into the stone, or so it appeared. What looked to be a rough edge was actually a slice in the rock. Straight on it appeared like a wrinkle in the stone, forged from the crushing pressure of the ice floes that had created the Trotternish eons ago. She turned sideways and slithered into the tight space. There was a grinding sound and for several heart-stopping seconds she thought she would be crushed. Then the stone in front of Rory shifted and she was freed. She stumbled behind him into an open area the size of a small courtyard. It was mostly a rock tumble, with towering stone walls all around.

She looked up to find the night sky twinkling above her, the moon had risen, bathing them in blue-white light, casting long shadows from the rocky spears above. She turned slowly. "This is amazing." She turned in time to catch a brief flash of pride cross his face.

"This is only the beginning."

He dropped her hand and stepped behind her, reaching into the passage. Seconds later there was the same grinding sound. Cailean's eyes widened as the boulder in front of her shifted and rolled, as if being pushed by some unseen hand. It stopped directly in front of the passage.

"An auld trick my ancestors learned from the Druids. Interesting lot, that."

He took her hand again, the combination of his smile and his strong hand in hers stilling any words she might have uttered. He stopped long enough to light a small torch, then led her through the open area through another hidden passage in a tumble of rocks directly across from their entrance. No moving stones this time, not that it mattered. She was quickly lost in the maze-like warren of passages Rory drew her through.

In the flickering shadows she saw other passages not taken and some others that had caved in. Occasionally they wandered briefly through an open moonlit area, only to quickly descend back into the stone passageways.

"It's no wonder no one found this," she said in hushed tones. She felt like she was entering a sort of sacred ground. Other than Rory, she was very likely the first person to enter this part of Scotland in several centuries.

Rory nodded toward the next passageway. "As I said, Stonelachen only gives her secrets to those born to her."

"When did you leave, originally?"

He paused at the entrance to another tunnel and looked back at her. The torchlight cast his face in harsh relief. "Right after the last MacKinnon fell. I wasna going tae be a conquest of no bluidy Claren."

He turned away and headed off to their left. Cailean stood for several seconds, unable to follow, unable to do much more than breathe. There had been hatred in his voice, and worse, in his eyes. Three hundred years was an awfully long time to nurse a grudge.

For the first time she questioned her safety. Would he drag her all the way in here to exact some sort of revenge? She hadn't thought so. Hadn't *felt* that. Her vision had said the harm he'd bring to her wouldn't be physical. In fact the only physical thing he'd wrought on her was pleasure— hot, sweet, dizzying pleasure.

She stared down the passageway, his frame cast in shadow from the flame held above his shoulder. "Tell me what happened," she said, suddenly needing to know before she went another step. "What happened that day, Rory?"

"I fought beside them. Calum was one of the first to die."

She drew in her breath.

"I was their Laird, then. They fought for me, Cailean, for the memory of my father. They gave their lives for me. But the Clarens—they kept coming . . . and coming. I was but one man. I couldna kill them all." His voice grew hoarse with emotion. "But God himself knows tha' I tried."

Vivid images of the battlefield that day blazoned bright and bloody in her mind's eye. She felt her stomach pitch and roll as she saw him, an immortal warrior filled with rage against his mortal enemies, and yet unable to claim victory against them.

"Rory—" She stopped as her voice broke.

He reclaimed the distance between them. "No. You will know it all now, Cailean, before we go one step further. I didna believe her, you know. I didna believe she could cast the curse of immortality upon me. She was possessed of the sight, as her older sister had been before her, but she also claimed she'd held forth with the *sithiche* and shared in their faery *druidheachd*, their sorcery."

"But—"

"She sent word that she wanted to meet me the night before we were to be wed. She wanted to tell me what had really happened between my brother Alexander and Edwyna. That we could not wed until I understood."

"Edwyna was dead by then," Cailean murmured.

"They blamed the MacKinnons but we did not slay her. Though there were many who would gladly have done it."

"What did Kaithren say?"

"She claimed Edwyna had given her heart to Alexander. She said Edwyna had seen his future and that whatever she had done, was done to save him from a far more horrible fate. She claimed she wanted to make sure the same horrible fate would not befall us." Rory scowled. "There was no love between us, but there was lust. She wanted us to commit our hearts to one another and I told her what she wanted to hear."

"She didn't believe you?"

"I didna think it mattered what she believed. She knew I did no' trust her. The loss of my brothers was a festering wound inside me and in my clansmen. I would have her commitment tae me, whatever it took."

"So you made love to her?"

"It was what she sought and I wanted to make sure the wedding took place. The future of my clan depended on it. Her talk of hearts bound and love meant nothing to me."

"She thought otherwise."

"Aye."

Cailean began to tremble. as she recalled his words to her when he held her in thrall. *This time I will be the conqueror.*

"I was deep inside of her when she put her curse upon me."

"Oh, Rory."

"It was revenge. For Edwyna and Mairi's deaths."

Rory's face was a mask of pain and rage, made more fearful by the rigid control he was exerting over both. "I did no' believe her faery spells and I demanded the wedding take place. She had to marry me now, her virginity was lost. She could have had a MacKinnon bairn already growing inside her. I thought I would have the final victory."

"You would still marry her, when you knew she hated you to the point of putting a curse on you?" *While you were still inside her?* Cailean could not fathom such manipulation.

His voice shook. "I would see our clan survive no matter what. Our union was our last hope." His control began to crumble. "She renounced me on the altar, claimed I'd raped her to avenge my brothers' deaths, even held up the bloody sheet we'd lain on. She cursed our union to eternal hell and called her clansmen to arms. They were prepared. They had been forewarned of her intentions."

"My God. What happened to her?"

"She died in battle."

"By your sword?"

He shook his head. "I dinna know which of my clansmen cut her down, but I saw her face as she fell." He began to shake. "She knew I understood her true power then. As men fell all around me and I remained standing, she knew I'd realized the curse was real. She smiled as her last breath escaped her."

The horrific images flooded her mind. Without realizing it she found herself reaching to stroke his face.

He caught her hand before she touched him. "I didn't believe and I have paid the price." He looked into her eyes. "I won't make that mistake again, Cailean."

"But I don't—"

"No." The word, sharp and commanding, rang against the stone walls, echoing until it faded into silence. She saw him clearly now as Laird of his clan, commanding men twice his age into battle, commanding them to their deaths.

"Understand this," he said softly. "I have no love for the Clarens. Hatred burns in me for what she did, for what her sisters did. But you are not here to pay for the sins of your ancestors. I want only for you to free me, so that I may join my clan, my father and my brothers. So that I may be finally free of this cursed earth."

He stepped closer and held her hand between them. "You will give this to me and I will use any means necessary to achieve my goal. I will not be thwarted nor tricked this time."

He turned abruptly and pulled her behind him. He wasn't hurting her, but his grip was firm.

They moved along at a swift pace that kept her almost at a trot. Then he turned into a tunnel lined with torches. He slowed and lit each one as they passed until he came to a stone wall. He reached for a sliver in the rock to his right. The sound of stone grinding on stone came again and the wall facing them shifted to the right. A gaping blackness lay beyond. The torchlight penetrated no more than a foot of it.

He turned to her, blocking the entrance. "We're here."

She tried to quell the trembling of fear and anticipation. "How do you remember all those twists and turns?"

"I grew up in them. Of course, we took the scenic route."

Cailean wasn't surprised. He would take no chances with her. He would do whatever was necessary to maintain full control of what would pass between them. She understood why, even if she didn't like it.

"Well, let's not stand here all night," she said at length.

"As you wish." He leaned in to light torches on either side of the portal.

Cailean stepped inside and her mouth opened in amazement. Rory moved along the walls, lighting torches as he went.

They were in a great hall of massive proportions. One

wall was lined with huge inset fireplaces, big enough to roast an ox. Or two. And they likely had. The opposite end of the room was raised up several levels higher. Broad stone stairs, each the width of a man, led up to that area. There was no furniture of any kind, only piles of rubble and rock where parts of the ceiling and walls had caved in over time. All in all, it was amazingly well preserved.

She turned, gaping. The walls were bare, but she imagined them as they once must have been, hung with tapestries and shields, armaments perhaps. She looked up. The ceiling was so far overhead, it faded into darkness.

Rory came to stand several yards away from her.

"How far beneath the ground are we?"

"Not as far as you'd think."

The depth of this hall alone put them a fair distance below the earth's surface. "How did you—your clan— carve this room out of stone?"

"These caves and caverns were mostly formed naturally, by the melting ice floes that created the Trotternish. There are other stories, of course, some legend, much of them myth, but even I don't know the full truth of the origins of Stonelachen."

"How far back do you know for certain this existed?"

"Is this Cailean the scientist asking?"

His question startled her, because she hadn't been thinking at all about the scientific import of this. She'd been thinking of the man in front of her, that this was his heritage and that she could well understand to what lengths he would have gone to save it.

She stood here and for the first time in her life she wasn't an awed observer. She felt connected this time. Personally connected. To something larger, something more important than the sum total of her own short life. It filled her with an entirely different sort of awe, and with a pride that stunned her. "No. I'm asking because this is my heritage too."

She'd expected the fury and she wasn't disappointed. She spoke before the rage in his eyes could spew forth. "I'm not my ancestors, Rory. I didn't betray you or slay your men. But like it or not, my heritage is mixed up with yours. My people—" Her voice broke on that word and she had to pause as the wonder of that truth washed over her. "My people were here too, even if their time of occupation was brief. Even if their occupation was ill-achieved."

He looked away and shrugged. "I hear what you say, Cailean Claren, but you will have to forgive me if I dinna like it much."

"I'm not asking you to like it. Neither of us is particularly thrilled with our current circumstances," she said pointedly.

He took her face in his hand and held her chin tilted up. She could have pulled from his grasp, but she did not. Her breath had deserted her like a traitor at his touch and she found she had no will to break the connection.

"Your heart beats faster when I touch you. Your pupils dilate and your skin warms." He moved closer to her and she vainly tried to moisten her throat. "You say you are not thrilled, yet you thrill easily and swiftly to me. Isn't that true, Cailean?

"The past between Claren and MacKinnon blood has been brutal and ugly. It doesna have to be that way this time."

His touch on her skin, the way the burr slipped in and out of his speech, his commanding presence . . . and the fact that she wanted more of all of it, combined to leave her trembling.

He stepped in closer, reaching over her head and shoving the torch he held into a stone sconce on the wall behind her. He leaned in to her, trapping her in the space between the cold stone and his very warm body. "Do ye tremble in fear, lass, or anticipation?"

"It won't matter," she managed.

He merely raised one brow.

"It will end badly," she said, her voice a whisper. "Unions of any sort between a Claren and MacKinnon always have."

"Ah yes, Lachlan and his legendary curse." He lifted his head, but did not step away.

Cailean was torn between the need to move away from his overwhelming presence and the desire to step forward and curl into the warmth and protection he could certainly offer her.

Protection? She blinked at the idea. How insane was it to want protection from the only man she'd ever needed protection from?

"How can you question it after what you told me of Kaithren?" Her head began to throb now, and she looked down, away from the light as she pressed her eyelids shut. "The curse on you is real, as is the curse on our clans. It all began back then—with Kaithren, with Edwyna, we may never know. But it exists."

He gently lifted her chin up to him. "All the more reason for us to find the answer, to end it once and for all. And I don't speak only of the curse on our clans. Do you not wish to end your curse as well?"

As the Key, she was an integral part to it all. She reached up a shaky hand and covered his as he caressed her cheek. He would guide her to the end of the curse; his, the clans', and hers. He would guide her to the solution.

"Maybe I will be the death of you after all, John Roderick MacKinnon."

TWENTY-ONE

Because he did not want to, he pulled his hand from beneath hers.

"Then we have an agreement." He wanted to know that he would be in control of everything that passed between them, and yet he could already feel her faery sorcery at work on him. Why else did his heart beat so strongly at the mere touch of her?

"Yer tired and hungry," he said, more gruffly than he'd intended. She stiffened and pulled away from him. "Come," he ordered, willing his body to cool, his pulse to slow.

"Yes, master."

His lips quirked at the sarcasm. She had a a sharp wit. And an innocent heart.

His pulse thrummed hot and heavy at the mere thought of how she reacted to his touch. Her kiss had been one of inexperience, which made no sense for a woman who was surely past her first quarter century. Was that the secret of her power? Was it her naiveté in that realm that called to him? He wouldn't have thought so. Innocence had never been attractive to him. He preferred to be partner, not teacher.

He grabbed a torch and headed across the hall, not looking to see if she followed. Another button pressed, another stone moved, and they were in another passageway. "Stay close, this area hasn't fared as well as others."

"It must have been hard to live like this."

"Everyone who lived within the castle knew their way." He turned sideways to shift around a pile of stone that had fallen in and caught himself just in time, reaching for her hand. She was in fine shape, fatigued though she might be. She had no need of his assistance, and still he felt the loss of the warmth he'd have gained from holding her hand in his. Conversation was a wise diversion and an easy one given her innate curiosity. "If you mean supplies, that wasn't as hard as you'd think."

"I figured that much. Those fireplaces in the main hall weren't designed for roasting marshmallows. I was referring to being underground. It's like living in a cave. A huge cave, but still. No sunlight, no way to mark the days from the nights."

"There are places of sunlight and moonlight." He turned another corner. "It is not entirely an underground fortress." He turned again and the passage became narrow.

Cailean followed closely behind him, staring into the succession of door-size openings they passed, but unable to see anything inside them but inky blackness. She was so intent on her surroundings, she almost walked right into him when he stopped at a wooden door.

She ran her hand over the cut planks. It was obviously newly made, the planks measured and cut specifically to fit in the misshapen stone doorway. They had been sanded and stained to a beautiful finish, all fastened together with broad brass straps. "You made this?"

"It's just a door."

If she wasn't so exhausted, she would have been amused by the nonplussed look on his face. "Does it work?"

"What? Of course it does."

"Then, can we go in?"

His face actually colored. The door swung soundlessly open. "Your chambers, madam," he said darkly, then swept an arm in front of him.

"I don't need much," she said as she quickly stepped inside the dark room. "A mat on the floor will do."

"I think I can accommodate you."

He swung the torch up and lit the sconces on either side of the door. "I'll get the fire going."

The sudden brightness made her blink, and once again, she was shocked into speechlessness.

She'd been expecting a medieval version of a bachelor's pad. A stone bench or two, some hay on the floor maybe, a fire and a cot or something.

Instead she felt like she'd fallen into a sultan's harem. There *was* a stone bench, which was actually a part of the opposite wall, and there was a rather large fireplace. Beyond that, nothing was as she'd expected.

Furs covered the area in front of the fireplace, but it was the amazing array of Persian, Oriental, and Turkish rugs, with their rich jewel tone colors and variety of sizes and plushness that caught her immediate attention. They were spread around the room, overlapping here and there, and simply rolled up in places where the stone walls weren't squared off properly, the intent being insulation, not affected décor. But the result was that of opulent decadence, which was topped only by the bed.

It sat in the middle of the room and aside from an armoire shoved over in the far corner, and a heavy wooden chair near the fireplace, it was the only piece of furniture in the room.

It had four thick posts that rose toweringly overhead, draped with layers of sheer silks that hung to the floor on three of the four sides. Through the filmy layers, she could see a massive carved headboard filling the remaining side. Pillows of all shapes and sizes, fashioned in a variety of colors and fabrics, were heaped on the bed, spilling off to one side where several lay on the floor.

"How on earth did you get that thing in here?" she said, her gaze fixed on the monstrous bed.

"Scots ingenuity is legend," he said, without looking up from the fire he was building. "I dismantled it, carted it in, and built the thing again. Not so tricky."

"But those posts . . ." She thought of the lattice work of passages they'd been through and it seemed an impossibility. Yet here it stood. "It's an awful lot of work for a place to sleep."

She turned to face him. He'd taken his duster off and she found herself short of breath again as she looked at him, truly looked at him, for the first time. It hadn't been the coat making his shoulders seem broad, they were indeed wide enough all on their own. His chest was deep without being massive, made more so by his lean hips and long thighs. He wore a cream colored shirt tucked into dark pants, both of which looked impossibly modern on her centuries-old warrior.

And yet he was still both, modern and ancient. Uncloaked, he was even more imposing. He stood there, arms crossed, ankle deep in furs, the firelight dancing behind him as he studied her.

"When you've lived as long as I have, a comfortable place to sleep becomes very important."

She understood then. "You sleep here."

"I did no' go tae this trouble for a guest room. I dinna have guests here." His brogue twinkled into his speech once again, making her want to relax her guard.

She stood up straighter. "What are you proposing then?"

He stepped from the furs. "I'm proposing we eat and go to bed."

As weary as she was, this was no time to allow him the upper hand. If he thought she was going to be the blushing maiden, he could think again.

She walked over and pulled back the curtains. She slid her backpack and coat to a small heap on the floor. There was a footstool she made use of, though she still had to jump to boost herself up on the side. "I prefer this side, is that okay with you?" It was the closest to the fire and the side with the stool and very obviously the side he slept on.

The bed was amazingly soft and pulled her in like a downy sponge. She could feel her eyelids grow drowsy even as she shifted to untie her boots and slip them off. As she sunk into the mattress, she discovered she suddenly didn't care about needling him.

She snatched a long velvet covered pillow and tucked it under her head as she stretched out. A long, appreciative groan eased from her as she allowed the bed to take over and pull her the rest of the way in.

As she drifted into sleep, she heard his dry voice.

"That side is fine."

RORY STOOD WATCHING her far longer than he should have. What was he to do about her? He sure as hell knew what he wanted to do *with* her. Christ in heaven but the expressions that had crossed her face as she'd examined the bed had made him hard as the stone bench he'd almost taken her on seemingly eons ago now.

His stomach growled loudly. He was ravenous, but too tired to want to do anything about it. Still, it was something to do to postpone the inevitable. He went to a small door on the other side of the fireplace, glancing at her once more before stepping into the small adjoining room.

She was curled on her side, clutching a long pillow to

her chest, loosened strands of hair falling in a tangle across the pillows piled under her head. He wanted badly to smooth those snarled strands and feel once again the softness of her cheek, trace that slight plumpness of her bottom lip.

He sighed in disgust. He would not let her leave until she'd found a way to lift his curse. But how long would he last before he gave in to this spell she had cast upon him? This curse of need.

He looked at her and felt himself jerk in awareness, even when all she did was sleep. The fires of hell were licking at his bootheels and he hadn't even begun to feel the heat. He swore heavily and closed the door behind him.

CAILEAN PURRED AS she shifted into an even more comfortable spot. These were the most exquisite accommodations she could ever recall having on a dig. She bolted upright.

She wasn't on a dig. She flipped pillows off and pushed the hair from her face. She knew immediately where she was . . . and why. She looked next to her and sighed in relief. At least she was alone.

From the looks of things, she had been alone all night. She pushed her hair back and peered through the silks. The chair was empty and the fire had gone to glowing embers. There were several candles burning and the torches by the doorway had been replaced with small kerosene lamps, both lit.

Where was he? And more urgently, where was the bathroom? She envisioned having to climb back through the long maze of passageways. There had to be something better than that.

She used the step stool to climb down from the bed. The floor was amazingly warm and she wondered how many layers of rugs he had in here. Then she spied the corner door. She knocked, but got no response, so she pushed it open.

This room was much chillier. She walked inside, leaving the door open to allow the lamps to cast some light inside. There was a wooden table, almost a foot thick and definitely not newly made. However, the chair placed next to it was a work of art. She ran her hand over the smooth curved back and admired the bowed dowel rods that ran from the rim to the seat. He truly was a craftsmen. *I guess when you live that long, you're bound to learn a few things.* Realizing she was caressing the wood, she quickly removed her hand.

This room was much smaller than the bedroom. Several cardboard boxes were scattered on top of the long, narrow table which stood along the opposite wall. In the corner was a small kerosene cookstove and several dishes. Now this looked more like bachelor digs.

She lit two lanterns with the matches she found and grabbed an apple and a bread roll. Then she noticed a small sink in the far corner with a pump handle. If he had running water down here, then there was hope for other indoor plumbing.

She finished off the roll, then primed the handle and was rewarded with a splash of extremely cold water. She managed to wash her hands, face, and do a cursory job on her teeth before she reached for the handtowel hanging from the bar on the side. It was soft and smelled sweet, making her wonder how on earth he did his laundry.

She crunched the apple and looked around. The ceiling slanted down to head height and she almost didn't see the smaller door under the stone eaves. She creaked the door open and sighed in relief.

As bathrooms went, it wasn't much. The very basics of archaic essentials. But it was far more accommodating than some of her desert digs and not bad for an ancient underground castle. Rory's talents were growing more amazing by the minute.

Feeling refreshed and wide awake now, she headed back into the bedroom. She was about to go into the hallway and call for him when she spied the narrow stone steps leading up the wall in the shadowed corner behind the headboard.

There was a small hole in the stone ceiling. As she emerged through the hole, the steps turned sharply left and went upward again. She was in a small tower-like structure, all stone. Dim light came from somewhere above. After several more short flights, she took a sharp turn . . . and suddenly found herself standing on the top of the world.

The sun was a glowing yellow ball just rising over the craggy peaks. There was a relatively flat area several yards square, beyond which the world fell. Standing on one of the higher pinnacles of the mountain, she could see for miles.

Rory sat several feet away, a fur wrapped around him as he watched the sunrise.

"You're awake," he said without turning.

"This is incredible."

"It's worth the visit."

She wanted to ask him how many times he'd sat here and watched this, but she suddenly felt like she was intruding. Which was ridiculous. He'd all but dragged her here. If anyone should feel intruded upon, it should be her. But at this moment, she only felt gratitude for this view.

She stepped away from the stone portal only to be almost knocked to her knees by a sudden gust of wind. Heart pounding, she grabbed the stone and debated going back down the stairs for her jacket. But the steps were steep, with no railing and the descent would be slow. She'd miss the show if she left now. She carefully sat down, leaning her back against the stone for support and a wind break.

"It's better from here."

"I'm afraid I'll get blown off the edge."

"Crawl."

"I beg your pardon?"

"Crawl over here. I'm no' planning tae toss ye off," he added, when she didn't respond. He looked at her for the first time that day. It made her toes curl. "I need you, remember?"

She held his gaze for a long moment, then moved carefully away from the rock. If she was going to find the key to the legend and end her visions, it looked like she needed him too. She scooted slowly over to him, the wind ripping at her braid.

Rory lifted his arm and held the fur open at his side. An amused smile ghosted his lips. "I won't bite either."

Biting wasn't her concern. Then she laughed silently at herself. As if she were some ravishing goddess that he wouldn't be able to resist. He'd made it more than clear yesterday that while he could play her like the finest violin, she was but one of many violins whose strings he'd chosen to pluck.

He'd also made it clear he'd just been establishing the boundaries to which he was willing to go. Since she'd more or less agreed to work with him, he wouldn't need to resort to seduction any longer to gain her cooperation.

She crawled next to him and he closed the cloak—and his arm—around her. They sat in silence and simply watched. He was big and warm and she was supremely aware of every contact point between them.

When the last particle of yellow broke free of the highest peak, he spoke. "You can see now why Stonelachen was undefeatable."

"I can see why you would give your life to save it."

"Aye, I did give my life."

"I see what you meant about not being so far beneath the surface. It's just the surface itself is so inaccessible."

"Exactly."

The sheer drops from the points below made it obvious why no climbers had found entrance into the castle either. Still . . . "With modern technology and all the professional climbers in the world, I'm still amazed that no one stumbled across this place."

"Most of the portals are blocked with moving stones. Unless you knew where they were and how to trigger them, it's unlikely you'd stumble into Stonelachen."

"It must fill a goodly part of this mountain." He nodded. "I guess I still can't get over the fact that something as big and unique as this didn't find its way into recorded history."

He merely shrugged. "Go figure."

A short laugh burst out before she could stop it.

"Wha' is so amusing?"

His question brought her attention to his mouth. She looked back out to the horizon. "Nothing. It was just such a modern thing to say."

"I'm a modern man." His tone was quiet, almost desolate.

"I can't imagine what it must be like for you."

"It's not something easily explained."

"I'm not asking you to."

Now he turned his attention forward once again. "Does the scientist in you want to analyze me?"

"Well, I'd be lying if I said that encountering a man several centuries old didn't trigger a few scientific queries. The DNA I usually examine is several thousand years old." A smile curved her lips. "Yours would be a lot fresher."

He didn't return her smile, but he did look at her again. "And yet you haven't analyzed anything. I have given you no proof that what I say is true."

Her smile faded and her heart bumped against her chest as she looked at him. "I know what you say is true," she said quietly. "Maybe I knew it even before you told me."

"I thought scientists were trained to accept only fact."

"Science is based largely on theory, which we spend our time trying to prove. But this isn't about theories or proof. It isn't even instinct. It's just . . ." She couldn't find the words. "Do you want me to analyze you? Take samples, run tests? Prove you are who you say you are? Haven't you spent several hundred years moving from one place to another to avoid that very thing?"

"There was nothing simple about it."

She stared at his profile. He wasn't classically handsome, his features were too harsh. Yet he was captivating and it was impossible to look away.

"I don't want you to run tests," he said abruptly.

"What?"

He turned on her. "You were studying me as if I were already on a glass slide under a microscope. I said I don't want—"

"I wasn't studying you as a scientist." Why in heavens had she confessed that?

"What is going on behind those bonnie green eyes of yours, Cailean Claren?"

There was a moment, a long, elastic moment when she knew she could evade his question and change the topic away from the tantalizing void that yawned in front of her. But she didn't choose that path. Maybe the choice had already been made when she followed him home.

"I was wondering what it would be like to make love with you."

TWENTY-TWO

"I'M NO' CERTAIN that is something we should find out."

"But you want to, don't you?" She felt his body tense, even as his eyes darkened further.

"Do no' speak to me of wants, Cailean," he warned.

She saw it then, the flicker of . . . was it fear?

"Why? What do you have to fear from me?"

"I am not—"

"Ah, but you are." She loosened her hand from the fur and brought it up to his cheek. He didn't flinch or move when she laid her palm against his skin. A muscle twitching in his temple was the only sign that her touch disconcerted him. It was enough.

"We have enough to work out between us," he said, his jaw tight.

His morning stubble rubbed against her palm. It made her skin twitch and her blood heat. "I think if we are to discover anything, we must work through this first."

Before she knew what was happening, he turned and laid her flat on her back, cushioned between the fur and his body. He pressed down on her and her vision was filled with his eyes, his mouth, his parting lips.

"You do, do ye?" he said. The menacing tone didn't frighten her. It thrilled her. He pushed his mouth close to her ear. "What do ye want to work out first, lass?"

She shuddered beneath him.

"Do ye want my touch first? Here?" He pressed his lips to the soft skin below her ear. "Here?" He trailed his tongue along the side of her neck. "Maybe here?" He nipped at her chin. "Or here?"

Cailean couldn't have formed coherent speech if her life depended on it. A moan slipped from her lips as he moved his mouth down the other side of her neck. He took one ear lobe in his mouth. She squirmed under him. "Please," she managed.

He nuzzled her ear, then bit the lobe, eliciting a small cry of pleasure from her. "Please what?"

"Rory."

He pulled his mouth away. "Open your eyes."

She did. The sun was at his back, casting his dark head in a golden halo. His face was a mask of desire, his eyes were bottomless. Her empty angel.

She reached up and stroked his face. "Come to me," she said.

The emptiness in his expression tore at her heart. " 'Tis *druidheachd*," he whispered hoarsely. "Only sorcery could make me want you so."

"I am not bewitching you. I'm responding to what you've made me feel. Perhaps you are the sorcerer and it is I who should be afraid."

"I am not afraid."

"Then what are you waiting for?"

He held her gaze for what seemed like an eternity as the battle raged in his eyes.

"Come to me, Rory."

A long groan tore from somewhere deep inside him as

he lost the battle and swooped down to claim her mouth in a crushing kiss. He didn't merely take, he plundered. He had no use for finesse or slow seduction, and in truth, she'd have been impatient with all that. This is what she wanted, this man with a raging passion for her, a man who had no thought in his mind but of claiming her.

He consumed her. His tongue was bold and direct, a warrior that invaded her mouth with an intent to conquer. He wasn't satisfied with that and pulled her into a duel. Parrying and thrusting, demanding that she keep up with him.

"Kiss me," he said roughly. "Take me like this." He took her mouth again and again, turning her head so he could plunge the farthest depths of her. He rolled so she was on top of him, swallowing her short scream with his mouth. Long strands of hair whipped wildly about her head, the chilled air burned her hot skin.

"Kiss me," he demanded again. He pulled her head down until their lips were barely brushing. "Kiss me, Cailean. Show me that you are part of this insanity, this need."

She sunk her fingers into his dark hair, her eyes burning into his as she leaned in and took his mouth, with full intent to conquer. She felt him groan beneath her and his hands came up to grip her hips. The fur was a tangle around them.

She kissed him hard and long. She bit his chin and suckled his earlobes until she felt him hard between her legs and she wanted nothing more than to claw away the clothes that prevented her from reaching what she wanted most. "Is that what you meant?" she whispered in his ear. "Do my kisses inflame you as yours do me?" He turned his head to take her mouth again. When she tore away, she traced the tip of her tongue along his jaw to his neck, and said, "Do you want to be buried inside me as badly as I need to feel you there?"

He pulled her hips tight against him and ground his hips into her. "Sweet God, yes," he said darkly, the confession sounding as if it had been ripped from somewhere deep inside him.

"Now," she demanded.

He rolled her back into the tangle of fur and pulled at their clothes. Her hands tangled with his. There was no finesse, no time spent exploring bodies. Just frantic haste. And then he was there, pushing inside her.

He groaned, long and low as he pushed himself fully inside her. She clutched at him with her hands and with her body.

It was fast, hard, and incredibly fulfilling. He shouted out his release, thrusting into her again and again as he convulsed within her. He raised his head, leaving her dangling on the edge.

"I said I'd make you scream," he said. He reached down between them and caressed her slick, aching need.

And scream she did.

Her body still shuddering, he moved to slide out of her but she caught him to her.

"This is no curse," she said intently. "This is no trickery here between us. Not for me."

He held her gaze silently, the flash of bleakness in his eyes making her heart ache. "Rory—"

He shushed her, then pressed his face in her hair. He turned to his side and, without a word, pulled her close. Something gentled inside her then. Not the ferocity of her need. She might be sated, but even now she wanted him again. And again. He had unlocked something in her just as he'd said he would. The bold, demanding woman she had just been with him was totally foreign to her, and it thrilled her to know she was his match. Ferocious. Yes, she was that. Perhaps there was warrior in her blood as well.

But this feeling, this new warmth when he'd pulled her

to him, this was a different sort of gentling. Oddly, it was now she began to feel nervous.

Before fear could fill her with doubts she reached up and pressed a soft kiss to his mouth until he returned it, slowly and languorously. His arms slid around her and pulled her tightly to him. Cailean felt her eyes burn. This was a new kind of need, a more treacherous kind of want. To be held, like this.

"Rory," she said. It was barely more than a plea against his lips. A plea for what she didn't know. She only knew she'd never been so terrified in her life.

He brushed his lips against hers. When he slipped his tongue inside her mouth this time, it was a request, not a demand.

She responded, then made a request of her own. "Make love to me, Rory."

There was no bleakness in his eyes now. But there was fear there. She wanted to reassure him there was nothing to fear with her, but knew no other way to tell him than this.

Rory looked down into eyes that were a soft, mossy green. There was sated desire there, and a confidence he hadn't seen before. Her passion had been a raw, honest thing that had stunned both of them. But this—what he saw in her eyes now—this truly made his stomach knot and his heart tighten. *Make love to me.*

Every image of his past fled in the face of this moment. Even Kaithren and her cruelty. There was no cruelty here, no revenge. No manipulation. He believed her. Because manipulation had no part in this for him either. Heaven help them both.

Make love to me. Her plea resonated throughout him.

"I fear that is exactly what I'm doing," he said. His hands were slowly memorizing her body, as if by their own accord, mapping each sweet valley and lean curve.

Lovemaking. He'd thought he understood the difference. Enough to know he'd been careful never to stray over the line. There was lovemaking as an art form, from which one could derive an astonishing array of sexual pleasures. And then there was the lovemaking that had little to do with learned finesse and much to do with the hearts of the persons involved. He'd had plenty of time to perfect the former and had managed to always avoid the latter.

His own heart thumped hard in his chest. What he did now would affect every second of the rest of his life in ways even Kaithren couldn't have fathomed. His hands faltered and stilled, eliciting an instant whimper of dismay.

"Cailean, I . . . we . . ." Dear Lord, he'd been inside her one time and she had him stammering like a schoolboy. And yet that little whimper, that instinctive little cry of dismay the instant he'd stopped touching her, beckoned to him. He should have been able to ignore it. He should have been able to ignore the leap of his pulse when she laid her hand on his. He should have been able to ignore the responding tug inside him that begged him to revel in the pleasure he and he alone could give her. Revel in the pleasure it would give him just to please her.

"Rory."

He looked away from their joined hands, to her eyes.

"If I am to be your key you can't run away from what is happening between us."

He tensed at that, wanted to deny that this was exactly what he wanted to do. But the words wouldn't come.

"This is all part of it. Don't you feel it? This exploration of one another, learning each other, binding ourselves together in this way—it's vital." She laid her hand on his chest. "Vital."

Hot and unexpected, anger clashed with desire. The anger came from knowing that she was right even as he didn't understand how he knew. "I just want this to be over," he ground out. "I hadn't planned on this. I hadn't planned on you."

Her eyes cleared and sharpened at his harsh indictment,

but she made no move to cover herself or shift away from him. It made her words all the more stark, the content all the more impossible to ignore.

"No," she said softly, "you knew I'd come. Maybe not consciously, but you came back here for a reason. Maybe we've been destined for this all along.

"What you don't like is that you can't control this and make it go the way you want, when you want, how you want. You couldn't control what happened to you three hundred years ago either. No more than I can control the visions that strike me." She tightened her hold on his hand. "If you run from this, from me, or try to impose your will on what is happening between us, then I am afraid we are both doomed."

Her fingers left him with a soft caress and absolute emptiness washed through him when she moved away from him and began dressing.

"What exactly are you afraid of?" she asked. "A man who wants to end his life shouldn't be afraid of anything."

He was forced to confront it then.

He was forced to consider what it would be like if he was never allowed to hold her again, or touch her or make love to her. And a fear the likes of which he'd ever felt before swamped him.

He looked back at her, her lithe body perched upon this pinnacle as if she were a mythical goddess and this was her throne, here, on MacKinnon land, high above the rest of the world. Her eyes looked directly into his, past his stormy denials and angry epithets, straight to his heart. And he knew what he was afraid of.

"I do want to end my life as a mortal," he said, his voice hoarse from the raw tightness of his throat. "But it will be easier to leave here if I do not care for anything."

She reached out a hand. "If you are to break the curse, maybe that is the first step you must take."

Rory stared at her hand, then back at her. He moved

toward her and finally reached his hand out as well. "God help me," he murmured. "I think I already have."

He expected to feel a doomed resignation, but when their hands intertwined, it was a shot of energy he felt; primal, a feeling of renewal. And a sense of hope. But hope for what? How could he feel renewal, when his ultimate goal was death?

"If it's any consolation to you, this terrifies me as well."

He said nothing, just pulled her to the portal and they climbed out of the howling wind and down the stairs. At the first sharp curve, she tugged his hand to a stop. "Rory, I . . ." There were so many things . . . She broke off and tried to gather her thoughts. "We have to talk. There are things you have to know, important things—"

He pressed his fingers to her lips. "Not now, Cailean. Let things lie for a bit." He continued down the stairs.

"No, really, I should have told you sooner, but—"

This time he turned and shushed her with his mouth. When he finally lifted his head, her heart was pounding and her mind was spinning and she had no idea what she'd been about to say. "Why did you do that?"

He looked so stern, it surprised her when he suddenly smiled. It wasn't the light, happy smile of a contented man—it was the dark, promising smile of a fallen angel. She shivered even before he spoke.

"If we are destined to learn about each other, as you say, then I plan to start our education immediately. And I'm nothing if not thorough when I want to educate myself."

"Rory, we really must—"

"Do much more of this." He turned her so her back wedged in the stone corner and leaned fully into her while he took her mouth in a slow, methodical seduction.

She didn't try and stop him—she didn't want to. But she also knew that she could never again let him think he controlled the situation between them. That much of their path she understood.

She slipped her hands between them and slid them down over his chest until she could grip his hips. He jerked involuntarily as she leaned into him and her hand closed over his buttocks, then slipped her fingers lower, brushing them between the backs of his legs.

She nipped her way to his ear. "Since we're talking about education, did you know that there is an aboriginal tribe in New Guinea that believes that . . ." She whispered in his ear.

His groan was very satisfactory. He took her mouth in a fierce kiss, then, when she was totally without breath, he grinned and said, "Did you know that in fourteenth century Russia, there was a band of Mongols who thought it was very pleasurable to . . ." He leaned up and whispered in her ear.

She experienced a slight dip of her knees. "You know," she said, sliding her hands around the front of him . . . and down. "Education is a wonderful thing. Why don't we go share our . . . bodies of knowledge."

CAILEAN HAD NO idea what time it was, or what day for that matter, when she finally roused herself. She stretched, then groaned as muscles whimpered. She thought she heard Rory stirring in the anteroom. Her stomach grumbled in response to the idea of food.

Her gaze drifted to the pile of furs in front of the glowing embers of what remained of the fire. She had no idea how long ago her last meal had been. She rolled to her back, the satin pillow she held feeling deliciously cool against the tender skin of her chest and stomach.

She felt decadent, like she'd been taken on an erotic journey to new worlds. And she had, all without ever leaving this room.

Her thoughts drifted languorously over the past hours and heat stole through her yet again. Several hundred years of practice gave a man a certain amount of stamina. She only wished the same could be said of her.

They had both been careful to keep things on an "educational" level. There had been no declarations and no epiphanies. But there had been other moments, like when she'd awoken to find them curled around each other. She remembered nestling against his chest, held there by a lightly caressing hand. Or the time when his face had been buried in the crook of her neck, his fingers having woven through hers as they slept.

She rolled to her stomach and pressed her face into the pillow. What on earth had she done? Falling in love with Rory MacKinnon was definitely not wise.

A rueful smile crossed her face. If Rory wasn't allowed to control the path he took to salvation, what had made her think she could?

The vision flashed through her mind again, along with the words she'd heard in her mind.

He will bring you pain.

Now she understood how.

He chose that moment to come into the room. He was freshly shaven and naked as the day he was born. He was supremely at home in his body, but then he'd had a long, long time to get used to it.

He carried a small wooden platter with some fruit and rolls and preserves stacked haphazardly on top. He was smiling. It made her heart ache.

"What's wrong?"

Everything, she wanted to say. "You were right," she said.

He laid the tray on the foot of the bed, spilling half the fruit across the tangled sheets as he sat beside her.

"This comes as no surprise tae me," he said, a twinkle in his eyes. He tucked a wayward tangle of hair behind her ear. She smiled as she remembered the hour he had spent stroking a brush through her long hair.

His smile faded as her dreamy expression faltered and she looked away. He turned her chin toward him. "What's the matter?"

She didn't want to look at him. Didn't want him to touch her so gently, so reverently. Didn't he know what he was doing? Didn't he realize what was happening to them?

"It's easier when you don't care." She'd meant to say it flippantly. Instead she'd sounded pathetically needy and bleak. She rolled from his touch, not caring if the fruit all spilled to the floor.

"Cailean—"

"No," she said. "Don't." She went to the fireplace and piled some of the wood onto the grate. She was fully aware that she was as naked as he was. Her lifestyle had made her less than prudish about nudity, something that had surprised Rory. She'd teased him and reveled in his response.

She heard him come toward her and knew if he touched her, she'd end up back in bed . . . or in his arms right here, clinging to him, saying things she wasn't prepared to say, admitting feelings, to herself and to him, she had no business feeling.

"We need to talk. Yesterday I told you that there were things you needed to know. Things you'll want to know. I should have told you already, but . . ." She very carefully kept her gaze away from the bed.

His expression had become unreadable. It pained her in a way she hadn't expected. He'd been more open with her over the last however many hours than she'd ever expected, certainly more than he had, she was sure. So this closing off, this shutting her out, hurt. It shouldn't have.

More proof.

"Well, if we're to have a civilized conversation, I suppose we should dress like civilized people." His King's English was as crisp and sharp as a freshly creased piece of parchment. "Will the dining room, such as it is, be appropriate? Or should we adjourn back to the main hall? I'm afraid our thrones are long gone, but you seem to have a distinct ability to command an audience, whether on a pedestal or not."

"The dining room will be fine," she said, suddenly weary. She pulled a blanket from the pile on the bed.

Rory didn't dress either, but gathered the scattered fruit and carted them back to the other room. He was angry. That he placed the platter on the table with utmost gentility before carefully seating her in the chair told her just how controlled a rage he was in.

"Don't be angry with me."

"Don't shut me out," he said shortly. He took a roll and leaned back against the long counter table.

"This isn't about us—"

"Don't be foolish. Everything said here, done here, is about us. Right now, there is nothing else *but* us." He started to take a bite of the roll, but ended up tossing it on the counter instead. He leaned over the table, fists planted on either side of the platter. "You told me we had to bind ourselves together. Consider me bound."

Her throat tightened at the bald, rawly stated admission.

He moved in even closer. "Tell me this, Cailean lass, did ye honestly believe I was tae be the only one caught in these deadly ties?"

"No."

"What di' ye say?" he goaded, cupping one hand to his ear. "I canno' hear you?"

She shoved the chair back, suddenly fighting to control her own rage. "I said no," she shouted. "No. You're not the only one bound. Okay? There, I said it. I'm falling in love with you, John Roderick MacKinnon, and I'm not any happier about it than you are."

They both stood there staring at each other, speechless as the echo of her words faded between them.

"But there is more to deal with in all of this than just us," she said hoarsely.

"Like what?" He was rounding the table.

"Your brother, Duncan."

That stopped him. His eyes narrowed. "What of Duncan?"

"I met him. And my cousin Maggie. In North Carolina. Last week." She slumped back down into the chair, weighted down by his incredulous expression.

"But he's—"

"A ghost."

TWENTY-THREE

R ORY STARED. "A ghost," he repeated.

"What, you don't believe me? Mr. Immortal?"

Actually, it was the exact opposite that had left him speechless. "Do you know," he said quietly, "that I have never told another human being the truth about what I am?"

Her expression turned thoughtful and her shoulders lost some of their defiant stance. "No, I didn't know that."

"I have spent my life evading any long-term contact with another person. If I'm around long enough, people start to notice things. Like they age and I never seem to. Oh, I could get away with it for five, even ten years. But eventually . . ." He walked toward her. "And then there is the problem with having to leave people you've grown to like. Over and over, again and again. It's simply easier to avoid the relationships in the first place."

She reached up and stroked his face. It was a simple gesture of comfort, yet it almost brought him to his knees.

"I chose long ago to never let myself get close enough," he said, his voice vibrating with emotion, "to allow even the simplest of caresses." He trapped her hand to his face when she would have pulled it away. "If I cannot share my life, my experiences, then why tempt myself? Oh, there were many who would have been fascinated, perhaps even believed my fantastical tales. Not one would have truly understood. Until you."

"We are not so different, Rory. Maybe that is why I knew, somewhere inside, who and what you are. I, too, have spent a life cutting myself off from those very same connections. When I begin to care, the visions start increasing. The pain and frustration is—" She broke off when he slipped her hand down to his chest and covered it with his own. She stared at their joined hands laid over his heart. "You understand that pain. It became easier not to get close." She looked up. "Until you."

"Then we understand each other." He dropped a soft kiss to her lips, then led her over to sit in the soft furs. "Tell me about my brother."

"It will be easiest to explain from the beginning."

He nodded. "I want to know it all."

"I was on a dig in Peru when I heard about my inheritance. This was the first I'd ever heard of Lachlan." She went on to relay the story, and in doing so, she talked about her past, her childhood, about her visions. She ended up telling him, with his encouragement, more about herself and her thoughts and ideas than she'd ever shared with anyone. It shouldn't have been so earth-shattering, yet it was. To share like this, to sink into a deeper relationship, to allow intimacy of an entirely different sort to blossom between them, was simply profound.

When she was done, Rory sat back, dropping her hand for the first time since she'd begun.

"Are you okay?" she asked.

He waved off her concern. "This is all beginning to seem too . . . real, I suppose," He turned to look at the fire. The flames flashed shadows across his face. "I suppose I thought you'd merely seen an apparition of him, a haunting of the place where he died."

Cailean hated hearing him sound so desolate. She didn't know what else to do except tell him the rest. "Duncan had saved Maggie's life and by then I'd read all of Lachlan's journals and realized that my path lay in this direction."

Rory suddenly sat up and gripped her arm. "Is Duncan still in North Carolina? Haunting this cabin?"

"I don't know, Rory. Maggie was certain he'd reappear after I left. But I'm not as sure."

Rory rose immediately. He grabbed a leather satchel and began shoving clothes in it.

"What?"

"We're going to North Carolina."

"Just like that? What about . . . what about your sheep?"

"They mix in with a herd in the valley beyond from time to time. The beasties will be fine. We canno' waste time. He could already be gone by now."

If he is there at all, Cailean thought. "Wait a minute. We?"

"Of course. We'll drive to Portree and check you out then head to Glasgow. If we're lucky, we should be able to fly out the day after tomorrow."

"I guess you have a passport."

He looked at her and grinned. It was silly, but her heart flip-flopped. He looked so young. For the first time, he looked like the twenty-seven year old man he was . . . or would have been, three hundred years ago.

"I have gone through more passports than you could pack in Lachlan's fabled trunk. There are very few places on this planet I have no' been."

She was struck again by the reality of his existence. "What of the curse, Rory? What of my role in it?"

"We can deal with that after I see my brother. It's not like I'm running out of time."

"I am. I can't stay away from my work, from my life, forever. I can't just put everything on hold."

"If it's money yer worried about, have no fears. I've mastered many a trade and spent one decade teaching myself finance and the laws of inheritance. I've been inheriting my own money, a steadily increasing amount, many times over, for well over a hundred years now."

"It's not about money—it's my career. I'll lose my place on this team for good if I don't return soon."

Rory flipped the heavy leather flap over the top and buckled it in place, then slung the satchel over his shoulder. "Can ye spare me another week, Cailean?" His eyes were hard, demanding. "Or am I askin' too much of ye?"

She wanted to tell him to go to hell, she wanted to wipe the arrogance from his face. But she couldn't. "I'll go with you. But then we have to figure out where the key is."

He frowned. "You're talking nonsense now. You're the Key."

"I mean the key to the curse. I may be a Claren Key and yes, I guess I possess the 'sight' but I've told you I do not have any other 'special powers.'"

"We will find a way. You are the answer, Cailean Claren. I feel it. I know it."

"I feel it, too. But Lachlan was convinced that the beginning of the Legend MacKinnon dealt with some talisman or something that the Claren women must have used. He spent his last years looking for it."

"I have no idea what you are talking of."

"Did Kaithren use something when she cursed you? Maybe something of Edwyna's. Was she holding something?"

His eyes flared. "Ye mean besides me?"

Cailean flushed, but she didn't back down.

"I canno' remember if there was a talisman. We were no' completely undressed, so I dinna know wha' she might have been carryin' on her." He took a moment and made a visible attempt to calm down. "And what if she was? Are ye saying we are to look for some small talisman held by three women over three centuries ago? How in hell do you expect us to find such a thing, even if it does exist?"

"The Clarens took over Stonelachen right after the curses were cast, and you said the castle was abandoned a few years later. Maybe it is here, somewhere. Maybe that is why we are both here, now. I feel it, Rory. I understand why you have to go, but I can't shake the feeling that it's wrong."

Rory stood silent, seeming to ponder all she said. Then he swore. "Are ye sayin' ye want to stay here and search for it while I'm gone?"

It had occurred to her that having him away from here and from her, as much as it was the last thing she wanted, might in fact be the wisest thing she could do. But wisdom was a tricky thing. "It would be easier with you here to direct me."

"Then I propose this. Come with me to America. Then we will come back here and begin our search." He gentled his voice. "As for your job, there will be other digs, will there not?"

She nodded. "It's not just about that, Rory—"

"I know," he said. "But your career will not live or die with this one operation. True?"

"It was an important project to me, Rory. One I fought to be involved in for a long time."

"Then I will give you another one."

"What do you mean?"

"I told you. I have been many places, seen many things. Just because I don't choose to form ties with others does not mean I don't learn, or that I don't listen. I can give you locations that will yield discoveries you and your colleagues would likely find quite interesting."

"Name one," she challenged.

"There is an ancient Aztec community in Mexico, almost intact but buried by centuries of jungle growth. Far bigger than anything previously recovered."

She gasped. "Really?"

"I'll lead you to it personally, if you wish."

"That would make my career for life." She noticed an odd emotion flash in his eyes, but she was too overwhelmed by his offer to pay it close attention.

"Then have it you shall," he said almost curtly. "Now that we've settled on a price, can we go? I have a reunion to attend." He didn't wait for an answer, yanked his bag to his shoulder and went to the door.

"I did not ask for payment," she warned.

Rory turned at the door. "But we have settled the matter, have we not?"

Cailean had already grown used to his domineering ways and would be lying if she said she'd really want him any other way. But it gave her a great deal of satisfaction to say, "You might want to do one other thing before we go."

With his patience obviously at an end, he sighed and said, "And that would be?"

"You might want to get dressed first."

CAILEAN WAITED, TOE tapping, as the stone slid to one side and they stepped out into the back corner of the cemetery.

"I can't believe you made me climb that mountain, then hike down all those passageways." Their trip out had been far more direct to say the least.

"I thought the scientist in you would appreciate the full tour."

She wanted to wipe that smile off his face. She wanted to drag him back to that bed of his and forget about the world, for say, a year or so. Instead she said nothing, stepped carefully past him and walked directly to her car.

He shut the door and the weirdest feeling washed over

her. It felt strange being in a twentieth century vehicle with him. She cast a quick glance at him, wondering, not for the first time, what it must be like to have hundreds of years of memories to account for.

He was looking at the rear view side mirror as she backed out. The impatience to be on the road and on their way fairly vibrated from him. They remained silent as she made the descent from the Quiraing, back to the narrow main road. She couldn't deny that seeing Duncan was more important than anything else, yet she couldn't shake the feeling that this wasn't the right thing to do.

"I'd love to hear about some of your travels." She caught his quick glance and smiled. "The scientist in me is interested."

"I'd rather hear more about my brother. And this cousin of yours."

Cailean sighed inwardly. She knew he'd opened up to her in ways he likely never had before, but he was still a tough man to penetrate. But then, he'd had centuries to erect some pretty strong walls.

"Okay," she relented. She spent the remainder of the trip to Portree filling him in on all the details.

When they pulled up in front of the hotel, a light rain had begun to fall. She turned to him, leaving the motor running. "If you want to wait, it will only take me a minute to get my things together and check out."

He was already opening his door. "I'll help you carry your bags down. We'll get away faster."

She didn't argue and let him hold the door for her to enter the small foyer. When the young desk clerk looked with great interest from her to the man stepping in behind her, she actually felt her cheeks begin to heat.

For heavens sake, she was pushing thirty years old! No need to explain herself or the company she chose to keep to anyone.

Cailean wondered if the young man knew he was having

a close personal encounter with The Remote. He could dine out in the pubs for months on that one. But he remained silent, finally shifting his attention nervously to her when Rory cleared his throat.

"Are ye wantin' to check out, miss?" he said, his soft accent relaxing her a bit.

"Yes, please," she said. "I'll go collect my things and pay you when I come down, is that okay?" She was already turning to the stairs when the clerk spoke.

"Fine. But you have a message here you might want to read. Came in late yesterday." He handed her the white paper, a shy smile on his apple-cheeked face which faded abruptly as he glanced at Rory. "Appears your cousin is in town and lookin' for you."

"What?" Cailean then spun to Rory. "She's here! Maggie has come. She must have changed her mind and left right after I did." Cailean couldn't believe she'd left Duncan behind so soon. A thought struck her. She spun back to the clerk, interrupting him as he tried to speak again. "Did she have someone with her? A big, tall man with long, dark hair?"

"No ma'am. Her name wasna Maggie. I wrote it down, it was somethin' unusual."

Cailean stared at him, confused, then uncrumpled the note she'd crushed in her hand. "Delaney Claren," she read. "I'm staying at the Skeabost Hotel. Please call as soon as you get this. It's urgent." There was a number after it.

Frowning, Rory took the note from her. "How many cousins do ye have running about?" he said.

"Oh my God," she whispered. "The third cousin." With everything that had happened, she'd totally forgotten about her. "She really exists." Stunned, she turned back to the young clerk, who was once again looking uncomfortable as he stared at Rory.

"Did you take the message? Did she give it to you in person? What did she look like? Do you remember?"

The man's head bobbed up and down repeatedly and then, at the last question, a broad smile split his smooth features. "Oh, I remember all right. Hard to forget that one. She was shorter than you, but, well . . ." He blushed furiously. "Curvier, ye know? She had short black hair and these unusual eyes. Purple they were. I never recalled seein' purple colored eyes before. Like Elizabeth Taylor, ye know? She reminded me of her."

Cailean stared at him for a moment after he finished babbling. "Did she say anything else?"

"No. Just that she was real sorry she missed you and for you to call as soon as you got in."

Cailean nodded slowly. "Thank you."

She turned to Rory, who was scowling. "Let's go upstairs. We can figure it out there."

"What's to figure out?" he asked. "I dinna have time for this—"

Cailean motioned with a small jerk of her chin. "Upstairs? Please?"

Once they were in the room, she watched Rory prowl around with an animal-like grace that made her shudder and ache. Staring out the window, she said, "I have to call her."

"You have to drive to Glasgow and catch a plane."

She turned and braced herself against the cool glass. "I will. Right after I call Delaney. When I looked at Lachlan's documentation of our parents' generation, there was a third child born to his nephews. I didn't know her name, or that she was still alive. I was going to try and track her down while I was here, but Lachlan's solicitor wasn't at all forthcoming. And then I met you." She turned back around. A headache was forming behind her eyes. Wasn't everything complicated enough?

"Then how did she find you?"

"I haven't any idea." She closed her eyes and rubbed her temples. "Let me at least call and find out what she wants.

A few more minutes won't hurt anything. We won't be able to fly out until tomorrow anyway."

She felt him come up behind her. Her fingers were brushed away and his own strong fingers took over the gentle massage. "Magic fingers," she said. "You could license them and make a fortune."

"They earned me a few pence here and there."

She opened one eye and turned enough to level it on him.

He raised one brow in return. "Jealous?" he said, a smile almost curving his lips. "Don't be. It was before you were even born."

That jolt of reality was enough to make her pull away. She smoothed the note once again and went to the phone. Her fingers hesitated just above the pad, a strange sense of foreboding washed over her. She tensed, half expecting a vision to overtake her, but it didn't come. She sighed in relief and quickly punched in the number. At the answering voice, she said, "Delaney Claren's room please."

As she waited for the connection, she looked up at Rory. He nodded once, just a slight dip of the chin. She gripped the phone more tightly at his show of support.

Then a sharp, take-no-prisoners voice invaded her ear.

"Delaney Claren here."

"Hello, this is Cailean Claren. You wanted to speak to me?"

"Cuz!" If it were possible, she was even louder now, but definitely more jubilant.

Cailean held the phone away from her ear, then placed it back again. "What?"

"You're speaking to your long-lost cousin, Delaney Claren," she said. "Old Lachlan left me some land over here and I finally got around to seeing it. It's gorgeous, but I can't afford to keep it. I talked to a realtor about listing it for sale and she's apparently a friend of a friend of Lachlan's lawyer's secretary and she mentioned something about another relative of Lachlan's being in town doing some family research and well, what a surprise, huh?"

Cailean sat there, reeling from the impact. Delaney Claren was like a tornado and Cailean was left feeling a bit windblown. "You're selling the land?"

"As far as I can tell, it's just a big pile of rocks. Oh, and a graveyard. Sort of spooky and maybe not something I should point out right off to a prospective buyer, but hey, we're family right?"

"Right," Cailean echoed numbly.

"So, you in the market for a piece of family history?"

Cailean stared at Rory and had to fight the sudden urge to laugh hysterically. "You have no idea," she murmured.

TWENTY-FOUR

CAILEAN HUNG UP the phone. "She's coming over."

Rory sat down, rattling the table next to him. "What?"

"I said she's—"

He held up a hand. "I heard you." He stood and began to pace. "And I suppose you can't wait to see her."

"If she is my cousin, then yes, I'd like to meet her. You might be interested in meeting her as well."

"Another bluidy Claren? I dinna think so!"

"I'm a Claren and you've managed to tolerate me well enough."

"I didna have a choice."

Cailean sat down, very carefully. "I see."

He stalked to the bed and stood towering in front of her. "Do no' take that tone wi' me. You know as well as I that our situation is different."

She'd come to think of them as far more than just a forced union, that their being together meant more than a means to an end. More fool she for thinking he felt the same way. She stood and pushed past him. "You still might want to reconsider meeting my cousin."

"I couldn't imagine why."

Cailean turned to him. "Because she's your new land-lady."

"What!"

"She owns the land you've been living on, including Stonelachen. Lachlan left it to her. I guess Lachlan bought his way into that cemetery fair and square."

"He doesna belong there," Rory thundered. "He doesna belong with the sacred remains of MacKinnons who gave their lives defending that very soil against him and his like."

"You yourself said that no man owns the earth, but is merely caretaker of it. Well, the Clarens took care of that land, too."

"Not too damn bloody well they didn't. They lost it to the MacDonalds before they could move into the place." He stormed to the door, then back across the room again. "Once I realized the battle was lost, I made sure they couldna take Stonelachen without more cunning than the lot of them had together."

"How could you protect the castle? The Clarens knew it was there."

"Aye, they knew. Angus Claren himself had feasted with my da many a time in better days. But they didna know all her tricks. I moved walls, blocked passages. I made sure they never found all of her." He folded his arms across his chest. "She was MacKinnon built and it was MacKinnons she protected. We were the ones who filled her with life, we were the ones who gave our lives for her. They might have conquered the MacKinnons, but I wasna about to let anyone else take Stonelachen without a fight.

"You can print all the pieces of paper you want and spend all the money you want. In the end, it all means naught. The land is owned by those who protect it and take their life from it. It's a partnership, with the land as the only enduring partner. Men will come and go, ownership as they see it will pass again and again depending on who is the most powerful or cunning at the moment."

The intensity of his gaze held her still as surely as if he held her there by force. "But Stonelachen belongs only to a MacKinnon, first, last, and always. She only gives her secrets to those that made her. Always has, always will."

"You're right," she said quietly, shamed by her earlier avowal. She had strong feelings for Stonelachen even she didn't understand. But it wasn't her heritage to claim, not truly, not in the ways that really mattered. "I thought that I understood the real power of family, of heritage. It's my job to understand the foundation it can create."

"Maybe it's because you never studied the one foundation that mattered. Your own."

"But I couldn't risk that it would make things worse."

His stance relaxed. He understood. "So ye form bonds with those whose lives have already been lived."

She nodded sadly, feeling pathetic.

" 'Tis understandable, Cailean. Dinna fash yerself this way. Ye are here now."

"You're right. Whatever my reasons for finally digging into my past, I *am* here." She walked over to him. "I have to tell you something. I know how important it is for you to see Duncan. But ever since we left Stonelachen I've had this dreadful feeling that we're doing the wrong thing."

"We will come back, Cailean."

"It's not that." She lifted her hands in frustration. The words she needed to explain how she felt wouldn't come. "I am the Key, am I not?"

He inclined his head stiffly.

"I appreciate the significance of Stonelachen to you, and I agree that while it is part of my past, there is no denying the claim you have on it, or the connection you rightfully feel. I understand why you did whatever you could to preserve her sanctity." She shook her head, amazed at the immensity of the task he'd taken upon himself. "You are like the lone sentinel, the only one who knows her secrets, the only one left to protect them."

She walked to him, pulling apart his stiffly crossed arms. "You've come back to her time and again. You've protected her for centuries, Rory. There is a reason you feel so tied to her. Somewhere inside is the secret that will set you free. I feel it, Rory. The answer is inside Stonelachen. We should be there, searching for it."

"I will see my brother first. If the secret has been there all along, it will remain there."

Cailean shook her head. "No—it's both of us being there, now. It's just something I feel, something I know." She gripped his arms. "The answer is there, but this is the first time all the elements have been in place to unlock it."

"Then we will both come back to it."

She shook her head, frustration mounting.

"I hear what you say, Cailean."

He pulled his arms from her and she let him go. "But you aren't really listening, are you? You're leaving anyway."

He sighed again, but his expression softened, his voice gentled. "You have an understanding of me that runs far deeper than I expected. This connection we have terrifies me as much as it tantalizes me."

He touched her face and she wanted to clutch at him, beg him to stay. She forced her hands to remain at her side, knowing what was coming by the sick knot of dread in her stomach.

"But I canno' do as you ask." He let his hand drop to his side and walked to the door. "I will see Duncan, with or without you."

"You underestimated the power of a Claren Key once before. Are you so ready to make the same mistake twice?"

Rory turned on her, a new light in his eyes. "Do not toss that out lightly, Cailean Claren," he said icily.

"I wouldn't dare. I might have been confused by it before, but I am certain of it now. It's that important, Rory."

"And when did freeing me from the bonds of immortality take on such importance to you? Or is it that you are merely in a hurry to end these visions of yours?" He leaned his face into hers. "You have lived with your curse for a far shorter time than I have suffered mine. If I am willing to wait, so shall you be."

"Even if it means losing the one chance you'll have?"

"If you honestly think I believe you'll leave me when you stand to gain as much as I do, well, perhaps you need to be more creative with your threats." If she thought his tone was menacing before, she was chilled to the bone by what she saw in his eyes now.

"I don't plan on going anywhere. But perhaps you'll be interested in knowing that Delaney plans on selling the land you now reside on, land that contains Stonelachen and the key to your immortality."

"What of it?" he said. "She will not find Stonelachen. Nor will anyone she might sell it to."

"You could buy it."

He bristled in outrage. "I willna be payin' one pence for land that is already mine!"

"Fine. *I* know where Stonelachen is. Perhaps I'll enlist her help in the hunt."

He went completely still. "You wouldn't dare."

"If you leave, what other choice do I have?"

He crowded her back against the wall, pinning her there with his arms braced on either side of her. He leaned in until his eyes were level with hers. The word unholy came to mind again, but for entirely different reasons.

"We all have choices, Cailean. It appears I've made another bad one. Three hundred years and I choose to once again trust a Claren. I must be more a fool than even I thought possible."

"Rory—" If there had just been the anger of betrayal in

his eyes, she might have withstood it. But there was pain there, well hidden, but there nonetheless for the person who knew where to look for it.

She reached up between them and cupped his face. "I'm not cowering before you. No matter how fierce you are. And, standing here I can fully appreciate how fine a warrior you must have made. Still make." She kept her hand where it was, stroking his cheek, his jaw. It twitched under her touch.

"I won't betray you," she said softly. "I couldn't. But you weren't listening and I had to get your attention."

"Ye've accomplished the task."

She would have smiled, but his gaze was still far too unyielding. "It's that important, Rory. If you have truly placed any of your trust in me then believe that we have to stay. It will work out with Duncan. I can't tell you how I know that, but I do. You have to trust me."

Someone knocked hard on the door, startling them both. Rory went to pull away and Cailean wanted to scream in frustration. If he left now, it would be over. She gripped his head in her hands and he stilled. "Don't go." She held his gaze tautly. "Promise me, Rory."

"Cousin Cailean?" came a shout from the hallway. "It's me, Delaney."

"Promise me."

He held her gaze and she clearly saw the battle that raged inside him.

"Until we talk to Delaney, at least." The knock came again. "Please, Rory."

"You talk to her," he said at length, "then we'll decide what is to be done."

"I won't let us down," she said fervently. She leaned in to kiss him, meaning for it to be a quick affirmation of her pledge.

He had her flat up against the wall and was deep in her

mouth before she could blink. She responded without a moment's hesitation.

The knocking came again, but he didn't seem to care. Cailean found she didn't either.

Rory finally pulled his mouth from hers. "No matter what happens, we are bonded in this quest, Cailean. We will see it through together, you and I. Wherever it takes us."

"I—"

"We will not part until it is done." He kissed her again, short, hard, and fast. "Promise me."

"I promise."

He moved away and she gulped in air and smoothed her hands through her hair. What a way to meet her newest relation.

She opened the door just as the small woman on the other side raised her fist to knock again. The woman quickly pulled her hand back and smoothly shifted the action into an offer of a handshake. "You must be Cailean," she said, a bright grin on her face. "I'm your cousin, Delaney Claren." Her laugh was deep and surprisingly rich coming from such a small person, and incredibly infectious.

"Hello." The woman's grip was quite firm, Cailean thought, as Delaney released her hand. "Come on in."

Delaney moved into the room with the same sort of feline grace she'd exhibited with her handshake maneuver. Her frame was on the petite side, but she packed a lot of curve into the tiny package. She wore black jeans that fit her like they'd been custom-made and a short jacket that emphasized her narrow waist, not to mention the upper part of the hourglass figure. Her dark hair was wavy and cut very short, with wisps that framed her face in a gamine sort of way. It was the perfect foil for those eyes. All in all, Delaney Claren packed quite a wallop.

"Oops, you're not alone," Delaney said, yanking Cailean from her musings. "Hi," she said, walking over to Rory, who was now standing by the window. "I'm Delaney Claren."

"So I've heard," he said.

Cailean turned. "This is Rory MacKinnon." She watched for a reaction to the last name, but there was none.

Delaney didn't seem remotely offended by Rory's less than enthusiastic demeanor. In fact, she grinned and said, "I've obviously intruded at a bad time." She shot a wink at Cailean. "Not bad," she mouthed silently. She turned back to Rory, appearing completely guileless, though she had to know he hadn't missed her little display.

Cailean should have been annoyed, but she found herself charmed despite herself.

"I'm really sorry to storm the place like this. It's just that I wasn't planning on staying long and I wasn't sure how long you planned to be here."

Cailean spoke. "Well, I was—"

"Just checking out actually," Rory interjected.

Delaney looked between the two of them for a moment, easily picking up on the undercurrents running between them. Not only was she charming and gorgeous as hell, she was sharp.

Delaney smiled brightly. "Well, then I guess it's good I caught you when I did. Can I interest you two in an early lunch, tea perhaps? I really want a chance to talk to you, Cailean. I had no idea I even had a relative, you or Lachlan for that matter. I have a million questions and who knows when we'll cross paths again."

"Where do you live?" Cailean asked.

"The world is my hotel," she said. "But originally, Kansas." She raised a hand. "I know, but please, no Dorothy jokes. I've heard them all."

Cailean was curious. "I travel a lot as well. What do you do?"

"I'm a liaison to Uncle Sam," she said easily.

"Another way of saying spy or agent," Rory added, just as easily.

Delaney turned to him without pause and said, "Actually no, I'm a civilian. I lecture and teach defensive training to both the military and the government. My specialty is antiterrorism."

Rory didn't blink, but he did incline his head briefly. "Interesting occupation."

She smiled. "I actually think you meant that. I didn't even hear the inferred 'for a woman' at the end of that statement."

"I would never make the mistake of underestimating the abilities of any woman." He didn't so much as glance as Cailean, but Delaney had no apparent problem in picking up on that underlying message either.

"What is it that you do?" she asked Cailean, smoothly shifting her attention.

"I'm a forensic anthropologist. I specialize in DNA analysis."

She raised her eyebrows. "Impressive," she said. "Wow, are we an interesting family or what?"

You don't know the half of it, Cailean thought. She wanted to tell her about Maggie, but while her instincts told her Delaney was on the up and up, she wasn't going to reveal anything until she had more proof than her word on it.

"So, you say you'd never heard of Lachlan before you got word of your inheritance?"

Delaney shook her head. "No, but that's not all that surprising. I was orphaned pretty young." She paused for a second. "What?"

Cailean hadn't thought she'd been that transparent. "Nothing. I didn't know him either. I was orphaned young myself." As had been the case with Maggie. Cailean didn't need further convincing that the curse was real, but it still gave her a little shiver.

"Isn't that a strange coincidence," Delaney commented. "I guess it took them a while to track you down too, then."

Cailean nodded. "Peru. I was on a project there."

"Bosnia and Kazakstan," she said in response.

"So," Cailean said, breaking the sudden silence. "You said Lachlan left you some land?"

"Yeah, he did. And I have to admit I'm more drawn to this place than I counted on being." She shot Rory a smile. "Lovely country you have here, by the way."

"We try," he responded, looking almost amused.

Cailean fought a smile. Delaney was getting to him.

"Well, keep up the good work," she shot back, then shifted her attention back to Cailean. "Anyway, I love the land and the area and as much as I find myself wanting to stay and dig around a bit, my schedule—and my whole life is a schedule quite frankly—just won't allow for it. And even then, I don't have the funds to maintain such a large chunk of real estate. The inheritance taxes alone would sink me. So, as much as it pains me, I'm going to have to sell it."

Rory stalked over to the window, dismissing them both. Cailean opened her mouth to make an apology for his rudeness, then closed it again. He could correct his own social blunders. Not that he would.

But then, he hadn't encountered one Delaney Claren. Cailean watched with avid interest as her cousin stood and walked over to him.

"It's not that I don't respect my heritage," she said to his back.

He looked at her then.

"I simply have no choice."

Rory looked directly over her head at Cailean. "We all have choices."

She followed his gaze, then gave him a considering look. "I suppose. But mine is to sell my inheritance." Delaney frowned for the first time. "Why does what I choose to do

with that land bother you?" Her eyes narrowed in suspicion and she turned toward him in what could only be
called a defensive posture. "Or did you think *she* would
inherit the land maybe? Is that what you're upset about?
That you'll have to pay for it instead of having it given to
you?"

Rory snorted in disgust, but Delaney shifted positions
when he tried to walk past her. Raising an eyebrow, obviously questioning her dubious decision to challenge him,
he remained where he was. "When I want something I
tend to be direct about it. But perhaps you have a point.
Perhaps it is time for the MacKinnons to take back what
has always been rightfully theirs. You Clarens never were
able to hold on to the place. If it will keep you from tossing
it about like a nuisance, then own it I will, in every way it
is possible to claim it." He looked passed her, dismissing
her easily. "No Claren will have to worry about 'maintaining the property' ever again."

Delaney jerked his attention just as easily back to her.
"You assume a great deal, Mr. MacKinnon." Gone completely was the warm, congenial charmer. Cailean wondered how often her opponents misjudged just how much a
threat she could pose. Cailean looked at Rory and fought a
smile. His mind probably held more knowledge about
more things than any other man on earth, yet, apparently
when it came to Claren women, he was destined to learn
the hard way.

"You assume the property will be for sale to you," she
said. "It is not."

"I don't believe I mentioned anything about purchasing
it," he said silkily.

Cailean expected to see sparks and flames when Delaney's temper blew, but if anything, her control became
icier and more rigid. A worthy opponent indeed.

"Then I assure you, MacKinnon, that if Cailean and I
come to any kind of agreement about this property, I will

have it drawn up so that you will never be able to claim ownership of so much as one pebble of it, even if she's foolish enough to marry you."

"There are other ways of claiming land that do no' include money or marriage, Ms. Claren."

"And what ways would they be?"

Rory leaned back against the window and folded his arms, the casual pose far more menacing than any in-your-face posturing. "Why, war, Ms. Claren. You know all about war, don't you?"

Cailean wasn't certain what reaction Rory had hoped to elicit, but gauging from his stormy expression it was not the broad smile that Delaney bestowed him with. "Why yes, as a matter of fact I do." She held out her hand. "May the best man, or woman, win."

Rory took her hand. And an instant later found himself lying flat on his back. The floor shook from the impact.

"Rule number one: Never underestimate your opponent." She bent over him, smiling sweetly. "And here I thought you didn't make that mistake." She turned to a gaping Cailean. "I'm so sorry, but he really was rude. Would you like to have that tea now?" She walked to the door. "Maybe we'd better make it a beer." She leaned on the door handle and massaged her lower back. "Damn, but he's heavy."

TWENTY-FIVE

CAILEAN MOTIONED DELANEY to a booth in a quiet corner of the small hotel restaurant. She swore she could hear Rory stalking the room above like a caged lion. His glare as she'd followed Delaney from the room burned in her brain.

But no matter how furious he was, she knew he was a man of his word. He wouldn't leave without her.

"What'll you have?" Delaney asked brightly as she seated herself across from Cailean.

"Oh, uh, tea is fine." She hadn't even noticed the waitress standing beside them. "Maybe some cheese and crackers, too?" She'd quickly come to like that particular Scottish favorite and right now she wasn't sure her stomach could take anything more than that.

Delaney ordered the roast special and the best ale they served. The young woman smiled as she jotted it down, and hurried off.

Delaney sighed. "I could definitely get used to eating here. These people are serious about their meat and potatoes. A country after my own heart."

"You'd have to roll me out of the door if I ate like that on a daily basis."

She leaned back and fiddled with her spoon. "I like you Cailean Claren. I'm glad serendipity worked in our favor."

Cailean's easy smile tightened a bit. "Well, I'm not sure how serendipitous this is."

Delaney's smile faded. "You mean because of that business upstairs? Listen, I'm really sorry about all that. You want to tell me what's going on with that?"

"It's not the simple story you might imagine it to be."

The smart smile returned. "There ain't nothing simple about a man like the one you got stashed upstairs. Where did you dig him up?"

Cailean laughed despite the knot of nerves in her stomach. "I met him here."

"You're recent acquaintances? Man, I'm rustier than I thought. I'm usually a dead-on judge of people. It comes in handy in my line of work. I had you two pegged as having quite an involved, complex relationship."

"Bullseye."

Delaney leaned forward. "So, spill. Was it one of those instant passion kind of things? He seems rather the instant passion sort, in a bottled up, super controlled kind of way." She winked. "Uncorking it can be pretty exciting, huh?"

Cailean just sat there.

"I'm overwhelming you, aren't I? Just tell me to butt out."

"No, it's not that. I guess I wouldn't have pegged someone in your line of work as being such a romantic."

Delaney wasn't offended. "I am most definitely a romantic."

"I would have thought, seeing what you must see, dealing with terrorists and that sort of devastation, that you'd be, I don't know, more cynical."

"Well then, I might as well give up if that was the case,

right? If the world has already gone to hell, then what's the point?"

"I never thought about it that way."

"It's because I believe in hope and passion and the power of love that I do what I do."

The intensity, the heart she imbued in that one simple statement spoke volumes for the woman she was. "I think I like you, too, Delaney Claren."

She grinned. "I'm hard to resist. Like the plague."

The waitress came back with their order and then Cailean said, "There are some things we really should talk about. Other than the property I mean."

"Shoot." Delaney made short work of her roast, then proceeded to demolish two rolls. She caught Cailean staring and grinned sheepishly. "I'm cursed with the metabolism of the Tasmanian Devil."

"I could think of worse curses," Cailean said.

Delaney paused in the middle of buttering her third roll. "You say that like you have a specific one in mind. So, what is your curse? Besides having gorgeous long blonde hair and a man to drool for?"

"A man you recently flipped like a pancake."

"Yeah well, you had to admit he had that coming." She laughed when Cailean was unable to conceal her grin. "You want me to teach you?"

"I just might."

She nodded approvingly. "Okay. We were talking curses. Spill."

Deciding bluntness would not be a problem with her new cousin, she did exactly that. "I have what's called second sight."

"Really? Meaning, what, like you see the future or something?"

Nothing fazed this woman. It was disconcerting, but also incredibly freeing. "In a vague, frustrating way, yes."

"And that's why you left Peru to come to Scotland?"

"No, I left Peru to go to North Carolina. That's where my share of Lachlan's legacy accidentally ended up."

"Talk about losing your luggage. How did that happen?"

"Well, I'm not your only new cousin. There's another one. Her name is Maggie. She inherited a cabin Lachlan owned in the Smokey Mountains. When they couldn't find me, they sent the trunk containing Lachlan's journals to her."

"More family? I love this! So, have you met her? Do we like her?"

Cailean grinned at the phrasing. "We like her."

"Oh, this is so cool. Is she still in North Carolina?"

"Actually, when I got your message, I thought it was from her at first. I begged her to come with me, but she's got some, well, loose ends to tie up."

"I know the feeling. As wonderful as it is to find out you had some crazy old relative who died and left you a mountain in Scotland, it's an amazingly complicated ordeal to sort out. Wait a minute." She frowned. "I get a mountain, she gets a cabin and all you get is a lousy trunk full of old diaries?"

"It's okay," Cailean assured her. "Actually, I think I got exactly what I needed to get. It all ties in." She put her cracker down. "There's more. It's complicated and sort of well, a little weird. Okay, a lot weird. You're probably going to think I'm nuts."

"No, I've seen nuts. Trust me, you're not it. So the journals are part of why you're here?"

Cailean nodded. "Lachlan spent most of his life researching what he called the Legend MacKinnon."

Delaney interrupted. "So the meeting with Mr. MacKinnon upstairs was no accidental bumping of elbows?"

"Actually, I had no idea he existed, or rather, still existed, until he found me. Lachlan's wife was a MacKinnon. He lost her when they were both young. He spent the rest of his life researching her history, and his—ours—and discovered what he believed is a curse that has lasted between our two clans for three hundred years."

Delaney dropped her roll. "A curse? Oh, this is better than stories around a campfire. And you believe it's real? What kind of curse?"

"Whenever MacKinnon and Claren descendants from the original clans have married, it has always turned to tragedy for one or the other or both." She explained her and Maggie's connections to the curse.

"Well, my mom was a Hainey," Delaney said, then her eyes went wide. "But, whoa, now this is really weird. My mom was adopted. So I guess it's possible she might have been a MacKinnon."

"You don't know?"

"I was too young. After my parents died, I went to live with a cousin from my mom's side of the family. We never really talked much about my background."

"Is anyone still living that would know?"

"No, but I have a some boxes of family papers and stuff. A bunch of it came from my parents' house and was stashed away. I never really wanted to look into it all. You know, move forward, don't tangle yourself up in the past. I kept it all, though. Maybe there's some reason for that."

"I think we just do what we have to. I've become a great believer in destiny. I feel like we've all been drawn here for a reason."

"What do you mean? Did you have some sort of 'vision' about all of this?"

Cailean sipped her tea then set her cup down. "Yes. The visions have become more intense lately, to the point that I couldn't ignore them. I had received word about my inheritance, but I was working on the project of my career and I didn't want to take the time to hunt the trunk down. But soon it became clear that if I wanted any peace of mind, I would have to."

"And then you met Maggie, found out you had a cousin."

"I'll tell you about her story later. She was also running, but for entirely different reasons. But she wasn't alone."

Delaney grinned now. "The plot thickens. Another man enters the picture?"

Despite her nerves, she almost smiled. "You do read situations well," she said. "Yes, a man. In fact, it's Rory's brother."

Delaney did a slight exaggerated shudder. "Now, that's too weird a coincidence."

"Oh, you haven't gotten to the weird part," Cailean assured her. "And it was no coincidence. That is what I meant by the destiny part. It's all tied up in the legend."

"The Legend MacKinnon. MacKinnon meaning these two guys. Maybe you'd better tell me more about this legend, or curse, or whatever it is. How does it involve me?"

"I'm not sure yet, except he left you the land and there's things about that you don't know about either. While I was still in North Carolina, I read all of Lachlan's journals and learned all about the curse. It started three hundred years ago, with three MacKinnon brothers."

Delaney was riveted as Cailean went on to explain the rest, including the three Claren sisters, ending with the cabin in North Carolina.

Delaney listened, completely enraptured.

"So, he apparently tracked down much of the property that was owned by Clarens at that time."

"Like my mountain here?"

"Yes. You own the land where the MacKinnons fought the Clarens for the last time."

"I need another pint." Delaney waved for the waitress and lifted her glass.

"When Duncan disappeared and didn't return, they betrothed the youngest son to Kaithren, who was said to be a far more powerful seer than her sister Edwyna. She was also rumored to be in cahoots with the faeries—"

"Did you say fairies?"

Cailean nodded.

"I've known cultures to believe in things just as fantastical. Why not, right? Makes a good legend."

Cailean was frankly amazed that Delaney was taking this all as well as she was, but that didn't mean she was truly believing it. Still, this was a better start than she could have hoped for. "Something happened between the two the night before their wedding. And Kaithren cast a curse on him and refused to marry him. A battle began in earnest then with the youngest son in the thick of it."

"What happened to them?"

"It was rumored that Kaithren fled to the faery world, but I know now that she was killed in the battle. The youngest son, Rory, survived."

Delaney grabbed her arm. "Did you say Rory?"

Cailean held Delaney's gaze firmly and nodded. "John Roderick MacKinnon, known as Rory, youngest son of Calum MacKinnon."

Delaney lifted her gaze pointedly to the ceiling then back to Cailean. "And the Rory presently upstairs? A descendant?"

This was the moment of truth. Cailean shook her head slowly.

Delaney stared at her. Then, very quietly, she said, "And the brother currently in North Carolina with Maggie? His name is . . . ?"

"Duncan." Cailean drew a breath. "Second son of Calum MacKinnon."

Her face paled and her eyes went wide. "You're not suggesting . . ."

"That's exactly what I'm saying."

"And Rory upstairs?" She slapped her palm on the table. "No way. He's as flesh and blood as they come."

"Well, Duncan is every bit as hot blooded and fleshed out, trust me. But Rory isn't a ghost."

"Ooookay."

"It turns out there is some truth to the rumors about Kaithren. I don't know the origins of her powers, but she did cast a curse on him."

Delaney slumped back in her chair.

Cailean smiled. "I know I'm asking you to take a lot in here, and much of it on faith. I think you should read the journals. They explain it better than I can. Maggie has them now. And you probably still think I'm nuts and I don't blame you, but, well, it's hard to refute the facts when they are living and breathing and inhabiting the bodies of some very realistic men."

"So Rory is . . . what?"

"Immortal."

Delaney let her head fall with a thunk to the table, drawing the attention of several diners around them. "Yeah, right. I knew that," came the muffled reply.

Cailean darted a gaze around, but there were no eyes on them now. "You must think I'm crazy."

Delaney was silent, then shook her head as she slowly lifted it. "No. I've met lunatics. They think they're logical and, in their twisted minds, they even think what they do has a rational, plausible explanation. But there's no doubting they're insane." She leaned back and blew out a breath. "You, on the other hand, are far too rational and sane to believe in something this fantastical . . . unless . . . unless . . ." She ran a hand over her short hair, making it stick up in all directions. "Unless it were true."

"I know this is a lot to take in. But wait until you read the journals before you make a final judgement. Please."

"Deal." Delaney seemed to relax a bit then. "What about Maggie? Does she know that . . . you know." She laughed again. "Christ, I can't even say it."

"That Duncan is a ghost? Yes, she knows." Now Cailean

smiled. "You have to meet her. She wasn't any happier about the situation than you are."

"And the two of them are . . . ?" She crossed her fingers.

Cailean nodded.

Delaney's suddenly went wide. "Oh! I just got it. About the mountain and Rory and his war comment. The land I inherited from Lachlan is—"

"Was, his. Yes. The Clarens defeated the MacKinnons that day and took their land and their castle."

"There's a castle? But the solicitor said it was just a mountain. He didn't mention any ruins or—"

"It's more complicated than that."

"Of course it is," Delaney agreed, though it was obvious she had no idea why. "So this is why he wants it back? Wait." She held up her hand. "Back up a little. Why did you come here?"

Cailean was relieved to see Delaney think like the strategist she was. She might not know it yet, but she believed. And she was just as involved as her two cousins. Cailean couldn't shake the feeling that this was all somehow preordained. "I wasn't planning to come to Scotland until I read his journals. Lachlan is convinced that there is a key to the curse." She explained about the Claren Key and Lachlan's belief in an actual key that would unlock the curse.

"So you took up his quest," Delaney said when she finished. "How did Rory find you?"

"I was at Lachlan's grave. He had himself buried in an ancient MacKinnon graveyard on what is now your property."

"And Rory?"

"Lives in the area as well."

"I guess he's really not happy about me being here then, huh? Or selling his heritage away."

"You could say that."

"And now the two of you are . . . ?"

Cailean felt her cheeks heat, which was ridiculous at this point. "Yes, we are."

"This is not a good pattern I see developing here. You of all people ought to recognize that. I mean, Maggie and Duncan, you and Rory, Clarens and MacKinnons—especially these MacKinnons. God, I'm open-minded, but even I can't believe I'm having this conversation."

"We're all here for a reason, Delaney. I am the key to all of this. If I can figure it out, maybe I can break Rory's curse, and mine too."

Delaney said nothing for a moment, then finally, "Does Rory know about his brother?"

"Yes. In fact, we were leaving for North Carolina when I got your message."

"Ah, so that explains the tension in the room when I showed up. I gather he's not too thrilled about waiting."

"No. But I was trying to convince him to stay. We need to stay here. I can feel it."

She fiddled with her napkin. "So, what can I do in all this?"

"I'm not sure. I just knew I had to meet you, see you, talk to you. I can't buy the land, Delaney. I don't have the money, either. But you can't sell it. I mean, to just anyone." She leaned forward and laid her hand over her cousin's. "Would you consider talking to Rory? He's never cared who owned the paper to the land, he has sort of different opinions on ownership and things like that. But I think he might change his mind now."

"After what went on upstairs you want me to offer to sell it to him?" She snorted.

"Please?"

Delaney scowled.

"Believe me. It will be just as humbling for him to admit he wants to own it in the eyes of the law as it will be for you to back down on your word and offer it to him."

"He has the money?"

Cailean nodded. "I don't think that is a problem for him. I don't know how long it would take to get his hands on it. I'm, uh, not sure of his banking methods."

Delaney opened her mouth to comment, then shut it again and slowly shook her head. "This is all starting to sink in now. I'm the truly crazy one." She laughed. "Okay. Maybe we can work something out."

Cailean beamed. "You won't be sorry, I promise."

"Don't make promises you don't know if you can keep," she warned, but she was smiling too. They sat in silence for a moment or two, then Delaney said, "You know, I'm not so sure I can just sell the land and walk away."

Alarmed, Cailean said, "What?"

"I mean, I *have* to sell it, I can't keep it, that's not what I mean. But I'm involved in this now, and I can't simply walk away and ask you to drop me a postcard and let me know how it all works out. I want to help you with the hunt. And I want to meet Maggie. We need to work on getting her over here. It makes sense, doesn't it? The three remaining Claren women? And Duncan, too. We have to reunite the brothers. Oh God, does he look like Rory?"

There was a sudden commotion at the door.

Cailean's heart stopped and a tingle crawled down her spine. This time it wasn't dread. It was pure unadulterated excitement.

"You be the judge," she said to Delaney, whose head had turned with the rest of the diners.

Maggie and Duncan burst past the poor desk clerk and invaded the restaurant.

Her cousin's eyes bulged. "Dear Lord have mercy," she breathed.

Grinning, Cailean got up from her chair. "Do they look like brothers to you?"

TWENTY-SIX

Rory heard the rumbling voice all the way upstairs and froze. *It couldn't be.*

"Duncan," he breathed.

His anger at the Claren women disappeared and emotion coursed through him, making his eyes burn and his heart clutch. He stormed to the door and took the stairs like a warrior descending to battle.

Only no battle lay in wait for him this time, except perhaps the battle for his composure. He was shaking so badly he almost tripped over his own feet as he skidded around the last landing. He felt laughter at his own clumsy idiocy bubble up in his throat and was startled by the sound. It was . . . joyous.

"Where is she, lad? Surely in a place this size it canno' be too hard to find one woman."

Rory found himself halting on the last step as his brother's voice boomed from the doorway just around the corner in front of him.

This was ridiculous, this . . . fear. Yes, it was fear. Absolute terror. She'd said he was a spirit, yet his brother sounded quite mortal. His beloved brother.

He stepped into the front parlor and had to brace his knees at the sight before him. Duncan, in his full kilted glory, stood in the doorway to the restaurant where he was presently terrifying the hostess. It brought a smile to his face. Spirit he might be, but he hadna changed so much.

There was a woman next to him that was no doubt Maggie Claren. She had the look of Mairi, she did. Eerie it was.

Duncan went to push past the young woman, who was well beyond speech at this point, when Rory finally found his voice. "Duncan." It was no shout. It was hardly more than a hoarse rasp of a word, but it was all he could manage. Yet his brother heard it.

Duncan stilled, then turned slowly. His expression turned from angry determination to stunned disbelief. "It canno' be," he whispered. He stared, as he took one step, then faltered to a stop. His voice broke. "Rory?"

His eyes swimming now, it was all Rory could do to nod.

A grin split his fierce features as Duncan let loose a war whoop that had several patrons scattering toward the door. It made Rory laugh. It was that exact moment he knew this was real. Better than real. This was goddamn fantastic.

"John Roderick MacKinnon!" The name rang from his brother's lips like a royal herald. Arms wide, he covered the distance between them.

Rory met him midway, wrapping his arms around his brother's shoulders. They held on, laughing while tears coursed unashamedly down their cheeks.

Duncan finally grabbed a fistful of Rory's hair and yanked him off. "Hardly enough fer yer enemies to take," he commented calmly, as if weeks, not centuries had passed since they'd spoken.

Rory laughed, choking on his tears, and retaliated with a hard right to Duncan's midsection. Pain sang up his arm.

He'd never felt anything so goddamn wonderful in his whole wretchedly long life.

"Enough for the likes o' you. Now let me go, or did ye intend tae snatch me bald headed?"

Duncan released him. "What in the devil are ye wearin', Rory MacKinnon? Where's yer plaid, mon?"

"I fear I've changed with the times. It's cold tending sheep in November wearin' naught but a skirt."

"A sheep farmer? Och, but I believe They have conspired a worse afterlife for you than even for me. What horrible thing did ye do tae earn such a wretched existence as that? Sheep." He laughed as he wiped his eyes, then clasped Rory in another hug. "Dear heaven what happened to ye, brother. Are ye haunting the mounds of Stonelachen?"

"I'm no spirit, Duncan." Rory stepped back and ran his gaze over his brother, drinking in the incredible sight. "Christ, ye look like yer goin' tae battle, Dunc. Dinna they let ye change yer kilt in heaven?"

"Ye incorrectly assume I ascended that high," he responded easily.

"Well, I doubted the devil would let ye out of hell on good behavior." Rory was having a hard time truly comprehending the sight before him. Despite his own supernatural state of being, he had a difficult time stretching his beliefs to the afterlife. Yet, here stood the proof. Sweet mercy.

Duncan's smile faded along with his. "How are ye here, Rory?"

" 'Tis a long story, brother."

"Time is no' something I have a tremendous lot of."

"Then we are in opposite places, brother, for time is all I have." Rory's attention was caught by the sight of Cailean. She had broken away from an animated discussion with her two cousins and was headed toward him.

Duncan followed Rory's gaze to Cailean and grunted. "I see ye've met the Claren witch."

Rory opened his mouth to defend Cailean, then shut it. The instinct to protect had been strong and instant. He shifted uncomfortably. It was one thing to pledge a bond between them privately, he wasn't so certain he was ready to proclaim the odd union to anyone else, most especially Duncan. "Aye, that I have," he answered, his attention still on Cailean. Her hair had somehow come unbraided. It struck him hard in the gut. He had flashing images of all that golden glory, spread on his pillow, sifting through his fingers, spread across his chest. She came to stand beside him.

"I see ye've more than met," Duncan observed quietly.

"We share a common purpose," Rory said evenly.

Cailean's skin had turned a delectable shade of pink, but he found himself silently applauding her for maintaining eye contact with Duncan. Not an easy task, even for him.

"Rory and I have met, yes," she said. "Several times in fact." Her gaze shifted to encompass Maggie, who'd come to stand beside him. Delaney stood just behind her. "You wouldn't have a problem with that, would you?"

Rory would have laughed if he'd thought he could escape his brother's quick retaliation.

"Ye think this is hilarious do ye, younger brother?"

Sharp as ever, Duncan was. "We might be able to work up a good argument over exactly who's the younger now."

Delaney stepped forward and held out her hand. "Nothing like being a fifth wheel. I'm Delaney Claren."

Duncan's eyes narrowed and he looked warily at her hand, then grunted when Maggie elbowed him in the side. He reached for Delaney's hand.

Rory's smile turned to a scowl. "I'd be careful with that one."

Delaney favored him with an even bigger smile, which Rory returned with a cool nod. "I only defend myself when pushed." She turned her charm on Duncan. "Be nice. I almost threw my back out with that one." She nodded at Rory.

Duncan looked suspiciously at her hand, then at Rory. "What did she do tae ye?"

Rory felt four pairs of eyes shift toward him. It mortified him, but he actually felt his cheeks darken.

Cailean rescued him by saying, "Rory, I don't believe you've met my other cousin. Maggie Claren, Rory MacKinnon."

"About whom I expect a full explanation later," Maggie said to her cousin. She smiled at Rory. "You have no idea how thrilled I am to meet you."

Rory could have kissed Cailean right on the spot for her timely intervention, which only unsettled him further. He didn't need a Claren to protect him. A partnership they shared, but he'd intended to control it. He now acknowledged that intent for the fantasy it was.

He scowled, but shook Maggie's hand. "Aye."

Duncan grunted and gave Delaney's hand a quick shake as well.

"There, now we've all made nice," Delaney said.

Maggie laughed. "Why don't we see if there is somewhere to sit and talk privately." She motioned with her eyes to the room behind them. The patrons all had their full attention glued to the little tableau in the doorway.

"Yes, why don't we," Cailean said quickly. "There's a small parlor across the foyer for hotel guests. The clerk said it's usually deserted this time of year."

In silent agreement, and to the not so silent dismay of the restaurant patrons, they moved to the empty parlor.

The petite Chippendale style settees and chairs looked like dollhouse furniture when compared to the MacKinnon men pacing around them.

Cailean, Maggie, and Delaney sat down as Duncan started a fire in the small fireplace.

"Now he feels better," Maggie said. This earned her a swift glare from Duncan, which Cailean noticed only deepened the adoring expression on her cousin's face. Uh oh, she thought. She'd known there was a strong attraction between them, but she feared it had gone much further than that.

And yet she could hardly criticize. She found her gaze straying to Rory, who was handing wood and kindling to his brother. Muscles that had been aching only hours before quivered quite deliciously. But it was the heart that dipped and fluttered in her chest that proved the real truth. No, she absolutely could not criticize when it came to matters of the heart.

"So," Delaney said brightly, "this is quite the reunion."

Maggie looked at Cailean. "Does she know?"

Cailean nodded as Delaney laughed. "She knows," Delaney said. "She's not sure why she believes, although when you look at those two, anything seems possible." She sighed lustily. "They just don't make men like that anymore." She turned her gaze back to her cousins. "So, what do we do next?"

"Lachlan left her the land that the MacKinnons and Clarens fought for," Cailean told Maggie. "Did you read the journals?"

"The ones that dealt the most with the time period. I brought those with me and read them on the plane." Her gaze darted away. "When I wasn't dealing with that one in a plane for the first time."

"We'll have to hear that tale," Delaney said, then caught Duncan glaring at them as he moved around the furniture. "Perhaps later," she said with a wink.

Duncan scowled then joined Rory by the windows.

Cailean turned Maggie's attention back to them. "Delaney has to sell the land."

"Oh no!"

Delaney winced at Maggie's instant horror. "I know, I

know, but I can't afford it. But I think we found a solution."

"What?" Maggie asked, immediately hopeful.

"Rory," Cailean said.

"He wants to buy it? That's great! Speaking of Rory, explain," Maggie said.

Cailean glanced at the brothers, both of whom had stepped to the other side of the small parlor and were deep in conversation. Her heart swelled at the emotions so clear on their faces as frequent hugs and back slaps, along with the occasional laugh punctuated their reunion.

"Kaithren cursed him," she said softly, then went on to explain the rest of the story. "I'm the key to the curse, Maggie," she finished. "All of it. His, mine, and the clans. We have to find the key Lachlan wrote about and figure out how to use it."

"I'm not sure what he thought it might be," Maggie said.

"Maybe some ancient tool the Claren Keys used back then, or some talisman." Cailean shook her head, feeling the familiar frustration taking over again. "I don't know. Neither does Rory. But I know it is up to us to find it. The fact that we are all here together, on the same ground where it all began, is proof enough that I am right."

"So, where do we search? Have you found any clues?"

Cailean looked to Delaney. She'd remained silent during the exchange, but it was clear she was just as riveted. She sent a quick glance at Rory and debated on how much to tell them.

She was saved the decision when Duncan let loose a thundering growl and turned on the cluster of women. "She claims to own Stonelachen?"

Delaney jumped. "Don't do that," she said, as Duncan stormed across the room toward her. "What in the blazes is Stonelachen?"

Duncan froze and sent a look over his shoulder to his

brother. "What madness is this? Did ye or did ye not just get done tellin' me that—"

"I didna get done tellin' ye anything," Rory said. "As usual, ye went stormin' off before I could finish."

"What is Stonelachen?" Delaney repeated. "Cailean?"

Cailean rose, her attention focused exclusively on Rory. "They all have to know."

"What of our promise, Cailean?"

There was complete silence in the room. "Our promise stands. We will do this together. But we need help."

"Duncan can help, if necessary. He knows her secrets even better than I. But I'll no' have them in Stonelachen, Cailean."

Cailean took the blow without flinching. She stood taller, her expression carefully smooth. "We have no choice, Rory. We are all part of the quest now. It must be that way." She held his gaze, ignoring all the eyes she could feel trained on them. "You will have to trust me."

Rory remained silent for some time, his gaze steady. "Trust is a commodity I have not afforded myself for quite some time." He briefly shifted his gaze to Duncan, then zeroed it back on her "I would lay down my life without hesitation, were it possible, for my brother. And for reasons even I am not certain of, I would likely do the same for you."

There was an audible gasp from Maggie. Cailean's heart began a hard, painful hammering in her chest.

"Rory,—" Delaney's speech was abruptly silenced with one raised hand from Rory.

"That may not be the trust you seek, but I'm afraid it is all I can offer you. I'm doin' my best, Cailean."

Shaken, Cailean took a moment to steady her voice. "We have no choice in this, Rory."

"We have spoken on choices before."

"I cannot give you proof, but I know that we will each play a part in the final resolution." She walked slowly, steadily toward him, shutting out the others in the room as surely as if she'd closed a door in their faces. "There have been Clarens in Stonelachen before."

"And tragedy befell the MacKinnons because of it."

"I survived it."

"You are a Key. And there is no proof that your intrusion won't result in more of the same."

"Intrusion? Is that how you view my visit there with you?" His eyes flared and her pulse sped up as if injected with a potent drug, still he did not answer. "If you cannot give me your trust, at least give me the truth. If you could reverse time, would you choose to have kept me from Stonelachen? Would you erase the time I spent there?"

"No." He'd said it clearly, without hesitation. That was something, she told herself. It was a start.

"I *am* the Key, Rory." She lifted her hand to his cheek, his eyes blazed into hers. "If we are to lift the curse, it is time for Stonelachen to welcome both Clarens and MacKinnons alike."

"Have you had a vision of this?" he asked.

She shook her head. "I haven't had a vision since the one in the graveyard, yet I know things. It's just there, in my head. Perhaps you were right. Perhaps I do have powers that extend beyond the sight. Perhaps I am the only one that can free you."

"I believe that you are. Just as I believe that we must do this alone."

"You are willing to bring Duncan into it."

"He is a MacKinnon. He knows Stonelachen already. He can pose no threat."

"You don't know that. We have no idea what forces are at work here. We would not all have been pulled here to simply break your curse."

"You were pulled here by a crazy old man who couldn't come to terms with the death of his wife."

Cailean dropped her hand. "Are you saying you don't

believe in the legend then? That you and you alone are the
sufferer here? What about your brother? Doesn't the mere
fact that he still haunts the earth tell you anything?"

Rory shut his eyes and dropped his chin. "I no longer
know what to think."

She framed his face with her palms. "Would you deny
your future descendants the freedom to love as they choose?
Would you choose to use me simply to gain your own
mortality and ignore the possibilities for the rest?"

He opened his eyes and looked deeply into hers. "Nay. I
canno'." He covered her hands with his. "We will do this as
you request."

Her heart swelled. "You have more trust in you than you
think."

"I would like nothing more than for that to be the
truth."

She went to move away, suddenly quite aware of their
little audience. Rory, however, had other ideas.

He pulled her into his arms and kissed her. It was neither hard, nor fast, but a deliberate, time-consuming seduction.

"Why?" was all she could manage when he ended the
kiss.

"I just needed to assure myself that I am not the only
prisoner here."

TWENTY-SEVEN

CAILEAN LOOKED UP from the journal she was rereading when the door to her hotel room opened quietly. She didn't have to look at the clock on the nightstand to know it was close to dawn.

"I didn't think you'd be awake," Rory said as he closed the door.

"I didn't think you were coming back tonight," she replied. Maggie and Duncan had decided to stay at the hotel for the night and Delaney had left for her hotel with a stack of Lachlan's journals. Rory and Duncan had left shortly after to go off alone and she hadn't known what to expect after that. He'd silently accepted the room key she'd handed him before leaving. "Did you enjoy your reunion with Duncan?"

"Aye." He started to speak, but then stopped and shook his head, a marveling smile crossing his lips. "Aye," he repeated more softly.

"I'm happy for you, Rory. I'm so glad they decided to come here."

Rory's smile widened. "Duncan's account of his first plane flight is not to be missed."

Cailean smiled. "Maggie visited me after you both left. Her account was also not to be missed."

"I can well imagine." He crossed the room and slipped out of his coat. "What are you up to there?" He nodded toward the journals in her lap.

Cailean felt a slow heat seep into her veins at the sight of him moving about the room. It was a dangerous thing, getting used to having him around. "Maggie and I were trying to figure out if perhaps we missed something Lachlan said about Stonelachen or the Key."

"Find anything?"

She shook her head. "If he knew about it, he didn't write it down in here. In fact, he says nothing about the land or the graveyard. He obviously spent a great deal of time tracking that down, but it doesn't show up at all."

Rory came to stand at the foot of the bed. "Odd, don't you think? For a man obsessed with recording every detail of his research?"

Cailean couldn't think. Rory was unbuttoning his shirt. His hair was damp from the constant drizzle outside and he just looked so damn sexy.

He looked up and caught her staring. "Something wrong?"

No, she thought. Not a thing. She managed to shake her head.

He paused, his hand on the next button. "Did you not mean for me to be here with you tonight?"

"I gave you the key, didn't I?"

He held her gaze for a long moment, then said, "Do you want me here, Cailean."

She closed the journal and laid it aside. "Yes."

His fingers resumed their task and Cailean's attention was held in rapt fascination as she watched him undress. In the dim lamplight he was nothing short of exquisite.

He didn't move away from the end of the narrow bed. "Your turn," he said.

She'd been naked with him already, unselfconsciously so. But this was different. This was . . . erotic. She discovered she liked it. A lot. There was a dark thrill in teasing him, taunting him.

She slowly unbuttoned the soft sleepshirt she wore. Not exactly a sexy peignoir, but you wouldn't know by his intensifying expression.

"You're a vision, you are." His voice was deep, dark and arousing. "You should be made love to under the moon and stars."

She thought of the mountaintop where they'd first made love and wondered what it would be like to make love with him under a summer moon. Pain pinched at her heart and she once again turned away from thoughts of the future. Right now the future was this night. This night was a certainty.

He reached down and gripped the covers, stripping them from the bed in one hard tug. He crawled onto the bed and straight up over her body. Her shirt disappeared under his hands and her head tilted back as he feasted at her breasts. She reached for him, pulling him to her, unable to wait. She slid down and wrapped her legs around his waist, pulling him insistently inside her, moving under him in a demanding rhythm.

"I do believe I will see stars after all," he said roughly, then took her hips and fulfilled every need she'd ever thought to have and few more she hadn't known about.

CAILEAN NESTLED AGAINST him, tucking her legs into his. She pressed her face to his chest and sighed as he stroked his fingers through her hair.

"I've wanted to do this since I first saw you," he said.

"You almost did," she said, the words muffled against his warm skin.

He actually chuckled and her throat tightened at the wonderfully warm sound.

"Not that, although it was a close second," he said. "I meant this." He dug his fingers deeper into her hair and massaged her scalp. "Your hair. It beckons me."

"You should have said something."

"One thing I've learned is patience." He continued his ministrations, sending tingles along her scalp and down her neck with each stroke. "Besides, I wanted it almost too badly."

Cailean lifted her head to look at him. "Is that such a bad thing?"

"Wanting? Needing? In most every case, yes."

"And this case?" She needed to hear him say it. Her heart was already dangling from a high precipice and she knew her hold was tentative at best. She wanted, needed, to hear she wasn't the only one hanging by a thread.

"In this case I had no choice."

Cailean tried not to tense, but she knew Rory sensed it. "Because you need me to reverse the spell?"

"Because I need you . . . period."

She wanted to revel in this, but the dark cloud that sent a shadow over her senses was getting harder and harder to ignore. Feelings of doom she didn't want to acknowledge were becoming stronger and she knew it wouldn't be long before she'd have to face them.

She closed her eyes, willing the darkness to the corners for one more night. Tomorrow they would all go to Stonelachen to begin their hunt for Lachlan's key. Once that quest was begun, she had a terrible feeling that the darkness would consume them both.

"What's wrong, Cailean? What do you see? We are partners, you must tell me."

She stiffened at his tone. "Is it simply the information you seek? Because my feelings aren't that conclusive. Partner."

He pulled her head back, not ungently, and lowered his face to hers. His eyes were black and fierce in the dim lighting. "That is not what I meant, and you know it. Partner isn't merely a word describing a business transaction. If you can think that after this night and what we just shared—"

"What did we share, Rory?"

"We are well and truly joined now, Cailean. There is no escaping it. Destiny? Fate? Perhaps. I do not know. I only know that for what time I have remaining, we will spend it together."

Her heart, flying high at his declaration of commitment, took a sharp dive as the final words sunk in. "Time remaining?"

"Until we reverse the curse."

"Your curse is immortality. If we reverse it, then you become mortal. To live out your days here, aging like the rest of us. You aren't that old, or weren't when she did this to you. You have many, many—" He quieted her with a finger to her lips.

"I've already lived my lifetime. Too many of them. Cailean, I am done here."

She sat up, horrified. "You can't be saying what I think you're saying." She scrambled from the bed, her heart pounding so hard she thought she might be sick or faint or both. "I won't let you do it, Rory. I won't." She pressed a fist to her mouth as her stomach wrenched.

He left the bed and came to her. She backed away, beating on his chest. "How could you do that?" she demanded. "How could you make me feel like this and tell me you feel bonded to me and—" She broke off, choking on a sob. She still fought him off. "I won't reverse it," she finally managed. "It would be like being an accessory to murder."

Rory dodged her flailing fists and pulled her to him. "Stop!" He tightened his arms around her. "Don't do this, Cailean, stop."

She didn't stop, she kept on, crying as if her heart were being torn into pieces. He'd done this to her. Shame rushed through Rory, as did anger, at himself, for being so cruelly thoughtless. He'd thought she understood.

Rory wrapped his arms more tightly around her and held on for dear life.

Dear life.

He pushed her into the corner, trapping her against him, his own eyes burning as the epiphany washed over him. Her pain was more than palpable—he felt it because he shared it.

"I didn't know," he said. "I didn't know." He repeated it over and over again as the fight slowly ran out of her. But the sobs and the pain did not. They continued in torrents that tore his own heart to shreds.

"I love you, Rory," she choked out. "How could you not have known?"

"Cailean," he said hoarsely. "I'm sorry, so sorry." Fear lanced through him. He'd known he had feelings for her, he'd known he was forming an attachment the likes of which he'd never allowed himself to feel. He'd known she was forming an attachment as well, but he'd thought she'd understood his plan from the beginning.

It stunned him once again, that this woman he held had given her heart. No trick, no ploy. And it was a gift he cherished.

"I won't do it." The words were beyond raw, as if dredged from the depths of hell. A hell he'd forced her to live through.

"You have to do it," he whispered. "Don't fight me anymore." He lifted her into his arms and carried her back to bed. He didn't give her a chance to escape. He slid down next to her, leaning against the headboard and pulled her into his lap.

He didn't say anything for a long time. He put all his efforts into soothing her, one gentle stroke at a time. He waited until her breaths were no longer hitching and her muscles had gone pliant.

Her quiet voice surprised and stilled him. "I know you didn't plan on this, Rory, plan on me."

"I don't want to leave you, Cailean. It will hurt me, too. I thought this was my price to pay. I didn't take into account the price you were paying." He tilted her chin. "I'm sorry, Cailean." He kissed her eyebrows and then her cheek. "I'm sorry."

"I won't apologize, Rory." She sat up and framed his face. "I've fallen in love with you, John Roderick MacKinnon. The one Claren on earth who should know better. I didn't delude myself into believing anything was going to come of it." She paused. "Okay, so maybe I'd begun to. And I suppose the more time we spent together, the more I'd have let myself do that. I knew it would hurt me, I knew it, but never did I think that you . . . that you . . ." Her eyes brimmed again and she couldn't get the words out.

"I've been here for so long," he began, knowing there was no way to make her truly understand. "I've known for so long that if I ever found the cure, that I'd—"

"But how? You can't just . . . just . . ."

"I never planned it all out, if that's what you mean." That wasn't entirely the truth. Early on, in his first century, he'd tried many times to end it, had schemed again and again for a way to trick destiny. "But I never had anything to regret leaving before and then when Duncan came back . . . well, the way just presented itself to me."

She sat up straight. "What are you talking about?"

"He only has a little more than a week left. When he returns to purgatory, if we've found the key by then, he said he'd take me with him."

There was no look of horror this time. Her face crumpled and his heart crumpled right along with it. "I didn't think about that. Of course you'd want to be with him, with . . . everyone. You'll be reunited with your clan. Of course you want to go with him."

She leaned back into his chest and his arms came around her naturally. "I'm the selfish one, lass. Och, what a great wreck we both are." He tilted her chin up and kissed her gently on the mouth. He felt his own eyes burn even as he smiled down at her. "Perhaps we were truly meant for each other. Who else would have us?"

A small smile hinted at the corners of her mouth as another tear tracked down her cheek.

"Ye make me feel as if the Lord himself has blessed me when ye smile at me, Cailean Claren." Her smile wobbled then, but he pressed it back into place with as gentle a kiss as he knew how to give. "Yer right, I do no' want to leave ye. I never thought of it as somethin' I had a choice over."

"Duncan, your father, your other brother, Alexander—Rory, I understand now. Your destiny—"

"I don't know what my destiny is," he said, kissing her again. He sighed deeply. "If I'd had yer mouth to kiss for all eternity, perhaps my immortal life wouldna hae been so much burden as pleasure."

"Rory—"

This time he stopped her with a shake of his head. "No decisions tonight. We'll begin the search tomorrow. When we find the key we'll talk of it then." He didn't tell her he had what might be considered prescient feelings of his own, feelings that had long told him that he'd die when his curse was reversed, that he'd have no actual choice in the matter. "We'll know more then." Dear God, he hoped.

Cailean seemed to accept that and he held her, stroking her hair until he felt the even rhythms of sleep in her breathing.

Staring down at her, curled so trustingly against him, he said in a soft whisper the words he hadn't thought fair to burden her with before. "I do love ye, Cailean. As much as a man like me is able." She sighed against his chest and he thought for an instant, she'd heard him. But she slept on.

"We'll find a way. Destiny be damned."

PART THREE

ALEXANDER

"The illimitable, silent, never-resting thing called Time, rolling, rushing on, swift, silent, like an all-embracing ocean-tide, on which . . . all the universe swim . . . like apparitions which are, *and then* are not. . . ."

—THOMAS CARLYLE,
SCOTTISH ESSAYIST

TWENTY-EIGHT

DELANEY CLAREN STEPPED cautiously into the small stone room. She turned on her flashlight and slowly scanned the walls and floor. Nothing. Again.

"Twelve down, twelve hundred to go," she muttered.

"You okay down there?" Maggie's voice echoed down the narrow passageway.

Delaney backed out of the room as Maggie's flashlight beam flickered toward her. "Fine. Another empty room."

Maggie stepped around the bend and aimed her beam under her chin. "Am I the only one who keeps expecting a vampire to pop out of one of these tombs, I mean rooms?"

Delaney laughed. Cailean had been right. They definitely liked Maggie Claren. "For me it's skeletons. I just know there's a dead body in here somewhere. And frankly, I've seen enough of those for one life."

Maggie smiled. "Don't let Cailean hear you say that. She made me swear not to touch anything if I happened to stumble across any bones. Like that's going to be a problem. They're all hers."

"She gave me the same lecture." They shared an exaggerated shudder, then laughed at themselves. "No luck?"

"All empty," Maggie reported. "Same for you?"

She nodded. "I know Cailean is convinced we'll find something in here, and I have to say, reading Lachlan's journals makes me feel like she might be on to something, but this is such a massive undertaking. This place is monstrous, with these endless passages connecting all over the place."

"I know, it's hard to take in, but when you imagine it full of people, with torchlight everywhere and well . . ." Maggie smiled wistfully, then laughed. "I'm sure I'm romanticizing it grossly."

Gross being the key word, Delaney wanted to say. She'd been in garrisons and fortresses in other parts of the world that equaled Stonelachen easily in terms of age. There was nothing romantic about poverty, disease, and filth. Maggie was most definitely wearing rose colored glasses, with really thick lenses. But Delaney wasn't going to be the one to yank them off.

"I think about the feasts they had in the great hall." Delaney recalled when they'd all stepped into the cavernous room and Rory and Duncan had lit the torches. She got goosebumps just thinking about it. Perhaps she had a little pink in her lenses too.

"Well," Delaney said, "I guess we'd better get back to it. We meet Cailean in the central passageway at three."

"I synchronized my watch," Maggie said, saluting with her flashlight. "We'll recon in two hours, captain."

Delaney smiled and saluted before turning back to her assigned wing. There was no logical layout to the castle, which made it both the perfect fortress, since no invading army could know where all the passageways led, and the most difficult to defend. She was glad she didn't have to work out a defensive strategy for this place. Hostage removal would be a real bitch.

Still, it was an awesome feat of nature and ancient engineering and she'd be lying if she said she wasn't completely fascinated by the whole thing.

She headed around the next bend, head still half in the past, and stopped short. "There's not supposed to be anything branching off of this." She tucked her flashlight under her arm and pulled out the map that Duncan and Rory had painstakingly drawn. Each person had a different map, with Rory and Duncan taking the quadrants with the most damage, trying to find ways around the smaller blockages to get to the rooms behind them.

She unfolded the map and held it against the wall with one hand, aiming her light at it with the other. "You are here," she intoned. She followed the beam past the room along the passageway she'd taken. "No Y in the road." According to the map, her passage should have continued curving around, with three more rooms—two on the right, one on the left—before connecting again to the main artery.

She let the map slide down as she aimed the beam down the unmarked passageway. "So what are you doing here?" It was entirely possible that Rory and Duncan had just gotten mixed up or forgotten it. There were so many levels and so many passages that, after all this time, it was pretty incredible how much they'd been able to recall. They may have missed a thing or two.

She walked a few yards and flashed her beam ahead, trying to see if there were any doorways or if it was a dead end. But the walls were smooth and solid and the light didn't penetrate far enough to determine the full extent of it.

She debated finishing her original search, checking in with Maggie, then coming back to check on this. She checked the glowing numerals on her watch. She really should continue as planned.

She went several more feet, half-hoping the beam of

light would reveal a stone wall dead ahead and put an end to the side trip. No stone wall. No rooms either.

She rounded one more bend. It widened out considerably, but still no rooms. No end to the passageway either. She walked a bit faster, flashing the beam of light back and forth so she didn't trip on loose rock. The passages weren't level, so she was moving up and down inside the mountain, with passageways above and beneath her at times, running every which direction as well and at times connecting with each other. Very confusing.

She rounded the next bend and skidded to a halt. "Holy, sh—" She swallowed the rest, along with her heart. Her toes dangled over the edge of what looked like a black abyss. Heart pounding, she flashed the light downward.

"Stairs," she breathed. This passage obviously connected with another lower passage, which would be included in another search. But wasn't this quadrant already in one of the lowest sections?

She stood there for another moment, then reluctantly turned to retrace her steps. She took two steps and stopped. *What was that sound?* She sat down on the top step so she could lean forward more without fear of pitching head first off the top riser. It sounded like wind blowing through trees, or, or . . .

"Water." Rushing water. An underground spring? Not surprising since the mountain was riddled with them. The MacKinnons had done a miraculous job of sealing off minor springs, or diverting them into other spring beds and harnessing the force of the water for power. From Rory and Duncan's descriptions, the engineering complexities achieved by such an ancient people boggled the mind.

Seeing as she was in a lower part of the castle, with these stairs leading lower still, it was likely that what she heard was the combined forces of several springs emptying out into the stream that led all the way out to Staffin Bay. If she could hear it this far away, then it had to be a pretty powerful flow, which tied into her theory perfectly.

She would have accepted that explanation, except for one thing. Rory had said the diverted springs had all been shunted toward the eastern side of the mountain, which was bayside. The problem was, she was in one of the lowest, westernmost parts of the castle.

She looked at her watch. "Damn." She'd spent more time here than she'd thought. As it was, even if she ran all the way back and skipped her assigned room checks, she'd be lucky to make it back in time.

She flickered her beam of light over the stairs one last time, then took the map out and drew in a rough sketch of the passageway, making a few quick notes about the stairwell. Duncan and Rory could probably explain it all.

She stood, dusting off her jeans, then froze. Cocking her head, she listened. Nothing. She knelt down and leaned out over the stairs. Still nothing. The sound of rushing water, or whatever it was, had stopped.

Okay, now was definitely the time to get out of here. She backed away from the edge and moved as quickly as she could back down the passageway. She rounded one bend, and then another. It hadn't seemed this long on the way in, she thought. She was the one who had lectured the group on the safety precaution of staying close to within shouting distance. She was beginning to wish she'd heeded her own advice a bit more closely.

She rounded another bend and sighed in frustration as her flashlight beam flickered over another long passageway. She could have sworn she'd only rounded three bends.

"Stay calm." She was trained to handle all types of high voltage scenarios, she could certainly handle one walk down a creepy castle hallway. There was no doubt that the gang had all reconvened by now and was worrying about her. Worst case, she reassured herself, was that

Duncan and Rory would backtrack along her route looking for her and realize they'd left off this passageway and come looking for her. She'd have to suffer an annoying lecture from both of them, but at the moment, it seemed a small price to pay.

She rounded what absolutely had to be the last bend in the passageway and came to a dead halt.

"No. This can't be." Her heart pounded harder. She backed up a step and played her light over the solid stone wall in front of her.

A dead end? Impossible.

But that was exactly what she was facing.

She purposely took several seconds to breathe deeply. There had been no other passage, of that she was certain.

Maybe this wasn't a dead end, but a closed door. Maybe this was one of those moving stones. It would explain the sudden lack of sound. Perhaps what she'd heard had been wind, and not water, and the closing of the passageway had stopped the flow through of air.

Duncan and Rory had opened and closed several Druid doors during their initial descent into the castle, but her enthusiastic pleas for instructions had fallen on grudging ears. So, she'd watched closely, and she knew there had to be a hidden switch of some kind that triggered the door.

She slipped her backpack to the floor and trained her flashlight along the edges of the wall, ceiling, and floor. It was impossible to tell, however, if the stone was a separate thing. But she knew the triggers weren't obvious. She moved closer and began a slow methodical search for a sliver in the stone, an opening of any kind that she could fit her hand into.

After three painstakingly slow circuits of exploring every cranny in the stone wall as high as she could reach, and as low as the ground, she had come up empty.

She gave in to the obvious, even though she felt foolish,

and just pushed on it. Nothing. She moved her way methodically across the stone wall, pushing every several inches. Still nothing. Scowling, she braced her hands on her hips. "Open sesame." Nothing.

She sat down and dragged her pack over, then leaned back against the stone wall. She pulled out her map and went over it again, and again, but there was simply no way she'd gotten turned around or that the passage she'd entered, and was presently trapped in, was on that map.

Which left a moving stone wall as the answer.

But who had closed it?

Could Rory and Duncan have conspired to trap her in here? Could they have purposely left the passageway from her map, knowing she'd attempt at least a cursory exploration? And if they had nefarious plans in mind for her, what about the safety of Cailean and Maggie?

No. Her instincts shouted that loud and clear. She'd seen the four together. Duncan and Maggie weren't in the least reserved about their feelings for one another. The big Scot could barely be parted from her for any length of time. And Rory and Cailean, while far more circumspect, only had to be within shouting distance of each other to scorch anyone else in the vicinity with the tension that smoldered between them. No, she could not imagine the MacKinnon brothers harming either one of them.

Whereas Delaney held no such fond place in their hearts. In fact, as heiress of Stonelachen, she basically only presented an obstacle to them. Rory had made it bluntly clear that money, or the lack of it, was not the motivating factor behind his tough stand in negotiating a sale with her. It was all about pride with that one.

But was his pride so immense that he'd remove her from the equation entirely rather than come to an agreement on the purchase of the property?

A moment of guilt came over her. She should have just signed the deed over to the man. It was his heritage, and Duncan's, absolutely. She wasn't looking to profit from an inheritance she hadn't even known about or wanted. But pride was a strong motivating factor with her as well.

And maybe Clarens and MacKinnons were just destined to clash over this mountain of rock for all eternity.

She swore under her breath. She decided to wait where she was for at least another hour. She checked her watch. This would give the group enough time to know for certain that she was missing and to come looking for her. If she'd somehow accidentally opened or closed this passage on her own, maybe Duncan and Rory would remember its existence once they began retracing her route and open it back up. This was the high percentage plan.

THREE HOURS LATER, Delaney was forced to reconsider. She'd already tried shouting, but she doubted her voice would penetrate the stone wall.

She scooped up her backpack. She'd already made a message out of several pieces of notepaper and placed them strategically in the center of the passageway with small stones on them in case of a draft when the wall finally moved.

That done, she took a deep breath and switched her flashlight back on. She blinked at the beam of light, then slowly moved forward. This time she carefully played the beam up one side wall, across the ceiling and down the other side, taking slow, careful steps and examining every inch of stone along the way for any kind of sign, either for the trigger, or for another possible passageway that had opened and closed without her knowing about it.

Another hour passed before she made her way to the top of the stairs. There had been no surprises along the way. There was still no sound of rushing wind or water. Delaney played her light along the walls of the descending staircase, but saw nothing new.

"Well, Delaney, you get your wish," she murmured. She moved to one side of the stairwell and, using the wall for balance, she carefully began her descent into the lowest reaches of Stonelachen castle.

TWENTY-NINE

DELANEY DESCENDED THE final step and paused to take a deep breath. The stairs were so steeply pitched they'd felt almost vertical. They had plunged onward and onward, until she was thankful her flashlight grew dim so she could only see a few feet ahead at a time.

The thin beam was almost gone now. The stone wall was clammier, but not cold. She had to be far down inside the mountain at this point. It should be chillier, but while the air felt more humid, it wasn't cold.

She crouched and slid her backpack gratefully from her shoulders. She took out new batteries and carefully arranged them before switching off her flashlight. She made the exchange quickly, relieved when the bright beam of light filled the landing.

A solid wall of stone was yards ahead, but the edge of the beam caught the continuing passage to her left. This one was surprisingly large, more a round-shaped tunnel. Judging by that, and the humid air, she guessed it had been formed by water. She checked her watch. A long time had passed. Were they following? She turned back to the tunnel feeling very alone.

Enough, she scolded herself. Think of this as a grand adventure. As a child, she would have been enthralled by the opportunity to explore such a mystical place. It was her yearning for such far-flung adventure that had led her into the military as an eighteen-year-old. It was the most direct way for a girl from Kansas to see the world. And see the world she had.

She hadn't changed much from that little girl. She still liked adventures, especially if they landed her in the world's hotspots. She thrived on the action. It made her feel vital. Right now, however, despite finding herself in a place even her fantastical childhood imagination couldn't have conjured up, she was having a hard time working up that enthusiasm. She was tired, hungry, and concerned for the rest of her group. She felt anything but vital.

She was delaying the search for the key because of her own stupidity in wandering off. If this had been a mission and she was team leader, she'd have chewed her ass up one side and down the other for pulling such a bone-headed move. And she would deliver that ass-chewing lecture, just as soon as she found a good spot to set up a makeshift camp for the night. It wasn't going to be on this stone slab landing.

She paused long enough to pull a package of cheese crackers out of her pack as she moved forward through the tunnel. After two slight curves, it ended abruptly, as everything the MacKinnons built seemed wont to do. This time, however, her gasp wasn't in fear, but in wonder.

The tunnel stopped more than fifteen feet up from the floor of a giant cavern. Weak light filtered in from small slits and crevices in the rock ceiling. It was close to dusk, so it was likely that it would be even lighter by day.

Weaving through the center of the ballroom-size floor was a stream, around which grew an amazing festival of plants, lichens, and moss that, even in the dim lighting, were brilliantly green. A tumble of rocks had caused the formation of a large pond in the center. Gauging from the steam pockets she saw escaping from some of the rocks, the stream was at least partly fed by a thermal spring.

There was about a ten-foot drop if she lowered herself in a full stretch. The big problem being that once down there, getting back to the tunnel would be difficult at best, impossible at worst.

She stared at the pond, visually tracing the feeder streams. *Something is not right with this picture.* It was as still as glass. Not all that unusual since the feeder streams were fairly narrow. But the feeder streams were flat as glass too. They should be moving, flowing, but all the water in the cavern appeared to be totally still.

She squinted again at the steam coming from the rocks and the trickles of water that ran down them. That water moved, but it wasn't enough to form the feeders on the cavern floor below, or to maintain such a large pool. Then she realized that the widest path down the rocks wasn't actually water . . . at least not at the moment. But it was evident that water often poured over that top rock. Not only was it still damp, but it was stained and permanently grooved by the natural flow of water.

And at the height of that top boulder, that water flow would have created quite a waterfall. A thundering one, in fact. The sound of rushing water she'd heard!

Delaney had to rub at the sudden wash of goosebumps on her arms. She noticed the water marks on the rock beds banking the streams, all much higher than the current water level. How do you shut off a waterfall? The same way you shut off a passageway, perhaps? With a Druid door?

She tried to see above the top of the boulder, but it was higher up than she was by quite a bit.

She had to climb those rocks and find the source of the waterfall. If it was a moving door, maybe she'd have some luck opening it. She took the time to write another message, and anchored it to the floor with the dead flashlight batteries.

She pulled her pack on, said a quick prayer, rolled to her belly and shimmied back over the edge until she hung by her fingertips. She glanced down, gauging the landing zone, inched over a bit to her left . . . and let go.

BY THE TIME she'd skirted the pond, it was full dark. She'd have to wait until morning to climb the rocks. She decided to reconnoiter the cavern floor instead. There might be a passageway she hadn't been able to see from her perch at the end of the tunnel.

Two hours later, she was exhausted and trying not to feel discouraged. The streams that she'd tracked each disappeared into a gouge in the rocks at some point. She flashed her light around in front of her, debating the best place to make a bed for the night, when she saw it.

She trained her beam on the jutting edge of something wooden. A crate? She moved closer and realized that the boulder in front of her actually curved inward, leaving a gap big enough for a person to move through. She walked around that curve and gasped. It was a crate all right. One of several dozen. Some were wooden, the rest metal. All modern. She played her beam over the writing on the side of the one closest to her. It was in Arabic.

"Wonderful." She had a sick feeling she knew exactly what was in these crates. She raised her eyebrows at the international kaleidoscope of languages she discovered. Whoever was amassing these didn't play favorites when making his—or her—purchases.

"Bingo," she said softly as she spied the American flag. She'd understood most of the labeling she'd read so far, but none of it had been conclusive until now. "U.S. Army," she read. Followed by a code number she knew well.

"An international black-market arms dealer, holed up in

a castle in Scotland?" It made no sense. Or maybe it made
perfect sense. Scotland wasn't on any of the United Nations
hot zone lists, nor did it show up on any Interpol lists in
terms of terrorist harbors. But this locale definitely had
some geographic plusses. Its close proximity to Northern
Ireland for one.

"Figures," she sighed in disgust. She'd come into this
marvelous, intriguing inheritance and had hacked time out
of her schedule to come and see it . . . and her job followed her anyway.

She was honor-bound, for several reasons, to check into
this more extensively. Not the least of which was that this
was her property! It also occurred to her that if the government, or worse, the media, somehow discovered that an
American antiterrorist specialist was found to be stockpil-
ing black market arms on land she owned in Britain, well,
this would not be a good thing. She had to handle this
with utmost caution.

"Lovely," she said sarcastically. "Simply lovely." She
cleared out of the gun nest and moved back around the
pool and made camp behind an outcropping of rock. She
was fairly certain she was alone, but there was no point in
being obvious in case Mr. Arms Dealer decided to show up
while she slept.

THE SOUND OF heavy panting roused her. The wet
tongue scraping her cheek startled her eyes open. But it
was the sound of a gun being cocked that brought her to
full alert status. She would have scrambled back and sat up,
but the muzzle pressing against her temple encouraged her
to remain still. The two-ton dog pressing her flat on her
back, baring his teeth in her face was another good reason
to remain put.

"Who are you?" came the rough demand. The speaker
was just out of range of her peripheral vision. And the

lighting, which indicated it was past dawn, was still weak enough to keep the immediate area in shadows.

"Your dog has lousy breath," she said carefully.

"He likes you," came the flat reply. "Can't y' tell?"

The accent was light, but distinctly Scottish.

"I like him, too. But I make it a rule not to French kiss on the first date."

The dog cocked his head at her voice, his tongue eventually lolling out of the side of his mouth. Drool splattered on her face.

"Balgaire, down," he commanded easily, but nudged the gun harder against her temple. "Move, and we'll end this date without a goodnight kiss."

The dog lumbered off her body, bruising at least half of her internal organs while doing so. "That's no dog," she said, grimacing as the last paw pressed against her lower abdomen, "that's a small horse."

"He's sensitive, thinks of himself as a lapdog, so watch what you say."

Delaney's heart was finally crawling back down from her throat. She was beginning to think clearly, so she shouldn't have been amused by his dry banter.

"Who are you?" he said sharply, nudging her again.

"A lost soul." She strained to see him, but he was a shadow. "Who are you?"

"Someone who doesn't take kindly to trespassers."

"Well, see, this is where we might have a problem."

"Not we, lass, you." He shifted further to the rear, sliding the muzzle of the gun to just behind her ear. "Put your hands on top of your head and sit up. Slowly."

He knew something about taking prisoners, she noted. She carefully did as he asked. Sitting provided her a broader range of opportunities. She went to curl her legs under but he nudged her again.

"Legs straight out in front of you. Heels on floor, toes to the ceiling."

Okay, so he knew more than just a little about taking prisoners.

He leaned in closer. She could feel his breath on her hair. "Your name."

"Is not something I offer up freely. Of course, in the spirit of sharing, I might be moved to be a bit more generous. You are . . .?"

"This place you trespass on belongs to me."

"Oh? When did you purchase it? From whom? Because I happen to know the owner. And it isn't you."

There was a pause. Good, she had him thinking.

"How did you enter the cavern?"

"Is there more than one entrance?"

"Enough word games!" He jerked her to her feet and pushed her, face first against the boulder. He pressed his mouth to her ear; the gun was pressed slightly lower. "Tell me who you are, who this supposed owner is, and how you entered the cavern." He held her hands above her head in one giant fist; one of her cheeks was pressed hard against the damp stone. His body—much taller and broader than hers—covered her almost completely.

"Or I will simply put a bullet through your head and toss you into the sea." He slid the muzzle of the gun down the side of her neck and propped it under her chin. "Your choice," he said, his voice dangerously silky.

"Delaney," she managed.

"Good decision."

She grudgingly admitted he was good, damn good.

She'd simply have to be better.

"Who is the owner you spoke of?"

"At the moment, I am."

That got her the break she needed.

He rolled her to her back, her hands still gripped in his, his body still trapping her against the stone. But her knees were free now. And she used one. Swiftly.

He had quick reflexes and her blow caught him in the

thigh, but his shift allowed her to duck and turn. Using his grip on her hands for leverage, she was able to use the force of her movement and his body to flip him. Unfortunately, he didn't let go of her hands and she went down on top of him.

She immediately somersaulted over his head and tried to leverage her way free once again. He would either have to drop the gun, or drop her hands. He let go of her hands. She continued her roll and as he swung the gun toward her, she executed a perfectly aimed kick and connected hard with his wrist. He grunted as the gun flew up and clattered into the rock tumble above their heads.

Both were quickly on their feet, circling the other as each looked for a weakness to exploit. She had a glaring one, her size. But she'd long ago learned to use it effectively. However, she didn't underestimate him. He was a big man, but he moved with a lithe grace that belied his size. She'd have to be quick. And accurate.

"Who sent you here?" he growled.

"I don't think you are in a position to demand anything at the moment."

"Think again," he said. "Balgaire, strike!"

Damn! She'd forgotten about the stupid dog.

She twisted in time to see the beast's massive body leap from the rocks overhead. She ducked his flying pounce, but wasn't able to regroup fast enough to evade her other opponent. He took her down with a bone-jarring, skin scraping tackle. Stars twinkled in her peripheral vision as he rolled her to her back and pinned her, hands on either side of her head. The dog stood over her, grinning and drooling on her, completing her humiliation.

"Retrieve," her captor commanded and the dog leapt effortlessly up the boulder pile. He was back seconds later with his master's gun. "Good lad."

"Yeah, a real wonder dog," she muttered.

Her unfortunate position did yield one benefit. She

could finally see his face. Well, sort of. He had dark hair that had been secured in a ponytail, but the front had come loose and hung in his face, preventing her from seeing him clearly.

She did see his grin. A quiver of recognition jolted her, but he spoke and the sensation fled.

"Don't let him hear y'. He'll gloat for weeks."

If she hadn't been so ticked off, she might have actually smiled back. It was hard to hate a guy who fought that well *and* respected his dog. But this was no time for professional admiration.

"If it hadn't been for the dog, I'd have taken you."

Surprisingly, he nodded. "I believe you might have. Someone trained you well."

He gave her little time to enjoy the compliment, as he transferred her hands into one of his and slipped his belt from his pants. He efficiently bound her hands and placed her back against a rock. He'd cleaned the drool-covered gun and trained it steadily on her as he sat back on his haunches. His hair still hung irritatingly forward, making her want to push it out of his face.

"Delaney. First name, or last?"

She stared at him for several long moments. "First."

"What are y' doin' down here? Who sent you?"

"Are there many people who know of this place? I was under the impression that Stonelachen guarded her secrets very closely."

That got his undivided attention. So, he hadn't just stumbled into this cave, unaware of the castle above it.

"What do you know of Stonelachen?" If she'd thought his voice cold before, it was downright frigid now.

"I own this place. I inherited it."

"No one can inherit Stonelachen." He straightened his shoulders, looking every bit as imperious as he sounded.

It all fell into place. Each hair on her body stood directly on end. "Let me see your face." She was unable to keep the words from wavering.

"Why?" But he was clearly unnerved.

"Show me your face."

Holding himself stiffly, he did as she asked.

"Holy mother of God." His face was sculpted differently, his mouth fuller, his forehead broader. But those eyes . . . "It's you. Alexander MacKinnon."

THIRTY

ALEXANDER FROZE. HOW could she know his name? He'd not told his true name to anyone in this time. But she knew Stonelachen, claimed to own it! And she knew him.

"What are you? Witch?" He had never been one to lend credence to the *sithiche,* until Edwyna had made a believer of him. He gave this one a wide berth.

As he moved back an inch or two, she also shifted and a beam of light caught her face, making him swallow hard.

"Faery eyes," he murmured. "Who sent you here?" This time the question was prompted from a different source. He no longer worried that one of the many men he'd dealt with over the last seven years had somehow traced him back to his lair. He had been supremely careful to build his arsenal as anonymously as he could. No one would ever surmise his true reasons for hoarding the weapons of the twentieth century.

But perhaps he'd been protecting himself against the wrong foe. There was only one person who knew where he was.

"Did Edwyna send you to me?"

He studied the sprite in front of him. She was faery. She had the gamine face, the lithe body . . . and those eyes that could not be of the natural world. She also fought like an underworld warrior.

In his seven years spent amassing weapons of destruction, he'd also studied everything he could find on the faery world. Edwyna had credited the faeries in helping her create the portal she'd tricked him into passing through. He'd hoped to divine the secret to open the portal back to his own time. He'd yet to find it.

But perhaps, it had found him. Perhaps this run he'd just completed was to be his last. Edwyna had claimed she'd tricked him for his own good, to save his life, his soul. Perhaps she'd realized her mistake and had sent this sprite to bring him back.

He would return gladly, but he would return triumphantly. He had planned for this every minute of the past seven years. Edwyna's clan would bear the brunt of the mistake she made in trying to spare him from the future she had seen.

"Edwyna is long dead," the faery proclaimed.

"She is perhaps long dead in this century, sprite, but she is very much alive in another time. You will show me the portal to it."

"I am no sprite," the faery said, heat coming into her eyes. Powerful, mesmerizing eyes. He pulled his gaze away, realizing that there may be powers there he would not be able to withstand. He certainly felt his control slip when he looked into them for any length of time.

"Explain yourself to me then. But you will show me to the portal. I have wasted too much time searching."

She studied him in silence. He began to grow uncomfortable as the quiet stretched around them. Was she weaving a spell? How else to explain the unsettled way her gaze made him feel? He'd stared down warriors, both in this time and in his own. They were men who would kill, and did, as easily as they breathed. Yet this one sprite challenged him, making him fight the temptation of a hasty retreat.

"How are you here, Alexander MacKinnon?"

Her sudden question caught him off guard. "You would know better than anyone. Edwyna sent me through the portal of time. She claimed to love me, wished to save me from death on the battlefield." He would have to be careful with this sprite. They were a tricky lot who craved war and enjoyed all its strategies. "Now it is time for my return. We are to wed."

"Oh, I don't think there will be a wedding."

His gaze narrowed. "What do you mean?" Could Edwyna know of his plan? Had she a way of spying on him from her place in the past? Had she sent faeries here before to spy on his actions and intents? He did not think so. Balgaire had a nose for intruders, no matter their origin or species.

"I can't send you back to your own time. I'm afraid you're stuck here."

"That cannot be," he demanded.

She shrugged. "Well, I can't say there isn't another way, but it's not with me. The only portal I came through was that tunnel up there."

He did not have to look away to see the passage she spoke of. "Impossible."

"If you travel back down the tunnel, you'll come to a set of very steep, wide stairs. Sound familiar?"

She had been in the tunnel. But he hadn't opened that door in five years. Calum had entrusted the knowledge of the secret cavern and its passage to the sea to his eldest son only after his betrothal to Edwyna. There was one lever in Calum's private council room, which was situated directly above the tunnel door, and another in the cavern itself, in one of the many catacombs. It was in those catacombs he'd hidden all but the most recent cache of armaments, sealing each one shut from the water that filled the cavern when he was gone. And Calum's council room was in a section of the castle that was now inaccessible due to rock fall. Unless someone had cleared it in the last five years. He hadn't been in the castle in that time.

Stonelachen had kept her secrets well these past three hundred years. Waiting, waiting for him to find his way back and change the bloody treachery she did not deserve. But it was clear now that someone had indeed discovered at least some of her secrets. "If you're not sent from the underworld by Edwyna, then how did you discover Stonelachen and the passageway to the cavern?"

"I told you, I inherited it."

"This land has been the legal property of many, but not one has discovered her."

"I had help."

Just then the bristly tan hairs on Balgaire's massive back lifted, a low growl rumbled from his throat. "What is it, lad?" The dog maintained his stance; his gaze intent on the upper tunnel. He was a massive shaggy beast, a deerhound whose origins Alexander knew not. He'd been but a pup when he'd made the leap through time along with his master. Alexander had come to be grateful for the animal's companionship and his innate ability to serve and protect.

If Balgaire sensed something was wrong, it usually was. Alexander didn't waste time. He hauled Delaney to her feet by her elbow and pulled her along. "This way. Come."

"Like I have a choice?" After stumbling once, she kept up with him as he moved swiftly around the boulders and into a catacomb.

"I never even saw this last night."

"They're not designed for easy detection."

Balgaire loped in behind them.

"Guard," Alexander commanded. The dog dutifully sat at the entrance, nose to the air, gaze searching the area.

"Spooky beast," she said as he pulled her deeper in.

"He is rewarded well for his service. In many ways, dogs make better compatriots than men."

"That's a cynical view. Especially for a Scot, and a clan chief at that."

He stopped short and pushed her up against the wall, his face inches from hers. "What do you know of my past?"

"I know that if you treat your compatriots as well as you treat your dog, you will earn their loyalty and respect. A loyal man will lay his life down for you."

"And what do you know of loyalty, little warrior? Have you tricked men into declaring fealty to you? Have you coerced them into giving their lives so you may go on to lure others with those fey eyes of yours?"

"I said nothing of trickery. I spoke of respect." She didn't struggle under his grasp, nor did she seem to have any trouble holding his gaze. "Perhaps that is why you must rely on a dog for a companion."

"I don't see anyone flanking your side."

She had no answer to that. Instead of enjoying the taste of victory, he found himself wondering about the taste of her mouth. He yanked away from her and shoved her in front of him. Trickery.

"Where are we going? What are you afraid of?"

"We are going where I can keep a better eye on you. And I am afraid of nothing." Alexander had been stunned to find anyone in his cavern, but Balgaire had known immediately after he'd returned from securing his boat that someone had invaded his sanctuary.

As shocking as the discovery had been, he didn't think anyone else had breached the lower sanctum. Until, perhaps now. He hadn't forgotten her words just before the dog's warning growl. She'd had help finding this place.

He kept them moving around another tight bend, then another, then pushed her into a small alcove. "Sit." He pushed as he commanded and she complied with no resistance. Wise, that one. She knew when to fight and had the patience to wait for her moment. His throbbing shoulder and wrist were constant reminders of her agility.

He lit a small kerosene lantern and sat on an empty wooden crate. The room was small, with a narrow rug, a crudely built table and the crate he sat on. There was another room behind this one with a narrow connecting passage that he slept in when he was here, which was only very briefly between voyages.

He laid his gun on the table and faced her. She sat against the wall, several yards from his feet. If her arms or hands hurt from being bound behind her back, she didn't show it in any way. Her cheek was raw, but there was no blood. She had borne his brutish behavior without a cry or a tear. She held his gaze easily, as if she were his equal, not his captive.

She was an underworld warrior for certain. No one else could have found Stonelachen, much less the cavern. Was he to be invaded with bluidy *sithiche*? "Who helped you?"

"My cousins," she responded.

Faery kin kept close ranks. "They know where you are?"

"What are you planning to do with the guns?"

Her question surprised him, but he managed to keep his expression even. "What guns?"

She nodded to the empty crate he sat on. "The ones that were inside that crate. The ones you have stashed amongst these little rooms. It's a dangerous game you're playing, you know, buying from the right and from the left. But then, you didn't plan on being here long enough to get caught in the middle did you? What is your plan, Alexander? To go back to your time and wage war with twentieth century weapons?"

He stood, shoving the crate back. "You say you are not faery, but you have the knowledge of a *sithiche*."

"No, I have the knowledge of terrorists. And that is what you will be if you do this."

"I come from a time of warriors, and a warrior uses

whatever tools he can find to defeat his foes. The battle goes to the most cunning. Edwyna made a tactical error and she and her clan will pay the consequences."

"You seem to have forgotten one small detail," she said. "How are you going to return? And how will you bring your pile of guns with you?"

He towered over her. "You will show me."

"How many times do I have to tell you? I am a twentieth century woman whose great uncle left her a pile of rocks in Scotland. In those rocks I found Stonelachen."

"With your cousins," he said skeptically. "You of the amethyst eyes are no more mortal than Edwyna. I will not be tricked again."

Delaney eyed Alexander. At any other time in her life, she would have been convinced she was dealing with a delusional psychopath. It said much for the experiences of the past few days that she knew him to be anything but. She was still stunned by the reality of his presence, but after reading the journals, she had no doubt he was Alexander MacKinnon. Born in sixteen-something. She stifled a shiver.

Her gut told her to convince him of who she really was and take him to his brothers. But she wasn't an idiot. She had to look at the big picture. He had every intention of going back and kicking Claren butt. And he might well decide to begin with hers. What if the key her cousins and his brothers were presently looking for ended up unlocking this portal he spoke of? What if he talked Duncan and Rory into going back with him? And what of Maggie and Cailean then? For that matter, if the MacKinnon brothers went back and changed history, would she and her cousins even exist?

She had no idea what rules of nature he was playing with or what was best. Should she allow him to believe she was indeed a faery and lead him on a wild goose chase to buy time? Or did she reunite him with his brothers and pray the portal never opened again?

She was saved making an immediate decision when Balgaire's ringing bark echoed down the passageway.

"Stay put." He grabbed his gun and left the room.

Delaney immediately rolled to her knees and stood up. If she could find a weapon, she might at least buy some time to think through a rational plan. First she needed to get this damn belt off her wrists. She moved quickly around the room, looking for his food stash.

"Aha," she breathed quietly, as she spied the two crates in the corner. She could hardly see the contents since the corner was deep in the shadows, but she spied the bottle of oil easily. She cast a quick look at the doorway. Alexander could return any moment. She turned and knelt with her back to the box and leaned back until her fingers grasped the long neck of the bottle. She moved to the table, then laid the bottle down with the cap hanging over the edge, keeping her eyes trained on the door as she unscrewed the lid. The oil would ruin her clothes, but it was a small price to pay for freedom.

The oil ran over her wrists and the leather, which she began working immediately. Her wrists were already chafed but she worked at the bindings heedless of the scrapes and the mess she was making. "Bingo." One wrist slid free and the belt fell to the floor. She immediately ran for the passage, but saw Alexander's looming shadow indicating his return.

"Damn." She spun around and spied the small door at the back of the chamber. She darted around the table and the oil slick on the floor and dashed into the dark passageway beyond just as Alexander strode in.

His roar filled the small room and filled her with no small amount of trepidation. She ducked around the narrow bend as she heard him pounding down behind her.

The passage ended around the next corner. There was a

room on either side. She dove left, hoping for another way out, but it was pitch black and she struck her shin on something big and hard. She swallowed the curse and ran her still slick hands over the object, hoping against hope it was a crate filled with guns.

"Delaney! You will not escape me!"

She started at the nearness of his voice, but stayed on task. The object was a table, or felt like one. Nothing was on the surface. She limped forward, hands out to protect herself in the total darkness and ventured deeper into the room, hoping he searched the other room first.

Her hands met air, but her shins met metal. She pitched forward before she could catch herself and landed with a thud on what felt like a padded slab of stone.

Alexander, who obviously knew the maze of rooms far better than she did, entered the room right after her. He had grabbed the kerosene lantern, which he hung on a peg by the door. A doorway he more than filled.

Delaney darted a look around the room but quickly saw there was no way out but the one presently blocked with about two hundred pounds of very angry male.

She looked down and found she was indeed sitting on a padded slab of stone. His bed? She looked back at him and tried to will her heart to slow down and get out of her throat. "Not exactly a Posturepedic. This can't be good for your back."

" 'Tis no' my bed, but Balgaire's."

His pronounced accent was an unexpected but pleasant surprise. The glint in his eyes as he closed the distance between them was not.

"Well, since I'm in the doghouse, this seems apropos, don't you think?" She tried a smile.

He said nothing, just continued coming toward her.

She resisted the urge to crawl backward and plaster herself against the wall. "Speaking of the dog, what was the ruckus about?"

"He is barking up at the tunnel."

She worked to contain her elation. Duncan and Rory must have opened the door and found her note! "Shouldn't you be checking that out?"

"I will know who enters here soon enough, but I knew better than to trust you to do as I asked."

"Commanded," she corrected.

He stopped a foot away and lifted one brow. He'd pulled his hair back into the tight ponytail again, giving her a chance to really see him. He wasn't gorgeous, but he had that same striking intensity as his brothers. Brothers he would be meeting shortly.

"You must listen to me."

"I will do as I please, not as you direct. Stand."

"I have to explain things before they get here."

"Stand!"

She sighed in frustration and slid off the stone bed, stepping over the gunstocks she now saw piled on the floor, the same ones she'd struck her shin on. "Figures," she muttered. Uzis, she noted. MP-5s. And other assault weapons that had recently been introduced on the growing international arms black market. This guy meant business.

"You will show me this portal before your cousins arrive." He moved closer and took hold of her arm. "I will tolerate no more games."

She looked at his grip on her arm, then back up at him. "You know, it's a good thing I'm not a faery, because I could really get into turning you into a toad right about now. Or maybe a pig."

His eyes widened for a split second and his grip loosened a fraction. The laugh burst out of her before she could stop it.

"You almost bought that, didn't you? Damn, I should have just gone for it." He opened his mouth to argue and she impulsively reached up and covered his mouth with her hand. "Listen to me," she said, but faltered to a stop when his eyes flared again. There was no fear of faery magic in them this time. This look was purely mortal male reacting to mortal female.

His mouth was firm, but his lips were soft and warm against her oiled palm. The jolt of awareness that shot through her wasn't remotely unpleasant. He didn't move and when she lowered her hand, he didn't speak again either. But the loss of immediate contact with his mouth only made her more excruciatingly aware of his hand on her arm, his chest brushing against her shoulder.

"I'm no faery, Alexander," she said, surprised at the hoarseness in her throat. "Believe it."

"Ye are witch to be sure, Delaney." She watched with a combination of terror and anticipation as he slowly lowered his head toward hers.

No, she told herself, *this isn't appropriate. He's an arms dealer. He's a MacKinnon! Stop, move, duck.*

"Faery eyes," he said, "but the mouth of a sorceress." He brushed his lips against hers, making her gasp. "Dinna burn me with yer fey fires, Delaney, until I'm done kissin' ye."

Clarens were indeed doomed to be drawn to MacKinnons. "Dear God, the curse is real," she whispered shakily.

He paused and lifted his head just enough to look into her eyes. "Curse?"

"Between our clans."

He straightened and his eyes narrowed. "And what clan would that be?"

"You never asked my last name."

"Faeries have no surname."

"Mortals do. Mine is Claren."

THIRTY-ONE

"**B**LUIDY HELL." He searched her face. "Yer lying. Ye haven't the look of any Claren I've ever seen. What trickery does Edwyna think to play with me now?"

Delaney sighed. Enough was enough. She yanked her arm from his and before he could grab her, she stomped on the butt of one of the guns at her feet and snagged the other end when it flew up. She backed away and leveled the gun at him. A nice little MP-5. He had his gun too, of course, but hers was bigger . . . and way faster.

She motioned to his gun. "Drop that, please. And kick it toward me."

"Now why would I do that, lass?"

"If you don't think I know how to use this, think again. I could field strip this in the dark, one-handed. So put the gun down, and kick it away."

"You can put together a dozen of them in the dark, sprite, but they willna work too well without ammunition."

She didn't even glance at the gun. She knew it was weighted with ammunition. "Nice try."

He tossed his gun to the floor. "But if you think I believe you will shoot me, that is a nice try as well."

"Just ten minutes ago you believed I could turn you into a pig, so I'm not real worried." She had the pleasure of watching his face turn a very mottled shade of red.

"And I'm done with all this faery nonsense. My name is Delaney Claren. I was born in Kansas, in the United States, thirty-two years ago. I am not now, nor have I ever been, in cahoots with a dead woman or anyone from faery land."

"Yet you so easily believe I am Alexander MacKinnon? For a mortal woman born thirty-two years ago who can fieldstrip MP-5s one-handed in the dark, I find your gullibility a bit difficult to buy. If you'll forgive me for saying so." He offered no smile, but there was amusement in his eyes.

Damn the man, but she found herself stifling a smile of her own. The way he slipped in and out of the rhythms of modern speech also snagged her attention. "Let's just say yours isn't the first incredible tale I've come to believe in the last few days."

"Explain."

"You give orders very easily, too. As one would expect from the chief's oldest son. You would have made a fine chief yourself, I think."

His eyes flashed steel. "There is no 'would have,' Delaney Claren. I will be laird."

"Do you honestly believe you can return to your time and alter history? Do you have any idea what that would do? This isn't some game you're playing here."

"I am well aware of that, sprite."

"Stop calling me that."

"Sensitive about your size, are you?"

She hadn't meant to give him that particular weapon, it had just slipped out. "I think I have effectively proven that my size does not hinder me in any way."

He ran his gaze over her in ways that inventoried assets which had nothing to do with battle worthiness.

"Even if you find the portal, you cannot go back and change things."

"I care nothing for this time or its inhabitants. If I change the past, then what is affected is affected."

"Even if it means my birth might never happen?"

His gaze held such intensity, she knew nothing could change his long-awaited plan of redemption. "If that is to be so, then you will not know of it, as you will never have been."

She shook her head in disbelief. "You are so callous?"

"I am that honest. I am not going back to destroy the future, but if there is a way to change what happened to my clan, I have to do that."

"And what if your guns do not transport with you?"

"Then that is as it will be. I have to try. I have amassed more than armaments in my time here; I have gained knowledge as well. If I am to go alone, then I will at least fight beside my father and my brothers with a greater understanding of battles and strategies. If I am to die in battle, then I will die." He stepped closer until the narrow muzzle of the gun pressed directly into his chest. "But I cannot and will not sit here in exile and do nothing."

"There is more at stake than you know."

"It cannot be helped."

"Even if it means your brothers' happiness?"

Alexander felt the hairs on his nape rise. A certain dread filled him and it was only now that his instincts spoke loudly in her defense.

"You are truly not sent from Edwyna, are you."

She shook her head.

Crushing disappointment blew a wide hole in his gut. He hadn't realized how certain he'd been that his path home had been found until now. "Explain everything, Delaney."

She sighed in frustration. "I have been trying to."

He knocked the gun from her hand with a swift chop that had her eyes widening in shock. He gripped her arms and trapped her legs as he spun her toward the closest wall. "Never let your guard down, sprite."

She grumbled, but she did not fight him as he moved to trap her. He did not mistake her docility for acquiescence.

"Ye'd have made a valiant warrior for yer clan, Delaney. It is glad I am, I think, that I did not have to face you across a battlefield centuries ago." He released her, boxing her into a stone corner.

"Tell me your story, Delaney Claren."

She rubbed at her arms as she studied him and he felt a passing twinge for his rough handling. He was not normally a brute with women, but then, he had seen her as crafty faery warrior, as messenger and guide, he had not seen her as a woman.

At least not until that stunning moment when the temptation of her mouth had proven too much. And if that had not been faery trickery, then she was even more dangerous than he'd thought.

She did not speak right away. Wise one, she was indeed. Her mind was always working, never jumping into the fray without first weighing all the options, and weigh them swiftly she did. Had her Claren forebears been the same, this predicament he was in might never have occurred.

"Time's up." They were coming. And he would know precisely who "they" were so he could prepare. "Tell me why you came here, how you claim Stonelachen, and what it has to do with my brothers."

"Have you looked up the history of what happened to your clan beyond that final battle? Do you know why your clan fell?"

He had indeed researched his clan, but much of the documentation had fallen into the category of private family documents, which he could not lay his hands on. It seems the historians had forgotten the existence of his MacKinnon clan. The private documents had proven difficult to track, and he'd had other plans by then. "I know the Clarens defeated my clan in a massacre on the wedding day of their youngest daughter Kaithren to my youngest brother John Roderick."

"Yes, they did. You obviously know Edwyna was a seer, with claimed connections to the faeries. Well, as it turns out, Kaithren was even more powerful. She wanted Rory to profess his love for her. He told her what she wanted to hear, but she knew he lied and so she placed a curse on him."

"How do you know of all this?"

"My great uncle, Lachlan Claren, whom I never even knew, spent most of his life amassing the personal histories of the Clarens and MacKinnons. It was part of his legacy to his heirs, who turned out to be my two cousins and me.

"I've read his journals. It's all documented. You say Edwyna sent you through the portal to save you from dying on the battlefield, but the MacKinnons believed Edwyna had you killed. There were any number of myths about how she did so. Most of them revolved around the faery world. She was forced to go into hiding for her own safety. The MacKinnons would not agree to another betrothal with her. Her sister Mairi was betrothed to your brother Duncan instead. She also refused to marry. Perhaps she believed her sister's tales of destruction, perhaps she also would not marry without a promise of an enduring bond."

"The union between the Clarens and MacKinnons was not over something as contrived as the notion of love."

"The Claren sisters did not see it that way. They felt that without at least the promise of a true bond, the union would prove to be worthless."

"You canno' force the heart to love, Delaney Claren."

She nodded. "That is true. But then it might also be

true that without that bond, your clans were doomed anyway. Edwyna saw this, as did Kaithren."

"What happened to Duncan?"

"Duncan followed Mairi when she fled to America. They both died in the mountains of what is now North Carolina."

He swallowed hard. So far from home, his brother could not be resting in peace. His heart constricted. He'd only come to terms with the deaths of his family and clansmen because he truly believed that one day he would return to fight by their sides. His throat was tight as he asked, "And Rory?"

"Kaithren had lost both of her sisters. After Mairi's disappearance and death, Edwyna was found raped and murdered. The Clarens blamed the MacKinnons, the MacKinnons claimed innocence."

News of her slaying brought Alexander sorrow, not vengeance. "She did not deserve to die a brutal death. I never felt love for her, and my time here in exile has not bound her memory fondly to me. But she acted on what she saw as truth. For that she did not deserve murder, much less rape." It took him several long moments to pull his gaze away from hers, to pull his thoughts away from the solace that he found there. "Did Kaithren curse my brother to avenge Edwyna's death?"

"Partly. She must have believed, as her sisters did, that there needed to be a deeper bond. Rory told her what he thought she wanted to hear but she heard the lie."

"He wanted the clans united!"

"Understandable, but Kaithren didn't see it that way. She not only cursed him, she cursed their union at the altar. She had apparently told her clansmen of her decision beforehand and they were prepared for battle."

"For slaughter you mean!"

"Yes."

Her easy agreement gave him pause. "Not spoken as one who should be loyal to her clan."

"I didn't even know I had one until recently. As it is, my clan now consists of my two cousins and myself."

"And it is they who are here in Stonelachen with you?"

She nodded. "Kaithren's curse has extended through time. Every union between a Claren and MacKinnon has ended in tragedy. We are searching for the key to end it."

"The key? You mean a Claren Key, such as Edwyna?"

She shook her head. "Not that kind of key. Lachlan believed that there was some amulet or talisman that Edwyna and Kaithren used when they cast their curses. He had hopes that if he could find it, he could reverse the curse that has plagued the two clans for three hundred years."

"Edwyna used no talisman that I can recall. And these cousins of yours—are they men?"

"No. Women. The last of the original line."

Once again Alexander felt the chill, like air from an open crypt door, pass over him.

"They are not the only ones who have come back to Stonelachen to search for the key." She took a breath and held his gaze firmly. "Your brothers were both cursed, just as you were. Each in a different way."

He went completely still. "Explain yourself."

She told him of Duncan's purgatory and Rory's immortality.

Alexander could not take in the magnitude of what she was saying. "Rory— He's here?"

"Duncan, too."

He began to shake, so uncontrollable was his reaction to such stunning news. He whirled away from her, trying to assimilate what she was telling him. Then suspicion crept in. He turned and stormed toward her, trapping her deep in the corner, his body looming over hers. "God save yer soul if yer lyin' to me about this, Delaney Claren."

She held his gaze. "I do not lie to you, Alexander. Your

brothers are here. In fact, they should be coming down those blasted stairs as we speak."

"They dinna know of that passage," he said, almost more to himself than to her. He struggled mightily to make some rational sense of it all.

"So that explains why it wasn't on my map."

He hardly heard her for the thrumming of his blood, pulsing past his ears, filling his head, quickening his heart. He grabbed her as it all sank in. His eyes burned and his throat ached with a joyous disbelief he couldn't manage to express. It tumbled out in a fury of confusion and rage. "Why did ye no' tell me immediately?"

"You are planning to return to your time and wipe out my clan. I was afraid you would convince your brothers to go with you."

"Aye, and that I will!"

"Then you will break their hearts."

He laughed. It broke free from his chest in a wild burst. "My brothers' hearts are firmly with their clan. They will return with me whether I ask it of them or no'."

Why in hell was he standing here arguing with her? He released her and turned for the door. He was reaching for the lantern when she spoke.

"My cousins might convince them otherwise."

He was of a mind to ignore her. His brothers! Here! But something in her tone pulled his head around.

"And how would that be possible? You say Claren women are the curse of all MacKinnons. My brothers would most certainly not bring that on themselves."

"Cailean is a Claren Key, but that is not the power she wields over Rory."

"A Key?" He strode into the room. "Your cousin has the power?"

"She also has Rory's heart."

"Bah! She will guide us to the portal. We will return triumphant!"

"Her powers are rather limited. Nothing like her fore-bears. And Duncan's heart is firmly in the grasp of my other cousin Maggie. He saved Maggie's life.

"I guess I'm hoping that if they find the key that ends the curse, the rest will somehow fall into place. Happy endings for all." She looked to him, a surprisingly hopeful look on her face.

"A warrior who is a romantic?" he scoffed. "I wouldn't have thought it of you, Delaney."

"It is my heart that makes me such an effective warrior, Alexander. You would be wise to understand that."

Her gaze held his in a vise grip. He was at once deter-mined to break it, and loath to end this sudden connection he felt to this woman.

Balgaire began barking just then. Delirious ringing yaps that echoed through the catacombs into their chamber.

"They are here!" He spun around, but her hand was faster and she swung him back to her. Her face was as fierce as any opponent he had ever faced.

"We are here together for a reason," she said. "We are here to find the key and reverse the curse. If we don't succeed, our clans will never again have a chance for free-dom."

"I am my clan's only choice for freedom."

"Your clan consists of three men right now. You, Duncan, and Rory. My clan is three women. It is their bonds, and the bonds of all those that will come that must be the focus of our attention. The rest is past and cannot be changed." He tried to pull away but she held fast. "You played in matters of the heart once before and lost badly. Do not rush in and make the same mistakes again, Alexan-der."

"This is not a matter of hearts."

"Then you have learned nothing. Because that is all this is about."

THIRTY-TWO

UNLESS SHE WANTED to be left in the dark, Delaney had no choice but to follow him. Alexander's much longer legs and familiarity with the catacombs made it a challenge. Balgaire was still barking uproariously.

Delaney wished she could untie the knots currently twisting up her insides. She'd done a lot of thinking during that time in the hidden passageway yesterday, but it had only really fallen into place when she'd explained it out loud to Alexander. Now, with the added story of Alexander and Edwyna, the pattern was clear.

Her heart clutched as she studied the man who strode so purposefully in front of her. The Claren sisters and the MacKinnon men had all made mistakes three hundred years ago. Mistakes that had impacted generations for centuries. It was obvious to her, as she knew it would be obvious to Maggie and Cailean, that the MacKinnon men had been given a second chance for a reason. And their second chance was connected specifically to three modern Claren women. One of whom was her.

A hot rush of anticipation mixed in with the dread. It had not escaped her attention that in the boy-girl boy-girl grouping she found herself in, there remained one boy and one girl that were, as yet, unhyphenated. And there was no denying she'd felt something almost . . . unnatural back there when he'd brushed her lips with his. Call it fate, call it destiny. She definitely felt like part of a grand plan.

Alexander moved out of the last catacomb, into the open cavern. The tunnel opening was just visible.

Delaney moved beside him when he stopped. A gasp, then an awed curse issued softly from his lips. She looked up to see Duncan, Maggie, Rory, and Cailean, all standing at the abrupt ending of the tunnel above them.

The last of the Clarens and the last of the MacKinnons. Reunion. Confrontation. Fate. Destiny.

She put her hand on Alexander's arm, pulling his gaze reluctantly to hers for a brief moment.

"This truly is the last chance, Alexander. For all of us."

His gazed seared into hers. "I'll do what I must, Delaney."

"Then factor this into your decision making." Without thought as to the consequences, she grabbed his head and pulled his mouth down to where she could reach it. And she kissed him like she'd never kissed a man before. She was stunned herself by the power and emotions that poured from her as she moved her lips over his. His initial reaction was shock, but when he made no effort to pull away she held nothing back. A groan ripped out of him and he clutched her as fiercely as she held onto him.

His kiss was a raw, powerful thing that snatched her breath away and whatever was left of her common sense.

"Mortal you may well be, but you are in league with the *sidhe,* Delaney Claren," he said, breathless himself.

"I am not magician or sorcerer, faery or witch, Alexander. What I am is your destiny."

She had been the deciding factor between life and death more times and for more souls than she wanted to count. But in that moment, as she looked into his eyes, his taste still on her lips, she understood that this time, there were centuries of lives hanging in the balance. A sensation rippled through her, filling her with a certainty she couldn't quantify. She simply knew. That it was up to her to make him understand. Her and no other.

He said nothing. When he stepped away from her and turned to face his brothers, his future, the two feet that separated them might as well have been the distance from the earth to the moon.

"We've only just begun this battle, Alexander." When he strode into the cavern, she was right beside him.

ALEXANDER MOVED INTO open view just as Balgaire came bounding down from the rocks, his frantic barks ringing off the stone walls.

"Balgaire?" It was Duncan.

Hearing his brother's beloved voice made him stumble to a stop. "Aye, it is the ragged beast," he shouted out.

John Roderick, dear Rory, who had been barely a man last time he'd seen him, had already turned to lower himself to the cavern floor. He froze at the sound of Alexander's voice. Duncan's head shot up, his gaze pinning Alexander instantly.

Somehow he found the power and control to move forward, and then he was running. Duncan and Rory turned and dropped to the floor, heedless of the rock tumble. Both stumbled toward him in a mad scramble.

The three brothers were reunited in a giant grasping of strong arms beside the cavern pool.

Tears coursed down Alexander's cheeks unabated. "Dear sweet merciful God I never thought to see your faces again."

They all held on tight, crying, until Duncan began to chuckle. His laughter grew until he threw his head back and cut loose with the force of his joy. Alexander felt it fill him as well. Rory was pulled in until they were all laughing like loons. Duncan finally reared his head back and filled the cavern with the ringing sound of a war whoop.

Wiping away tears, filled with an indescribable joy, Alexander stood back and assessed his long-lost brothers. "Ye look like ye just left the field of battle, Duncan." He eyed him up and down. "And lost." At Duncan's laugh he fingered his youngest brother's jacket. "Rory here has at least adopted some civilization." His smile turned misty as he studied the miracles in front of him. "I'd no' believe it was true if I weren't seein' you with my own eyes."

Rory nodded. "Aye."

Delaney had said his youngest brother had been cursed with immortality, yet he didn't look the worse for his long journey on earth. Until you looked in his eyes, Alexander noted, with a pang. "Ye used to be the one with all the smiles, John Roderick," he said softly. "Has your lengthy stay here taken such a harsh toll?"

"You know of my curse?" he asked.

Alexander nodded. "Yours too, my brother," he said, turning to Duncan. His mouth kicked up in a smile, even as his eyes burned. "Though ye dinna look like any spirit I'd expect in the yonder world."

Balgaire loped up and nudged his head between Alexander's arm and his side.

"How are you here, Alexander?" Duncan asked. He reached out and gave the dog's scruffy head a good rub. "And why in hell did ye bring this bluidy beast with ye?"

"Which are you, ghost or immortal?" Rory asked.

"Neither. I am a traveler through time. Edwyna thought to save me from death on the battlefield. She foresaw the end of our clans and wanted to spare me."

"I dinna believe ye'd leave us if ye knew our final battle was pending," Duncan stated.

He shook his head. "She tricked me through a portal of time. Balgaire leaped through behind me." He gave the dog a pat on the head. "I've been thankful for his companionship these last seven years. At times I've felt like he was the only familiar being in a foreign land." His mouth tightened. "Even if this land is my home."

"Ye've been here seven years?" Rory asked, frowning. "In Stonelachen?"

Alexander nodded. "Though only for short stays. I haven't been up in Stonelachen proper in years. I've been busy making plans for my return to our time."

"I've been here off and on." Rory shook his head. "I canno' believe we both resided within her and knew not of the other's existence."

"Maybe you weren't meant to cross paths until now."

It was Delaney's voice. Alexander turned to see her standing just behind him. Rory scowled and Duncan simply stared at her. An amused smile kicked at the corners of Alexander's mouth. "I see ye've met one another."

Delaney shot him a look. "We have to talk. All of us." She held out her arm to encompass Maggie and Cailean.

Alexander grasped the arms of his brothers. "Aye, that we do." He saw Delaney's intent and had every intention himself of cutting her off before she could launch into her speech of destiny and fated hearts.

His lips still burned from her unexpected show of passion, and, och, the lass knew how to kiss a man. But he had to withstand the pull in his loins. His brothers' reactions to her gave him something to latch onto. Hope began to grow within him. His destiny lay on the other side of that portal, not in the arms of a twentieth century Claren lass.

However, his brothers' individual expressions as the two remaining Claren cousins joined them gave him a great deal of pause. Delaney spoke of hearts taken and happiness crushed, but he'd given her words no consequence. He knew his brothers, he knew their loyalties would ultimately lie with the clan and with him. Or he thought he had.

The honest emotion he saw on both men's faces rocked him. On top of the throes of emotions their reunion had wrought, this realization was almost too difficult to take. If he could withstand the power of a Claren woman, so could they. He would change their minds. He was their laird. They would do as he asked for that reason alone. That he was their blood brother would only cement their decision.

"I'd like you to meet my cousins," Delaney was saying.

"Edwyna," Alexander said in a stunned whisper, as he looked at the two women.

"Cailean," the tall blonde corrected as she stepped forward and offered her hand.

He shook it, but quickly broke contact. He could feel her power. It fairly vibrated around her. He didn't need Delaney's declaration to know she was indeed a Claren Key.

"The resemblance is striking, I understand." Her voice was steady and calm. That it soothed him in such a tumultuous moment proved she had dangerous magic indeed.

"She has the look of Kaithren as well," Rory said. "Or so I used to think." At Alexander's frown of disagreement, he added, "You never saw Kaithren as a woman grown, Alex. Take my word for it."

"I'm Maggie," said the smiling brunette. She held up her hand. "I know, I look like Mairi. It's okay, I'm getting used to it." She offered her hand to him, which he shook, even as he shook his head in bewilderment. "We haven't figured out where Delaney popped out on the tree," Maggie went on. "She doesn't look like any of the original Claren women as far as we can tell."

"He's convinced I'm in cahoots with the faery world," Delaney said with a grin.

Cailean rubbed her arms. "Edwyna claimed to have faery ties." She turned to Alexander. "How are you here?"

She asked the question so easily, her expression open and expectant. He looked between the women, and his brothers, and realized that they had already faced the shock of their unnatural existence. It was odd, but he felt truly at home for the first time in years.

Alexander took a steadying breath and explained the curse to both Claren women with Delaney filling in any details he'd omitted.

At the conclusion, Maggie and Cailean were both slack-jawed. Delaney nodded. "I know. It all fits now."

"What fits?" Alexander asked.

Surprisingly, it was Rory who answered. "There is a pattern to the curse." At Duncan and Alexander's frown of confusion, he elaborated. "We have all been doomed to some form of exile for failing to exhibit a true desire to bond with our original betrotheds."

"Bah!" Alexander replied, though he knew by the dread shifting in his chest that his brother spoke the truth.

"I tried to tell him," Delaney said, "but he wouldn't listen."

Cailean stepped forward and placed her hand on his arm. It was all Alexander could do not to yank his arm from her power-laden touch. "If you don't believe, we have no hope."

He did pull away then. He backed up several steps from the entire group, working hard to corral his control. He must convince them. *That* was their only hope.

"This is not about bonds forged between men and women, this is about bonds forged between clansmen," he said, struggling to keep his tone moderate. "I have spent my time in the future wisely. Delaney speaks the truth when she says we are here for a reason." He turned from her surprised look and directed his gaze toward the blonde witch. "She is our path back home," he said, pointing to Cailean. He turned to his brothers. "I have the means to win the final battle, to save our clan from destruction." Fervency crept into his voice. "We will go back brothers, and we will triumph over the Clarens once and for all!"

"No!" All three Claren women shouted in unison. The

suddenness of it made Balgaire bark. The ringing sound echoed through the cavern as they stared at one another in defiance.

Duncan stepped forward. "Surely this is not something we must decide right this very moment."

"It is not something we can let linger," Alexander said. "Your time here is limited, is it not?"

Duncan looked to Maggie. The bleakness was so clear in their eyes that Alexander felt his hopes slip another notch.

"Aye, that is true."

"Then we must find the portal before then. Once you return, history will change. Your trip to purgatory will never have taken place." He turned to Rory. "Your immortal soul will once again be inside your mortal body. All will be as it should have been three hundred years ago."

"No," Cailean said, looking horrified. "You cannot change history. It would wreak havoc on so many lives."

Alexander pinned her with a gaze. "How do you know that? If we return and avoid the curse that started this whole bluidy thing, perhaps all those tragic clan unions would end in happiness and prosperity. We could be rewriting history for the better."

Cailean shook her head, unswayed. "What is done is done. You can only affect your future. And that of every Claren and MacKinnon yet to come."

Alexander stepped forward. "Of which all are represented in this very space. If we return, who is to say that our clans would not have flourished throughout time?"

Rory stepped forward. "We have much to discuss. But it has been a long day for us all. We should ascend back into the castle and take the remainder of this day for ourselves." He looked at his brothers, a wet gleam in his eyes. "I never thought to see you again, Alex, and I have only just been reunited with Duncan. Surely we can take this one day to celebrate such a joyous miracle."

"Aye," Duncan echoed. "Give us this day, then we will sit and discuss what shall be done."

Alexander wanted to force the issue, to get it all decided right then. He had worked so hard, so single-mindedly, that now that the goal was within his grasp it was almost impossible to step back from it. He did want to rejoice with his brothers, but if he had his way, they'd have the rest of their lives to do so.

That snake in his gut told him that giving them any time would undermine his plan. He found his gaze drawn to Delaney without his will or consent. She was staring at him, the message in her haunting violet eyes clear.

He sighed and pulled his gaze back to the group. "Fine," he said. He was chastened further by the relieved expressions on everyone's face.

Duncan clapped his hands. "Good. Now, is there another way from here other than those bluidy stairs?"

"Speaking of those stairs, just how did you find me anyway?" Delaney asked. "Alexander said you didn't know about the passage."

"We didn't," Rory offered. "On our search yesterday, Duncan and I cleared the rubble and found our way to the council chambers. We found the door lever by accident, but didn't know the location of the door it operated. It wasn't until this morning that we discovered it."

"I must have gone in when you opened it," Delaney said, "and then couldn't get back out when you closed it."

Duncan turned to Alexander. "Why did you know of this and not us?"

"Calum told me on the eve of my wedding to Edwyna. I had not had a chance to even explore it. This cavern and the connecting passage had been constructed as a safeguard should Stonelachen be invaded. From here you can gain entrance to the sea."

"Impossible," Duncan said. "We are in the westernmost bowels of this mountain."

"There is another Druid door, up there." Alexander motioned to the large slab positioned above the top of the tumble of boulders. "It blocks a natural, spring-fed waterfall."

"Waterfall?" Rory looked up, as did the rest of the group.

"Aye. The spring beyond is fed by a much larger one. I have a boat docked there. If you know which streams to follow, you will find yourself emptying out into the sea just below Kilt Rock. There is a natural cave. You can only go out or come in on high tide."

"Why the moving door here? And the hidden lever for the passage door? How does it work from such a distance?"

"This door is to block the natural flow of water and allow entrance into the catacombs below. There are crevices in the rock that will allow the water to drain off. There is a swinging walkway from this boulder over to the tunnel end stowed in the tunnel behind the door. There is a side passage for safe travel along the stream. If you open the door fully, the water will flow faster than it can run off and will eventually fill up much of the cavern. With the bridge withdrawn, you could make your escape and your enemies could not follow. By the time the natural run off levels it out, you will be long gone."

"And what of the other door? The one atop the stairs?"

"There is a lever below, in the catacombs. It is directly below the door. I know not how they put it all in, but it works. Only a strong pair of lungs could reach it once the cavern is full. And the swimmer would have to know its exact location."

"Did Calum tell you of this, Duncan?" Rory asked of his brother.

Duncan shook his head.

"If we had been under serious threat of invasion, he would have told you," Alexander assured them. "He only told me because he didn't fully trust the Clarens. Once wedded to them, they would understandably gain fuller access to Stonelachen. He wanted me to be prepared for any eventuality. I don't know why he decided against telling you. Perhaps he didn't trust the weddings to take place."

"See, even Calum realized that marriage might not be enough to end the wars between you," Delaney said.

Alexander turned to her. "There is no certainty to any aspect of life, Delaney. He hoped the union would buy us time to build our strength. None of us truly believed the union alone would end our wars. It would be up to our leadership, our cunning, our—"

"Stupid male testosterone," Maggie put in. She threw up her hands. "Haven't you learned anything?"

"Apparently not," Delaney offered.

"Enough!" Alexander shouted. Even Duncan and Rory straightened. That heartened him only a little. He turned to find the Claren women all staring at him with their arms crossed over their chests.

A formidable lot. They could give their ancestors a run for certain. He shuddered at the very thought.

Delaney turned at the bump of Balgaire's shaggy head against her elbow. She stroked his neck making the dog groan and drool in foolish pleasure. Traitor, Alexander thought, even as he envied the disloyal beast her touch. He scowled.

Just then Delaney looked up and caught him staring at her hands, slowly moving through Balgaire's scraggly fur. There must have been something of the yearning he felt in his expression because she grinned audaciously at him and winked. Winked!

He was mortified to feel his cheeks darken. He had to get himself and his brothers away from the influence of these Claren women. It had been their downfall before and would be again, he was certain of it!

THIRTY-THREE

ONCE THEY'D REACHED the castle proper, it was late and they were all tired and hungry. It was decided that the brothers would bed down in the castle and the women would spend the night in the hotel in nearby Flodigarry, where Duncan, Maggie, and Delaney had taken rooms the day before. When they'd begun the search for the key, they had all decided it would be smarter if Duncan, Maggie, and Delaney relocated closer to the castle. Cailean had quietly moved her belongings into Rory's chambers.

For the night, however, the Claren cousins had decided to allow the brothers to reunite in private. Delaney had watched the couples' parting kisses and some of her concerns about this set-up abated. Duncan was open and lusty about his feelings for Maggie, whereas Rory and Cailean had that simmering-about-to-boil-over type passion arcing between them that was obvious to anyone with eyes in their head.

She'd kept her attention studiously averted from Alexander during the prolonged good-byes. Her feelings for him completely disconcerted her. The more she thought about it on their return trip, the more confused she'd become.

She'd also worried that leaving the brothers alone together was a tactical error. It would give Alexander all night to convince his brothers of his plan. There was no doubt that was his goal, and why he'd been the first to encourage the sleeping arrangements. She had caught his eye then. He'd boldly held her gaze like the clan chief he was, all but daring her to comment. She had held her tongue, but had played her own trump card by insisting that Cailean pack a bag and return with the other two women, to allow the brothers their reunion in complete privacy.

The tightening around Alexander's mouth had been signal enough that he'd understood her greater goal of keeping the Claren Key away from the MacKinnon brothers. Without Cailean, they would not likely find the portal on their own.

But upon witnessing their good-bye kisses and private whisperings, she'd also begun to think that Alexander might have a more difficult task set in front of him than he had thought, clan chief or not.

Now it was the following morning. The sun had made a stunning debut over Staffin Bay and the three cousins prepared to head back to Stonelachen.

Despite their wish to get an early start, Delaney had talked them into stoking up on a big breakfast first. "They'll still be there when we get back," she'd teased, but the two women had only mustered weak smiles.

Maggie slid a piece of toast from the crisps rack and crunched on it, her expression turning thoughtful. "Are you saying that you don't feel any, you know, electricity, between you and Alexander?"

On the trip down to Flodigarry, she'd told them about the guns and Alexander's plan, but they had been so exhausted she'd been spared talking about her feelings toward

Alexander. A good night's sleep hadn't rendered her any more ready to discuss him now. "Electricity?" she responded wryly. "We met when he was holding a gun to my head and his three hundred pound dog was drooling in my face."

"And you're holding that against him? Believe me, it's not hatred I see in his eyes. Frustration, yes. Lots of that." Maggie laughed. "But I've seen the way he looks at you when you aren't watching him. Which isn't often, you know."

Cailean smiled at that, but hid it by quickly taking a sip of her tea.

Delaney hadn't missed it. She dropped her head on folded arms. "It's true. I know I stare. I can't help it." She lifted her head and peered at them both, a grin curving her lips. "But did you get a look at those arms? And that backside? I mean, come on, I'm only human!" Her grin left her and her shoulders rounded a bit. She couldn't do this. Her cousin's smiles faded as well.

"What is it, Delaney?" Maggie asked.

She shrugged, hating the helplessness she felt. "It's hard to explain. I have always believed in the power of true love, real love, you know, soulmate stuff." She stopped, not sure where she was going, but knowing it would be better once she gave voice to it. "Okay, I joined the military when I was eighteen because I craved adventure as a child, and figured that was the best way to get it. I discovered I was a good strategist and I got into the terrorist aspect of things when I was invited to join a task force being implemented to look into ways of dealing with the growing concern. By the time my tour was up, I was hooked. I was helping people in the worst of circumstances. Bringing about some happy endings and getting adventure all wrapped into one. I went civilian because it gave me greater latitude." She took a breath and tried to organize her thoughts. "In all this time, I always felt like it would be my turn at some point. That true love would just knock on my door." A small smile came out. "Well, almost-love and wish-it-were-love came knocking a lot, but that one special, you-know-it-when-you-see-it love. It's silly, but I've just always known . . ." She trailed off, unable to explain.

Cailean laid her hand on her arm. "I understand all about unexplainable feelings."

"It's Alexander, isn't it," Maggie said in a hushed tone. "He's 'the one'?"

Delaney slapped the table, making them jump. "See, that's just it! He can't be 'the one.' Can't be. He makes me crazy. Not to mention the fact that he was born just a few years before me." She dropped her head to the table. "It makes no sense. I waited all this time for him?"

"Who said it was supposed to make sense?" Cailean said.

"Why did you crave adventure?" Maggie asked quietly.

Delaney lifted her head, frowning. "I'm not sure. Maybe because my parents were gone when I was so little, I was left to my own devices a lot. I was always creating wild, fantastical worlds."

Maggie grinned. "See? Now you have a real fantastical world. Maybe this makes more sense than you think."

"You've accepted us into your life fairly easily," Cailean said.

"Yeah, but you guys are flesh and blood normal."

Cailean rolled her eyes at that. "So you say." She grew serious. "You've accepted that we've all been brought together for a reason. A larger than life reason. Why not accept that maybe Alexander is going to play a role in that as well."

"Because I can deal with rescuing other people's lives and making the ending work out right. That's much safer than thinking about my own. I can't control that as much." She swallowed. "Nuts, huh? Handling terrorists is safer than handling my own life. What in the hell does that say about me?"

Maggie leaned forward. "It says you like to be in control and when you lose for someone else, it isn't as hard as when you lose for yourself."

"I hate to lose period," she said, scowling.

"Make-believe worlds and make-believe love are easier to believe in, to trust in," Cailean said.

"I certainly deal in real enough life! As real as it gets," Delaney shot back defensively.

"But that's an unreality of it's own, don't you think? Keeps you from doing the white picket fence thing." Her tone gentled. "The normal mom and dad thing."

She opened her mouth to argue, then stopped and leaned back in her chair. "Okay, maybe you're right. But it doesn't mean I'm ready to accept that my future is meant to be tied with a . . . to a . . ."

"Actually, I think he makes perfect sense for you," Maggie said, then raised a hand. "So it's not totally perfect, it would be nice if he were born in this century." She smiled and deflected Delaney's half-hearted smack. "But look at your backgrounds, your training, everything. Finding yourself attracted to him makes perfect sense. And it's obvious he's never met anyone like you."

Delaney scowled. "Attracted is one thing. It's the feeling that we're linked somehow, that it *has* to be him. I don't like it."

"And you think we did?" Cailean asked. "Your destiny is as intertwined with Alexander as mine is with Rory and Maggie's is with Duncan."

"What happens if I don't want it? Hell, maybe I don't know what I want or what is right for me. I'm thirty-two and single for Christ's sake."

"So? All three of us are single. It doesn't mean we're losers. We've all given a great deal of attention to our careers," Maggie said. "That doesn't mean we can't incorporate that into a fulfilling relationship and do the happily ever after thing if the right man came along."

Delaney snorted. "And these are the 'right men'? Come on! We should all run screaming for the hills."

"So why haven't we," Cailean said seriously.

"I hate it when you do that 'Key' thing. Gives me goosebumps."

Maggie shook her head. "It's not about 'is it normal and is it easy.' It's about whether you could walk away without trying. If you can walk away, then that's your answer right there. It's when you can't walk away that things get interesting. I know I might be in a no-win situation. Believe me, I'm terrified as much by never seeing Duncan again as I am about trying to make it work and failing. But the other alternative, to just walk away now, curse or no curse, is simply not an option. What I feel for him—" She broke off.

Delaney covered her hand. "I'm sorry, Maggie. I didn't mean to make you hash through all of this."

"It's okay. But do you understand? Am I supposed to ignore it because it's not what I imagined true love to be? How I feel, how he makes me feel, all of it, is so incredible, and so different than I've ever felt before. We both decided we'd rather have it for whatever time we can than not have it at all."

"I'm not sure we ever really have a choice when we meet someone who affects us like that," Cailean said quietly.

"You mean fate?" Delaney asked.

"Not exactly. Certainly we are all free to make the choice to follow our feelings or not." She looked at Delaney. "You could walk away right now and not look back. I believe we have many potential destinies depending on the choices we make as we go along. But there are some paths that will bring greater fulfillment than others.

"As to what you feel, well, it doesn't seem to matter if it's an inconvenient time to feel them. The right person comes along and bam, you feel it. You have a reaction like you've never had to another person. Time doesn't matter, place doesn't matter, propriety doesn't matter, nothing matters. You may not like it, but you can't change that, any more than you can make yourself feel something for someone just because he has come along at the right time, at the right place, and fits in perfectly."

"I'm not sure what my feelings are," Delaney said, even more confused.

"Well then, you'll have to decide if you want to find out," Cailean responded.

Delaney groaned. "You make it sound so easy."

Maggie and Cailean both laughed. "Oh yeah," Maggie said dryly. "Piece of cake."

Their food arrived and they all fell silent as they ate, each lost in her own thoughts. What did she feel for Alexander? It wasn't anything simple enough to put into words. They were finishing up when she spoke quietly. "He gets my attention. Like no man has ever gotten my full and undivided attention before." She stopped, but couldn't find any better way of putting it. "He drives me crazy, totally frustrates the hell out of me. I want to wring his neck every other second, but I can't take my eyes off of him. Or stop wondering what he's thinking, or what he will do, or say. Or if he'll ever kiss me again." Her cheeks flushed at that unplanned admission, but Maggie and Cailean simply smiled and nodded.

"We never said it was all bliss and birds singing," Maggie said. "It can be that and more, but all your emotions are engaged. Full scale chaos."

"Sounds like something you should get a shot for," Delaney muttered.

They paid their bill and were in the parking lot when Delaney spoke again. "Well, whatever happens, at least we'll have each other to hang on to. And that's already more than I've ever had before."

Maggie and Cailean agreed and they moved into a brief, tight embrace.

It was then that Delaney noticed Cailean looked a bit paler than she had moments before.

"Are you okay?"

Cailean looked up, almost startled by the question. "Yes, yes, fine. I'm fine."

Delaney shared a quick look with Maggie. "What is it?" She led Cailean to a bench overlooking the lawn and Maggie followed. "You felt something, didn't you?"

Cailean kept her gaze focused on the water.

"Cailean," Maggie said. "You can't keep this inside. It tears you apart, and it's not fair to us."

Her gaze swiveled to Maggie, eyes flashing. "Not fair to *you*?"

"It's our lives too, and you're part of that. Maybe we can't do anything to help, maybe it will just make us more scared, or whatever. But we are family and we will stand with each other."

"She's right." Delaney put her hand on Cailean's shoulder. "You don't have to suffer through this stuff alone anymore."

Cailean's shoulders slumped and her chin dipped as a weary sigh slipped out. "I don't want to suffer with this stuff at all, alone or together."

Maggie slid off the bench and crouched in front of her, taking both her hands. "Just tell us what you saw. Don't take it all on yourself."

Cailean looked first to Delaney, then to Maggie. "We're going to find the key."

Maggie's mouth dropped open then quickly shut. Cailean tried to stand but both Maggie and Delaney held her back.

"When?" Maggie asked.

"That's just it. I don't know. Maybe today, maybe not

for a few days. But we will find it. Soon." She did stand then, turning to stare up at the craggy pinnacles of the Quiraing that loomed in the distance behind the hotel. "And then we will see what is to become of all of us."

THIRTY-FOUR

ALEXANDER PACED THE length of Calum's council room, which he'd turned into makeshift quarters for himself. Delaney had asked to meet with him privately before they all sat down as a group.

He was tired and not a little frustrated. He'd planned to present the Claren women with a united front when they returned this morning. However, neither Rory nor Duncan had complied. They'd listened to his plans, they'd asked dozens of hard-hitting questions, and hadn't been at all reticent in voicing their doubts. For all their joy in being reunited and their interest in what he had to say, both men had been preoccupied and it hadn't taken a genius to determine the source of their distraction.

If he weren't so frustrated, he'd have been forced to admit to a little distraction himself. Delaney might be mortal, but she had an unnatural hold on his attention.

She chose that moment to stride into his chambers. Despite his determination to maintain strict control, or perhaps to purposely mock it, his attention was pulled directly to her mouth.

She'd been making a point yesterday, when she'd slipped

her fingers through his hair and tugged his mouth down to hers. He'd allowed it, had thought to prove to her that it was he who wielded the power between them. But the strategy had been a tactical error of startling proportions, one that had only proven that the game they played was far more dangerous than either of them expected.

"Good, you're here," she said.

"I believed this was something of a command performance, was it no'?"

She laughed. "Don't play the pompous clan chief with me, Alexander. I asked to see you and here we are."

His scowl deepened. "Pompous am I now?"

"At times. I imagine it would serve you well as laird, but it's really not necessary now."

He didn't know what to think. She never let his mind progress in a rational, straightforward manner. One word, one look, and his thoughts were all a jumble. Dangerous game indeed. "A shift through time does not change what I am, Delaney."

"Nor am I to be blamed for what my ancestors did before me. But this is the twentieth century, not the seventeenth. You are not a ruler, you're just a man. So can't we unbend a little and just have a conversation without all the posturing?"

Posturing? He wasn't posturing. As if she'd read his thoughts, she cocked a skeptical eyebrow and looked pointedly at him. He looked down to find his arms crossed over his chest and his legs braced in a commanding stance. He scowled again, but refused to shift to suit her sensibilities. "A conversation about what?" he demanded instead. "The portal? You know where I stand on that issue. I imagine that you've already rallied your cousins to your way of thinking."

"As you have rallied your brothers to yours, no doubt. That is why I asked to speak to you before we all talk. There's something you and I need to get figured out first."

Alexander badly needed to pace the floor, to burn off the excess energy that seemed to spike within him every time he was around her. Instead, as a test of sorts, he remained still. "And what could that possibly be?"

Delaney blew out a breath. "Why did I know you'd make this difficult?"

He narrowed his eyes and studied her. Beneath all her forthright speech, she appeared almost flustered. "What on earth are you talking about?"

"You see? Normally, I have no trouble communicating with men. Until you, that is."

He raised his eyebrows at that, but wisely remained silent. What was she about now?

"Normally, when I'm not interested, I have to spend at least half my time making sure I don't send out the wrong signals, because, face it, some men think breathing is a signal. The other half of the time, when I am interested, I have to make sure I don't come on too strong, you know? I mean, I'm small, but I can pack a pretty mean punch, so men are kind of surprised when they get to know me. And I refuse to play dumb and weak so they can feel all strong and protective. It's a stupid ritual and most times I have no patience for it at all, which is probably why I'm still single. But I've never, once, had to explain what the signals are in the first place. Most men get that much." She looked up at him, absolutely serious. "Are you with me so far?"

Alexander nodded, just to be safe.

"Good." She propped her hands on her hips. "So, what are we going to do about it?"

He blinked, half afraid to ask. "About what?"

"Us!"

"Us?"

"You didn't hear anything I said, did you?" She turned and began pacing. He was sorely tempted to join her.

"What does this have to do with finding the key?"

She stopped and turned to face him. "I'm not talking

about the damn key." She placed her hands on her hips, opened her mouth, and then closed it again. With an aggrieved sigh, she let her hands fall to her side and shook her head. "Never mind. Maybe you're the type who has to have a picture drawn." She strode across the room, her expression so intent and determined, his immediate instinct was to back up. He had no desire to end up tossed on the floor again. She was upon him before he could match thought to deed.

She reached for his head before he could duck and he found his mouth welded to hers an instant later. He gripped her arms, intent on putting her off of him, but just then a low groan issued from her throat and her dominant kiss turned pliant and wondrous. And just like that, he was once again lost in the infinite pleasures of Delaney Claren's delectable mouth.

He held on to her arms, as she did his head. Her fingers kneaded his scalp, making him tighten his own grip against the overwhelming need to pull her against him, to feel her body flush up along his, to hold her in his arms as they took one another. And it was a joint taking, of that there was no doubt. Perhaps all the more intoxicating for their lack of contact beyond that of their hands and their mouths. She tasted sweet and salty and he discovered, to his astonishment and pleasure, that he rather enjoyed the fact that she wasn't shy in enjoying his mouth every bit as much as he enjoyed hers.

He was quite breathless when she broke free and stumbled back a step. She stared up at him, her eyes deep violet now, and her lips sweet and puffy from his kisses. He found himself reaching for her, but her reflexes were sharper than his and she danced back just beyond his reach.

"Cailean is right, you MacKinnons do pack a wallop."

"Yer looking at me like ye've never seen a man before." He was as fascinated by his reaction to her as she apparently was by him. She was a warrior just as he was. His brothers had talked of her antiterrorist background and it had only served to increase his fascination. A woman who understood the mind of a broad range of warriors, who comprehended battle strategy in all its forms?

Had he not already met her, not squared off against her, he would have doubted that someone of her stature and sensibilities could play such a delicately balanced role in the violent world of political and religious warfare.

He had no doubt of it now.

She had passion for what she believed in and it infused her with an energy that was infectious. Och, that someone with her strength of conviction could believe in him, stand for him and by him. With her by his side, he would feel unconquerable. The revelation stunned him.

"Maybe I've simply never seen a man like you."

"Am I so different from the men in your world? I know of your career and I would think you've gone up against warriors before. I would think one such as you would seek them out, as they would you."

She seemed stunned herself by his statement.

He stepped closer and was mightily intrigued when she instantly retreated a step. "Haven't you?"

"I . . . I said before, it's a ritual I have no patience for. Strength, both physical and intellectual, and femininity make an odd mix, I've discovered. But as you said, it's what I am. I can't change that. For anyone."

"Perhaps you simply haven't met the warrior who understands and appreciates those traits. A man who would revel in that power rather than attempt to diminish it." He took another step. Her eyes widened somewhat, but not in fear. And this time, he noted, she stood her ground.

"Perhaps not," she said, a slight, unsteady thread weaving through her voice.

What was he saying? That *he* was that man? Preposterous. And yet, the very thought of another man attempting to join his life force with hers sparked a reaction inside him that was so virulent, he could scarce contain it.

But she hadn't approached another man. She'd come to him. She'd stormed his castle and staked her claim on him. Surprisingly, the idea of being claimed by her fortified him.

He stepped closer and heard her soft intake of breath. He reached up and traced the delicate line of her cheekbone and jaw. "Why me, Delaney?" His voice was a dark whisper. "Do ye think I am your match?"

"Maybe I was wrong after all," she said shakily. Then a slow smile curved her lips, shocking him into an instant state of almost painful hardness. She stepped closer and ran her fingers along his lips as well. "You did read the signs."

His heart pounded beneath her touch. His body screamed for release. " 'Tis a dangerous journey we embark on here."

"Answer me one question."

Surprised but curious, he nodded.

"Right now, if you were given the chance to walk away from me and never go beyond this moment together, would you take it?"

With his gaze steady on hers, he shifted his mouth and slid his lips over her fingers. He pulled them into his mouth, then pressed his teeth slowly into the soft pads of flesh. She held his gaze boldly, then curled her fingers, skimming them across his tongue, deliberately scraping the length of them along the edges of his teeth as she slid them free . . . and then she placed them in her own mouth.

He groaned and muscles locked as desire the likes of which he'd never felt slammed through him. "I canno', would no', walk away from ye, Delaney. We are well and truly matched. Maybe too well. Perhaps ye are destined to be my doom."

"If I am to be your doom, than you may well be mine. One thing I do know is that we are bound—through time, through the past, through the present." Then she moved into his arms and took his mouth even as he was taking hers.

ALEXANDER HAD NO idea of how much time had passed when a sharp clearing of a throat brought him jarringly back to earth.

It was Duncan. "I am sorrier than ye know to ruin this moment, but the others were gettin' worried."

"About which one of us?" Delaney asked, forming an easy smile despite her less than steady breath.

Duncan laughed. "That is still under discussion. I was elected to enter the lion's den." Duncan's grin grew wider, if that was possible. "I see you two are still grappling with the issues of control and leadership."

Delaney grinned in return. "And quite enjoying the power struggle, too, I might add."

Alexander felt his cheeks begin to heat, but Delaney held fast to his arm and would not allow him to step away. Damn the woman! He should have known better than to allow her to weave her faery magic on him, mortal or no. But even as the thoughts warred in his brain, he knew he had no real desire to be anywhere other than right where he stood.

"What is it, Duncan?" he demanded, willing his warming cheeks to cool. Duncan missed nothing and was obviously enjoying his older brother's discomfiture.

"Well, it has been some time since you sequestered yourselves. Even Balgaire was getting restless." His smile dimmed somewhat. "We are all gathered to discuss what is to be done."

Delaney squeezed his arm, then released him and stepped away, far too easily for his peace of mind. "I think you are right," she told Duncan.

Suspicions formed, unwanted but undaunted in his

mind. Had she thought to cloud his mind with desire, hoping to cloud his judgement as well? He placed his hand on her shoulder, holding her still, but turned his attention to Duncan. "Tell the others we will be there shortly. Send my apology for keeping them waiting."

"No apology necessary. I'll tell the others you will be along." He looked to Delaney and winked. "Don't be overly rough wi' the man, Delaney. He's no' accustomed to a strong female who knows her mind—and his." At Alexander's gargle of outrage, Duncan flashed him a victorious smile, but spoke with full sincerity. "It's no' a thing to consider lightly, brother."

He was gone before Alexander could put together a coherent response. Delaney broke free from his grasp and turned to him. "You cannot retreat into your laird mode every time your brothers do something to make you feel uncomfortable."

Alexander pulled his attention away from the empty doorway and looked at her with honest surprise. "I was not retreating into anything of the sort! I am their eldest sibling as well as their clan chief. They look to me for guidance and leadership in both roles. I was merely—"

"You were merely feeling threatened by what we were sharing and by the fact that Duncan obviously pegged it so you assumed the cold laird pose and issued orders and took control of the situation." She stepped closer and patted his shoulder. Patted his shoulder!

"I am not a pet or a small child to be placated with a pat to the head."

"No, you are a man who is dealing with some very serious issues, not the least of which is handling your family. Which, I see now, might not be the easy task that you envisioned. Am I right?"

He blustered for a few seconds before releasing a deep sigh. He broke away from her infernally reassuring touch and paced the room. "Aye," he said, filled with disgust. "Aye, yer right."

She walked up behind him. "Things have changed for them, Alexander, they are changing for you, too. Your brothers aren't the men they were before. They aren't second and third in line to the chieftainship, or even loyal clansmen, worried about the fate of their clan. They are dealing with other, very difficult realities. You cannot simply command them to follow you wherever you think it's best for them to go. What is best for you, for your clan, for the past you want to return to, may no longer be what's best for them."

Her words pummeled him like arrows and stones. They stuck, they hurt, they got his attention.

She took hold of his arm and turned him to face her. "But you are and always will be their elder brother. They will always want to do what is right by you and for you. If you think this is an easy task for them, to make this decision on what to do, you are wrong. They are as pained by it as you."

"Yer sayin' I am makin' it harder for them still?" He leaned away from her touch, frowning. "I canno' shake my loyalty to what I was born and bred to do, which is to do whatever I must to save my clan. If I have a chance, no matter how narrow, I must try. And as their brother and their chief, I must insist they return with me. The date on the calendar, the realms of this world that they exist in, matters naught. Their loyalty to their clan, mine too, shouldna waver in the face of anything. If ye canno' understand that—"

"Oh, but I do," she said quietly. "Sadly, I do." She dropped her chin and was silent for a moment. "I deal with fanatics all the time."

"I am not lunatic or despot," he exploded, stunned by the accusation and startlingly hurt by it.

"Ask yourself who you are really doing this for, Alexander." Her eyes were flashing now. She stormed closer. "For all intents and purposes, you are dead in the past. You disappeared from that time and time marched on. It is history now, fact and final. For you to even consider going back and changing, or attempting to change the outcome, because it enrages your personal sense of right and wrong, is arrogant and selfish in the extreme."

"And what of your quest? This one you embark on with your cousins? What if you are able to lift this curse? What if you are able to give my brother Rory his mortality? Will that not change some future sequence of events? Isn't the very fact that my brothers and I are existing in a place out of time already a sleight to nature and history? Who are you to determine what is okay to toy with and what is not?" His chest was heaving by the time he finished his tirade. He fully expected her to erupt in return. To his further amazement, she did not.

The fight left her. She looked like that small, fragile woman she so vehemently denied wanting to be. He wanted to rage at her to fight back, to argue the point with him and loudly. He wanted her to give him a dozen reasons to make him believe she was right and he was wrong.

He wanted her to give him a reason to stay.

That truth rocked him so hard he could not think, could not speak, could not move. Panic rushed to fill the gaping holes she'd just blown wide within him. If she'd wanted to cloud his judgement, it seems she had well accomplished her goal.

"Perhaps we should take this discussion back to the rest of the group," she said quietly. Too quietly.

He turned what he was very much afraid was a wild-eyed, desperate look in her direction. "Delaney—"

She didn't answer; she merely turned and left the room. Everything he'd ever believed in had just been turned upside down. He needed this time alone to piece it all back together, to right the world she had so swiftly and easily upended.

Dammit, don't walk out on me now. Come back.

Dear God, come back.

PART FOUR

THE KEY

". . . Love is indestructible."
—ROBERT SOUTHY

". . . And all that life is love."
—JAMES MONTGOMERY

THIRTY-FIVE

DUNCAN GRINNED AS he watched Maggie slip from the room he'd been examining for the key. She'd snuck up on him and he was still breathless from the assault. His grin remained as he returned to his work, but he had to fight to keep it there, to keep his thoughts rooted firmly in the here and now.

His time was almost up.

He and Maggie had come to a silent agreement not to mention it, but he'd felt the quiet desperation in her kisses just now.

After hours of arguing with Alexander, which had gotten them nowhere, they'd all decided to put aside the decision of what they would do until the time came for them to make it. If that time ever came. He was very much afraid it would matter little whether or not he and Rory thought they should accompany Alexander back into the past. He would return to purgatory this time tomorrow unless they found that key. Duncan himself wasn't certain what finding the key would have to do with his returning, but there was naught else to pin his hopes on, naught else to keep his heart from shattering.

They had spent long hours in Stonelachen this past week, looking for the blasted thing. He was very much afraid it did not exist, no matter how certain of its discovery Cailean was. She felt it more strongly every day, she said. But he'd seen those same desperate looks she'd sent Rory's way and wondered how much of her knowledge was second sight, and how much was merely her heart's desire.

Three hours later, he'd finished examining a half-dozen more rooms with nothing to show for it but a brutal headache and a growing sense of panic.

With a low curse, he swung away from the next appointed room and retraced his steps. He knew Maggie would likely still be in the north passage. Coming back to Stonelachen, tracing her many twisted corridors and passageways had been a gift to his soul, one almost as sweet as that of Maggie's love. Och, but he'd missed this place, aye he had.

But even warm thoughts of his childhood home could not quell the rising tide of fear, or dampen the growing ache within him. By the time he reached the adjoining corridor, he was all but running. He swung around a corner and skidded to a halt. She was there, just ahead of him.

"Maggie," he said, out of breath.

Startled, she spun toward him. Her expression lightened immediately at the sight of him, but as she ran close enough to see his face clearly, her smile faded. "What is it, what's wrong?"

He pulled her tight against him and just held on. The tide rose further within him. How on earth would he survive without her in his arms this way?

She struggled against him. "Duncan, you're scaring me."

"I didna mean to frighten ye, Maggie mine. I simply had to hold ye."

It took no more than those simply spoken words to make her understand. Her expression crumpled and her eyes turned glassy. "Oh, Duncan." Her voice wobbled and she buried her face against his chest.

His heart shattered. She sobbed and he had nothing in him to make her stop. She cried his tears as well.

"What are we going to do?" she demanded, almost angrily. She pounded on his chest. "Why did we spend all this time apart looking for the stupid key?"

He held her fists and kissed each knuckle until she looked up at him. What he saw in her eyes broke what was left of his heart.

"I want more, Duncan. I'm not ready to say good-bye." Her face crumpled again and she gulped on a fresh sob. "God, I can't bear this, I can't."

Duncan was afraid, deeply afraid, that he would break down and not be able to pull himself back together again. He had to act; he had to do something. And there was only one thing he could think to do with his remaining time. He swung Maggie up into his arms and marched down the passage.

"Where are we going?"

He slowed enough to look down at her. "We've looked for the key and it isn't to be found. I willna waste the rest of my time here on an empty search. I must say my good-byes to my brothers." He was forced to pause as a painful lump lodged in his throat. "Then I want to return to our rooms and spend every last second alone with you."

She nodded as fresh tears coursed down her cheeks. "I can walk, Duncan, you don't have to carry me."

"Yes," he said quietly, "yes, I do."

Rory and Alexander strode into the main room from opposite passageways just as he entered himself.

"What's wrong," Rory demanded, immediately crossing the room toward him. "Is she hurt?"

Duncan shook his head and reluctantly let Maggie slip from his arms to stand tucked by his side. "She's fine. I need to speak to both of you."

Alexander's expression was tired and worn as he crossed the room to stand before them. Duncan knew that he and Rory had made things difficult for their elder brother and the familiar guilt snatched at him again. "I'm sorry, Alexander, I hope you can find it in you to forgive me. I must abandon the quest."

To his utter surprise, Alexander moved forward and caught him to his chest in a tight hug. " 'Tis all right. I know the time has come." It was a long time before he released him and stepped back.

Rory stepped forward and took his hand in a hard shake, then pulled him into an embrace as well. "I dinna know what to say, Duncan. I feel as if I just found ye."

"I know, Rory. I know. But I will fully ascend one day, and when I do, I'll find Da and tell him you both continue to do him proud." Somewhere he found a grin, which he sent to his elder brother. "And you can rest assured he will box my ears clean from my head when he hears I didna follow yer orders, Alexander."

"If I thought it would help, I'd box them off now." Alexander managed a small smile, but it did not come close to warming his eyes. He sighed and gave up all pretense. "Och, Duncan but this is a fine mess. I canno' find the words and I canno' deal with the pain of yer leavin'."

"Ye'll still have Rory." Duncan said, his throat raw from the effort of keeping his words steady. "No' that this is a great consolation I realize." His laugh ended abruptly in a choked cry and they all somehow ended up in a tight embrace of arms and tears.

"Are ye leavin' Stonelachen?" This came from Rory.

"Aye. Maggie and I, we need—"

"Ye dinna hae to explain."

"No," Duncan said, deeply moved, "I suppose I don't. Thank you, Rory."

"Can we talk you into spending your time here?" Alexander asked. "Rory's chambers will afford ye privacy and that way we can keep the search up to the last minute, in case—"

Duncan raised his hand. "I appreciate the gesture, Alexander. But the search, for me, is over. I'm no' too certain that findin' the key would have changed my destiny anyway. I made a deal with Them in order to have this time here and I wouldna go and change that even if I could. I've had more than most men." He looked to Rory. "I know your curse still stands, but I can ask Them when the time comes—"

Rory held up his hand. "No. I will deal with that on my own." There was desperation beneath the confident tone, but Duncan could say nothing to ease it.

He knew Rory's feelings on ascending had changed from the time when they first spoke of it. He also knew his brother feared that his ascension might already be preordained, if they were to reverse his immortality. He could become a more than three hundred–year-old man in the literal sense, which would mean his mortal life would end right then and there. Perhaps his immortality did not seem as much a curse to him now that he had someone to live for. But he also knew that at the end of either path lay sorrow.

He pulled his brother into one last embrace. "God be with ye, John Roderick," he said close to his ear. "When yer time comes, whenever that may be, I'll be waitin'."

His brother could only manage to nod and tighten his grip. Then the two stepped apart and Maggie stepped to his side once again and took his hand in her own. He looked at her. "Do you wish to find your cousins before we leave?"

Maggie nodded. "Please." As if summoned by the force of her will, Delaney and Cailean entered the room together.

"What is this? Another round of *Family Feud* and no one told us?" Delaney joked. But she quickly noticed the sobering tension and crossed the room. "What's wrong?"

Cailean said nothing; it was obvious that she had immediately understood what was taking place. She moved to Rory's side, close to Maggie. "Are you going?"

Maggie nodded. "We don't want to spend what time we have left searching for the key. I'm sorry, Cailean."

Cailean shushed her. "No, don't. I understand." Her expression was more worried than Maggie had ever seen it. "I'm sorry I took you away from each other, but I really thought—" She broke off and put her hand to her mouth to stifle the tears that swam in her eyes. "I thought we'd find the answer."

Now it was Maggie's turn to shush her. "I thought we would too, or I wouldn't have spent the time looking. We'll still find it, Cailean. You know we will find it. And who knows, maybe it won't be too late." But Maggie didn't really believe that and she knew that Cailean didn't either.

Maggie's time with Duncan was at an end.

Delaney stepped forward and pulled her into a short, tight hug. "Go on, we'll keep looking. I wish I could do something to make it easier."

"You are. Just being here helps. I'm going to need you." She looked to Cailean. "Both of you."

They nodded, squeezed hands, then let them go.

"I don't know when I'll be back, I—"

"It's okay," Cailean said.

Maggie looked to Rory and Alexander. "Thank you," was all she could say. But she knew from their expressions that they understood she was thanking them for giving her their brother's final moments alone.

"We must be off," Duncan said. Then he scooped her up in his arms. "Hold tight, lass."

She clasped his neck. He looked to his brothers and nodded, they each nodded solemnly in return. Then he looked to each of her cousins. "Ye take care of her or I'll come back to haunt ye both, ye understand?"

Both women nodded through watery eyes.

Then he pulled Maggie tight against him, and they disappeared.

SHE SWORE SHE'D done little more than blink, and they were in their room in Flodigarry. "Wow. I thought you'd stopped blinking in and out." His ability to do that had waned as time had marched on, to the point where he didn't even try it. Maggie hadn't minded. It made him seem more mortal, more real.

Duncan seemed winded. "It was no' so easy. But I dinna want to waste the time driving."

She kissed him on the chin. "I'm glad you did."

He carried her to the bed and they fell into the soft downy duvet together. Clothes seemed to disappear like magic. Maybe it was. Maggie didn't waste time questioning it. Their urgency was a raw, driving thing, their need to be bonded in the most intimate of bonds was all-consuming, driven by the heartache and desperation they both felt. When he entered her she screamed in exultation, then clung to him as they rode the fierce wave to its crashing conclusion.

Shaken deeply, Maggie wondered how she could feel so complete and so achingly hollow at the same time. She curled into Duncan's chest and tried to block the pain and fear. But there was no pleasure great enough to keep such a deep, abiding pain at bay.

They clung to each other with his body wrapped around hers. It was a long time later that he finally spoke. "Ah, Maggie, what will I do up there without you?"

"Oh, Duncan." Her eyes burned and her throat ached, but there were no tears left to shed.

"Do ye regret the decision ye made back in that cabin, Maggie?"

"To spend these last few weeks with you? No, not for one single moment."

"But?" He tilted her chin back to his when she tried to duck his knowing gaze. "Tell me, Maggie."

"I can't. It's selfish in the extreme. I mean, I wouldn't wish you to have not seen Scotland again. Just seeing your face as you entered Stonelachen again makes any pain worthwhile. And then reuniting with Rory and Alexander." She shook her head. "I would never take that from you."

"But? What selfish feeling do you have? Because if it concerns me, then I have to say I am feeling much the same as you. Tell me."

She swallowed hard and looked him in the eye. "I thought I'd be able to handle this, but it's harder, so much harder than I ever dreamed and I—" She swallowed another gulp of air, then blurted, "I wish I'd taken your offer and gone with you that night, before Judd found me."

"Och, Maggie, love." Duncan cradled her to his chest and rocked her gently. "I have had the same thoughts. I wished shamefully that you were mine to take with me forever. Even though I would be robbing you of your life on earth, of your reunion with your cousins. Robbing you of the full life I'm sure you've yet to live."

"But, Duncan—"

He placed his fingers on her lips. "Ye see that we feel the same. Ye'd give up this life and all the gifts of it, as would have I. Even my brothers, even Stonelachen. For you, I would give up anything."

She could only nod, stunned by the depth of the feelings this man had for her, this man she so cherished.

"Perhaps this is what was meant for us," he said.

"You can't mean that. This pain? No. I can't believe that."

"What I meant was that perhaps it took the incident with Judd and these last weeks, for this love of ours to grow. If we had gone when They first made the offer, perhaps our eternity would have been one of misery and mistrust. This time we've spent together has made certain our legacy is one of love." He kissed her again, then pulled her close. "I would wish eternity with you, Maggie. But I wouldna give back this time we've had, short as it was, for an eternity of anything less than this." He kissed her slowly, deeply, with infinite patience until they both could only cling to one another. "This is a love that will last for eternity. 'Tis more than most ever have. We are well and truly blessed."

"I love you," she whispered.

He framed her face in his large hands. "I love you, Maggie."

And then it happened.

A blinding white light filled the room.

In her heart, in her soul, she must have known what was happening because she screamed. "NO! I'm not ready, no! You can't have him yet."

Though she clung to him, and was still cradled in his arms, she could already feel him becoming less solid.

"Cry naught, sweet Maggie." He kissed her fiercely. "I am to fully ascend. Your love has released me from purgatory."

"Oh, Duncan," she sobbed shamelessly. She could feel only the lasting impression of his lips on hers. "Wait for me," she whispered before breaking down completely.

And then he was gone.

THIRTY-SIX

CAILEAN CAUGHT UP with Delaney just outside the main room. "Finished?"

Delaney's shoulders slumped. "Yep. No luck." She put her hand on Cailean's arm. "I'm sorry. So sorry."

"Me too." They'd all been in a morose fog after Duncan's exit, but had ultimately decided that continuing the hunt was the best thing they could do. For themselves, and for Duncan and Maggie. "Are you heading back to Flodigarry?" Cailean asked wearily.

"I'd planned to, but my room adjoins Maggie's and I don't want to feel like I'm intruding. At the same time, if . . . if it's over, I want to be there for Maggie."

Cailean saw the anguish in her cousin's eyes and felt the same ache behind her own. "It's pretty late." She didn't have to add that it was probable that Duncan was already gone. "Do you want me to go with you?"

"No. You need to spend time with Rory right now."

"But I—"

Delaney's expression was adamant. "But nothing. I've seen the way you two have tried so hard not to look at each other since Duncan left. The tension between you is like a hot wire. You need to reassure each other."

"I'm not sure I can after today. What if we never find the key? Rory has been shutting himself off from me these past several days. I think he's afraid his curse will never be reversed."

"But the feelings you get—"

"Are useless!" she snapped, then quickly got a grip. If she didn't maintain tight control at all times, she'd unravel completely. "I'm sorry. I know I've felt certain we'd find it, but maybe I'm not interpreting it right, maybe I'm just superimposing my own wishes. Maybe—" She broke off and began to pace. "Maybe I'm losing what is left of my mind. All I know is that if Rory does decide that his curse is as immortal as he is, then he will pull away from me totally rather than suffer the consequences." Her voice broke. "I can't blame him, even if it is tearing me apart."

Delaney pulled her into a hug. "I wish I knew what to say. I wish I could tell you it was all going to work out."

"All I get are these vague, disquieting thoughts and this sense of impending change, big changes, for all of us. It seemed a positive thing, but nothing about today was remotely positive."

Delaney gave her a slight shake. "Listen, I want you to go find Rory and talk to him, spend time with him. I don't have your second sight, but I do know when two people need to be alone together. You saw Duncan and Maggie today. They were in agony, and yet they wouldn't have traded one second of their time together. If you and Rory aren't meant to work this out for happily ever after, then take what time you do have. You'll never forgive yourself later if you don't."

"I hear you, Delaney, but it's hard." She released a shaky sigh.

"I understand," Delaney said quietly.

Cailean heard the underlying confession. Over the last

week, Delaney and Alexander had sparred like the bitter enemies that the Clarens and MacKinnons had been centuries ago. But no one been fooled by their constant bickering. There was no denying they disagreed on most topics and both had a real problem with letting the other one be the leader, something which they'd been teased about mercilessly by Duncan and found not in the least amusing.

But the true tension that sizzled between them wasn't fueled by anger. No one had dared tease them about that, yet she knew they all understood it for what it was. They were all in the throes of the same overwhelming emotions; Alexander and Delaney were simply having a more difficult time coming to terms with it and finding boundaries within it they could both live with.

For all their protestations and debates, the two were, more often than not, off hunting for the key in the same general location. Cailean had caught them both looking at each other when neither suspected they were being watched. The heat and desire in their eyes would light a thousand torches and still have fuel to light a thousand more.

"Why don't you take your own advice?" Cailean suggested gently. "You and Alexander waste too much time being defensive, when it's obvious to the rest of us that you are dying for one another."

Delaney gave a hollow laugh, then the smile slid into the most desolate expression Cailean could ever recall seeing on her cousin's usually animated face. "I don't know, Cailean. He is such a hard man to get close to. I know he feels this same explosive thing there is between us, but he can be so damn hardheaded and he wants to run everything and tell me what to do and—"

Cailean found her first real smile in what felt like days. "Not that you'd have any understanding of that personality type or anything."

Delaney had the grace to smile sheepishly. "Maybe we're

too much alike, I don't know. But it feels like it's because he *is* like me that he's the only one who really gets me, who really understands what motivates me. I catch him looking at me sometimes, Cailean, and my entire body turns to hot mush." She fanned her face. "He's annoying and frustrating and autocratic and pompous and—"

"Stay here, tonight," Cailean interrupted. "Stay with him. All those things you said about Rory and me apply to you as well. I know it's scary and maybe it will make it hurt later, but like you said, could you forgive yourself if you walked away now?"

"God, I hate it when you're right."

Cailean laughed, but she caught Delaney in a hug.

"What about Maggie," Delaney said.

Cailean stepped back and squeezed Delaney's hands before letting them go. "Maggie will need us both, I'm sure, but tonight it's probably best to leave her alone and let her grieve privately."

"How can we go off when she's alone and in such pain?"

"Do you think she'd rather we were alone, too?"

"It's just so damn unfair."

"I know. Go find Alexander. Do you know where he is?"

"He's trying to clear rubble from the passageway leading to his old rooms. You know where Rory is?"

She nodded. She knew where he was supposed to be searching, but she had a very strong feeling he was somewhere else. "I think so."

They made plans to meet at eight in the morning and Cailean watched Delaney head out of the main room.

CAILEAN FOUND RORY right where she'd thought he'd be.

She pulled the fur tighter around her shoulders, and stepped away from the stone portal and into the moonlight.

He sat in the same place he had the first time she'd found him here. That sunrise seemed ages ago now.

The wind was screaming and he couldn't have possibly heard her arrival. Just the same, she hadn't taken two steps when he turned and lifted his arm for her to join him.

She made her way carefully to his side, then tossed her fur around them, as he shifted his across their laps.

They sat and stared in silence at the growing array of stars. The sky was remarkably free of clouds and the temperature was almost balmy. Not warm, but there was no winter bite in the air.

"What are ye thinkin' upon so hard, Cailean."

His voice immediately soothed her and just as immediately it jacked up her fear. Something wasn't right. "I'm not sure."

That elicited a surprised chuckle from him. "Yer thoughts are so confusing ye know no' what they are?"

She liked it when his burr flavored his speech, as it did almost all the time now since his reunion with both brothers.

"Something like that," she said, feeling the relief of a smile curve her lips. But its warmth was short-lived. "I'm feeling sort of pummeled by all these feelings and I'm not sure I want to deal with trying to figure them out anymore. I worry that I'm leading everyone on this giant goose chase but I can't stop trying because—"

"Cailean, stop." He pulled her close, then rested his cheek on her hair as they both continued to stare at the night sky. "Ye knew where to find me, so yer feelings must be more on target than you think."

"I knew you'd be up here because I know you."

He turned to her then. "And what of me do ye know? Why di' ye come to look for me here?"

His sudden demand startled her. "If you'd rather be alone, I can—"

"I dinna want to be alone. I came up here because I

needed to say good-bye to Duncan. And yet all I have thought about is you."

She didn't know what to say to that.

His tone gentled. "I've been needin' ye, Cailean. And you came to me."

"It was Delaney who made me come find you."

Rory scowled. "Well, you'll forgive me if I dinna seek her out to thank her."

Cailean smiled, craving the much-needed warmth it brought her. Rory and Delaney made a great show of seeing who could out-insult the other, but she sensed that underneath it there was a growing respect for one another, grudging though it may be. "She was worried about you." At his snort, she added, "Alexander, too."

"Worried that she won't have a sparring partner perhaps. The two of them are more suited for each other than any two people I've met. Surprised they haven't killed each other. But she does keep him from sticking his nose in my business every second, so for that I suppose I do owe her a great debt."

"Not that you'd ever share that with her."

"And dinna be tellin' her yerself either, or there will be no livin' wi' her."

Cailean laughed. "And ruin all the fun? I wouldn't dream of it."

She noticed he kept his hold firmly around her. Cailean pulled that feeling of security around her even more tightly than the blanket and used the strength it gave her to say what was on her mind. "I feel like you've been pulling away from me. It scares me."

He looked at her with honest surprise on his face. "How can ye say that? I'm all but on top of ye."

"I don't mean physically. I mean emotionally."

"Dinna go and get scientific on me, Cailean, it's been a very hard day for all of us and I—"

"You really need to listen to me. We've been physically close. A lot. And I revel in that connection, Rory, I do. But it's in all the other ways. You don't look at me for very long. It's as if you're afraid I'll see something you don't want me to see. I feel like a freak enough as it is and I don't want you to be uncomfortable around me in any way. But it hurts when you close yourself off like that. I'm not just a Claren Key. I'm a woman and that's who it hurts. It would be easy for me to let you do that, to pull away myself. After today, I thought maybe I'd do just that. But Delaney said I should fight for this time we have, that we should——"

"Delaney says, Delaney says," he exploded suddenly. "What d' *you* say?"

"I say I love you," she shouted back. Then they both sat back from one another, as the words hung there between them. Those words she had said before, those words he had shown her in every possible way that he felt too, but had never once spoken. "I witnessed perhaps the most wrenching scene of my life today when Maggie and Duncan said their good-byes. It made my heart hurt so bad I thought I wouldn't survive it, and that terrified me."

Rory's expression was totally unreadable. "Why would it terrify you?"

She hadn't missed the return to his excruciatingly correct English accent. "You're doing it right now."

"Doing what? Asking you a question?"

"Distancing yourself. It scared you, too, didn't it? This whole week, the sensation of time ticking away, all of it." She worked hard to keep her voice steady and try her best to explain it. "It terrified me because I feel those same strong emotions for you that I saw in Duncan and Maggie and because I have this feeling, this sick, dreadful, nauseating feeling that our time will come just as theirs did and I'm not certain I can bear it. Maybe you feel that too and it's why you're pulling back. Maybe that's why there is always this part of you that is tucked away. I wish I could do that, keep one part of me safe and whole, to cling to later when the rest shatters around my feet. But I can't step back from this, from what I feel. And maybe that is what scared me the most. Knowing that I've given all of myself, everything that matters, over to a man who might not want to keep it."

She started to tremble as she looked into his still impassive eyes. "When Duncan offered to take you with him, I thought I'd fall to the ground, and die right then." When he said nothing, she doggedly pushed on. "When you refused him, the relief was so profound I almost passed out. You want terror?" she said fervently. "That was terror. Because I knew that you didn't refuse Duncan because you wanted to stay here and make this work. You refused him because you don't really believe your curse can be reversed." She felt as if her whole life was slipping through her fingers and there was no way left for her to hold on. "I guess I had hoped that I was worth fighting for, too. That you would have faith in me, even when I don't have any in myself."

"I do have faith in you." He spoke so quietly, so suddenly, she had to hold her breath for the words to reach past the sound of her pounding heart. "And that is precisely why I've done what I've done. Terror is a pale description of what my feelings for you do to me."

Cailean's chest began to burn and she trembled at the depth of pain and anguish in his eyes.

"It is not the continuation of my immortality that I fear. And it is precisely because I felt those very same things when I watched my brother and Maggie today that I knew I had to preserve and maintain what little was left of myself. It was both selfish and unselfish." He dipped his chin and fell silent, then slowly, as if by force of great will, dragged his gaze back to hers. "I willna be able to bear our end, Cailean. I knew the anguish you felt in watching them, I saw it in your eyes as you watched them and could no' bear you lookin' at me the same way when my time comes. And come it will. You were right in that."

She cupped his cheek, held him there when he would have looked away. "What are you saying? You can't mean—" She broke off on a gasp. "You can't still mean to end your own life when the curse is lifted, not after all we've—"

"No, no." He slid her hand to his mouth and kissed her palm deeply, then curled her fingers in his and held her hand to his chest. "But I'll go anyway, Cailean. I know it to be true, though I can't explain the how of it. Maybe I have some of your sight myself, or maybe it's part of the knowledge that comes with living with this curse as long as I have. When the curse is lifted, my time on earth will be done and there will be no choice in the matter." He brought her hand to his lips and kissed her fingers, then rested his forehead against them. "There is no future to fight for beyond now."

She knew he spoke the truth. This was the reason for the black chill she'd felt earlier. This was the impending doom she'd feared. But she'd also felt hope, felt that there was goodness to come. Had that changed? She was so jumbled now she didn't know what she felt. "Then we simply won't find the key."

He pulled her into a tight embrace. "We have no choice there either, Cailean. Ye know that as well as I. Ye've been feeling its discovery and it will happen soon whether we choose it or no'."

"No." She wanted to shout it, defy what she knew was the truth. "We'll stop looking."

"I dinna think its discovery is in our hands. It will find us."

He looked into her eyes again. "You have been the brave

one, while I wasted time runnin'. I'm sorry, Cailean. Yer right, I regret no' usin' the time we had to its fullest. I have been both fool and coward."

"We're just human. No matter how many years you spend on earth, you're still human. But our time isn't up yet and I refuse to believe there won't be another choice. It can't just end."

And yet, hadn't it done just that today for Maggie and Duncan?

He kissed her until her trembling stopped, until she relaxed enough to give in to what they had left together.

"I would fight for you," he said against her lips. "I would spend all eternity fighting for you."

She cried. And when the flow of tears finally started, they came in a great hot torrent and there was no stopping them. Rory held her and rocked her, his own tears streaming down his cheeks to mix with hers.

She felt desolate. "Wait for me."

"Och, Cailean, ye dinna know what ye—"

"Promise me," she demanded, needing to hear him say it.

He kissed her hard and fierce until she moaned with it. "I'll wait for ye, always, ye know that. But dinna give up yer life waiting for it to end. There is much out there to see in this world and I want to discuss it all wi' ye when we are reunited. That you must promise me, or I dinna think I will bear it. I want ye to fight for that like you fought for me, do ye understand?"

She could only nod as fresh tears washed over her again.

They clung to each other and time finally ceased to have meaning. What existed was each moment. He kissed her, stroked her, and held her until the moon was high in the sky. Then he laid her down on the furs and made slow, maddeningly, unbearably sweet love to her, their salty tears mixing with moans of pleasure.

He pulled her tightly to his chest, wrapping his body around her. He kissed her tenderly on the lips. "Forgive me for not saying these words sooner." He held her face and looked into her eyes. "I love you, Cailean."

And then it happened.

THIRTY-SEVEN

DELANEY FOUND ALEXANDER that night in what used to be his chambers. He'd cleared the rubble, but there was nothing else in the room. "Not very homey," she said, leaning in the doorway.

He had been staring sightlessly into the centuries-cold fireplace, but didn't seem startled by her presence. "No, it's not."

She frowned. There was a hollow, almost vacant tone in his voice. Perhaps Cailean had been more on target than she gave herself credit for. She wanted to go to him, console him on the loss of his brother. She couldn't conceive what he was thinking or feeling or, worse yet, what he would do now because of it. For the first time in many years, she felt supremely inadequate.

So she took a different tack altogether. Maybe they would find the way together. "How do you have a fireplace inside of a mountain? Where does the smoke go?"

He answered in the same toneless voice. "There are fissures in the rocks that have been vented for such a purpose."

"And the smoke that rises from the mountain, how is that explained?"

"I don't imagine it much mattered back then since our mountain peaks couldn't be scaled. I suppose Rory has had to deal with the modern problems of helicopters and such, but there are enough hot springs with steam vents on the surface that I doubt anyone would pay much mind, if they happened to see it."

Now she was getting angry. She'd never heard him so emotionless, so empty. She wanted her passionate, opinionated man back. She wanted him to be angry, she wanted him to fight.

"I'm surprised to see you just give in like this."

That got his attention. His gaze fixed on hers. "What is that supposed to mean?"

"It means that you're a man with a mission. A man who is willing to do whatever he must to return to his clan and fight for their continued existence. No matter the cost." She sidled into the room, moving closer to him despite the fire now brewing in his eyes. Good. Fire was good. "I know you lost Duncan today. But I didn't expect you to take his leaving so hard."

"That is a harsh thing to say, even for you."

She took that arrow in stride. "These are harsh times. You were willing to lose your brother on the field of battle. I would think you'd be happy that he is reunited with his clan right now, with your father. Or are you just upset that you've lost a capable warrior?"

He spun on her so fast she gasped even though she was hoping he'd react.

He took her arms and shook her. "How dare you speak of Duncan that way? Have you no real soul in that body of yours? For a self-proclaimed romantic, your heart is a cold place indeed."

She made no attempt to break free. "I am not heartless

and the last thing I am is cold. Especially when it comes to you, Alexander."

"We'll see about that, indeed we will." He spun her to the nearest wall and pinned her against it. Had she wanted to, she could not have fought her way free, so securely did his body pin hers.

"Kiss me, Alex."

He growled something beneath his breath, but take her mouth he did. It was a punishing kiss that had more to do with control than with passion, but she could withstand the assault and would do that and more if it would reach him.

She kept her mouth soft and gentle, her responding kisses coaxing and reassuring. She had no idea that she was capable of such softness. Her assault was far less brutal and far more devastating to his defenses than his assault was to hers. His anger was spent quickly as she kept her mouth as pliant under his as she was able.

And then he was kissing her as if his life depended on it. Taking from her, feeding from her mouth as if his life force emanated from there. He groaned and leaned into her and she thought her heart might actually break so anguished was the sound that issued from deep inside him.

"It's okay," she whispered against his cheek when his lips moved from her mouth to her jaw and on to her neck. He still had her hands pinned to the wall and she slowly slipped them free and wove her fingers into his hair. His hands curled into fists by her head as she continued to stroke him, to rain sweet, soft kisses along his cheek. "It's okay to grieve, Alex. You don't have to be in control all the time. Not with me. Never with me."

He slipped his arms around her and pulled her tight against him as he reversed their positions. He slid down the wall enough to pull her between his legs and angle her head so that he could take her mouth again. He did not speak but let his kisses communicate his torment for him.

She found herself moaning as well. "I want you, Alex. Tonight."

He was devouring her. And she reveled in the taking.

"If you cannot cry, cannot let it go, then spend it on me." She looked into his eyes when he lifted his head. "Spend it inside me."

"Dear God, Delaney you have bewitched me for certain."

"Then we have both been bewitched. I have never wanted a man like I want you. This is no sacrifice I make. It's a pledge."

"I canno' take yer pledge, lass. No' when I'm questioning everythin' I've been about for seven years."

"You don't have to decide tonight. Come to me and leave the rest of the world and all the decisions. They will be there in the morning."

He looked as if he was going to speak, but after a long, searing look into her eyes, he merely pulled her against his chest and tucked her head beneath his chin.

She felt small and protected. And strong. Stronger than ever before. He may have had the bigger frame, the more powerful body, but they had equal strength where it mattered. She protected him as well.

Together they found sanctuary.

"I fear the morning will be too late." He pressed his lips against her hair. "It has begun. I know it, I felt it the moment Duncan disappeared. I need to be decisive about this now, yet I find I canno' be. This is no' the mark of a true chief, Delaney."

"No. It is the mark of a great one. You care, Alex." The torment in his eyes tore at her. "You care about the people you are sworn to protect. In this century and in your own."

"I canno' hide in your arms."

"Seeking solace isn't hiding. You are not a better laird, or even a better man, because you shoulder every burden alone."

"Aye, you are one to speak of shoulderin' burdens alone. Have ye not done that all yer life?"

"More than I realized. But because of my new family, because of you, I'm realizing how lonely an existence that has been. I've spent my life helping others and I'm proud of that. But somewhere along the way I began to use that as an escape. I was afraid to risk failing in something I've always wanted so badly for myself. Maybe I was right to protect myself until it mattered enough, when I couldn't protect myself any longer."

She faltered, but pushed on through the knot that was tightening in her stomach. "I don't want to spend the rest of my life questioning what we might have had, might have shared. Even for this one night. You matter enough, Alexander. Take me to your bed. We'll face the morning together."

Alexander looked into her eyes and knew the answer had already been decided for him. She had bewitched him, but the magic had been purely her own. "Yer heart is a warm, generous place. Glad I am to be held within it. Even for this one night." He lifted her into his arms and carried her from the room, stepping over the piles of rubble, then ducking into his own chamber.

He laid her gently on the thick furs he'd borrowed from Rory. "Leave your troubles at the door with my own. This night is to be ours."

ALEXANDER SMOOTHED THE short, tangled hair from her brow. Even in sleep, Delaney looked capable and ready to do battle. There was energy vibrating from within her, as if she could spring to action, at a moment's notice, ready for anything.

He wasn't ready for her.

He pressed his lips into her hair, then felt his heart squeeze when this slumbering warrior snuggled closer to him, tucking herself into him, instinctively knowing that she could sleep peacefully in his arms.

Peacefully, yes. But securely? Alexander felt a wash of fear run through him, freezing his blood, chilling his heart. The time would be upon him soon, he felt it. He had a decision to make.

That his firm resolution to return to the past was now something he viewed as a choice was a warning in itself.

His loyalty lay, first and foremost, with his clan, did it not? His brothers had made other choices. He wished he could summon up outrage or even a small sense of betrayal. But the sleeping woman in his arms made that impossible as well.

Och, what he'd felt when he'd thrust inside her for that very first time. It was a sensation that was carved on his inner being for all time. Never had there been anything so perfect, a place perfectly meant for him.

He frowned. Yes, he'd given in to the temptation of thinking of talking to her about coming with him once they found the portal. But even though the world had turned upside down for both of them this night, he could not, would not ask that of her. Whether or not his clan was successful in battle, he would likely not survive long in the past once he returned. Such was the time he lived in. He could not subject her to a life of strife and difficulty she did not deserve when he could not swear to her that he'd be by her side to guide her and protect her. He almost smiled at that. She wouldn't take well to his willingness to protect. But it was more than her physical self he wanted to protect from harm. His smile faded and there was a stabbing sensation in his heart.

How am I to leave you? Never had he suspected such a woman would exist for him.

Delaney shifted in his arms and placed a warm kiss to his chest, just over his heart. Her wide violet eyes, even more magical when filled with the softness of recent slumber, lifted to his. "What goes on behind those stormy eyes of yours, Alexander?"

He knew he could pull her beneath him, bring her finely tuned body to a peak of quivering need into which he could pour himself without restraint. Aye, but she was made for him she was, as he was for her. But there would be no more escape into the mind-numbing pleasures of lovemaking this night.

She reached up and smoothed her hand over the rough stubble of his jaw. "You were supposed to have left your worries at the door," she chastised gently.

He looked down into her eyes for a long time, felt his heart grow heavier with every beat, his throat grow tighter with every breath. "I find I canno' leave it go," he managed. *I canno' leave you go,* he added silently.

"Alexander—"

He placed his fingers across her lips. Smart, seductive lips he had sipped from until his head reeled like a drunkard. Lips he would kiss no more once his decision was made, once the portal was found.

Worry creased the corners of her eyes, pinched at the edges of her perfect mouth. "Tell me," she said, her gaze steady and unfaltering.

He wasn't going to, had planned not to. It wasn't fair to either of them. But his mouth opened and the words began to tumble forth. "The portal will open soon. I am no Key, but I feel it as surely as I breathe."

"I feel it too."

Her response only made the knot tighten in his gut and further crumbled his good and noble intentions. "I fear we have little time left to us. And I find I am no' ready to part wi' ye."

"What are you saying? That you're not going back?"

The hope that had sprung into her eyes, despite her attempts to remain strong and steady chewed his guilt to ragged ends. He was handling this badly. Very badly.

But was there a good way to say good-bye?

"I have to go back, Delaney. I have no choice."

A series of fissures shot through his heart, splitting it apart, as he witnessed the death of hope. She was valiant, for she did everything she could to protect him from her pain. But suffer she did.

"I understand. Perhaps more than you realize."

He did no' deserve one such as she.

"You know how I feel, but my reasons for not wanting you to return aren't all motivated by my beliefs of right and wrong." She took a breath and her steady expression began to shatter. It was a slow destruction that stole his will and decimated what was left of his control. "I don't want you to return for reasons that are purely personal and every bit as selfish."

The tears came then, slicing him clean through in ways the sharpest blade never could have. He stroked her hair and felt tears of his own slide from his eyes. "If I dinna return, I will never forgive myself. Even if it is all for naught and I die just as Edwyna predicted. Stuck here in the future is a similar death, but worse still for being alive and still useless."

Her head came up then and he was almost happy to see the violet sparks shoot through the tears. "You would not be useless here. Not to me."

"I know. And that is why I canno' put my worries aside. You fill my mind as well as my arms. I canno' stop thinking of you, of what we shared this night. Of what we could share if I were to stay. But you must realize that I could no' live with myself if I chose my own selfish desires over the needs of my clan. I am laird after my father Calum. I have been raised to think of my clansmen first, myself second and last."

"You're right. How could I expect you to come to love me when you were bred only for honor and loyalty?"

He gripped her face between his palms. He felt raw,

exposed. "In this you are wrong. Aye, you have described my life well, my emotions and the reasons for them. And until this moment I would have fought to the death to defend them for the righteous creed they represent." His hands began to tremble. "It is precisely this weakness of the heart that my da sought for me to avoid. It can cripple common sense, undermine good judgment. And yet I have fallen victim to it." His pulse pounded in his chest, in his head, in his throat. "A willing victim. Perhaps I am filled with that supreme selfishness ye spoke of, for I canno' look into your eyes for another second in time and not utter these words to ye."

He brushed the gentlest of kisses along her lips and leaned his forehead to hers on a whispered curse. Then pulled back and looked deeply into her eyes.

"I could come to love ye, Delaney. With all the heart that God has seen fit to bless me with."

Her mouth dropped open and he knew a moment of stark terror. And coward he discovered himself to be, for he could not wait for her to answer. He took her mouth with all the primal force of man joined to his perfect mate, the other half of his soul.

And she returned his kiss. Damn them both, she did.

And then it happened.

THIRTY-EIGHT

THE SKY WENT white with a flash of light so intense it made Rory and Cailean shield their eyes.

"What the he—" Rory broke off when the light shrunk down to one narrow sliver from which a young woman stepped. "Kaithren," he breathed. He pulled Cailean to him, wrapping them both in the furs. "Why are ye here, Kaithren? Have ye not wreaked enough havoc in my life?"

The specter merely smiled at his words. He searched but spied none of the spite and hatred there that had carved her features the last time he'd seen her face. That moment had remained indelible in his mind's eye for three centuries. It would remain so for all eternity.

"I am no' here to curse you, John Roderick." Her voice was soft and gentle, not at all how he recalled it.

He could still hear her strident screech of rape echo through the chapel. She might look the angel now, but he trusted her naught. "Then ye must be here to kill me." The final irony—and victory—would be hers after all. After three centuries of hell on earth, he'd come to the moment when he wanted most to live, and instead, he would die. "I'm no' ready to leave as yet, Kaithren. Leave me be."

"You misunderstand, Rory. You have spent these years in a purgatory partly of your own making."

"It was no' I who placed the curse!"

For the first time, her serene countenance slipped a notch, but while there might be a touch of frustration, there was no hatred, no vengeance. "It was you who lied."

"I would have told you I'd capture the moon for ye if I had a thought it would save my clan."

"I knew better than ye what lay in store for us all. I couldna make you understand and nothing I said would have made ye listen."

He wanted to argue the point and had there been even a thread of condemnation in her tone, he might have. But Cailean chose that moment to tighten her hold on his waist. He looked down into the wondrous expression and her gaze immediately shifted to his. He felt his heart expand and his will ignite. He looked back to Kaithren and could only speak the truth. "You are right. I would no' have heard."

"Ye've had three hundred years to right that wrong, John Roderick and ye never did it." She stepped closer, the halo of light stayed with her, clung to her. "Until now."

Rory did not have to think on her words to understand. "What of your wrong, Kaithren?"

"Yer no' the only one who has spent time in purgatory. It has been my duty and my penance to follow the course of your life and do what I could to create the opportunities for you to learn from both of our mistakes."

"I dinna recall too many of those," he said.

A smile curved the corners of her mouth. "I canno' say that I was thrilled with my lot either, Rory. I wasna much more a willin' pupil than you. When I cursed our union, Rory, I had no intent to curse all MacKinnon and Claren unions, though if ye'd asked me that day, I'd have gladly made that part of it. I have done penance for that as well, but have been woefully inadequate to the task." Her gaze shifted to Cailean. "Until this one was born. This Key. Then I knew."

"And have ye found redemption, Kaithren?"

She looked into his eyes. "No."

"How have ye failed?"

"I was to see to it that you understood the true meaning of the bond I sought with you, one I only now understand could never have been ours. My final lesson is a difficult one, as I realize my goals were just as selfish as your own. It was no' you I truly loved, Rory, it was what you represented to me." She hung her head and her shoulders rounded. "My final punishment was to observe you finding that bond, knowing I'd never have that."

"Are ye so sure that there is nothing awaiting you of such magnitude?"

She shook her head. "No, I am no'. But that is no longer in my hands." She took a breath and straightened to her full height. "I was sent here to congratulate you on ending your purgatory. I am to personally escort you on your ascension, then await judgment on my own fate."

Rory felt Cailean grab at his waist. "No," she pleaded. "Don't take him now." She looked up to him. "I can't do this, Rory. I thought I'd be strong for you, but I can't and— Oh, God." She buried her face into his chest.

Rory felt his own heart ripping apart. "Kaithren, it has been three centuries, surely you can grant me time."

"Ye didna allow me to finish," she said gently. "I was to come as yer escort, John Roderick, but as difficult and painful a journey as this has been for me, I knew there was one last atonement I must make if I'm ever to find peace within my own soul." She stepped forward and knelt before them, bowing her head low, as if in fealty. "John Roderick MacKinnon, who would have been laird of his clan if no' for my treachery. Your leadership would have been short-lived, but it was no' my place to alter your destiny or your chance to change it." She raised her head. "So, as a final act in my quest for full redemption, I have asked that I be allowed to give you the choice of destinies now. Only you must choose this moment."

Rory felt Cailean tremble in his arms, then realized he shook too. "What are my choices?"

"You may ascend with me this moment, to reap the glory and all the rewards that await you." She paused and looked to Cailean, then back to him. "Or you may reclaim your mortality and live on this earth as mortal man from this day forth, vulnerable to the whims of fortune and fate. And love. Choose now."

Rory pulled Cailean tight into his arms and kissed her deeply and long. When he could, he pulled away and looked to Kaithren, feeling a pang in his heart as he spied the true hurt and regret in her eyes. "I forgive you, Kaithren Claren. We both acted as only humans can, though it has taken us a long time to truly understand the responsibility of our own actions and on whose shoulders that mantle lies. I hope you ascend to those rewards you spoke of. I think you have earned your redemption well." He looked to Cailean and felt his heart burst wide open with a joy that was insurmountable. "But I willna be escorting you there this fine moonlit night."

She bowed and smiled, albeit wistfully. "You have chosen well, I think. God be with you, John Roderick."

Both Rory and Cailean spoke. "God be with you, Kaithren." But the sliver of light had evaporated into the night mist as if it had never been.

"Mortal," he breathed, trying to wrap his thoughts around the gift of life he'd been given. "I dinna know how long it will take to comprehend it."

Cailean's smile and laugh quickly turned into sobs, of soul-shuddering relief and of limitless joy. He curled her into him and lowered her to the furs. "Dinna cry now, Cailean. No' when we have a lifetime of love and laughter in front of us."

"Oh, Rory, I thought you were lost to me forever."

He shook his head, smiling in wonderment as the truth fully blossomed within him. He brushed the tears from her cheeks. "We'll never be lost to each other. We have our lives on earth, and ever after in the heavens above."

Cailean nodded and pulled his head down for a kiss.

"We should go down and make use of that nice soft bed," he murmured.

She shook her head. "No, I want to make love to you under the heavens. It seems the perfect way to begin our lives together."

He shifted her onto her back and moved over her. "Aye, it does, lass, that it does." The stars winked as if in approval as he moved deeply within her.

ALEXANDER AND DELANEY sat up, furs clutched to them, mouths open in awe as reality shifted. The very air surrounding them seemed to shift and bend, then become almost wavery and tactile, as if one could touch it and feel it, pass through it. Liquid.

They watched in amazement as this liquid air shifted to a wavery panel of light at the foot of the bed. The colors inside the panel shifted and altered, as if a window were evolving. A window to the past.

"The portal," Delaney whispered.

Before Alexander could respond, the colors solidified into a scene. But it was no one-dimensional painting he sat witness to. The edges wavered, beyond was his chamber, the same as always. But within the window was a small courtyard, walled in stone, carpeted with green grasses and wild heather. A courtyard he knew well. It was the place Edwyna had met him in that final fateful afternoon. As if the thought had conjured her, she appeared within the window and stepped to the edge.

"It is finally time for you to return," she said.

Alexander could not move, could hardly find his breath, but a single word found its way past his lips. "Edwyna."

"You have discovered the bond, Alexander." She spoke calmly, as if she'd been waiting moments rather than centuries, for him to come to his senses. "You now understand what we must do."

And he did understand. "You are right, Edwyna."

A strangled gasp came from Delaney, but he caught her with a strong hand before she could bolt from the bed.

"Do not make me watch you go," Delaney said on a strangled sob. "You cannot mean to do that to me." She was almost begging him and it shamed him to the lowest part of his soul that his warrior would lower herself so for him.

"Come then," Edwyna said. Her visage was smooth and calm as it always was. He realized now how irritated her perfect mask had always made him. He had no idea what went on behind her glass-green eyes, no idea what went on inside her heart or mind for she carefully kept her emotions hidden, even from him, the man she'd professed to love.

"I have learned of this bond of love, Edwyna, it is true. But I dinna think you understand it well yourself."

Even then she did not look shocked or hurt. Or even particularly angry. "Oh, but I do understand." Her gaze shifted to Delaney.

Delaney immediately sat up straighter, as if determined to meet this new foe with full battle armor in place. Her nakedness did nothing to diminish her strength, in fact it did the opposite. Alexander's respect for her flourished in that moment. He released her and sought her hand, which he wove his fingers through. He felt her gaze touch his face, then felt her fingers tighten within his.

Edwyna's gaze riveted to this joining in a flash, then shifted back to him. "One such as she will be of no help to you, Alexander. She cannot return with you."

"I cannot return through the portal either."

Delaney's grip on his hand tightened almost to crushing. "Alex," she whispered. "Your clan."

Pain did lance his heart, a deep wound from which he would not easily recover. But there would be time for the grieving he had never allowed himself. Delaney would be there by his side as he endured it. And lived through it.

"Yes," Edwyna echoed. "Your clan, Alexander. This is your destiny. Together we can forge a union that will bring peace to the MacKinnons and Clarens. You understand now."

"I do understand, Edwyna. And it is precisely because I do that I now know I canno' return wi' ye. It will be of no good use. To any of us."

Her expression began to shift then. "But you must. It is your destiny."

"You say you loved me, Edwyna, but you do no'. No' in the way you must love. I wouldna ever hae understood this if you had no' sent me here. I have spent seven years cursing you and plotting my vengeance. But that is what it would be, vengeance, no' destiny. I never thought I would be grateful to ye, but grateful I am."

"This is nonsense. Return to me at once! I have saved your life. Given you the opportunity to learn of love."

"Aye, that you have. But Edwyna, there was your mistake. For true love is not a learned behavior, nor one that is earned as a debt paid from a lesson learned well. It exists between two souls that come together because they can naught be apart. You canno' make it so, it simply exists. It doesna die. It will always be. And it canno' be transferred to another on a whim. I will always be grateful to you for putting me in its path, Edwyna, but I do no' love ye. And I never will, in this time or that."

"Yer making a mistake Alexander, one that you will pay for with the lives of your clansmen. Can ye live with the guilt of this decision? All your planning and you change yer mind on a whim?"

"It is no whim. It is simply that now I see where before I could no'. My clansmen are already dead and gone, Edwyna. You have altered the future and because of it, I canno' come back and alter the past. It will change nothing then, and everything now. I finally see that."

"What of me, then?"

For the first time, he felt sorry for her. "You have given me a gift beyond price and it is sorry I am that your plans have not concluded the way you wished. But I do have the benefit of future knowledge and I wish to give ye something in return for all ye have given me. A warning."

Her brows furrowed. "Warning? I am a seer, I—"

"But ye dinna see things for yerself clearly, Edwyna. I know of your fate and it is no' a good one. Be wary of the knolls and braes around Stonelachen and dinna travel alone."

She straightened and folded her arms across her midsection as if chilled. "I thought you were no' willin' to affect the destiny of others."

He shook his head. "No, I am merely accepting my destiny as it has happened. Call on the faeries to help ye as they have in the past. If ye can create a portal for yerself, maybe you can change your destiny as well. Save yourself, Edwyna."

She shook her head. There was true resignation on her face now. "I thought to change our destiny to my liking. I see now that it was wrong. Though I did it in the name of protecting my clan, I should have known better. Perhaps the faeries knew of this when they agreed to help me. They are great ones for playing mortals for the fools they are."

"Then maybe we have both grown wiser for your deed. I can only wish you Godspeed."

There was a pause, then she nodded. "And yersel', Alexander. Godspeed in that future time." The panel wavered, the colors blurring. The air shifted, then settled. All was as before.

And nothing was as before.

Balgaire bounded into the room, barking furiously.

Alexander found himself bursting into laughter. "Och, what a poor watchdog ye make, ye great shaggy beast." He shooed him off the bed when the dog tried to make amends for his failure by drooling all over them. "Be gone wi' ye."

Balgaire sauntered back to the door and resumed his watchful post.

"What have you done, Alex?" Delaney's voice was small, but steady.

He turned to her and knew in that moment, when his heart filled with nothing but pure bliss, that he had done the right thing. "I have done what I had to do." He pulled her to his chest. "I will grieve for my clan, Delaney, but as you have tried to make me understand, they are well and truly gone. I am here and beyond giving them assistance. When I saw Edwyna, heard her words, I knew. I knew in a way I couldn't have otherwise. Things have been changing for me since I met you and I could not sort them out. I have spent a long time preparing for what I thought was my only choice. It was impossible for me to consider anything else."

He kissed her and felt his heart piece itself firmly back together. "I had only to look at her to see and understand that were I to go back, my clan's history would not change."

"What of her? Do you think she escaped that brutal death?"

Alexander shook his head. "I dinna know if we will ever know. Perhaps we willna until such time as we ascend." His heart grew heavy. "But I suspect it will happen as it is written in the annals of history. We feel that we are making choices, that we have a hand in our own fate, but I wonder, do we really?" He pulled her close and kissed her deeply.

She slid her arms around his neck and pulled his head to

hers and took his mouth in a way that laid claim to his heart and to his soul and everything that lay ahead for them both.

"I will spend my life making sure you never regret your choice."

"I had no choice. It just took me a while to believe in it. I love you, Delaney."

She rolled him under her and mounted him, her eyes filled with fierce light, her smile blinding him with her joy. "You can believe in it. Believe in us. If this is our destiny, then it will be a damned good one because I love you, too, Alexander." She bent to her task and took him to heaven and back. And to heaven once again.

Their joining was at turns fierce and soul-shatteringly gentle. When it was done and she lay tucked beside him once again, it was her chuckle that roused him as he drifted toward sleep.

"What is so amusing?"

"Well, we have one little thing we need to clear up before we begin planning our lives."

He lifted his head. "What would that be?"

"Well, there is the little matter of, oh, a few thousand weapons in the basement we need to discard."

He laughed, amazed that he was so carefree. After a lifetime of nothing but worries and concerns, it felt like no small miracle.

Suddenly Balgaire set off to barking once again.

Both he and Delaney froze, then laughed at themselves. "No more portals, no more curses," she said. "I need normal."

"I need to kill that damn dog." He pulled trousers on and stormed to the doorway.

"Don't shoo him off," Delaney said. "It must be morning. Maybe Rory—" She stopped and shot straight up. "Rory! Alexander, oh my God, I hadn't even thought—"

Her questions and her frantic attempts to drag on her

clothes and race after Alexander tumbled to a stop at the loud shout that echoed down the hallway.

"Rise you lazy MacKinnons! There's celebratin' to do and this fine first December day is a short one."

She and Alex gasped. "Duncan!" they breathed.

"Where are ye, brothers of mine? Get up, get up!"

Balgaire was running through the passageways, barking incessantly. Delaney quickly dressed and raced barefoot on the stone floors. It couldn't be. She caught up to Alexander in the main artery that connected to Rory's chambers.

Rory came tumbling out with Cailean right behind him. He ran to Alex and the two raced off.

"It can't be," Cailean said. Her flushed skin and tousled hair brought a smile to Delaney's own love-struck eyes.

They ran toward the main room, heedless of the cold floor and stubbed toes. "I have so much to tell you," Delaney gasped.

"Me, too. Oh, what a night."

Delaney could only grin at her as they maneuvered through the dim passageways. They all converged in the cavernous hall just as Duncan and Maggie strode to the center of the room.

"Duncan," Alexander breathed in a hushed tone, his hand held to his heart. "What— How?"

"They have given me a second chance." He pulled Maggie up into his arms. "And dinna think ye can pull me away from this one. It was her eloquent prayers what brought me back. We are well and truly bound. We are marryin' this day. I want my brothers as witnesses to this finest moment and I'll hear no arguments."

Alexander crossed the room and clapped his brother on the arm. "Ye'll get no arguments from me." Duncan slid Maggie to a stand beside him as his brother pulled him into a tight hug. "Och, Duncan how did ye come back to us? I thought never to see you again."

"It's because of Maggie. She is my miracle." He set

Alexander at arm's length, his smile fading into as serious a look as Alexander had ever seen on his face. "I know this is no' the time to speak of this, but we are all here and I feel it is together we should stay, Alexander." He looked to Rory, who had come across the room and hugged him hard.

"I am no' goin' anywhere," Alexander said. The room fell into a hushed silence. He turned to face them all. "We found the portal this morning. Edwyna called me back. I have learned what she sent me into the future to learn." He took Delaney's hand and looked down at the woman by his side. "To love. Fully and completely." He looked to the assembled group, wide smiles on all their faces. "My commitment to unite the Claren and MacKinnon clans and ensure their long and healthy future remains my goal. Only I will be accomplishing it here, in this century." He turned to Rory. "We have yet to find your key, but we will free you, John Roderick. It is our legacy to flourish."

A broad grin split his own quiet countenance. "We have already discovered it."

There was a gasp from the group.

"We each had the key," Cailean said. "It was inside us all. We had only to discover it to unlock the curse."

"Love." Maggie and Delaney spoke at the same time.

"Exactly."

"So it is over?" Duncan asked. "All of it?"

"I am mortal," Rory stated. He pulled Cailean into his arms. "And I plan to spend my future with this Claren women, legendary curse or no'."

Cailean smiled at him. "I have a feeling—" At Maggie's gasp of dismay she turned to her with a grin, "Not that kind. But this one is stronger than any feeling I have ever experienced. I don't need a vision to predict this future. Lachlan's mission has been accomplished. The Legend MacKinnon will flourish for centuries to come, only this time with stories of the startling success of the unions of the clans."

The three MacKinnon brothers pulled the three Claren cousins into their arms, their kisses a binding promise to her testament of their future.

Duncan was the first to break free. He swung Maggie into his arms. His brothers followed suit. Delaney, Maggie, and Cailean laughed and held on tight.

"I believe that chapel will be booked full this afternoon," Duncan said. He looked to Rory and winked. "Then the only question will be who shall be the first to propagate the clan?"

Maggie touched his cheek and pulled his face to hers. "I can answer that question."

Duncan looked as if he'd been struck over the head with the flat of a mighty claymore. He all but staggered. "What is it yer sayin', my Maggie?"

"I'm sayin' that is pretty sure I am that yer goin' t' be a da, Duncan MacKinnon."

He placed his hand over her stomach, a look of rapture and wonderment creasing his face. He lifted his head and turned to the rest of them. "We are all blessed."

Then his face split into a wide grin as he thrust his fist into the air. With a mighty shout that rang in the hall for long after it was done, he cried, "Long live the legend!"

EPILOGUE

LACHLAN LOOKED DOWN and watched the unfolding scene below him. He could scarce believe it. He hadn't understood himself what it was he sought when his time to ascend had come, other than to right the wrong that had surely happened between him and his beloved Louisa.

He could only leave behind all he had found in hopes it would find its own way. He could not have dreamed in his wildest imaginings that it would unfold as it had.

Love was an elusive sprite that did not always guide its subject down the right path. But succeed they had. And in glorious fashion. Without their boundless love for one another, the curse could never have been reversed. The three couples were well and truly matched.

He could well imagine the joy Cailean would take in sharing her travels and discoveries with John Roderick. He would help her to discover a world she'd never have found on her own, and the knowledge they would share with their eventual offspring warmed his heart.

Alexander and Delaney would also take no small amount of joy in bringing a shiny new slice of peace to a world they both knew could be fraught with ugliness and hatred. He had to wonder if they would not work for that greater cause a while longer before starting their own family. The troubled spots of the world would be well warned that there was a formidable team about to enter their lives, and make the wreaking of global havoc much more difficult to achieve.

Och, and the final couple, Duncan and Maggie. His heart warmed to overflowing when he looked down upon them. Aye, there would be MacKinnon-Claren offspring to fill this world and these two would play no small role in that endeavor. Stonelachen's great halls and winding passageways would be filled with the ringing laughter of children yet again. Perhaps their destiny lay in finding a place for Stonelachen in this modern world. He could not wait to witness it.

Now the Legend MacKinnon would begin a new arc in its existence. A glorious path into a future filled with the happiness and fulfillment of future generations of each clan and their joined progeny. Aye, his eternal contentment was assured. He could finally rest in peace.

Motion caught his attention and he reluctantly pulled it away from the tearful and ecstatic unions as the three couples became man and wife in a wondrous joined ceremony, steeped in the traditions of both past and present.

He shifted his observations outward across the heavens and was stunned beyond thought and deed by what he saw. He'd been so overjoyed with the earthly successes, he'd not given thought to the otherworldly effect their achievement might have.

He observed in awed silence as Claren souls, dozens, nay hundreds of them, crossed what once were unbreachable divides to be joined with their MacKinnon mates. The heavens rang out with the wonderment of true love rediscovered. And from the midst of the convergence, a woman's earthly image emerged.

It could not be. He could not withstand the illusion were he to discover it were only that. "Louisa?"

She smiled upon him and filled him with a warmth he'd thought never to feel again.

"Lachlan. My dear, devoted Lachlan. At long last."

Och, dear glorious God in heaven but it was her. He cried tears he could not feel, but knew them each and every one as they fell.

She came to him and it was a blending of souls, a supreme fulfillment. He had reached the highest pinnacle. True peace and eternal happiness.

They looked down upon those who had made possible this ultimate glorious gift.

"Long live the legend, indeed."

ABOUT THE AUTHOR

Nationally bestselling author, Donna Kauffman loves to travel. Usually this involves a passport and plane tickets, but she has always believed that some of the best adventures can be found between the covers of a book. Born and raised in Maryland, Donna currently lives in Virginia with her husband, two sons and two Australian Terriers.

*What happens when the clock strikes twelve and a
former secret service agent gets trapped in an RV
with the daughter of an ex-President?*

*Find out in Donna Kauffman's short story
and ring in the new millennium with*

YOURS 2 KEEP

*a collection of five original stories from
some of your favorite romance writers.*

Coming from Bantam Books in December 1999